The Air Cage

The Air Cage

PER WÄSTBERG

TRANSLATED FROM THE SWEDISH BY

THOMAS TEAL

DELACORTE PRESS / SEYMOUR LAWRENCE

Originally published in Swedish under the title LUFTBUREN
by Wahlström & Widstrand, Stockholm
Swedish edition Copyright © 1969 by Per Wästberg
English translation Copyright © 1972 by Dell Publishing Company, Inc.

Library of Congress Catalog Card Number: 79–37659

Designed by Joel Schick

Manufactured in the United States of America
First printing

Library of Congress Cataloging in Publication Data
WÄSTBERG, PER.
The air cage.
"A Seymour Lawrence book."
Translation of *Luftburen.*
I. Title.
PZ4.W1264Ai   [PT9876.33.A3]   839.7'3'74   79–37659

CONTENTS

The Water Palace

ONE

THE ANTIPODES

SOMEONE MUST also describe Jan Backman. He was above medium height, bony rather than muscular. His hair was ash-brown, gray under certain lights, and cut short because he thought it grew thicker that way. There was baldness in the family. He was usually pale but blushed occasionally. His ring finger, especially on the left hand, was longer than his index. The veins on his thin hands stood out clearly and separately.

He often sat bent over, his chest sunken. He had gestures, bad habits: rubbing his cheek with the backs of his fingers when subjected to an unexpected question, running his thumb along the outer contours of his ear when he thought or talked on the phone, pinching the back of his neck as if he were surprised that his hair didn't grow down his back. There were gestures he had given up, but they had been replaced by others.

His blood group: O. Good enough for anyone. He knew his social security number by heart. He saved his canceled bankbooks and passports, old ID's as well as swimming badges and report cards. He was never behind with the rent. No one could complain. He didn't think of himself as conscientious, but derived a pleasure from these confirmations of his citizenship, these testimonials to his right to exist in Sweden.

Other people observed him. He also looked at himself—a face that was gentle and cold, appealing and rejecting, extroverted and inhospitable. So he described himself, choosing terms that seemed accurate at the moment, confusing the issue and leaving a false trail. He could see a picture of caressing arrogance and confined chaos. A desire to remake reality, but also a desire to float away in it like plankton in an ocean current, touching down in its grass as timidly as a perception.

He liked this picture very much. For what he most often felt in the presence of this face with its restricted colors was a banality so intense that he doubted others had even shared it. Even Gertrude had her experience, her talent that she utilized so little, her dark illuminated thoughts. He admired most things about her without envy.

He liked to think of the antipodes—ever since he found out that if he dug straight down in the front yard of the Water Palace, or lifted a paving stone and happened to find a ladder, he would come up in New Zealand, head first, though he went down feet first. Somewhere there was someone who was he—the other end of a playing card that could never be called either "other" or "end." Maybe someone, who was he to a slightly higher degree than he himself, wanted to unite with him. At times he felt this someone was on his side when no one else was, no, not *on* but *by* his side. His antipodean body, his missing link. He whose shadow he was himself, and the other way around.

He often played with the thought, to him the feeling was real. Should he go out and dig someplace where it was so quiet he could hear grass growing over other grass, so quiet he could hear roots groping around among the dead? Later, when he had met Sten Tidström, he returned to the thought in another form: an antipodean conscience, a guilt on behalf of his opposite, a training in empathy for what was remote and nevertheless was he.

Someone who was his opposite and outside himself, yet magnetic, bound to him in a polaric dependence that could never be questioned. That dream led him to Gertrude.

Theirs was hardly the eternal story—that story of stimulated vanity giving birth to love that then grows inward, of casual words being weighed and interpreted and pondered in anxiety and hope, of looks and expressions almost too threatening to solve, the story of fluctuations between happiness and despair, of the murmur—to quote a book they both had read—"of the conflicting tones from which love one day arises despotic and indisputable, with dreams and fragrance beneath whose weight the lover would gladly die, as if beneath white bird-cherry falling across his eyelids on an evening in May."

This whole process, which erases the dead points in a person's emotional life, which makes everything quiver with a thousand impressions and fancies, which increases his susceptibility to what is blessedly unendurable, which makes trifles glitter because they've been changed into harder currency—this process was not theirs, not Jan's and Gertrude's. It was rather as though they had come to each other directly, without hesitation and fear, and they saw love not so much as an adventure but as a shield against the world.

They were siblings, half-siblings. They had the same father, half a common heritage. The other half was different. No one else knew anything about it. Their father had lived abroad for a long time and had no friends with whom they associated. Their own acquaintances thought they were married in the usual way, and when they were asked how long they'd been married they named the year they'd decided to live together.

Their common name was on the door. Gertrude said she had always been afraid of getting a new one, and so it remained the same as before. She could still see herself standing in a row at the boarding school in Lausanne and could hear Mademoiselle Gudasnes ticking them off: Marie-Clair Ange, Louisa Auer, Gertrude Backman, Catherine Bonmont. . . . The roll was called at the end of athletics day. They had run cross-country, lifted large rocks, crept along hedges, smelled burning leaves, and been chased by a bird dog. Then their teacher stood there under the pale sky and read from her green directory, where they were all locked up with their original names.

Was there a family resemblance? They were the same height. Gertrude had thin brown hair, she was slender, her throat soft and straight, her legs slim, with a few dark hairs that faded or fell off in the summer. They were no more alike than many other people.

The Gertrude Jan loved was the one who didn't resemble him. The Gertrude he so matter-of-factly lived with was his sister.

So it was not himself he loved in Gertrude. But what he felt at home with, in a way he could imagine with no one else, what gave him peace with her—that was the sisterly element, he told himself, that was himself in her.

How strongly did they require a common origin, Jan asked himself. Does the adopted child lose interest in his parents' families when he discovers he is not of the same biological extraction? Such a child often refuses to take on a different family, wants to have his own even if it consists of ribbon clerks and thieves. Where does he belong?

Why should anyone be more curious about the history of his own family than that of other people's? Jan was curious but had no family. Gertrude was closest. They adopted each other.

Once they had chosen to live together it appeared they had consciously done something few people dared. There was something forbidden in their life together, an ancient erotic magic that would have frightened and shocked people had they known. They were given the unknown and the sinful in the form of something very familiar. They were, from the beginning, within the family and yet on forbidden ground. Each stood face to face with himself and at the same time with someone else. That was the way they jokingly spoke of it when they tried to see themselves from outside.

For Jan, Gertrude was the puzzle piece that was missing in himself. But she was not the object of an eager or an agonizing search. He had never, really, discovered her. So he had no need to own her, grasp her, conquer her—the tiresome tricks and propensities of love. He didn't have much of a past that wasn't also hers. It was an odd situation; they came from the same direction and he had nothing that was really his own.

And it occurred to him that perhaps he had missed something in the fact that they had never had to conduct an agonizing exploration of each other. They had never met as strangers, but rather in a kind of smiling complicity, with the innocence of playmates. How much of that was cowardice? Did they share a fear of leaving the innermost circle, of going out into the world to adopt other ways of life, of breaking their biological solidarity?

They had protected, not tested, each other. So much unspoken understanding flowed between them. A person doesn't need to know much about his antipode. If you remember that it casts your shadow in the opposite direction, then almost everything else falls into place.

"I'm your double," Gertrude had whispered once. "No, I'm you. I don't look like you, but I have a part of you in me. I'm partly a man. If I had a sister I might love her like I love you. A sister, too! It would be wonderful to be able to manage two or even more, to feel they were like me, people I had to have around. Like children."

There were only the two of them. And they were close. For long periods they spoke with the same voice. But no one really understood that but themselves.

One day Jan realized, with surprise and a surge of helpless jealousy, like a mother who sees her daughter make use of her womanhood for the first time, that it was up to some other man, from his greater distance, to search out Gertrude, project her against his world, be taken in by her unfamiliarity, and feel her gliding away irretrievably just as he reaches out for her, like a child reaching for his image in a mirror.

THE END OF THE WORLD

THEY WERE TWELVE and fourteen. No one paid attention to their life together; they were the children in the house. There was no one else to play with.

Mrs. Tapper, the housekeeper, went on a short vacation, and a lady from Stockholm who lived in a summer house a little further away promised to look in on them now and then. Food was piled up in the pantry and the root cellar. At the store they were allowed to take what they wanted on account. It was like a scout camp. They were independent, had to learn to take care of themselves. They were not like other people.

Gertrude was the leader; she was so much older. She made all the decisions. She had turned up at the Water Palace and it was as if she owned it. She had thin, hard arms. She wasn't as strong as he, but she had greater endurance.

Jan worshiped her childishly and unreasonably. He was in her service and asked nothing in return. She was his sister, whom he loved. No one else could offer that combination. It was like having a precious stone in your pocket.

"Go outside," she'd say in the mornings when she was about to get dressed. "Go on!"

Her green eyes commanded. She stood in her loose pajamas with the tight elastic around the waist. He ran out into the empty house that had become theirs, he saw the carpet that writhed down the stairs from the hall, he stopped and could go no further away. He wanted to make up a song about her—he would have if she hadn't called out to him. He broke the habit of his loneliness, of himself. Then she came out to him, teeth brushed, dressed in shorts and a sweater. They drank cocoa and washed their cups; they were adults. The whole house became different because they were doing everything for themselves.

Though they had no need to hide from anyone, they liked the attic best. It was dry and warm up there, almost airless. Dead wasps. An empty landscape under wooden beams. Mattresses piled up and covered with sheets. Discarded encyclopedias.

A white deal dresser with smooth worn stones and shells on top, dusty, no sound of the sea. The biggest silence of all, the silence in a shell.

The enormous erector set with each metal strip perforated like a coded tape, now a completed construction and consigned to tedium.

The bulb on its twisted cord. A black trunk blocked a window and held out the sun.

An eye chart—who could have brought that home? A, the beginning of everything, stood at the very top with its legs astraddle. At the very bottom: "Printed by Isaac Marcus."

A plaster statue of a Swiss boy in knee-length shorts. Jan and Gertrude broke off his nose and prepared a poison powder.

Off in the gable, separated by a high threshold, was the hideout Gertrude had chosen. Fruit was stored there for the winter, spread out on newspapers that had become funny and strange with their headlines about old wars and old death. The papers lay there and made everything meaningless, or else the reverse, because the evil had lost its point for those who remained and couldn't imagine all those things, and therefore time did not seem consumed and lost but rather subjugated and defeated. Fruit from former winters—no one knew when—had rolled aside, shriveled up in the innermost corners of the eaves, hardened or rotted depending on its original succulence, and spread a smell of freshness and mortality, of nature and epochs gone by.

He kicked aside apples, stepped over the threshold into his own world, which ended in her. She was his sister and friend: the end of the world. Beyond her nothing. Everything he had to do with others was unreal. Her life in Switzerland—a blurred plate in a geography. With her he was himself, spherical, tentacles withdrawn. She existed in him, for all eternity he wanted only this.

"Smell my hair," Gertrude said. "I just washed it."

He leaned toward her, closed his eyes, smelled. Her hair was long, thin, tickling.

"Egg shampoo," she said. "Sometimes I talk most when I don't have anything to say."

She said they ought to have a Conversation. The words approached from a distance but slowed and stopped in her. When there was a lot you couldn't say, it was good to have a Conversation, something prearranged.

"It's hot," he complained.

"We'll take off our clothes," she said softly.

But it was she who undressed him. She handled him like a wonderful toy. He submitted, frightened and fascinated. She unbuttoned his checked shirt and pulled his short pants down over his hips like the time he had a fever and had to go straight to bed. He went along with the game though he understood nothing, he was the instrument of her imagination, words, and promptings. If she didn't make use of him she would be powerless—that's what he hoped. Anything at all, so long as it was him.

She undressed herself as well. While she was doing it she didn't look at him, he was irrelevant. He knew what her body looked like and yet was curious all the same. She stood on tiptoe and stretched up her arms so they grazed the rafters. Her breasts had filled out around her nipples, which were so much larger than his. Her belly had a different shape than his, which didn't begin with a definite waist. Light, downy hair almost covered the slit between her legs. Never afterwards did he see a body more sharply. And yet nothing was unfamiliar to him. He had studied all the anatomical cross sections in the Scandinavian Encyclopedia.

She took several leaps, laughing at her own lightness. He sat on the sill and she came up to him in one long stride, crouched down in front of him and ran her hands over his shoulders and down along his upper arms, came back to his neck, ran her finger along his collarbone and down his chest. Shivers ran through him.

"Feel me, we're different," she said.

She pulled his hands carefully to her breasts and he felt that they were as soft as her bottom and fit the palms of his hands.

Though their bodies were different, they belonged to one another. All at once everything started to be wonderful and strange, and they clung tightly to each other so no loneliness would slip in through a hole. They burrowed their noses into neck and collarbone. They sat motionless, felt warmth, smoothness, cramp, and numbness. To move was treachery.

She held him hard. What breasts she had lay flat against his ribs. It was as if terror drove them together, alone in a big house, with no parents. Maybe there was something helpless in their way of pressing themselves against each other. She looked as if she were about to cry. Then she laughed, pulled loose, danced around on the splintery floor, was the leader again whom he obeyed without comprehending.

It seemed to him she was more guarded and distant when she was naked. Her head seemed a little too big for her body, just like his own when he looked in the mirror. She looked at him with wide-open eyes, and he felt how he clenched his fists in a kind of defense. There was liquid blue in her eyes, it shimmered of power and arrogance and wanted to divide him up, tear him to pieces.

He sat, she moved. Her legs chased past his face, like algae driven forward and back by an eddy. He smelled her sweat, or his own, he didn't know. He couldn't move, the blood poured down to his thighs and knees and made him heavy.

Then she suddenly got dressed and rushed down to the kitchen for crackers and cheese. He heard her footsteps disappearing down the creaking stairs toward the rooms where they lived another sort of life among the summer furniture. Then he waited. At last, when he wanted to run away himself, he saw her again, creeping across the attic floor. His heart started to pound with joy and fright. He was bewitched, but ill at ease. They ate in their attic hideout, nibbling like mice inside the walls.

"Do you like me?" she asked commandingly, and there was power in her eyes.

"Of course I do."

"Say 'I like you, Gertrude.' "

He said it.

"Don't you like my name?"

"Yes. But it's not very common. You're the only person I know with that name."

He didn't merely like her. He loved her. He was exhilarated. Their house was the core of a giant pear. Everything became more vivid: the transparent skin of the sour cherries, the glitter of sunset in the currants, the gas pipe with its brass tap, the Baltic herring with their red eyes encircled by dark rings.

He touched her carefully and tremblingly. Then they sat in total silence. The slope of the roof made a tunnel with one of the inner walls. It was like a tent. They crept together on the rough attic floor and heard birds rustling in their nests up under the tiles on the roof. It was very dark, but their eyes slowly adjusted. When one cannot see, one can imagine all sorts of things. It made them freer. A spoken word was quickly blotted out, the pressure of a hand or a caress vanished as though it had never occurred, yet had its effect all the same.

He could dimly see his hands. He'd read about how your fingerprints stayed the same no matter how old you got. He saw the gleam of Gertrude's eyes. He didn't know why she was the one who decided everything. Something in him was changing, something he couldn't bear. He knew exactly how she would look at him: confiding and yet superior. It made him want to run away. He couldn't take it. If only he could pull a cap of indifference down over his face. He wanted to be daring and free, but she held him captive, she measured out his steps. It was as if all the strength he had was needed for her, or as if only her strength was left in him.

He watched her buckling her sandals, leaning over her knee with her hair falling over her forehead. He gave her a shove so she toppled forward. He needed to fight, to show her somehow that he wasn't helpless without her or that he could do something against her. He wished she'd hit back. But she'd skinned her knee and it started to bleed, and then his cruelty was torn apart by sympathy. He had no words for it, but a tenderness rose up inside him. What was he supposed to do? She turned to him full of rage, just when he expected this new tenderness to be returned. She licked her knee and ignored him. He forgot his useless compassion. To kill the love within him he shoved her again and she started to cry, but didn't hit back.

A day in the attic held time for so many different things.

And something had to be put away in the darkness where they lived, something had to be preserved from their time together. Their father's old luggage, most of it no longer used, stood there with its memories of diplomatic travels, labels from the Hotel Britannia in Budapest, the Europé in Leningrad, the Bristol in Sofia, the Palace in Madrid. Jan got the idea of putting something in a suitcase.

They took a piece of hard bread with soft cheese, a piece of boiled salami, a dessicated field mouse they found in a corner on its back. The sort of secret messages to the future in which they conspired against the world could only be buried outdoors or sent off by bottle-post. In the attic there were other rules: it had to be something disgusting, mixed with spit, sweaty-sweet, something that would disappear in its hiding place in the suitcase, where there was a vague smell of hair tonic and dusty timetables.

They also packed away an old, discolored book called

A Journey to Central Asia. But first they read a little of it and looked at the chapter headings.

The Author Enjoys the Hospitality of Nur-Ullah, an Afghan —The Author's Fear of Discovery—The Character of My Recent Host—An Ungrounded Fear of the Wild Ass—The Author's Final Blessing to the Khan—The Afghan Proves Vexatious— Spies Sent Out Against the Author—Excessive Customs Duties —The Forsaken Author's Plight—The Author Travels to London, His Reception in that City.

And so they also had something to laugh at together: the eternal travels hither and yon of authors such as these, their reception at various British embassies, the way they sent messages ahead about who they were. The way the whole world existed for their enjoyment.

But it existed no longer, that world, it might just as well be locked up in the suitcase with labels from hotels that had changed their names. It existed only in words, in tables, of contents. Now there was another world, with fewer words. It existed at the same time as they themselves but in another place. Jan didn't reach that far. It wasn't for him. He felt a great loneliness around the two of them in the attic, for if he was to keep Gertrude then he was forced to choose loneliness. No one could enter their sibling circle without changing everything.

When the suitcase was opened, maybe not for years, the Water Palace would ring with cries of horror, followed by the silence of speculation—where had these objects come from, how could they be dated? In this way Jan and Gertrude created the summer's secret. That he himself might be suspected never occurred to him. Mere accusations could never expose the impenetrable.

Something was taking place inside the suitcase, and Jan felt himself a friend to both growth and decay. The process of disintegration, clambering mold, a web being spun of something fine and indescribable. It all remained undiscovered,

uncompleted like everything else. And that was the best part—
he was an enemy of things that ended: his summer with
Gertrude. His comfort was that they were brother and sister.
That could never be changed, it was a door to her that no one
else had.

They found a cubbyhole Jan had never seen before. It was
full of skirts and blouses and dresses from the twenties, of thin
chiffon and flimsy artificial silk. Left from someone's past, or
several people's. Maybe they'd belonged to Jan's mother when
she spent her pregnancy at the Water Palace sculpting figures
from the sea.

He'd been naked, now Gertrude dressed him in a blouse with
a lot of frills and a long yellow skirt. He blushed, it all
seemed so dumb. She tightened the skirt around his chest, he
was too small. He was barefoot and had nothing on underneath. As she fussed over him, he felt his penis stiffen suddenly
and invisibly. She kissed his arm below the puffed sleeve.

"What are you doing?" he asked.

"You're the kind of boy girls like," she said, and kissed his
arm again.

"You think up so many things."

She had an atomizer full of toilet water and sprayed him
with it.

"Now you smell like a lady," she said teasingly.

He smelled like lilies of the valley. She put a little on her
neck, they smelled the same.

Gertrude treated him like a doll.

"Would you like a cup of coffee, my dear?" she said in an
affected voice. "Don't tell me you're expecting!"

"Expecting what?"

"A little one. An addition to the family, my dear."

"No, it's just this outfit that looks that way," he said seriously.

"So you're not actually in the family way?" Gertrude per-
sisted.

They acted out grown-up melodrama, kitchen table talk, gossip.

He would have felt silly in women's clothes if they hadn't been laughing and teasing each other. They traded shoes, they wore the same size. They felt they were very like each other because they could wear the same clothes. But Jan had shorter hair.

Gertrude looked delighted, fussed with him, pinched him, ruffled his hair to make it curlier. He looked at the veins that wound along her wrist and felt excited and confused. It was like a dream they seemed to be dreaming together. He didn't want to ask her about anything, he only hoped he was the largest letter in her eye chart, that she measured every letter, every person, against him.

"Kiss my hand," she commanded.

And he bent over it, courtly as a character in a novel.

She put chocolates in his mouth and ran her finger over his lips. He liked that.

"I dreamed about you last night," she said.

"What'd you dream?"

"You were an ugly fish." She laughed. "You were chasing me down the street. You caught me. Did you expect something else?"

She hugged him. He was used to that. But then she kissed him on the mouth, and that was the first time. He didn't like it, but he pretended they were becoming blood brothers, with spit instead of blood. He wondered if she only kissed him because he looked like a girl, girls regularly carried on like that among themselves. Did she kiss anyone else, some terrible rival? He'd been in a children's play at school where a girl had rushed up to him and shouted, "I love you, you are mine." Her voice had been shrill and cross. But she didn't love him, why should she? Who was he after all? A little boy in the play, no one in particular, a person who hardly existed. The teacher's eyes had glittered horribly. It was an untrue play.

When Gertrude kissed him, he was filled with a dreamlike desire. But what was he supposed to do? Something that hurt, or was shameful and dangerous? Pull her hair? Push her foot in her face and tickle it? Something that made her cry or laugh? First she was cold, then eager and excited. What did she want? They were halfway to something they couldn't reach.

"Do you think I'm pretty?" she asked.

"Yes."

"I have an ugly turned-up nose. But they say it'll straighten out in time. Can't you say something that'll make me happy?"

"We're having the same summer," he said right away, since that's what made him happy himself.

"We're having what?" she said.

"I mean we'll remember the same things."

"You're pretty," she said, and kissed him loudly on the neck.

He grabbed hold of her, embarrassed and happy, and time stopped, as in a photograph where a foot is lifted one inch from the ground to take the next step, but eternity holds it back.

And time *had* to slow down. He knew that already, how serious everything was, and how childish his love, doomed to pass ungratified into something else. It bore within it the seeds of separation, distance, indifference. Adults had decided his and Gertrude's fates: children couldn't stay together, they had no money, they couldn't make their own lives. Children in love can't marry. They know that, but it's no comfort. Somehow, he must make this love live on, overpower what was fated.

Gertrude undressed him, decked him out in cast-off dresses, did things with him. And he was utterly at her disposal, he had no other purpose. Without her none of this would be happening. It took place between them. That thought lived in him. He did not exist for himself, he was not separate. He was ruled by things outside himself.

He hoped she noticed that what they were doing was real and couldn't be ignored. And then a shiver of fear ran through him that maybe in spite of everything she was inaccessible, that she lived a secret life he couldn't know about. It mustn't be that way—he mustn't run parallel with her, but intertwined with her. Everything would be different after this summer, whatever he and Gertrude experienced would be different. But the new had already begun, he felt it. From the edge of the lens it moved toward the center and grew.

THE BOOK-FISH

GERTRUDE HAD A boyish body, strong and slim, freckled shoulders, a tendency to sunburn easily. She was light on her feet and her movements were quick, but sometimes she complained of headaches and lay on her stomach on the bed and never looked up, though Jan knew she wasn't sleeping. At such times he had nothing he could say to her. They could talk about most things. But there was a good deal that touched them and their lives that they didn't discuss. It was too strange and too obvious.

They were friends, with a kind of calm in each other's company. She was often slow to become sexually aroused, he was sometimes tired of making a particular effort. They lay down affectionately close to each other at night, and there was something monstrous in that. When their bodies built bridges to each other it occurred to Jan that they had met before, in their father's body. Maybe that wasn't enough. But it was enough so they could never really meet again for the first time, as strangers, as I and you.

There were so many desires. Her face told him that, not her words. An indescribable tenderness. A desire to hurt. A desire to protect carefully against all evil. A desire to be perverse, unfaithful, wild, in order to see if she would still be loved. He could see it more easily in her than in himself.

The best of all, when intimacy and desire came at the same time. When they found the words that dealt with themselves. That was harder than a person imagined. Thin as web and wind, it tears in two, it blows away. He told her about talking animals, about fungi that got lost in the moss, about the smells in different movie theaters—but it was dangerous, it was easy to forget her for the story.

Jan believed that because of him Gertrude could move without the fear of spaces. He was her freedom, so she didn't have to test herself against the unknown and the society around her. She didn't need to leave her original circle, worm her way in and submit to other people's terms. And those who found her lively and gregarious never noticed that she looked on the outer world as a difficult machine she would never learn to operate.

She leaned back against the past, against what she had experienced, her childhood, her father. But that was almost nothing, the past hardly existed after all. She was enthralled by the Water Palace, by the image of a more solitary, stable life, beyond adaptation and relearning. It occurred to Jan that she'd never been out to visit him at Arlanda, though he'd suggested it often. She went no further than the Academy of Sciences.

He'd grown used to her always being there with him, to the fact that she did little on her own. Everything that ended in a definite result, and therefore presupposed the beginning of something new, seemed to frighten her. But she was at home with things that continued for a long time and still remained unfinished, like complicated research projects. It was as if something had happened to Gertrude a long time ago. Something she must continuously return to, something not yet over and done with and decided.

So in many ways they were different.

And still he saw them as the winning number in a lottery, chosen in advance. No reality could wipe out their life together, no dream could gild it, no winter freeze it. They talked, but sometimes with their mouths so close that the words could not be understood. Pass through me, not beside me, they pleaded, with the same voice from the same place. If there was something alien in them, then it was built into both as common property.

Everyone must notice it, Jan thought, this almost tangible, visible feeling that just they, he and Gertrude, belonged together. Their faces betrayed nothing, but they were united by a thin sheet of ice that would bear only them. There was time between them, silences, pauses, but it was the same time. The objects that stood expectantly around them seemed to know this.

It was as if these two human beings each held a die in his hand, but however they threw them the two dice always showed the same number of eyes—and it didn't matter if it was good luck or if the dice had the same number of spots on every side.

They had moments of dizzying intimacy. He sat and watched her in the bathtub. She lay deep in the water, her hair, which she would shampoo later, floated in coils on the surface and was washed aside as she moved. Her knees drawn up, her pubic hair almost invisible against the first tan on her stomach. She breathed. Her breasts, light as balloons, tried to rise. She looked at him, undaunted but a little sleepily. Her glance didn't waver, though she said nothing.

"Stand up," he said finally, and helped her.

She stood in the tub and was taller than he. He washed every inch of her from her bottom and the hair between her legs to her neck and shoulders and finally got under the shower himself to wash off the lather. He stood behind her and crossed his arms over her breasts and felt her body like his own. It seemed to him she was his double. She was close to him without his having to create the closeness. No one else could touch her exactly as he did.

"I stayed in too long," she said. "I feel weak."

She braced herself against the tile wall, climbed out of the tub. She looked happy and knowing. She went into the bedroom whistling a pop melody they liked:

> Now when the light of reason fails
> And fires burn the sea
> Now in this age of confusion
> I have need of your company.

Vaguely, he thought: We are two people, quite young. We can do what we like. Now we're here, which is what we've wanted. We've always wanted to do things with each other.

She leaned against the end of the bed and took his penis in her hand.

"Come in me right now," she said. "Just for a minute."

He lay on top of her; her bath had left her dry inside. He hardly noticed that she helped him in. Her legs closed around his hips, she tightened her belly around him.

"Don't move," she whispered.

She grew quiet under his caresses and he stopped his hand. Her face almost went out. Her eyes darkened and lightened indiscriminately. The yellow fleck in her right iris.

"You're so warm in me," she said. "I'd like to come into you too. I'd like to huddle up inside you."

He was so close to himself in her that it was no effort to feel what she felt. He thought he knew.

"Stay in me," she said afterwards. "Don't leave."

But suddenly he was out anyway, and so they lay on their stomachs next to each other, elbows touching, she drawing her toes sleepily along his calves. He recognized everything in her, their smells were mixed, they scraped against each other so their noses grew red.

She jumped up out of bed naked, he watched her go around straightening up, pretty but not exciting him.

Later they sat down at the white leafed table by the window on Upplandsgatan and worked the puzzle Vanity Fair, eight hundred pieces. It was almost cloudy above the bustle of the fair, and the sky pieces were the same on both sides and grasped at each other lovingly and fussingly. Jan and Gertrude helped them find each other. They sat on opposite sides of the table, it was like a contest, but they worked together to complete the painting.

When they'd eaten supper and drunk red wine and decided to spend the evening at home, Gertrude started to cry, and it was the second time recently. He didn't understand why. He was tired of asking. He told himself that people behaved all different ways, explanations only existed to cover up their behavior. He ignored it. He was powerless, absent.

She and he—life's experiment. He saw them from outside: goodnight Jan. And a hand inside him took the ballpoint pen from his brain and laid it on the night table. Say something instead, then you won't hear Gertrude's misery, people's misery everywhere.

Finally he said, "Don't be unhappy. Don't cry. I like you very much. I'll read to you out of the Book of Marvels."

He took off her shoes and made her sit against one post of the canopy they'd bought at the city auction and covered with green striped linen. And he read.

" 'On the 23rd of June, 1626, at the marketplace in Cambridge, a codfish was sold, which when it was opened proved to contain a book in its stomach. It had been covered with sailcloth but was much soiled.' "

E THE WIND FROM THE SUN

ARLY MORNING AS Jan hung away his raincoat and looked at the empty papers on his desk, Arlanda's runways were white with dew, and when he looked out over the silent airport he saw flocks of wood pigeons browsing unmolestedly in the shadows of jet turbines.

He had the morning tower watch, took the elevator up to the meteorology stage, and then climbed the stairs to the platform. All the orders sent out during the night were preserved on tape for a month, but Jansson gave him a verbal report as usual. He'd seen the smoke from a forest fire in the west toward Sigtuna, the inexpensive night flights just beginning their season had arrived and departed with no delays.

It was a clear morning. There had been northern lights during the night. The planes showed up tidily out of the nothingness: Alitalia's night Caravelle from Rome, Finnair 791 from Helsinki, SAS 765 from Moscow, SAS 042 freight from New York.

There was a little morning dew on the wings of the first SAS plane. Had there been any radio disturbance up there, turbulence, undue roughness? Jan didn't bother to ask. He had signaled clear for landing, the captain could take care of the rest, vision was good. The plane had been at thirty-three thousand feet. How much different was it at sixty-six thousand? There is of course no real clarity and emptiness.

Full of charged particles, the wind from the sun sweeps like a broom across the earth. Then lightning flashes in the floorboard nails, then the aurora borealis and the whisper of the ether push through the cracks down beneath the flooring where we live.

Radiation beams out from every distant star system, moving in all directions like a telegraph net, like sound waves between the bodies of people talking, like notes and intonations.

The earth has its magnetic pole. Which has its place in a larger magnetic field, which in turn has its place in a larger still—growth rings in an immeasurable world.

The atoms have a common origin. Everything living and dead hangs together. Atoms dance in the hair of dead pharaohs, in breakfast bread, in the kneecaps of opera ballerinas, in the meteor that fell in northern Siberia, in the pupils of our eyes. And in that sense we've been given our eyes by a once-exploding star, and something of those eyes is found in space wherever we go, as are molecules of water from the breath that passes between our faces.

Everything is names and words, myths and inventions, attempting to encompass what exists and find descriptions that will make us first see it in a new way and then recognize it later. But terms like "charged particles" or "wave motions" can still only bear witness to a partial sight. Maybe they are really something else, unities that could be described in other ways and thus find other forms and meanings.

Jan picked up his binoculars and looked at the wing bolts on the plane taking off for Tokyo. They too held together a universe that wanted to explode. The flight plan had been filed, the checkpoints on the Stockholm-Copenhagen route had been advised. People were climbing aboard. Some of them were afraid of dying, a few felt claustrophobic. But they didn't panic, because their faith in the wings, in the bolts, in what they didn't understand but had learned to accept, was stronger than their imaginations and emotions, which they'd grown used to mistrusting.

Science changes our picture of the world, technology alters the possibilities of life. New facts populate space and rob words like light and dark, evil and good, of their meaning. Matter will encounter antimatter, light from far-off galaxies will one day turn us into energy ourselves. Until then we're only containers.

The vocabulary grows, old clichés are abandoned. Even the planes coming in to land are dependent on the laws of thermodynamics as we now understand them. The mind stands still in an instant of admiration for the new creation taking shape. Then everything continues as before and we try to feel at home. Those large-eyed children from the underdeveloped countries don't walk our streets, the patterns in living organisms can't be observed with the naked eye. We only care about what we can see. And we never seem to be able to learn to see.

Jan played his field glasses across the blackened mouths of the jets, the curved propellers of the smaller planes. All the inventions, thoughts, lines on tracing paper, patterns translated into metal, all the hands and machines that had been set in motion through the centuries in order at last to achieve these creatures, designed to transport people here and there to other people.

And what remains of the wasted thoughts, the successful plans and ingenious ideas are the small things people see: the plastic trays of chicken, the salt and pepper pouches, the profile of the stewardess, the way you make the seat go back, the door closing on its springed hinges, the way the toilet functions in the air.

So the plane appeared to the people climbing out onto the steps from Air France's machine from Paris. This was Icarus, the spirit that had become a tray of food and a roar at the sound barrier, the dream that had become tax-free whisky and seat belts for a little while between takeoff and landing.

And still it was the same world, the world of the senses where we were born and will die and where things move or seem to lie still.

Through the green-tinted window Jan watched the planes landing and taking off, the people streaming in and out. They blew away—the vapors of breath, the thin fumes of the oil heat, the blue spirals of exhaust, the smoke from smoldering refuse plants. . . . A million activities and movements rose into the atmosphere.

Arlanda was like a city, one of those new towns that spring up around a mineral deposit, a railway junction or a deep-water harbor. It was a society of outsiders, in which merchants and craftsmen, ships' captains and entrepreneurs, fly in from places with different customs, and complicated regulations and a lot of cooperation are required to keep cleanliness, precision, and morality from breaking down and a bad reputation from spreading far and wide.

The lines of communication met here. Like the airlines crossing each other on Jan's wall map, human beings seemed always on their way between landing places, temporary lodgings which they leave in order to return to. And the patterns they describe seem as fixed as the routes marked out by company headquarters.

The ground hostesses called out their flight numbers over the loudspeakers at the gates. *Embarquez s'il vous plaît.* . . . Final call for Lisbon, Monrovia, Rio de Janeiro, Sâo Paulo. . . . The passengers sit, on tenterhooks, in the transit hall. Carts of black umbrellas stand ready at the gates out to the field. Personal call for Mr. Fairweather at the information desk. Mechanics are summoned here and there. Chimes sound over the faint background music—SAS flight 875 to Copenhagen, Düsseldorf, Vienna. . . .

ESSA—Europe Sweden Stockholm Arlanda.

And in the midst of all this energy, this activity, this journeying to and from each other, Jan was on the lookout for a purpose.

A MEETING

WOMAN WAS standing outside the Arrivals door as if she were waiting for someone. At first there were people around her, a delegation that drove off in a couple of embassy cars. After that she was alone. It was during a space between planes; the bus to Stockholm had gone and Arlanda lay abandoned among the grave mounds on the plain.

Jan saw her as he drove out through the iron gate and waved to the guard. It had rained, the sun had been reflected in the skylights, but the clouds had closed in again. The loudspeakers were looking for someone, a man's name.

He drove around the parking area and stopped in front of her. Not even any porters were in sight. She was wearing a light gray raincoat and an elastic bandage around one ankle. She didn't notice him at first.

"Do you want a lift into Stockholm?"

"Yes, thank you. I got held up at customs."

She was carrying a green cloth suitcase which he put in the trunk, and a vinyl bag with a zipper which he put in the back seat. She got in beside him. He helped her fasten the safety belt.

"I came on the London plane," she told him.

"I know. I brought it down. I work here."

"I thought they had electronic brains for all that."

"There are still a few human beings coupled in. But we feel pretty unnecessary. We even keep the log on a computer."

"It's funny to think that you, that someone I meet right afterwards, brought down the plane I came on. And you're done for the day now?"

"I worked from seven to three today."

Where the single lane turned off to the north for Uppsala, he looked back over his shoulder to check for merging traffic and his glance passed quickly over her face. She had light, almost straight hair, and a short, broad nose. He didn't see the color of her eyes.

"Do you often give people rides like this?"

"I generally drive alone. Almost always."

"I think best when I'm driving. I'd never pick up anyone."

"What do you think about?" Jan asked.

"When I'm driving you mean. Or now? Just now I was thinking of opening the glove compartment. It's always full of things that tell you something about the driver—extra spark-plugs, advertisements, free postcards from restaurants, candy."

"Go ahead, open it! There's nothing special, I'm nobody special."

"No, there's not much here. Some maps, a bottle of wind-shield defroster, an owner's manual, a pen. Not much of a description."

Fog was blowing across the highway where the ground was marshy. It was like having cigarette smoke blown in your face. Mechanically he turned on the windshield wipers, which didn't help.

"I sprained my ankle my last day in London," she said. "Outside the Leicester Galleries, on the steps. Lucky it happened then. I usually walk for miles in London."

He saw shapes like bridges and piers in front of him. He drove more slowly than usual; it didn't seem there was any rush.

"Tell me what it's like in the tower. I've been listening to so much nonsense the last few days, meetings and things."

He told her about a fog in Copenhagen and how the passengers for Kastrup were brought up to Arlanda. There were seven hundred of them. There weren't any beds and in the end they spent the night in the barracks of the Svea Guards, who were gone on maneuvers. He said he liked Arlanda best when it was as deserted as it could get: technicolor sandwiches drying out under cellophane, paper cups and forgotten gloves, cast aside copies of *Playboy* and James Bond, *You Only Live Twice.*

"Do you?" she said, and suddenly there was laughter or flirtation in her voice, and he turned far enough toward her that he could see her eyes were slightly lopsided and apparently brown.

"What?"

"Live twice? Or live and let die?"

"Oh, you read James Bond."

"Everything. And then throw them away just like you said, on a chair at an airport."

He pictured her at London Airport, Heathrow, wearing the same coat. She was standing at the counter buying tax-free whisky. She was alone, she took care of herself. Or was there someone with her? She was wearing a ring on her left ring finger, but not an ordinary engagement ring, a thin gold ring with a smoke topaz. An unusual combination, he imagined, because the stone and the ring were almost the same color.

"On the plane I was reading Emma Göring's memoirs. There was a thing in there. . . . She tells about seeing Göring for the last time, and when she's leaving the prison she asks them if she can't avoid the photographers, so they take her back through the room where she'd been talking to Göring. She goes past the chair where he was sitting and runs her hand across the seat, and it's still warm."

"The only thing that concerned her," Jan said.

"Yes, after all the farewells. Like a table in a restaurant . . . with a spoon lying crooked, an empty glass. Or a hotel bed with the blanket turned down, and the person who slept there won't ever come back."

"I know exactly," he said with awkward emphasis.

"Do you really?" she said, in a tone of voice as if she wanted that piece of information for herself.

"Were you working in London?" he asked in return.

"My plane left there at twelve o'clock. Early this morning I was in the East End—a sort of street market. The kind with Jewish women in gray shawls, quarreling. Africans whistling at girls. Cafés with jukeboxes, and someone had written the names of the latest hits in chalk on the stone wall outside. I was there with a woman who works for an After Care Society that takes care of girls who've just come out of prison. They go back home, or to their boyfriends, in those long buildings with entrances from A to H, you know, and three hundred numbered apartments inside."

"That's what you've just seen," Jan said. "It's curious how people have completely different memories of things that just happened to them."

"Otherwise I work at the Department of the Environment."

There was a trailer truck in front of them. Red county buses passed in the opposite direction. Jan slowed down. Forest, lakes, remote estates, tract houses laid out around Väsby. The old Uppsala highway had wound its way along through a more varied countryside.

"Would you mind stopping for a minute?" she asked. "There's a turnout up ahead."

She disappeared a short way into the woods. She limped a little, with the elastic bandage around one ankle. Then she was back, out of breath, with laughter in her eyes and raindrops on her coat.

"I got a chill in London," she said. "A cold. Now I'll make it into Stockholm."

He noticed her glance pass over him, circling like the beam from a lighthouse, and continuing on across the countryside.

"I'm in England a lot," she said. "I usually take the boat and work on the way. Reports and that sort of thing. Then I thought, if I fly I can save a couple of days."

"Save them for what?" Jan asked.

"One day less away, one more day at home," she said. "But it's stupid really. I don't need to save time."

"The time goes anyway. You just do different things with it."

Jan liked conversations like that. About time, for example. He said that if she hadn't decided to save a day she wouldn't have come by way of Arlanda, and that would have been a waste. It sounded affected, so he added, "Now you'll have to go back to the office earlier."

"Working's no punishment," she said seriously. "And anyway I don't think you can put days away in a piggy bank."

It was late in the afternoon. He had driven out to Arlanda early, dawn on the Uppland plain. Royal grave mounds and the new hospital, the old churches and the truckers' cafés. Morning didn't care about the people who'd died during the night. Nothing worth reporting had happened that day. A plane had landed.

His passenger said, "Have you ever had an experience that suddenly made you happy?"

"Happy?"

"Yes, why isn't that just as good a question as what part of town someone lives in?"

"OK. But who can think of anything to answer?"

"You seem pretty used to answering questions."

"Yes. I've been sort of obedient ever since I went to school."

"Tell me then."

He nudged the rear-view mirror and looked at her more or less from in front, her eyes seemed to be watching the asphalt disappear beneath the wheels. He twisted to one side and saw her hands resting on her skirt. She was probably a perfectly ordinary person, he thought. He was annoyed with himself for even thinking that way, it didn't happen with other people. She was calm, spoke almost in a monotone and without any attempt to ingratiate herself. And yet he was giving her power over him. But of course she didn't know that.

"Let me think for a minute," he said.

He turned on the car radio. A music program ended with "We're gonna go fishing." Then Stig Järrel started reading the young people's serial for spring. "The Mysterious Island. Chapter One. 'Like a ball borne on the tip of a whirlwind, gripped by a swirling pillar of air. . . .' "

"A brick was put out to dry," Jan said. "That is, a piece of wet clay, sometime in the fourteenth century. A cat walked across it before the clay hardened. Now its footprint is built into an oven. And I saw it."

"And?"

"That's all. It made me feel happy all of a sudden. What more do you want?"

"No, nothing. If you're serious and that's not something you thought up just now."

"You're funny," Jan said, uncertainly.

"The same to you. You think I'm silly?"

"No. I'm glad you're sitting here."

He tried to smile at her impersonally, like when giving a gratuitous compliment, but he couldn't bring it off. They were silent, as if they had known each other a long time, or as if they had nothing further to say because they were strangers to each other, which was true. But he knew if she said anything he would for some reason believe it and trust her.

He turned off the mumbling radio serial and said, a little reproachfully, "We haven't even introduced ourselves."

"No, we don't know our names," she said illogically. "What's your name?"

"Jan Backman."

"Jenny Jeger."

Wood pigeons flew up from the ditch. A hedgehog lay dead on the yellow line, as flat as if it were airing its pelt. The tower of Sollentuna church could be seen beyond some woods; over there was the old road to Uppsala, and that was where the marathon runners had turned in 1912, all except the Japanese, who stopped for coffee and stayed forever.

Jan noticed her hand resting against the heater controls between the seats. If he had to turn it on he would touch her.

A shiver ran through him. He noticed how a thought that sensuous made him curious about this woman named Jenny Jeger who was a hitchhiker and career woman and had picked up an inflammation of the bladder in London. He wanted to start investigating her, as a game along the way, he told himself, an innocent whim, since they'd certainly never meet again. He looked at her hand again and was amazed at himself.

"Will you be going back to London soon?" he asked.

"It's not decided. But I go there every now and then."

"Fly again next time."

What a stupid request! Would he be driving her to the airport? Or home? Was he going to sit in the tower and look for her on the steps of every single London plane, in other words six times a day? Or did he, in some vague way, want her to belong to the Arlanda world and show up there again?

"Here's the Haga Terminal," she said. "I can get out here."

"Where do you live?"

"On Nybro Quay."

"I'll drive you home."

It was a dirty-brown building between the Academy of Music and Arsenalsgatan. In front lay the Nybro Pavilion, the water, and Strandvägen. On one side was Berzelii Park.

"What a tremendous location," Jan said. "You couldn't live in a better spot."

"The building's not modernized. They'll tear it down for sure."

"But it's right in the middle of town. Everyone comes by here."

He carried her bags to the street door.

"Thanks for the ride," she said, and took his hand. "It was pleasant, and very fast."

"Anytime."

He could give rides to hundreds of women, he thought, but this would never happen again. Whatever he did now, or failed to do, was equally irrevocable. If he did, he might regret the consequences. If he didn't, he would regret the loss but might forget the whole thing.

They stood for a moment beneath the building directory. Her name told him nothing. She was a stranger.

The world was changing its skin. He smiled helplessly. Maybe all of it was something he'd invented for himself.

He was filled with a tenderness that embraced everything, and a despair as if he were about to let go and fall.

Jenny looked at him as if she already knew there was nothing she needed to know.

"You must be tired after your trip," he said.

"Not tired," she said. "But thoughtful."

"I want to tell you something."

"Don't," she said.

"Yes, something else."

"Tell me then."

But he was silent. She had unfrightened eyes. He shook his head slightly.

"I can't go to prison for *this*," he muttered to himself.

And flooded by a feeling that everything was slipping away and would never return, he ran the tips of his fingers over her hair and pressed his palms hard along her neck and shoulders, against the arms of her raincoat and down toward her thighs. As if to capture her contours, set up boundary markers.

She took a deep breath. A door slammed high up in the house, steps approached.

Then she walked quickly away.

J OUT OF REACH

AN LEFT HIS CAR where it stood and went into the Riche Bar for a whisky. No familiar faces. He looked at an empty TV screen in the corner behind the bartender.

When he came out again it was cooler, and there was a mist hanging over Nybro Bay. It seemed to him he was standing between two landscapes. One of them he saw dimly through the mist—it belonged to the past and he didn't want to abandon it completely. The other was the quay he stood on, the city he'd come to, and a little further along the air was clear and he saw gulls on the bollards and piles of sand and automobiles.

There were two cities eating their way toward each other, so that as soon as they met they might break their frames and shatter. He belonged to both of them and wanted to store them both within himself.

He got into the car, drove home, and put the car in the garage. He took his briefcase from the back seat, then left it where it was. He checked the keys in his pocket, he had everything.

I can't possibly go home yet, he told himself. Nothing was different, but something had happened. He was trembling, not with desire but from lack of conscience, from being threatened, from a secret joy, from being taken back to a beginning. We're gonna go fishing, he thought.

He walked up to Observatory Hill. There were more flowers than his last time there, the leaves were larger and greener, but just as few people. A protest singer with his guitar was sitting down among the tables outside Corso's restaurant. He was wearing jeans and an open gondolier's shirt and singing a song about The War Which Is Attacking Others For What We Cannot Do Ourselves. The sky, clear again, showed signs of evening. Shifting colors like a smoke topaz, it arched over the home of the astronomers.

The tip of the tongue against the lower teeth, the back against the palate—the phonetics of her name. He had no other ground to stand on, no justified prospects. But it wasn't a question of that. He didn't want to make Gertrude unhappy. It was just that he felt absolutely certain that this person was thinking of him too, and that if they met again it would occur with inexplicable mutual understanding and they would never have to speak to each other in code.

It struck him that he'd felt this way before—or maybe not he but Gertrude, in the attic of the Water Palace when they undressed and dressed each other up—it didn't matter which of them it was. He could suddenly feel Gertrude's ecstasy like his own, together with the adoring submission and helplessness that he had felt himself. All of it had already taken place, in a shameless but accidental and irresponsible way, far off in an independent world of feeling that bridged over to the everyday world only by chance and for fun. He saw Gertrude naked in the attic, he saw himself naked.

There was a lack of anxiety in everything, as if he'd decided from the outset that nothing had happened. There was a children's song whistling in his head and molding his lips, he couldn't make it go away. "I've got sixpence, jolly jolly sixpence . . . ."

He was filled with a joy that was tiring and almost anguishing. He didn't want to think about it, didn't want to see its face. But his senses were awake. He saw the green roof on the School of Economics and the colors of the newspaper placards down on Sveavägen, he heard the traffic, he felt as if his body had become ten or why not twenty pounds lighter and he wanted to go high-jumping. The only paralyzing thought was that all this hadn't really happened, that at any moment he would look around and not understand a thing.

It occurred to him that he was spending his life in a single place, in a single job, with a passive, unexamined feeling for his role. Sten Tidström went to Africa and was socially conscious and involved, he understood that other people existed independently of what he happened to think of them. Tidström functioned rationally and clear-sightedly. Jan sat in his tower at Arlanda and still he saw nothing. Or he stood on the tarmac like an old Junker aircraft that couldn't get off the ground.

He grew frightened for himself, for his life, for his happiness. And his sensation of happiness lay perhaps in the fact that after this long day he felt himself a stranger in the world, and therefore freer. He couldn't force his way into it, it remained unfamiliar as if intended for someone else, and still *his* world lay before him.

What was this pounding artery in his midriff that filled him with feelings he didn't want to define? Is the person who tries to pinch himself awake awake already? And if he was awake, how could he go on living in this violent pulse?

Why had Jenny shaken her head? Not from aversion, certainly, but as though after a dizzy spell or getting rid of a distraction?

He was already asking himself questions about her. She was not the least bit mysterious, he told himself. She was a flash from the expected. Calm down, he said, she's in the same city, that's enough. Yes, he was calm. He was not beside himself. There is no moment when you are outside yourself. There are only inflexible actions.

He ran down Observatory Hill and took Sveavägen south, toward Nybro Square. He belonged to no one, not to Gertrude, not to this stranger. His life led him from one moment to the next. He seemed to be the same person, he didn't deny his reflection in a shop window, but he was also someone he couldn't reach, something he couldn't fulfill.

It was as if he couldn't hold this trembling within him. He felt joy and melancholy in such a curious mixture that it made him defenseless. It seemed to him the streets were as empty as in summer, and the air was clearer than usual. He felt very exposed and wanted to go into a doorway, crouch down in the shadows of the buildings like a thief who was too tall, amazed at the clatter of his own footsteps as if he no longer had a right to the sidewalks, to the city, as if everything he undertook was suddenly illegal and inexplicable, something there was no answer to and no meaning in.

When he looked around to compare things with the way they were before this feeling, before this afternoon and the ride into Stockholm, he couldn't remember anything. And where he was headed and what he meant to do there—he didn't know that either. It was like glimpsing a momentary flash of light from some object in a window or in a thought which he didn't have the strength to grasp.

He ran down Hamngatan from Sergel Square, which was still unfinished, its southern side blank walls. His face burned as if what he was going through didn't want to stay inside but had to get out and show itself. Still he felt embedded in himself, out of the reach of other people, with a new secret in his possession, a man in town on a mission. The people whose glances he met halfway had other missions. And the next day on the radio there would be a new episode from The Mysterious Island: "Like a ball borne on the tip of a whirlwind. . . ."

He had come to Jenny Jeger's building. There was a light in a window high up and he'd seen on the directory that she lived on the fifth floor, higher than he could throw a stone. It was dark in the beer café on the street level: they closed early. It was dark in the laundry next door. He glanced for a moment toward the telephone booth by Tornberg's clock. He walked around Nybro Pavilion. The secret, unbuilt Stockholm grew in there in white plaster: wonderful bridges and viaducts shadowing small buildings and invisible human beings.

He tried the door to the building, it was open. He climbed the stairs and examined every nameplate on the way as if he were looking for someone. He stood outside her door: Jeger. A name in white on a narrow black tape.

He had walked with the soundless steps of childhood, he wasn't out of breath but his mouth was dry. He had been transported to another world and hardly cared what had brought it about. He waited passively for nothing to happen.

How much would be different if she knew he was standing here? More than he wanted? For everyone else he remained the person he had been before, even for her, Jenny. Only he himself knew how his landscape, his people, had stopped at the cry of the photographer. Now they were still, very distinct, in the strong light of distance. And he himself was standing there with them, a stranger he could see at the edge of the picture, one among the others.

A building in Stockholm. A door with a name on it.

On both sides of that door there is oxygen being changed to carbon dioxide and a blind production of eggs and sperm. The machinery goes on. Why care about one person in this swarm of people? People are all alike. Why advertise whisky unless hundreds of thousands like it, or photograph naked models unless . . . or publish serials about inheritances, family intrigues and mistaken identity. . . . Almost everything is universal. Except for a little bit, some imperceptible divergence in the ads, preferences, smells, and that little bit gives rise to such an uproar and senselessness.

The everyday world that circled around him with its facts and figures and routines ceased, and the silence that was left filled up with something very complicated, and he was tired and his collarbone ached and he thought of Gertrude and how people can love the people they have to hurt, hurt the ones they love. "People"—not he, not I. He had difficulty imagining the days to follow—he looked into rooms that didn't belong to him, rooms where he didn't live.

Very near, just a door. But far away.

Your days are full of unknown moments. It was to her, this stranger, that he spoke, not to Gertrude, not to himself. As if you were holding your hands over my ears—I can see your face, but not your days. You—a commonplace, a meeting. Like me maybe, therefore this lack as if I ran around looking for my own tail. Unlike me, therefore this sensual pleasure like a dog with his head stretched forward and his sinews taut, picking up a scent he has to follow out. Unknown to me, and therefore this twisting navigation through the streets.

You know nothing. Think if you knew . . . there, at a distance of about ten yards. I've blocked the door you go through, I've raised the sill and still you don't stumble. Because you don't know. If you only knew how many doors you've run your head against and how many sills you've tripped on. I've stolen something in you, I have it here with me—a picture, a sign, a ball in my hand. And when you're feeling most unfettered, free as a bird, you'll notice you're being nailed to the ground and you'll realize you're my prisoner that I'm setting free.

When he came out to Nybro Square he looked up at the fifth floor. It was dark.

He stopped at Humlegården on his way home. He thought he'd bring Gertrude a surprise. With his fingers and a penknife he dug up a flower from a flowerbed. It resembled a hydrangea, he didn't know its name. No one saw him.

In the hall at Upplandsgatan there was a note from Gertrude. He guessed she'd gone to the Water Palace. But she'd gone to the movies. It was almost eleven o'clock. She'd be home any minute.

He didn't know exactly what he should do. He opened a closet door and looked at her dresses. He'd helped her buy a lot of them. Her taste was his, they knew each other so well. A decision could be made with the wave of a hand, as if it wasn't they themselves who decided things, merely a silent mutual understanding.

It could have been anyone at all, he thought. I could have adapted myself to someone else, then I wouldn't be who I am but someone I don't know anything about. People are undefined. Things become real for them by chance. But he had imagined that his relationship to Gertrude was safer than his relationship to anything else in existence, because she was his sister. Nothing bad must happen to her. He smiled at the darkness outside the circle of light. She was out there. He felt generous and rich.

You are with me in everything I do, he thought. It is you who act in me. Do you know that?

But this nameless thing that usually lay silent and dead and now suddenly began to eat its way up through him—what was that?

He sat down on the floor. On the bottom shelf of a bookcase were his and Gertrude's old schoolbooks, the ones they'd saved. He looked at the physics books while he waited. The clumsy drawing of a flask and the liquid that had stopped halfway up the tube, not yet hot enough at the moment of the drawing to have made it all the way, despite the petrified flame of the bunsen burner.

He suddenly smelled damp chalk, as if crumbled between his fingers. Happiness and self-effacement flowed through his veins like a wave of heat, an experience that would turn into nothing if he divulged it, however much he would like to.

He looked at the picture again. The liquid had not risen in the tube in spite of the fact that the heat seemed stronger.

He heard a key in the lock and then Gertrude hanging up her coat. He put away the book as if he'd been doing something forbidden, but at the same time he had to put her and the picture together in his mind, since it was only now, while waiting for her, that he'd smelled the chalk and felt the heat of the bunsen burner in his body—as if all these things had happened simultaneously and were collected in this one instant as the sound of her steps reached him like cautious hammer strokes against a flask.

"Hi. Are you here? I went and saw *Knife in the Water* at the Eriksberg. I didn't bother to call and find out when you were coming home."

"You hardly ever call Arlanda." He smiled.

He gave her the flower and said he'd swiped it in Humlegården. They looked at each other in surprise.

"What an idea," she said. "You don't generally do things like that. You must have been crazy."

He recognized her. Something in him sang like a bird. Nothing had changed. He loved her. But he couldn't tell her what he'd been doing.

THE WATER PALACE

THE NEXT MORNING Gertrude said, "I'm taking the day off. I thought I might go out to the Water Palace for a while and work."

She was packing their largest bag.

"I'll come along," he said.

"You have to be at Arlanda in the morning," she said calmly. "And I'm thinking of staying a long time."

"Doing what?"

"Out there you mean? I'm going to sit down with my ferns and see if I can get somewhere. I haven't worked on them for a long time."

He was glad she'd decided to go. She was less at ease in Stockholm, in this building that was eventually to be torn down. The city changed too fast; she always seemed to be standing in the shadows of new viaducts. And the Academy of Sciences was only a temporary retreat. Only at the Water Palace was she inaccessible. It was a place to hide. Was it the only one?

He knew how she would sit out there, looking at the birds outside, and they in turn would look at her and know that she was there. Her feet, brown and sinewy, would run down to the bay, she would put the rowboat in the water and red paint would scrape off on the rocks and stay there till next summer, she would clear away the reeds that had washed ashore. She would hardly bother to comb her hair and her face would take on the unguarded expression of a woman who forgets to look in the mirror.

The thought filled Jan with a painful, unsettling realization that he was necessary to her—just as the banks of a channel give relief to a boat that on the open sea would disappear from sight.

And so both of them went out. They picked up the laundry, stopped at the filling station, and shopped at the Co-op in Gustavsberg. When Jan came direct from Arlanda he usually drove across Vaxholm, took the ferry to Rindö and then the military ferry between Oscar Fredriksborg and Värmdö. The last stretch of four hundred yards there was no road, only a twisting path down a steep hill.

Early June. They had arrived like this many times. The bags from the supermarket went beside the sink. Gertrude opened the taps where rusty water had collected, she threw out a can of anchovies that was about to burst and some juniper twigs that had gone yellow in a kettle. Jan opened the windows on the second floor and raked the leaves out of the eaves with the handle of a broom.

The house was still full of shut-in winter smells, wood and linoleum, damp and age, something hard to identify and wonderful. Jan looked at objects, relentlessly long-lived, ready to let themselves be inherited once more and become the building blocks of other people's lives. They brightened up every time someone died. Now they could perform their drama again, and they'd learned a thing or two since last time.

Some furniture had nevertheless been sold at auction. Jan remembered certain things from other rooms, in other positions, as if he were seeing them through that yellow transparent sun-streamed water you find only under docks, the clearest water the Baltic had to give. The marine charts had been put away, *Information for Mariners* as well. Gone was the description of Swedish lightships, various hydrographic reports for the coast of Blekinge, a stuffed black-throated diver that moths had gotten into.

And as if by common consent—without their having mentioned it—the picture of their father had been removed from the desk they both used. Maybe Jan had moved it a bit, pushed it halfway behind a vase full of pens and pencils, or else Gertrude had taken it away and Jan realized he'd wanted to do the same thing that same day. He was now out of sight, with the dark moustache he'd had in those days to hide his weak upper lip.

Jan and Gertrude walked through a house with closed-eyed walls. They were silent. Early summer had begun with Darwin tulips on the lawn, buttercups still low in the meadow, dandelions and candle flames on the chestnut trees. But the inside of the house was haunted by an intangible world of shadows. Jewish refugees whom their father, with his fear and shortsighted nationalism, had prevented from coming to Sweden at the end of the thirties. The ever-present memory of a conservative and disloyal man many people had considered realistic and conscientious. Excuses.

Jan and Gertrude often felt small in this big house with its tile stove and polished friezes in the dining room, its more simply beamed white ceiling on the porch, its white and wine-red linoleum floor in the kitchen. It had been built at the turn of the century for a family with a cook and a maid. They lived here childless, somehow forgotten, at the tail end of a long evolution. Two grandfather clocks ticked out free moral advice.

The Water Palace—the shell around a vanished family feeling, the feeling in old novels where relatives visit one another and cousins grow up together.

The lilacs stood white and pale violet at this time of year. If you found blossoms with five or more petals you were supposed to swallow them and make a silent wish. Jan found one with six petals, Gertrude one with seven, and they wished. Jan found another and Gertrude asked him to make a wish out loud unless it would cancel his first one.

"An ability to accept experience."

"How do you mean?"

"Not to grow rusted over and become a virgin in reverse, a person who's left unmarked by whatever passes through him."

And then he found time to empty the water barrels that stood brimful at the corners of the house, to fix the Ping-Pong paddles where the rubber had come loose, and pick nettles that were almost out of hand. His fingertips didn't notice the sting until afterwards, they didn't burn but tingling bubbles crept under his skin, like touching something forbidden. A white butterfly with red at the very tips of its wings floated across the lawn, until a wagtail came tearing along and swallowed it.

Château d'eau. Named after a small district in Paris which is also a metro station. Jan and Gertrude's grandfather had lived there just before he built the house with the help of so-called volunteer labor during a convenient year of famine. And thus the authorized translation from the French—the house in the reflection, the sky beneath your feet, the tree roots over your head—Sweden.

As a child, Jan imagined a palace under water, shimmering blue. Children played by the shore and were lured down to the palace by sea witches and never heard of again. They enjoyed their life down there, they forgot everything else.

Now he had taken over the Water Palace. Who was there to force him up to the earth again? The old house lay fastened with green-slimed anchor chains to a bottom that bound his imagination in comfort and repetition and idleness.

A symbol must be broken open by other symbols like the egg by the sperm in order for propagation to occur.

One of the differences between him and Gertrude was this: at the Water Palace Gertrude was at ease and free and well-rooted, while Jan had a vague feeling of captivity. He saw objects clearly, they forced themselves upon him, never changed their positions, seemed to be nailed to the floor. If you tried to move them dark spots were left on the floors and carpets, places the sun had never been able to bleach.

Houses were like people, people sometimes like background. Gertrude lived out here in a tranquillity she had built up around herself, at home among things that were her parachutes. She didn't try to explain what probably couldn't be explained. The landscape was hers. He ran after her along a path, caught her, grabbed her hard by the shoulders—that was nice. She stretched out her hands that would soon be brown from the sun. They were ringless, Gertrude didn't like jewelry.

Later they sat on the enclosed porch. Gertrude had papers with her from the Academy of Sciences—engravings of ferns, Humboldt, a city map of Bogotá in the 1820s when the Swede Gosselman was there. She had taken her project from the fringes of the history of learning. She liked a certain amount of mystery in what she did. Where other people revealed themselves she was secretive, what she wanted to talk about was always something else.

Jan sensed that she wanted to screen off an area for herself, for both of them. It was this she had been doing all along.

Did he understand her work? He would interpret the reports from the German weather bureau more quickly than Gertrude's data. He heard her mention scales and natural sizes—how were botanical and zoological observations and measurements transferred to illustrations during different periods? How faithful to reality were the drawings, how strongly did they reflect the education and background of the observer—what the observer was looking for and therefore found, while other things remained in the shadows waiting for other angles of vision, other tools?

Gertrude saw the tree built into the leaf of the fern, the fibers that represented the next stage in evolution. No fungi, no diseases on the leaves—those belonged to different plates. She saw the mosaic bird come loose from its setting and fall to pieces the moment it flew instead of merely *represented* flight.

The channel passed outside their porch—boats to and from Stockholm on the route to Öresund and the southern Baltic had to pass this way. They watched them, made out their names through the binoculars, and the wakes kept pounding against the rocks for hours, almost without interruption. Then you could hardly hear footfalls or birds. But in the waves themselves there was such a multiplicity of vibrations that sometimes you heard footsteps in them, sometimes birds.

He wanted to lift Gertrude's face to his, there was tenderness in his open hands. If she were in a void, then she would find that he was also there, they would wait together, nothing that happened to her would not at the same time happen to him. They lived beneath the same umbrella, in the same danger.

He spelled out her life backwards as if in a mirror. Their helplessness . . . . There was so much he could tell her, so much she would have to go through, welding heat, freezing wind. Could he be asbestos and windbreak for her?

There ought to be a windier sort of security, which she would reach without him.

Go your way to the land of the ferns. Then I'll see you approaching me again, sister mine.

But he didn't dare say that.

He wanted to meet her in a world of touch where people could take hold of each other and where he would find her hands, quick, arranging, slightly flecked with age. And he saw her, how she came in with a spray of wild appleblossoms or bird-cherry and put it in a pot. A face as if mirrored in water, he thought. Artless, experienced.

And Gertrude in turn looked at him as if he were something to depend upon.

From their wicker chairs they could see a tapestry their father had brought from France. A tall, slender lady was riding on a lion. They filled almost the entire space. The lion was looking to one side, the lady slightly to the rear. They both looked a little uneasy, as if they were being watched or were gripped by an urgency they couldn't obey as long as they were caught in the cloth. They seemed, at all events, to be allies in the same predicament. Over their heads was a ribbon, on which was written in French, "We will soon be out of the forest."

Jan read that sentence often. Who was saying it to whom? What awaited them outside the forest, what different fates? Was the forest the lion's enemy too? Had the lion rescued the lady?

The forest—it consisted of a few dim trees. The simple words took up much more room. The trees yielded to the words. We will soon be out, soon. . . . And time passed and the lion wore the same unchanging expression.

"I'm going to wash the windows," Gertrude said. "They're streaked with rain. Here we sit. We could go on like this for a long time. Sometimes you need no space at all, sometimes you need whole prairies, streets that never end."

Jan didn't answer. He was thinking of Myra, the girl in school who'd always moved in the class photo.

"The windows are streaked with rain," Gertrude said again. Her dress was synthetic linen, yellow to brown hair.

"I think I'll go to South America this fall," she said without looking at him.

And so those words were said. The screw was twisted one more turn.

That night he dreamed he was standing in Jenny Jeger's closet. He'd never been there. He didn't know how many dresses she had. The door was closed but it was light inside—a green sunlight shone in from behind as if through leaves. Thin fabrics had been chosen and sewn together to encircle her. It was all by chance that they'd wound up here and belonged to her and he could smell them against his cheek. One was light brown with white dots and a broad belt, cotton for summer. One was dark red and rough as sackcloth and lined. He could see the seams in the sides above the waist—a dress can't be the same in front and back. He could hear Jenny's voice: "not tired but thoughtful," though the words weren't directed to him.

He woke up. A bright early summer night. Gertrude was asleep beside him. At first they'd had separate rooms, Gertrude in their father's, he in the room he'd had as a child. They would meet by the rusty water heater in the bathroom. In an unspoken way they had been more brother and sister out here than in Stockholm, something was left of their father, and their own games. At Upplandsgatan they met body to body, out here they met with the house all around them, which they held in trust. But that was a long time ago, and they had soon moved in together, curled up in the same wide bed, and left the rest of the house empty.

Jan couldn't go back to sleep. He was surprised. He felt as if he were some stray emotion, an emotion he failed to recognize because it was pure novelty. He was driven out into the quiet house.

The floor paint was worn into paths between the doors. He walked hesitantly, almost on tiptoe. But he was filled with a desire for action that usually had no place in him. Not a sense of purpose or effort, just a tightening inside, a knot. He was gripped by a sensual pleasure that made him see distinctly. Tenderness radiated out into the night. His fingertips found their way over unfamiliar skin. His life was close to a bursting point.

He didn't know how he should behave. His fear that for some reason everything would fall apart, his hope that everything would work out whatever that might mean—they canceled each other out and became indifference, as if he had turned over his fate to foreign embassies.

In looking back, people's lives, history itself, deal with moments when something happens, with crises, turning points and their consequences. But most people's lives consist of arming themselves against dangers that never materialize. To waste so much time and energy on useless preparation—what a trial when nothing happens. What really happens is always something else. And when it does, as always, the Achilles heel is unprotected.

On the way back to his sleeping sister he went past the door to the attic stairs and his mouth filled with the taste of that strange summer when he was twelve—his palate dry from physical excitement or from the warm air up under the tiles on the roof. But it wasn't the attic that reminded him, it was rather the warmth inside him that called forth Gertrude's games.

Gertrude was all he had. Mother dead, father often away, other people who didn't exist in earnest. When Gertrude was there everything was as it should be. And she was there, holding him in a tight grip in which there was something of the cradle.

Up in the attic of the Water Palace he had been on a peak, he would never get higher, there he had lived, and the way down was the way away from Gertrude and out into separation. Without noticing it, he had begun to cry. He always wanted to feel that she was there. Only between the two of them was the space open and navigable. All around them was the closed world.

This particular experience marked his life. It was his. A varnish of strangeness over everything, and then Gertrude's eyes—there was the familiar; there was where he had to be; he had to feel her fingers in order to feel everything else. Otherwise he slipped on the varnish, he couldn't get under it, not anywhere.

Everything protected itself against him, against his lack of touch. Only her face was open to him.

You can live without touching. But this is what he'd wanted —Gertrude's dance around him, her preoccupation with him, his with her, her hunger for him. The way they circled around each other, insects blinded by light, giddy from the heat, so close they were not entirely within each other's reach.

Did that greed still exist?

These hands that stretch across an abyss though they're perfectly still.

The one hand forgets and lets go, then the other grips convulsively.

They could stand opposite each other and breathe heavily in a long silence, while bewilderment drew over them.

Most of the things they'd done together as children had lost their immediacy. Once she had buried him in the sand, which was harder to imagine than the time he had tried to strangle her. Suddenly he saw her as she was then, the girl with the long slim limbs and the quick wild movements, sureness and strength, the girl who'd been his master. Then her features weakened, blurred a little as if behind a candle flame, and with dizzying speed his memories of her slipped into nothingness.

You are half of someone else who will maybe never come, he thought.

He went to bed, watched the dawn gnaw a hole in the

window and let in the sun, then closed his eyes without sleeping and listened to the wood pigeons starting their distant jungle drums and to Gertrude's breathing that he'd listened to for years.

They got up together. Gertrude looked at him as if she knew everything and it didn't surprise him; it was usually that way. He felt afraid and amazed at himself. In the mirror he caught a glimpse of a madman with a glassy stare, a criminal in early middle age who had just heard his sentence. Summer went on with iris and swallows outside the house.

Gertrude let the day float by. She worked with her material from the Academy of Sciences and sent Jan to fix the pump in the well-house—because of his job he was supposed to have a way with machines. She mixed pieces of chicken with iceberg lettuce and poured on cheese-flavored dressing and that was their lunch.

He wandered around their grounds, stopped under the wide tent of the bird-cherries, rescued a capsized beetle that glistened in the short grass. He saw the way the landscape came to a stop, like traffic at a railroad-crossing gate, or like Gertrude on the steps, squinting into the light blue smoke of morning.

Then it was afternoon and time to drive back. It was as if he were leaving half a century of overstuffed chairs, private lives, grandfather clocks, broad-minded respectability. Something to describe in novels—and then maybe never again.

He let his eyes travel over the house as if it were for the last time. But he knew that wasn't the case. The Water Palace wasn't childhood, though it lay like a magic mountain in the forest of the past.

RUNNING TAPE

HE GAVE Gertrude a long kiss when he left the Water Palace and she met him with her whole body. He could feel her knees against his, her breasts beneath the soft, much-washed bra. Her hands were hard and uncaressing as a child's. He noticed questioning and doubt in her sometimes, but they weren't there now. Their faces were so close they were invisible to each other. This was the face he got most from, he thought, he knew it better than his own.

A parting with loss and relief in it. He looked at her like a storyteller who is constantly forced to interrupt himself. There was a great deal he hadn't said.

He drove in as fast as he dared on the hopeless Värmdö road. The brakes were still a little loose, the snow tires still on, worn as they were. It was chilly, the time of the iron nights early in June. He saw no hitchhikers, but a lot of traffic in his own direction. He drove through forest succeeded by fields, houses, summer cottages, and occasional manors that were being farmed.

The driving itself was a solitary, pleasant activity. He felt he'd become a new person. A bolt of lightning had blown all the fuses, he didn't know quite how to function. Everything was flowing toward him and he was free to receive. At the same time he was captive. He saw Gertrude growing smaller, encircled by the round black contour of the telescope. It was like being torn in two.

The Danvik drawbridge rose up in front of his radiator; he glimpsed a freighter with farm equipment on its deck. Then the bridge went down again and passed him into Stockholm.

He drove along the city quay but couldn't see a phone booth. So he stopped at a harbor restaurant called The Frigate and called Jenny on a greasy telephone you weren't allowed to use for more than three minutes. He looked up her number in the book; it was the first time he'd seen her name in print. For a second he expected Gertrude to answer.

Jenny was neither at home nor at the Department of the Environment. He waited by the phone as if she knew where he was and would call at any moment. It was four thirty, almost dark inside the old customs shed. There were lifebuoys hanging from the walls and a fishnet below the skylight. A slot machine clattered in one corner.

Jan Backman began to have doubts about what he was getting himself into. But at the same time he was prepared to watch her house, interrogate the people in the laundry, sit down with a bowl of pea soup at the beer café and ask if they had noticed Jenny Jeger who lived on the top floor. But then he would have betrayed his interest, and he didn't want anyone to know. He was a secret cog in a piece of machinery he couldn't operate.

He stopped by the Finland boats on Skeppsbron and called her again. No answer. He didn't know where she could be. She wasn't waiting for him. She was involved in something else, as he was himself. No one is the first for anyone.

And then he was at Nybro Quay. He could see her door from the car. He felt no desire for her body but an almost crushing curiosity about her life. Two days before he'd run his hands one short moment over her shoulders and down her sides. . . .

There are unavoidable moments, you behave in a certain particular way but can't remember later how or why. You become willing to take risks. Everything happens in a quick transition, as when a casual dance is transformed into a thing of decisive importance in the very minute the music goes into its final bars, and you didn't want it nor intend it, but there you are helpless, broken open by a soundless storm.

He drove out to Arlanda. Forest again. And then across the treetops he saw the water tower, the radar equipment, the traffic control tower, all the familiar things that were his work and his responsibility.

. . . out of the forest.

That evening he dialed Värmdö. Gertrude didn't answer. Maybe she was sitting down by the water. He couldn't picture what she was doing. Then he called Jenny. Silence. He had never seen her apartment.

He was alone. He'd left Gertrude at the Water Palace. He couldn't find Jenny. There was no web of intrigue binding these two together. They had nothing to do with each other.

He wanted to write a story for Gertrude. It would be about herself when she was most shy, most timid, and didn't want to leave her room and go anyplace with anyone. At such times a book was more comfortable than a human being and someone else's printed words more real than the words she heard and the faces she saw. A story about her resistance, so her resistance would collapse when she heard about it, just as the story would be altered by her hearing it.

He caught glimpses of Gertrude, but he couldn't take stock of someone that close to him without counterfeiting his own senses. He lacked the laboratory of emotional distance. Pictures displaced one another. Blueprints—his was the last and the fuzziest. Like using someone else's discarded text as backing, and it imperceptibly blends in with what you've written yourself.

What he wanted—to spread out in every direction, to sink to his own antipodes, so that coercion and constraint, dictating in code would lead him to an unknown freedom.

But it was instead as if he'd lost in both directions. Gertrude, Jenny. . . . He was a jar full of fog. He didn't choose his experiences. He didn't shape things himself. He thought about the programmed and the animal side of man, and how nevertheless it was possible to change him.

At the same time he was fond of his intoxication.

Almost nothing was happening at Arlanda. The airport seemed abandoned. Visibility from the tower was limited. His senses were much more helpless than the reconnaissance instruments in the control room. Now when the traffic was slow his mind wandered off to other things. For example, he imagined that every day for five months he would observe and note the habits of a dying colony of penguins in Antarctica. Those expanses of ice meant confinement. He felt loneliness freeze up inside him, but he also felt possessed—these doomed birds, he knew this was the final stage of their long existence, *they* presumably did not. He was in the midst of them and yet he only looked out from his hut. Revelations of love and cruelty.

Lack of freedom existed. It did not follow from that that freedom existed. There were meetings and farewells. Magnetisms. Contacts. People found and lost one another. That's what everything was all about.

Nothing unexpected happened. He counted more tank trucks than airplanes down on the field. A hangar door closed—someone had pushed a button somewhere. Jan made a list of things to do in the next few days. He'd promised to write a petition to the landlord with copies to the local housing committee and the real estate office. Install side mirrors on the car. Have an extra key made for Upplandsgatan and leave it with the woman at the cigar store. Write to Sten Tidström in Africa.

The runner came in from the forecast room with the latest weather map, cluttered with symbols: red triangles for rain three hours back, black triangles for present rain, spirals for cyclones. Arrows traced the movements of the winds upward and down. Within the course of half an hour every flight control in Europe would have the same information. You looked at the triangles, assessed them, and acted accordingly.

Everything was at stake as usual. Nevertheless you went on living as if nothing had happened. It was almost always that way.

Jan Backman sent the tapes from the two previous watches

down to central: the traffic-control tower's official log, which now consisted of automatically recorded orders, instructions, position reports.

Once in a while he added a summary, comment or explanation at the end of the day.

The tapes were filed but never written out.

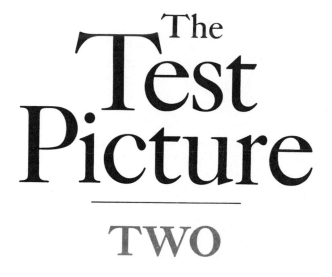

The Test Picture

TWO

FIVE THINGS

ASTRAGAL.

Jan Backman was working the crossword while he waited for the phone to ring. He hypnotized his gray cobra. It stared back with its little holes. But Jenny Jeger didn't call.

Astragal. What was that? The word was in the first volume of the encyclopedia. The oval stamp on the inside cover—Government Property.

No one knew. No one at Arlanda had any idea of his secret position. A girl came into his office and poured thin thermos coffee into a paper cup.

Dictionary. Lists. There were five things that could be called "astragal."

1. Dice, a game of dice.

A cart with a hundred roast beef sandwiches rolled out to a chartered plane. The way everything functioned! There were so many people to call and alarm if something went wrong.

2. The talus or anklebone. A caster-shaped bone resting on the heel bone and constituting the point of attachment between leg and foot.

Bulldozers were crawling around on the outskirts of Arlanda. Thunder—a bumpy descent for the tourists from Rhodes.

Right at the moment I live to find out more about Jenny.

Right at the moment he lived to find out more about Jenny. They'd seen each other for the first time a couple of days before—a ride, chance.

3. A forage plant of the pea family. Sweet milk vetch the most common in Sweden. Yields gum dragon, an effusion of sap and rubber produced by the reconstruction of the pith cell walls. Gum dragon swells in water without dissolving and is used by pharmacists and confectioners as an effective binder.

What meeting Jenny had been like—he'd never be able to describe it. He didn't live through it bit by bit like a tapeworm. He was inside a globe with yellow light, in a narrow endless cave.

Loanwords all of them. There was much that didn't exist until it was described. But if he were to tell about this most important thing in his life he would fail it, the story would be about something else. He couldn't handle the word order of emotion.

She'd been standing under the Arrivals sign, in the middle of a frame and the film had stopped. That was all.

4. The molding that separates the capital from the shaft of a column, pillar or pilaster.

His picture of Jenny wasn't only of her but also of himself and others. No one can be stripped in order to make her more herself, she only becomes more someone else becoming someone else. Living in Unattainability along with all the others.

5. Common name of an instrument of torture resembling a pair of tongs, used in French colonial prisons to elicit confessions.

Astragal. According to the reference books.

Sweden is divided into four flight information regions for the control of air traffic..

Radar doesn't *mirror* reality. With symbols that have no counterpart anywhere else, it describes part of what's happening out there.

Can the world be quiet enough to let the song of the astragal be heard? No. No one ever wanted to discover that bird. So silence is no help.

Jan's desk was comparatively clean, most of his papers were stuffed into files, arranged in folders. He felt as vapid as the barely patterned light yellow curtains found in so many government offices. Jenny didn't call, and he wasn't even sad but anonymous, unborn and dumb.

Airplanes climbed and descended. People streamed in and out through the glass doors. Cars drove in to various long-term parking lots. He didn't feel like a coherent human being. He functioned. He read the newspapers, thoughts arose and left him when he turned the page.

Nothing unexpected happened.

The astragal was still five things: dice, as well as a throw of the dice; the easiest bone in the body to break; the sap or cement that makes two surfaces difficult to separate; a transition in stone from one architectonic form to another; an instrument for making people talk.

He went over his life—a tranquil exterior, a well-paid government routine, a mask of law-abiding regularity, the traffic rules along the road from Stockholm to Arlanda.

It was as if someone else made all his decisions.

He was forced to accept the fact that Gertrude was his sister as a given, something he could not check or criticize or question. And yet something in him was secretly susceptible to disorder, licentiousness, and shame. He didn't have the strength to figure out if it was just an internal itch or a desire to put the inexplicable, vague, and alluring into decisive action.

Weather report: twenty-five-hundred-foot ceiling, NOSIG (no significant change).

Maybe astragal was an abbreviation.

He looked at several new books that passed across his desk: C. L. Stratonovich's *Topics in the Theory of Random Noise*, Balakrishnan's *Advance in Communication Systems*. They could go back to the library.

Jenny Jeger ought to call. He paced back and forth in his office. It was stuffy after the thunderstorm. It was summer, the window was open. Gulls in the air, shaking exhaust fumes from their feathers.

His FM transistor was playing the catalogue aria from *Don Juan*: his ten thousand and three women. The magic of numbers—what's a lot, what's a little? Hairs on a head, the cars that will line up at Norrtull this evening, the sandwiches in the SAS kitchens? Every time your heart beats three babies are born, according to the UN. He'd read a sociological study that said it wasn't unusual for a prostitute to have thirty thousand men in the course of her career. But no one is more than one person, though he sometimes felt like two—playing card, centaur.

Every person is on earth to fill a need, otherwise he's superfluous. That's what he'd been taught, but had never found a place where he was indispensable. Maybe with Gertrude, but not even there, inevitable was more like it. What would stop functioning if he didn't exist? Who won when he lost? He himself. Who lost on him? No one.

A list of watches looked like this: PM, AM, PM, AM, night, free. Or: AM, free, PM, night, night, free, PM.

What did he *do*? What am *I* doing here? What was he doing *here?*

You are always at a point. The points lay tight and rattled against each other like wind in barbed wire. Points of time. A point is defined as having a position in space but no dimensions and consequently no parts.

And soon the year would be over, the day would be over, it'll soon be over, you'll see, it'll soon go under.

He stared at the telephone. The girl poured more coffee. The morning was over. Jenny didn't call. He worked the crossword.

Astragal.

He seemed to be full of dead bones. So it wasn't easy to fly off to meet anyone. He couldn't leave the runway. He was both the cry and the silence. He had an apathy inside, a brick, a cat track in hardened clay.

But also a passion—which wore away the stone and weathered the pawprint free.

INVENTION

"IT'S JAN BACKMAN. First I thought I wouldn't call."

"Where are you?"

"Arlanda."

"First I thought I'd call you," Jenny said. "But I never did."

"Why not? I've tried to call a number of times."

"In order to be sure you wanted to see me. Why are you calling?"

"I thought I could be of use to you . . . I mean. . . ."

Silence.

"What do you see from your office?" she asked.

"The fire station, tank trucks, fences. Papers on the desk. It's soundproof. There's a charter flight landing, it was due this morning. Do you want more?"

"Later."

He felt his tone of voice change. He was collecting her words.

"Are you free?" he asked.

"Yes."

"Let's decide on something."

"Fine. Dinner on the *af Chapman?* We'd have to be on board by five."

Jan swept slips of paper with names he was supposed to call into the wastebasket. It's inconceivable I could be happier, he thought loudly and clearly. Still he'd only exchanged a few words on the telephone. He couldn't help it, he started skipping around in his office, then he locked the door and lay down on the sofa with his face in his hands and started a new conversation that no one heard and added new ps's to what he had said to her.

He drove in from Arlanda at a Sunday speed of fifty. He looked around more than usual. The lonesome junipers, the stubby fields, the barred-up roadside stands reminded him of basic training at Järvafält. He saw himself with spruce branches on his head, muddy from crawling across a hillside in full view of the enemy, machine gun oil under his nails.

All his life he'd let arbitrary factors take command, he had performed his duties and done what he was told. He'd never taken the trouble to be a Personality who couldn't be treated just any way at all, but neither had he been a sail that was sensitive to every breeze, nor a blotter sucking up letters and symbols, even if backwards. He was a sieve, it blew right through him, some of it caught on the edges.

He had telephoned Jenny quite readily. He hadn't wanted to cultivate a one-sided infatuation. He whistled with relief, he was no longer afraid of making himself ridiculous. He was filled with an undefined hope. About what? That this would come to an end? More nearly that it had never begun, that it was a dream being dreamed by someone else while he himself went on reading the newspaper, checking flight plans, receiving timetables for consideration, walking on the solid ground that consisted of other people's trusting expectations.

In actual fact he was already moving quickly in advance of himself. He was into something, inside, like the way certain toy carrousels or old-fashioned magic mirrors reveal figures, coherent shapes, only when they start to revolve, and as soon as the motion stops the shapes again become abstract designs, suggestions, puzzle pieces.

He drove in along Sveavägen and saw the sun glittering on the flat glass walls of Hötorget. He had the feeling that Stockholm was letting its old clothes flap in the breeze for the last time. This was the sale, the tumult on the eve of the actual change of displays. This was the new era when you could take your suit to a dry cleaner's in the subway, fall asleep in a berth to the underground whisper of pipes and fans, wake up to fresh clothes, and sluice yourself out into daylight.

Jan parked on Skeppsholm and sat down on the grass where one road led off to the Modern Museum and another to the ship. Jenny came walking across the wooden bridge. At first he hadn't wanted to look that way but be surprised, now he leaped up, she'd seen him, she was hurrying. He stood almost still and yet moved toward her.

They climbed the gangplank to the *af Chapman*, single file, not touching. They stood in line at the counter—sliced beef and beer. A foreigner asked them about dancing places and they suggested Gröna Lund, Domino, Gyllene Cirkeln for jazz. The man looked from one of them to the other, he thought they belonged together. It was like talking to each other through him. They sat down on a part of the deck where there was still some sun. There was a smell of tar from the planks. They leaned their trays against a black-pitched chain. Jan took off his coat. Jenny put her purse against one leg of the table.

"So here we sit," she said. "What is it we're doing?"

"Why not this as much as something else? After all, we chose to come. It wasn't some dark power that drove us here."

He sounded confident. And she suddenly burst into such glad and friendly laughter that it made him uneasy.

"No, none of it's the least bit remarkable. Everyone eats dinner after all."

"But it is remarkable," he said. "And there's one thing I can't tell you."

"Tell me then."

This time she wanted him to. In the doorway on Nybro Quay a few days before there was something else he'd wanted to say, and hadn't.

"Later that evening I went up in your building and stood outside your door. I don't normally go snooping around. I was acting so oddly I was afraid for myself, or afraid I'd made the whole thing up. Or afraid that what had happened was meant for someone else."

"What'd you do then?"

"For some inexplicable reason I was sure you were thinking of me too. I was standing hidden on the stairs talking to you, illegally sort of, and I couldn't imagine the days to come."

"And then?"

"I went home. My wife thought I had a fever."

He didn't mention the flower he dug up in Humlegården and gave to Gertrude. Jenny stopped eating and was silent for a while. He looked at her hands.

"You're taking a risk in telling me that. Do you always behave this way? Do I have to think about responsibility and dependency and that sort of thing? And be afraid that from the beginning you've made me into someone I'm not? Made a mistake? People mostly make mistakes, and they apologize and go. Or they slam the door. I've been through that."

"And still it doesn't scare you?"

"No. Maybe it's your laugh. I don't suppose you see me as I am, but it doesn't matter. It was something like that for me. I was at home alone. I tried to read but I couldn't. But I went right to sleep. I could feel your hands on my hair and shoulders. Other people have done much more, so it wasn't inexperience."

"I shouldn't have been so feverish and excited," Jan said.

The sun stood between Jacob's Church and the skyscrapers on Sergel Square. The Stockholm city flag was flying from the bow. He watched her eat. She was wearing a pleated skirt and a white blouse with a flowered pattern in pale brown.

"It's like this," Jenny said. "I'm legally separated from a man I have very little in common with, and I have a lover who lives in London. I have an interesting job. I'm not afraid of living by myself, I have friends. My mother is very fond of me, so I have to keep her a little at a distance, otherwise she sacrifices herself unnecessarily. She means well, but she doesn't understand who I am or who I've been, and since she's my mother I can't demand it of her. All that's a part of my natural habitat, as we call it at the Department of the Environment."

"My wife's name is Gertrude," Jan said. "We've known each other a long time, we're very close, though maybe you think that sounds dumb. I'm not lonely either, I've never felt the need to make up for something. Gertrude doesn't lack anything I'm tempted to look for in someone else. My best friend has gone to Africa. I have an apartment and a summer house and I'm not going through any emotional crisis as far as I know."

An Indonesian boy was polishing the copper fittings. He worked very carefully, never looking up. Through the net to the crow's nest they could see clouds dancing.

"Before I left London I had to run an errand at the General Post Office," Jenny told him. "There are potted plants in the windows above the built-in letter boxes. A thin man who looked like our waiter climbed up on the benches and watered and sprayed the plants. And then he took a sponge and very carefully wiped off each leaf. While the rest of us in there were bustling around."

Then she described her job. She had a good salary, higher than his—she didn't hesitate to mention it. She's doing well, he thought, I don't need to steal her time and money. As if he'd had any plans of taking something from her.

"Do you know what we're doing?" Jenny asked. "We're sitting on the *af Chapman* inventing each other. Look at the waves as they wash up along the quay. They're bottle green."

Jan gestured sweepingly.

"They're wearing away the granite, making sand for the future. . . ."

She smiled almost compassionately and disappeared behind a pair of sunglasses.

The neon lights at Saltsjö Mill were burning when they left. The lamps along the harbor were lit in plenty of time for dusk. They were a clear day-blue, as if a little of the sky were left in them.

"My car is behind the National Museum," she said. "I rent a place at the BP station. Mostly I walk."

"Mine's up by the Modern Museum."

They went there. The museum was closed.

"Shall we go to a movie?" Jan said.

"Don't you have to go home?"

"I'm on the evening watch."

"It's funny," she said. "Somehow I thought you'd told her you were out with me. Does there have to be such a difference because I'm a woman?"

"No," he said, "and Gertrude isn't like other people. But I didn't want to. I usually tell her everything. But I got the idea this had to be protected."

"That sort of thing is dangerous," she said. "I have to be sensible for your sake. It's easy to want to protect more and more. It shouldn't have to be that way."

"We can talk about that some other time," he said.

The Children of Paradise was playing at the Bostock. Jan parked the car in an empty lot. They each paid for themselves.

The main feature started right away. Night after night Garence watched thin, innocent Pierrot from her box. For a long time she had loved him from a distance. In the neighboring box sat the great actor, who had had an affair with Garence but never loved her. Now he saw how she looked at Pierrot and his jealousy was aroused, but not his passion—all at once he knew how he would play Othello.

Jenny was wearing white summer gloves. He touched her elbow, put his hand lightly on hers and slid his forefinger inside her glove. It rested there for a moment as if in a sheath, then she took off her glove, their hands met, his finger moved lightly across her palm. It went on like that throughout the film, but nothing more.

He looked at her without moving his head. Her neck was bent slightly back and her eyes looked straight ahead, she might have been looking above the screen. The film seemed clipped, half invisible, overgrown with wisps of fog.

Pierrot appeared on a platform outside the theater. This time Garence was watching him from a crowd of people. Standing beside her was a rich man with a watch chain. A master villain whose regular business was the removal of dignitaries had the day off and was devoting himself to picking pockets. He took the watch chain. The rich man accused Garence, and the police were ready to take her away. Then Pierrot interfered for the first time—he showed in a pantomime exactly how the thief had done his work. That is to say, Pierrot had had his eyes on Garence the entire time. The audience laughed and knew it was true.

"There was a lot I didn't understand," Jenny said afterwards.

"My legs are weak, as if they'd gone to sleep," Jan said. "It must be this astonishment."

"I know. As if we'd known each other for a long time."

"I would have made a hundred excuses in order to see you," Jan said.

"Would you?" she said with comic surprise. "Do you see how many people there are everywhere?"

She existed among them, he thought, in this combination . . . this incarnation. . . . He had to tell himself incessantly: I don't know her, this undercurrent of trust is my imagination. And still he felt this odd desire to tell her everything. And since the desire was there, there was the possibility of getting to know everything.

He took a deep breath.

"You breathe thirty quarts of air a minute," Jenny said.

They were standing by Jan's Volvo. There was a shifting light over the city. It had density and weight and you could see it move.

"Shall we go someplace?" Jan said.

"Do you mean to my place? No, better sit outside and talk."

He drove up Sturegatan. They hadn't agreed on any place to go. He turned off at General Lying-In where he was born.

"I know this road," she said. "I won't get lost here."

"Let's park the car and take a walk," Jan suggested.

It was warm. All of nature seemed to have moved indoors. The stock doves sounded like motors in the distance. Jenny kicked a brown leaf and it unfolded into a tortoiseshell butterfly.

He held her hand, passively, afraid she would pull it back. The trampled rifle ranges lay unnaturally pale. Above them the sky was water streaming over the white stone of the moon.

"When did it happen?" she asked. "In the doorway after you put down my bags, after the ride from Arlanda, just when you ran your hands over my shoulders? I always want to go back and find the exact minute."

"You felt the same thing I did," Jan said.

His voice trembled. There was something he had a hard time controlling.

"It frightened me when I understood. As if I'd been given the responsibility for what you felt."

Jan took off his raincoat and they sat down.

"We're putting out antennae," she said. "We're snails. Oh, this seems good and right. This is no toadstool."

She ran her little finger quickly across the back of his neck. They sat silently.

"There's where you cut my throat," he said finally.

They stood up at the same time. He put his arms around her hard. They didn't kiss each other. He felt her hair and her right ear against his lips, like in a dance. His mouth was dry.

"If we want to we have lots of time," she said as if consoling him.

It got darker. The light was as thin as skim milk and about to disappear completely. Jan felt disguised. Signs were tattooed under his skin, invisible, the bruises not yet showing. A bold sensuality in everything, a craving that expressed itself in an attentiveness beyond all bounds. He watched her with a clarity and fervor and kindness that were meekly self-assured. He presupposed an identity, what he did to her he did also to himself.

They walked along beneath the heavy power lines around the Hjorthagen freight station. The power lines stretched over heaps of slag and imported coal, piles of lumber and the gas-works. Someone had told Jan that birds sometimes flew into telephone wires in the dark and cut themselves in two. But the strange thing was that birds perched on the lines between the tall iron masts and a hundred and fifty thousand volts did them no harm. They were poor conductors. But electricity filled them. They flew off with one hundred and fifty thousand volts shut up in their bodies, an imperceptible burden, and when they landed the current rushed out.

They took paths where the only light was the face of Jan's watch. Beyond the empty boxcars at Värta station, in the thick cylindrical shadow of the gasholder, the familiar world ended. Hawkweed gleamed on littered hillsides, pipes and cables for a piece of subway construction lay in piles.

Further away one could still see the contours of cranes and chimneys, a horizon that at any moment could be drawn up around them like a lasso.

They went back to the car. Again he embraced her hard, almost stiffly, as if he were going to lift her off the ground.

He let her off outside her door. He was going on to Upplandsgatan to sleep alone. He hadn't told her that, nor mentioned Gertrude.

He got out of the car on Nybro Quay. They didn't touch each other. The paving stones they stood on were like the squares of a chess board.

The light from an airplane rose like a bubble up through the darkness.

THE TELEPHONE

As if i were leaning against a wall that was giving way . . . . As if I were a seed wanting to be hurled out of a hard pod and yet not wanting to . . . .

He was on his way to the telephone to dial a number, five words, then hang up—a secret telegram. Requiring no information in reply except the knowledge that she had heard, that she knew. Why should she know? He could probably keep quiet. Still how glad he was she knew. He would tell her everything, so that nothing was left. The hard part starts when you have nothing more to reveal. That was a risk he wanted to take.

Jan Backman stood in the cafeteria line at the Gyllene Mutter, by himself. A girl sat down at the same long table and filled in the crossword puzzle in a weekly while she ate. He was thinking about Jenny Jeger, who wasn't there and whom for the time being he couldn't see. She had a lot to do she'd said, overtime. He sought out places—the lavatory, the newspaper room, the meteorology stage—where he could think in peace without being spoken to.

He called her from Arlanda. She called him. They found the time to talk a lot. There was something in her voice he never tired of. He told her what he was doing. He hardly knew when he was talking to himself and when to her.

He felt he'd become a third person, he lived the life of a dragonfly and the sun glittered on his wings. It was as if he'd finally had his glasses focused.

Sometimes an elusive feeling of being at home came over him at Arlanda. His desk was equipped with gray metal boxes on runners that were as heavy as armored cars. In them hung labeled folders: a ministry of factual reports, comprehensive information. Everything there was unshakable. The air did not shimmer with uncertain illuminations. The film cleared away.

Jenny told him, "I was in the other room; my secretary answered the phone and I heard through the wall it was you. My hands started trembling. Like in a slushy novel."

"I'd be embarrassed if it weren't the same way with me," he said.

"What can you see while you're talking?" she asked.

He described the wall calendar, the traces of rain on the window, the police helicopter overhead, a practice run by the firemen.

Between conversations he sat in his chair, went through her tones of voice and wrote letters to her in his head, letters it was impossible to send. They were all about how he drank tea, read this or that in the newspapers, called Gertrude at the Academy of Sciences, thought about watching something on TV, had his car fixed by a flight mechanic with whom he had a small illegal deal.

He had begun to report things to her in a quiet, beautiful insanity, it was a story to which he could really see no end. It was an activity, a work, his collecting works.

Sometimes it was as if he lived without will, an iron filing in a magnetic field, a sperm cell helplessly wriggling its way through narrow canals. He was conscious of his breath, of a tightening in the muscles of his calf, of the ease with which unexpected noises produced a fluttering in his heart.

At other moments he was struck by something more concentrated. Her existence became a form of knowledge in him, a painful beam of light directly into his brain. It was like the moment when you understand, physically, wordlessly, that you are going to die, that something will take you by the arm and lead you away without a trace and that this is the only real unknown.

This happiness that sought its source outside himself, in another human being, made him feel inaccessible. He had often thought of himself as unchanging in a world of shifting images. Now he was moving quickly, with long strides. He felt open and nevertheless alone, a loneliness in the middle of a square; he was visible to everyone and unreachable.

Because no one took him for what he was but only noticed the roles he played, the activities that characterized him, the conversational tone they were used to. And there was really nothing else to grasp.

Now for the first time he left them behind, the roles, himself. Now for the first time began the confusion. No one noticed that he was calm and yet vibrating. He lived in the inexplicable and acted with unmotivated strength.

He wanted to grab hold of all that was eluding him, these fragments of sunlight, these splinters of clarity and wonder, and weld them to an unknown metal that nothing could destroy.

SACKCLOTH

JAN HAD PUT IN the morning watch at Arlanda and then stayed on to write a memorandum on the new safety regulations for night flights. He had driven into Stockholm and parked his car by the synagogue in order to do some shopping.

He made two circuits of the Nybro Pavilion for reasons he kept loudly to himself. The new Stockholm waiting around the corner gleamed plaster-white inside. He figured it interested him—Arlanda was included in the latest regional plan, Värmdö and the Water Palace as well.

He began torturing himself with suggestions. How much would it be worth for Jenny to show up, even if only for a moment and with someone else? What was he prepared to sacrifice? For what? He didn't really know what he wanted. Going up to her apartment would be too forward. He said her name slowly and went cold, as though standing naked on a rock after a swim. And the next second he grew warm as though he were standing in the forced air current at the entrance to a department store.

Then it happened. Jenny came out her door, alone, with a large handbag and a briefcase under her arm. He pretended to hurry toward her as if he'd caught sight of her from a long way off.

"Hi Jenny."

She stopped, saw him, smiled. Everything went as he'd hoped. He didn't have to sacrifice anything. It was the middle of Stockholm, there was nothing odd in his passing by. You could explain anything that happened on Nybro Square.

"I had a feeling something nice would happen," she said. "Everything tastes good today. I licked a stamp until it was limp. I never liked it before."

"Where are you headed?"

"To the Academy of Engineering on Grev Turegatan."

"At this time of day?"

"We can't get people together until after working hours. You look doubtful. Well it's simply a meeting. And even if——"

"That wasn't what I meant," he hurried to say.

"There are two of us from the Department of the Environment. We've just set up a coordinating committee with some other research organizations. I'm the secretary."

"Have you got time to have a beer with me?"

"I thought I might get a quick bite at the Corallo up there. Why don't you come along?"

"Sure, I'll have a beer and watch you eat. I'm going out this evening. There's a travel bureau having a PR party. I go around sometimes and give lectures on popular and exotic places to visit. For the money, and because it's fun to talk. My job is kind of quiet."

"Buttons and signals and telephones," she said thoughtfully. "A lot of languages. My job is to deal with prognoses and planning. And international cooperation. We have to get so many things done in a hurry. People and institutions and countries are starting to get used to being questioned and giving out information."

"It's safest to be asking the questions," Jan said.

At Corallo they sat way at the back of the room where it was already dusk. She ordered an inexpensive spaghetti plate.

"I've been at home all day writing a proposal for setting environmental priorities," she said. "Though that doesn't have anything to do with this meeting. What we're going to talk about now is an alarm system for air and water. And if it's good the department will submit it to parliament and to a new UN committee for the preservation and utilization of the world's natural resources."

She sounded enthusiastic when she talked about her job.

"It's important, what we're doing," she added.

Her eyes looked through the long narrow restaurant out toward the traffic. He caught a glimpse of everything he didn't know about her. Thirty years is time enough to tie up a life—nets for protection, nets for capture.

"If you'd been a Mayan girl on a bus in Yucatán instead of a city girl getting a ride from Arlanda, I wouldn't know what to say. We never would have met even if we'd been sitting next to each other. At a bus stop you would have disappeared into the jungle, on your way to an isolated hut. There's a lot we've been given free."

"If we'd met years ago, at a party, a tour, at one of your lectures, would we have *seen* each other then?"

"I don't know," he said. "If we only had a little more time. Right now I mean."

She put down her fork and spoon.

"We have time. I've had enough to eat."

Out on Grev Turegatan. She examined the buildings and stores.

"What are you looking for?" Jan asked.

"A doorway. No, a watchmaker's, actually."

There was one. She wanted a watchband. He bought it for her; it was the first thing he gave her.

There was a building being replastered. The workmen had gone for the day. Heavy sackcloth hung from the scaffolding. They stopped, looked at each other quickly and went inside. No one noticed them.

It was the first time they'd kissed. She didn't close her eyes, so he didn't either. He tried to see her face as it was now, and there behind it the face that had been hers the many years he hadn't known her. Then he closed his eyes.

He was very happy. He was sailing free, without identification, insurance, or set tactics. Escape artist. Not moored fast to her, but his drag anchor at home in her waters.

She drew back from his lips. He saw a picture of sparse heat collecting on the underside of a leaf.

"Do I taste of spaghetti?" she asked.

"Tomato a little."

"Doesn't anyone still live in this building?"

"Maybe they've cleared it out for the summer."

The sackcloth was the building's skin, the scaffolding its ribs. They were there inside.

He caressed her face, her hair, her neck—only there.

He closed his lips on the cool lobe of her ear. They saw people passing like shadows on the street. Feelings of lust and cunning shifted back and forth in an optical illusion. Another city . . . the buildings changing their facades and faces. The caryatids gazing down with veiled expressions.

They looked at each other, and their pupils enlarged until even the darkness brightened and the cave became an open sea. Stockholm stretched itself out, wires crossed each other in the weave.

"So long as we have words in common," he said. "Then it probably doesn't matter that we haven't known each other long. You say something and I know."

Without answering she put the palm of her hand on his face, spread her fingers and let the tips grope their way along. So the details wouldn't be erased. So that what felt elusively present and threateningly transient might leave its impression in her fingertips and allow itself to be studied afterwards. That was how she expressed it later on.

She told him she had scratched his initial on the wall of a building between an umbrella shop and an antique store, like a teenager. Lightly and quickly, a couple of days before. He wouldn't find it if he went to look. It was like picking a book at random in a gigantic library and sketching a figure in the margin. It was there somewhere.

"Did you really?" he burst out.

It didn't seem like Jenny, but he didn't know what was like her. He thought of the letter as a punctuation mark or a hyphen of uncertain life expectancy, written in chalk on a tremendous piece of slate.

A glass-clear sharpness carved in skin, only alive as long as the blood didn't harden. To have the scratch wiped out, the giddiness supported by a soft pillow—that was to go on living.

The scaffolding over their heads. A pail forgotten three floors up. Poles and pipes set crosswise, planks screwed fast with bolts. They felt like children having fun by not answering when their parents called. Unseen themselves, they watched other people through the loose weave of the sackcloth.

"Insist on a little freedom," Jan said, "to keep me from surrounding you."

"The meeting! I have to go. For that matter there they come, over there across the street."

"They can't see us. No one will guess where you've been."

"I might start laughing," Jenny said. "That man over there's from the Academy of Sciences Environmental Protection Committee—that's one of the places we send our proposals."

"Gertrude works at the Academy of Sciences," he said. "Did I tell you that?"

"No," Jenny said, and looked at him as if she expected him to go on. "We borrow a lot of books from them."

"What we do to each other only we can judge," Jan said. "Measured by other people's standards it might seem evil or good or stupid. What I do has no significance until it bounces off someone else."

"Yes," she said. "That's roughly how I argue questions of ecology too. We determine our own responsibility. And now I have to run."

She'd put her purse and briefcase on a plank. She had on a thin beige jersey suit and a white blouse. She was wearing the ring with the smoke topaz.

She threw her arms around him quickly, nibbled his upper lip and rubbed her cheek along his chin. A hare leaped through him from his shoulders to his toes. An octopus writhed in his stomach. He didn't want her to go.

"We have to see each other soon," he said firmly.

"Stay behind the netting until I'm inside the building," she ordered.

He kept his eyes on her. He imagined things about her. He told himself she had the cunning persistence of a person seeking something out of reach. She walked as if she had a long way to go and wanted to be sparing of her movements. She walked as if she were holding something explosive or very serious under control.

When she got to the door she turned around toward the draped building. He made a movement, but he knew the sackcloth looked like a wall from outside. She suddenly seemed exposed, like a single human being on a broad boulevard early in the morning.

But that too could be something he imagined about her.

He wanted her to see him, so he stepped out onto the sidewalk. It was early evening on a narrow street. Several people looked at him. She had disappeared.

NIGHT WATCH

Glass screens and instrument panels of blinking lights in the traffic controllers' cave, like a city seen from thirty thousand feet.

Jan Backman hurried out to the telephone.

"Are you alone? Can you come out here? It's crazy to call at this hour, but I had to. I've got the night watch, but Jansson can take over for a couple of hours."

He notified the guard to pass a gray Saab station wagon. Then he waited. On the radar was a Pan American ship at a high altitude with no intermediate stops, and a night exercise of the air wing at Norrtälje. When he went outside she was waiting.

"Drive just a little way," he said, and got in beside her. "There's a road past the oil tanks and out into the woods at the end of the runway."

"How much time do you have?"

"Till four in the morning. But I can't smuggle you into the stewardess barracks."

A chilly summer night. Clear over Uppland—the ceiling meters at the north and south ends of the runways had nothing to measure. The weather radar hadn't reported any precipitation within a radius of one hundred and twenty miles.

"Deutscher Wetterdienst is our backbone," Jan said.

"You could navigate by the stars tonight."

"Fliers aren't any good at that. Did you know there are stars that don't even have numbers for names? I think there must be words no one has heard. It would make you happy to know their names."

Jenny found an open place among the blackthorn and hazel. They put down the back seat so there was room to lie down. There was a vinyl bag full of tools, a couple of blankets, a sleeping bag.

"I didn't know what to expect," Jenny said. "I threw in everything. I didn't have time to make a thermos of tea, but I've got a little whisky in case we get cold."

They stood in the glade outside the car and kissed each other.

"Is the ground wet?"

Jan felt it. It was dry but chilly.

"Lie on top of me," Jenny said. "With your clothes on. Just for a minute. I want to feel your weight."

He lowered her to the ground and lay on her, his knees against hers, thighs against thighs, his mouth against her throat —they were almost the same height. They didn't caress each other, just breathed while their eyes got used to the dark, to the dog rose and the sheep dung.

It seemed to him the blood was leaving his cheeks. The skin was tight across his temples. She moved. Her hands for the first time against his thighs, on top of the rough cloth. One finger searched hesitantly a few inches in over his stomach. Then she let her hands fall on the moss.

A beetle woke up and crept up between her fingers and capsized. She turned her head and looked at it.

"Our smallest common denominator," she said.

"It's after midnight," Jan said. "Why don't we get undressed?"

They spread out blankets in the car. He rolled out the sleeping bag as a mattress. He unbuttoned the waistband of her skirt. Her bra was loose and he lifted it from her breasts. She was wearing a white half-slip and white underpants. He undressed in silence. He pressed his mouth against her waist. She was cold.

"Crawl into the sleeping bag," he said.

She did. He sat on his heels in the back of the car, where the floor was ridged with little rails. He looked at her face, and since he couldn't recognize himself in what he was doing, he tried to think of every action as impossible to set right afterwards.

Jenny looked like an olive-drab mummy. He opened the zipper on the sleeping bag. She laughed.

"I feel like there's light pouring out of me."

He was naked and crept down beside her. They were hidden under a lid of night.

This was real, her presence a grip on his shoulders as strong as her absence. The naked arch of her foot against his foot. He had seen her face everywhere, in his plate, in the air behind a candle flame. A thousand opportunities a day.

He ran his lips like a caterpillar across her throat and breasts and arms. He said he was thirsty from the salt he'd licked from her skin.

Jenny said, "When you pulled your finger out of my glove at the Bostock, I wanted you to glide out of me the same way soon."

"Have you got a diaphragm?" Jan asked.

"I've started taking the Pill."

She kissed him slowly to feel his lips, an inquisitive experiment, she took his upper lip between the two of hers. He let go of her and looked at her searchingly.

"You make me laugh and long for you," she said. "As if it were the same thing, laughter and lust, and I've never felt that way before."

She burrowed her nose in his hair.

"Do you know you smell like clippings from Allers Journal?"

They rolled down the windows, which were foggy from their breath. The sky arched over them, a blue-gray bird's egg they saw from inside. Several tree trunks away began the plain. A land of flatness, security, rich soil that was regularly turned. No heat from the depths tried to lift this roof. No earthquake had ever tipped the brim of its hat in this place, driving cats up trees and making horses bolt.

It was only the car that was bouncing a little beneath them. Jenny's head rested against one corner of the front seat. Jan braced his feet against the rear door. They were pressed together as tightly as if between two slices of bread.

He wanted to have her with open eyes, because when he closed them and tried to incorporate her into what his body felt she was not the person she usually was but a dream that exploded in him and through him, a frenzy of closeness that was cast out and away. And in the instant when membranes met and his seed streamed up into her womb, he was on the point of losing her and being left alone. In fear he clung to her tightly with fingers and nails and opened his eyes to see if she had changed and become unrecognizable—he feared it and wanted it both at once.

After a long time, with surprise in her voice, she said, "We wanted all of this. A little while ago we didn't even exist for each other. And still it feels so strangely uncomplicated."

He looked at her outside the threat and dim vision of habit. He touched her with the gentle shyness of a lover, though he'd been so close to her just now.

She had neither length nor width but an angular roundness that was measured by his arms around her. She had a night-pale face, he saw it peering up from the blankets. He thought about how a stay in prison can make people into mummies that can never be unwound. Then he began to unwind her.

She was naked under his gaze. Something pounded in the hollow of her throat. Her nipples had smoothed out, and he rubbed the back of his hand along her ribs and thighs. And with sudden greed he wanted to share in her life, all she contained of memories, conversations, cities, work. All at once he no longer had a clearly defined life at his disposal, it had extended into hers.

In the glow of the ceiling light they compared the nets of veins on their left hands. An airplane thundered in its landing pattern overhead.

"A charter flight coming in late, probably," Jan said. "No regular flight at this hour. Arlanda is the end of the line for most of them. We never get any traffic after midnight."

They didn't see the plane. Stars burned in the sky like distant cabin windows.

"That's how you arrived," he said.

"Before you land you go the lavatory to get yourself together. You look awful in the fluorescent light. And afterwards you smell of airplane soap."

"It may be a while before we see each other again. Pinch me as hard as you dare. I want to have a tattoo from you."

She pinched him shrewdly under the hair on the back of his neck.

"I'd like to bite off your largest birthmark," he said. "So no one could recognize you by it if you have to be identified someday."

He told her about certain insects that flew around like delirious shadows when exposed to a strong light. There was no instinct or magnetism left to guide them. Their feelers fluttered, they couldn't find their way back to their hive, or crack, or cell.

Jenny smiled and said he'd find his way back where he wanted to go, he wasn't homeless and neither was she. What they had together was remarkable, but it was best to reduce the enormity of it so it would be a symbol for them, something usable, filled with nourishment.

The symbol of a possibility—called forth as carefully as a whisper. Like letters taking shape under the celluloid surface of a "perpetual tablet," on which the letters can be wiped away by merely lifting the sheet, though it's called a perpetual tablet. Something untested, maybe with no strength to bear them.

He wanted to tell her everything, in endless, trying detail.

"There's no reason for it," Jenny said. "I'm very calm and happy by myself, I have an interesting job. And now here we are. Friendship? But unless you really want to see someone a thousand practical things can get in the way—distance, working late, children, and bother. So you rarely see each other. Life is short, and if you see someone once in a while you think you see a lot of them."

"Curiosity," Jan said. "Like the first letters in a long alphabet."

"A while ago, eternities ago, I was working with a committee on a thing that would map out the future and make it inevitable. It didn't bother me. I was doing it for what I considered a good cause. And then this happened. I didn't expect it."

Jan tried to think of Gertrude, his sister whom he loved. It seemed to him she was smiling at all of this with an understanding he wouldn't have dared give her credit for. But he knew that picture was only a wish.

Jenny licked him between the eyes and said, "Something we are is being exchanged for something that's come along. There's a helplessness about it."

"But we're not attracted by most of the things that come along. We're usually unreceptive."

He lay on his back on top of the sleeping bag and it seemed to him a shining tent was spread above them, protecting, expanding. She lowered her head toward him.

"It worries me to be this happy," she said. "Watch out. I don't want to fall in love with the wrong person. Because all I want is to stuff him in my pocket."

"The wrong person?"

"I destroy things for people, I know I do. You don't know how oddly programmed I am. And I'm in your way. Gertrude . . . ."

That was the first time she'd mentioned Gertrude's name, Jan thought. Someone she's never seen.

"No," she went on, "that's your business. Everyone gets his chance. We're not children. I hope we don't hurt each other. Any of us—however many of us there are."

"Jenny," he said, "I want to tell you everything, whatever it costs. There must be a kind of recklessness that doesn't hurt, if only we knew its terms."

"Could we sleep with you inside me, really sleep?" she wondered.

"No, we have to use what time we have, otherwise there'll be nothing left."

Then she lay on top of him and pressed her knees against his thighs and burrowed her nose in the hollow of his collar-bone.

"Lie still," he said.

She smiled down at him seriously. He felt the heat deep inside her. Outside was the Swedish landscape, the tops of spruces writing in pale ink on the line of the horizon. A thin fog wandering out toward the fields. The voice of an owl testing how far the night extended. Arlanda's radar revolving high above the level of the creeping things on earth.

From having Jenny's body so close and yet lying still and looking out at the late arriving dawn while she shoved her nose further and further in toward his throat, he felt his muscles suddenly contracting beyond his will. He didn't have time to warn her. She laughed when she felt what was happening.

Then he wrapped both blankets around her. He himself put on Jenny's Iceland sweater, violet with white splashes, crocuses in the snow. He caught the odor of her skin and the face cream in the neck band. He shivered with the intimacy that belongs to a borrowed piece of clothing—something uncouth, conspiratorial, a secret orgy.

He cupped his hand over Jenny's sex, the lips had closed but were still damp. He himself was worn and tender. He didn't think he'd ever felt such desire for anyone. He knelt in front of her so his head pushed against the padded roof of the car and, just as in the doorway at Nybro Quay, he ran his hands quickly over her head and shoulders and arms. Neither of them mentioned it.

"I've got to get back to my job. And you've got to sleep."

"Let me into the parking lot and I'll sleep a couple hours in the car," Jenny said. "I'll drive in in time to wash and eat before eight."

"You'll have a tired day," Jan said. "It's nice to know you'll be sleeping near me."

After listening to Jansson's report and working a couple of hours, he went out to the parking lot and looked for the gray Saab. There was an empty place between a Fiat and an Austin.

"Did you see her drive away?" he asked the guard at the gate.

"Did you think she'd vanished into thin air?" he answered.

Jansson came out in the morning light, yawned, and said, "I know a steward who sprinkles after-shave in his shoes every time he goes out. He's got ambitions."

The night flight from Rome, a Caravelle, landed with the brake flaps lifted on its wings. A few sparks on the concrete, which over a period of time had become streaked with soot and kerosene fumes. But no inscriptions, no ineradicable tracks.

THE ROOF PARTY

JAN WAS INVITED for seven thirty.

"I can't say for sure it'll be just the two of us," Jenny had warned him, but it was just the two of them.

"I didn't wear a coat," he said, and started to go into her apartment from the front hall. He'd never been there before. She stopped him and handed him a wicker basket.

"We're going to eat on the roof," she said.

Just above her apartment was the attic, and from there a ladder led out onto the black sheet-metal tiles of the roof. Jan hung his jacket on a ventilator, slipped, took off his shoes and socks, and the soles of his feet were immediately black with soot. Jenny's face bobbed up through the trapdoor.

He opened the basket and took out a bottle of red wine, tumblers, a towel full of dinner rolls she'd warmed in the oven.

She was carrying an ovenproof casserole of pancakes stuffed with shellfish and dill.

"That's our dinner," she said. "This is the first time I've ever been up here." She said it quietly but her delight was clear.

"Here we are right in the middle of town," Jan said, "and no one can find us. But we're living on the brink of a volcano."

"Of a chimney at least."

"These tiles are hot," he said. "We'll have to find someplace to sit."

The whole roof sloped. The huge Agfa sign threw a pattern of stripes across part of it, and they found they could sit behind its iron skeleton and peer down at the city like snipers.

From the peak of the roof they could see the churches, almost all the steeples in the inner city: Hedvig Eleonora's and Oscar's, St. Klara's and St. Jacob's, Johannes Church and Katarina, Engelbrekt's and St. Sofia's, Stockholm's sacred and less sacred couples. The Royal Dramatic Theater was just opposite, with its lanterns, and a foreign flag on the roof for a guest company from abroad. The lampposts were freshly painted gold. The resident company was on vacation.

Jan drew out the cork and threw it down toward Nybro Bay. The gas lights had been lit outside the Hotel Diplomat on Strandvägen. They drank out of Duralex glasses, and finally found a spot where they could brace their feet, against a splice that ran like a rail across the roof. Jenny was wearing tennis shoes.

"The men who clear the snow up here use safety lines," he said. "They're more careful than we are."

A grain of soot landed on Jenny's nose. The bric-a-brac on Berns glittered in the sun. And under the colored lanterns on Berzelii Terrace there was dancing every night.

"Can't people see us from the other buildings? Someone's liable to call the police."

"Maybe from the roof terrace at the Strand," Jenny said.

"But they don't expect to see anyone. People don't see things they don't expect to see."

"I'll hook the trapdoor, so no one can come up unless they knock."

"There probably isn't anyone in the building. It's mostly offices."

"You're one of the few people still living down here in the traffic and the fumes."

"It's part of my job. Can you smell the wind from the water? Somehow it's stale and fresh at the same time. And I've got Blasieholm Square, which is quiet. And from the kitchen I can see the ballet students practicing across the court."

"I walked around the block on my way," Jan said. "I didn't want to come too early, in case you'd invited anyone else like you said. You've got an all-night clinic and the Linnea Café, and a stationer's, and a travel bureau, and an antique store that's closing down. The house where Gertrude and I live on Upplandsgatan, they're going to tear down that one too."

"They have to get you another place first," Jenny said.

"Are we always in someone else's power?"

"If that's the way you feel. Unfree, predestined, encapsulated in society. And if you run away, then even the way you run is determined by the society you're running from."

"I'm really pretty loyal," Jan said. "Anyone could do the things I do at Arlanda, but a lot of people depend on the fact that somebody does them."

"We're civil servants," Jenny said. "Negotiations, policies, settlements—that's the language we speak. If you're involved in the goals of an organization, you never feel your lack of freedom."

"But I still have my own life," Jan said. "Or did Gertrude take it? Or did I lose it to you?"

"I don't know. Right down here in the doorway that first evening, you put your hands on me and even then . . . as quickly as that I mean. Just one motion. And ever since, a feeling that *now* will never end. Something happened to us that we don't deserve."

"I feel more experienced, and more childlike," he said. "Though you can't learn anything from experience except how to make a bed or fold a napkin. The rest of it fades out, you forget."

Jenny was wearing blue jeans, a white blouse, and tennis shoes. Her legs were bare beneath the tight, worn legs of the pants. She took out a plastic carton of Romanian raspberries with no Romanian worms. There were a few unfilled pancakes and Jan used them as a plate to crush the berries on.

"One drawback to being married," Jenny said, "is that the man's life always takes precedence. You marry his job, his habits, his demands. A man hardly ever chooses a woman because she stands for anything besides herself."

"I feel like I'm about to throw myself into something terribly dangerous," Jan said. "Break my routine completely."

"It's funny how people can change. There are so many combinations."

"We live in a society that has the power to send us out to die. I have duties, and one of them is dying for my country. If I refuse they can shoot me. Society can do whatever it wants with me, if things really get tight. I can't do what I like with myself, or with you."

"Even if we did something unexpected or unbelievable," Jenny said, "we'd be able to understand it in each other. Something outside the conventional barriers. We could handle that—don't you think we could?"

It seemed to Jenny that over the years she'd become more and more like an open window—words and odors drifted through, and the wall didn't know if it was facing in or out. She made better use of herself. She told him how she'd eaten breakfast of graham crackers and coffee with hot milk, how she'd gone to work at nine, bought cologne and Tampax and a green scarf on the way. She'd eaten lunch at the Department of

the Environment in Solna, read the newspaper, bitten by accident into a hot Spanish pepper, and gone dashing around like
a fire engine.

Sometimes, she said, the days went by as quickly and lightly
as animals through high grass—just a slight rustling around
them. She was surprised when she found herself singing Jan's
name to melodies on the radio, when she could feel his fingers
on her ribs.

"Do you see over there," Jan said, "the tiles make a sort of
hammock, in that corner under the chimney? We'd be safer
over there I think. Only watch out for the gull crap."

Jenny leaned back against the side of the chimney. Jan sat
down between her legs and rested his back against her breasts.
Her nose vacuumed his hair, one of her hands was on his thigh.

Whirlpools of drainage from the Strand Hotel ate at the
anchor chain of the showboat *Useful*, soon she'd have to cast
off for blacker water. The dormer windows along Strandvägen
glimmered like bird droppings on dark fields. Jenny had made
all this wide and quiet city hers, and for that reason Jan felt
himself at home.

"It could even be that I love you," she said against his neck.

He didn't answer.

"I won't let anything happen to you," she said. "I don't
want to shake your balance." And she shifted slightly away
from him on the sloping roof.

"Everything inside a person changes, of course," she said.
"But I still wanted to say it, right now."

"I love you Jenny," he said. "It's true, if you want to hear it.
It's funny we never said it before. But I wanted to be sure.
We've loved each other the whole time."

"It seems ingenuous. Unprincipled too, of course. Like something nobody else would understand."

He leaned back his head and she was there. His forehead
brushed against her chin and she ran the tip of her tongue
across his eyelids. He turned his body so he lay against her.
They lay still.

"What's smoking?" he said.

Not the chimney, it was the thermos at their feet. Jenny had taken out the cork when they changed places and now the coffee was cold. Jan wanted to leap up, shed some clothes, and dance on the warm tiles of the roof, but she tightened her arms around him like meridians.

He looked at the date on his watch.

"Did you know this is the summer solstice?"

"I'd forgotten. So this is as light as it can get, no lighter."

The sun was going down in the northwest, beyond Sture Square and the crown of Engelbrekt's church and the red tile roofs of the student apartments. The light was horizontal, on a level with them, six stories up.

He started to unbutton her blouse. She shifted nervously.

"The police helicopter is gone," he reassured her. "The gulls and the pigeons are down on the street. We locked the trapdoor. We're the roofwatch and the weathervane. No one can see us the way we are—we don't need to hide."

"No, I don't want to hide. I want to be covered only by our secrecy."

"We're hidden by the back of the Agfa sign, and the camera's blind."

He bent down over her, resting his knees against either side of the little tile valley, helped her off with her jeans and stuffed them underneath her back so no sudden gust of wind would carry them out over the trees in Berzelii Park. She left her blouse on.

The redness of the sun lingered in the houses in lower Östermalm like runic inscriptions on a gray surface, indecipherable at a distance. It was still light enough for them to see the ventilators and pipes on the city's roofs—Stockholm's organ. Except it didn't play.

"Passion is a word that never had real meaning for me," Jan said. "Like 'trinity' and 'resurrection.' But now I think I know. You're inside me, though physically it's the other way around. And I'm conscious in advance of a sense of loss, as if it were against some law for this feeling to exist. It's as if I already have to start getting used to living without it."

"Our feelings are facts," she said, looking very unfrightened. "They're there right now, and they agree on what they want."

"I want to lie on top of you. You won't have to worry about being seen."

"Do. Bodies know right away what they want."

"If we lived together we might not know we could want each other as much as this."

Then he bent down over her and let his forehead and cheeks become as wet as the insides of her thighs. Her smell was on his fingers. Warmth rose in him like a column of quicksilver.

He placed himself carefully on top of her, folded the blouse toward her armpits. She was lying with her shoulders forced together by the angle in the roof, and his chest touched her breasts through the light material of her blouse. Her inner arms were white, with several small birthmarks. She stretched them above her head. He kissed her armpit—nipple, mouth and armpit made a triangle. His hand glided along her arm to the palm of her hand. He pressed his lips against the hollow of her thumb.

"Everything happens in the face," he said. "My fingers and my eyes know the lips of your womb, but it's your face that excites me, and your voice. Sometimes it's enough to hear you on the phone. That's why I have to close my eyes and keep myself from coming too soon. Your face is unbelievably exciting. And you display it naked to the whole world. It ought to be veiled. The rest doesn't matter."

They were being carried high on the city's back, a city of drifting islands. The traffic had stilled and let the smell of water through. They were being carried. It seemed to Jan his body was filled with oxygen and bubbling and burning heat, and laughter seemed to fill his mouth.

"If we don't move no one will see us," she whispered.

"You're moving inside."

"You're in me so deep."

She pressed her fingers against her stomach and he could feel it. They prolonged their pleasure—he could stay inside her for an hour, it was a kind of sleep. Her muscles tightened around the tip of his penis.

Never before—at least not since the attic of the Water Palace with Gertrude—that feeling that's supposed to be the sinner's special privilege: having a sensation other people have never known.

"Come," she said. "Come now if you want to."

They were lying with their backs against opposite sides of the fold in the roof. Their eyes were open and he looked directly into her mustard-yellow pupils. At the same time he was dimly aware of lights in the distance, like quotation marks —what did it all say?

Hinges, two human beings hooked into one another. But when their bodies are closest, exchanging fluid, they are also closest to nothingness. He lay utterly motionless as his semen left him slowly, without spurts, confirming a pleasure not measured in peaks and crests.

The sky was pale violet like midsummer flowers. The streets breathed in the night. The buildings leaned in the quivering light, silently, as if they had asked for a time of reflection before their destruction.

"Now we've put a period to things," Jenny said after a while. "Now we exist."

Jan felt her knees against his, her hips as well—they hadn't moved apart. He looked at the grains of soot on the tiles. The roof was still warm. The paint was scaling.

"You can make a period smaller," Jan said, "but it doesn't disappear. The eye can ache from looking at it, and won't adjust to the focus. But the point is still there. It can get as small as possible, instruments can see it. And when not even the instruments . . . then it's still there anyway, though we've lost contact with it. There's no such thing as blank paper. It consists of points. Haven't we talked about that?"

The roof was damp where they'd been lying. Several patches were drying alongside gull droppings and splashes of rain. When Jenny moved he saw a diagonal line across one of her buttocks—so she'd been lying on a tile joint beneath his weight.

"Lie still," he said. "I've become a terrible voyeur. I want to be a plate and have you engraved on me with acid so I'll never forget you."

"Forget me if you can't remember me," she said.

"The important thing is to remember that this *is*. What exists now has existed and will go on existing someplace, like the fish in the sea's great nets. You exist, in the time in my brain. You swim in my blood like little fish, and you don't come out."

"Like your spermfish in me. Although they do come out, unfortunately. I guess people aren't safe deposit boxes for anything."

"Tomorrow, today will be yesterday. And people chew their yesterdays like cuds. Even today you're already a mass of yesterdays inside me. I'll never get rid of you. I remember you, but I remember myself as someone else than who I am now. I'm already changed, and so are you."

"That's you and your timetables. . . ."

He noticed her foot and was seized with a particular love for it because it was located at such a distance from her face.

"Childhood ends when you get your first watch," Jan said.

"Or when I got my first watchband from you."

"Let me look at you, bit by bit. I need to look at you through the wrong end of binoculars, and through a microscope."

"I'm perfectly ordinary."

"That's what makes it so irrational. Don't flirt with the ordinary. Alcestis crops up in the world just as often as a new model car. Lie still."

Jenny's mouth was softly open, she lay on her back with her

legs slightly spread, one knee drawn up. Her nipples were trying to sleep, arms along her sides, a kind of lankiness. He considered the fact that women often have shorter arms than men,
that they can bend th   gs to a larger angle because their
hips are made that way.

There she lay, with her eyes closed as if she were dead,
willingly dead. He, the voyeur above her, the observer, the
sniper, he felt as if he were embalming her with his glance,
as if he were committing something unforgivable and irrevocable.

"I'm on the verge of falling asleep," she murmured. "But
I'm getting cold up here."

She sat up quickly and looked straight into his eyes. Her
smile wavered in the corners of her mouth.

"And you've eaten all the raspberries. You know what I feel
like doing? Peeing in your hand."

THE STONES

THEY WALKED. Block after block. Moment
after moment. Labels and signs: barber perfume fashions bank.
The Institute for Rational Education. Gas station. They
walked.

What existed before she existed? All sorts of things, nothing
in particular. Things went fine then too. Now they both existed.
Block by block, stone by stone.

They followed the shoreline of Kungsholm, past the piers where the excursion boats tied up, past rows of small-boat buoys below Kungsklippan.

"Tell me some things you want," Jan said.

"A Finnish dress I saw at NK," she said. "A bowl baked out of ice-age mud from when they built the subway. Shrimp every Thursday. And other things I'll tell you about later. You?"

"A trench coat from the First World War. A very small tape recorder. Underwater binoculars with a built-in light."

"We've got time to get all of it."

"Or stop wanting them, before. . . ."

There was a before. They kept telling each other there were no guarantees, as if in fact they would rather have been automobiles with a five-year warranty. There was a great treachery in the very middle of the world, and for many it was life's largest experience.

"So let's remember the closeness," Jan said. "The spark of contact, the hidden rituals, the dizzy joy that's hard as flint, the things we'll never feel sorry for."

The Hong Kong Restaurant. German waiters served them chop suey and chow mein, half a portion each, rice and tea. The cars parked along the quay gleamed like ice flows.

Jan had told her about himself, about what he'd read and experienced, about his father in South America, about his mother's death and Mrs. Tapper, about his childhood on Brahegatan and out at the Water Palace, about how young he and Gertrude had been when they met. But that she was his sister, he couldn't say that.

They drank white wine. They were alone in the restaurant. Clouds were piling up over the Central Station as if a locomotive had just passed below the horizon. A sight-seeing boat with a girl guide went by on Klara Lake.

"Stockholm is situated on seventeen rocky islands. . . ."

"Tell me about yourself," Jan said. "I know it already, more or less. But tell me anyway."

Jenny's first love

I was nine, she was old, maybe fifteen, maybe twenty. I don't know why I thought of her the way I did. She probably wasn't even pretty. My feeling for her was my whole life. She was chewing gum once and spit it out on the gravel, by mistake I think. And then I thought, or I said to myself, "I'd like to pick it up and chew it myself, since she's been chewing it." Otherwise I was particular about food and things. I was disgusted by a lot of things that don't bother me any more. I took it all very seriously. I wasn't happy or exhilarated. It was love. No one noticed.

Jenny's childhood

Most of my childhood isn't a part of me. I'm not especially nostalgic. I've destroyed old letters and diaries. I like living in Stockholm, you can be anonymous here. You can be depressed in peace. I remember one summer at my aunt's in Viborg— that was before the war. Her husband was a doctor and had died in a cholera epidemic in Siberia. Viborg was an old city, built on grass and skeletons, my aunt said. She was really my father's aunt.

Mama taught Swedish and history in Västerås, in the summers she taught summer school. She was very frugal, kept newspapers for months in our old woodshed, put her small change in a box. My father was a lawyer and not like her. He embezzled some money, it wasn't much, he said it was to help a close friend. It was discovered, he was disbarred, the family was going to move to another town.

But he killed himself before we could move. They didn't tell me until long afterwards. That was the summer I was in Finland.

For many people it's too much trouble to be in love. So they decide that what they can't feel doesn't exist. My mother was a capable woman, she didn't find it hard to work, but anything outside the routine scared her. What my father did was unexpected and out of her control. She was proud of her profession, she could provide for a family. "Conscientious" was one of her favorite words. "Weak" and "peculiar" were words she used about my father.

I don't think she loved him, love belonged in the operettas that came on tour. But I don't know, people often imagine wrong things about their parents.

My aunt's hands hovered among white and blue cups in Viborg. "Lucky for you your mother is so strong," she said. "You can always start over," was another thing she said. Our life together sang, and grew in the evenings to a tree. There was something called spiced Viborg buns, and there was cold milk with crushed strawberries in it. When Viborg wound up in the front lines, my aunt moved to a yellow house in Lovisa on the Gulf of Finland.

Jenny's growing up

It was at summer camp, a bunch of girls living together in a cabin. I was sharing a bed with another girl. She started touching me, it was nice. I didn't do anything, I was passive. It was like touching yourself. Her body didn't interest me, only what I was feeling. The remarkable thing was that she was doing that to me. The next day I looked at myself—two flaps of skin, a little hair that was coarser than on my head. She took me by the arm a few times, we never talked about it.

I was sixteen then and I didn't want to study or go out dancing with the other girls. I felt I had to be in on The Great Event, but I didn't know what it was. The war had been over a couple of years, nothing had changed. People just bought cars, and the girls in my class drank rum with Coca-Cola so you couldn't taste it. I read books about the war. I kept asking myself, How can people stand to go on living? And why did I survive when all those other people died?

It didn't seem to me anybody was doing anything. Nobody was avenging the dead. Nobody cared about justice, nobody even stayed awake. And I didn't have anyone to talk to, they didn't understand. Truth wasn't so important, but some kind of justice. . . .

In the lavatory at school all they talked about was boys. Just jabber, never any clarity. Whether you had to take your clothes off, and who did it first . . . whether you slept together all night long or only a couple of hours . . . about how long a boy's thing could get, you could see it on horses of course, and if it came up into your midriff then you'd probably have to vomit like you'd been hit in the stomach. You were always in danger. If a boy kissed you with his tongue it was best to be standing against a wall, because your knees got weak.

One girl described it like this—you suddenly notice you've got two hearts, a pounding starts below your navel. And your breasts feel like they were made of porcelain.

Hitler wasn't mentioned in the textbooks. No one talked about him. A Moral Rearmament priest came down from Stockholm and preached about purity and the atom bomb and godless communism. I didn't believe all that. It seemed to me everyone was hiding things. Having something to believe in was beautiful, of course, even if it was only that it was right to sell your body on the street or put fluoride in the drinking water. But all I believed in was that nothing happens twice and that nothing stays the way it is, everything changes and gets forgotten and passes and dies.

Jenny's studies and lovers

I never went to bed with anyone until I was out of high school. I didn't trust men, maybe because I'd been told so often that my father was an unsuccessful weakling. Then it got a little better. I studied architecture at the Institute of Technology for two years, but I decided I didn't have any talent, so I quit. I got my degree at Stockholm—political economy, statistics, sociology, and cultural geography.

For a while I had a job with the City of Stockholm Regional Planning Commission. Mama thought my life was going well, she was conservative and noticed what people did rather than why they did it. She kept my letters behind the clock on the desk. I had a room on Surbrunnsgatan over a laundry, up toward Valhallavägen and Roslagshörnan's Café. We'll go there. I ate there a lot.

I got engaged to a law student. He was going to get a job at a bank when he got his degree. He drank. Sometimes he slept with other girls. I thought it would be better to see each other without feeling bound, so I broke the engagement. He fell apart, I was scared and moved back in with him for a while. Now he's married and has a lot of children and looks happy. I've caught sight of him in department stores a couple of times. It's nice when things go well for people you've liked.

I met a new man. He was an architect with the City of Stockholm, and he was headed for a great career. He wanted to see me once a week, the rest of the time was for his work. Now he's married, but he travels most of the time and doesn't see any more of his wife than he did of me. Still, he had a way of convincing me he needed me. I was furious with myself, but I didn't want to lose him. Every time he called I was happy all over again.

Jenny's marriage

I slid into my marriage. I was in love of course. Still, I didn't want to break up with this architect I'd never loved; we got along so well together, mostly sexually. So I was unfaithful to the man I thought I loved. Naturally all that was before he'd asked me if we should get married, before I'd openly admitted that I loved him. But I did love him, and still couldn't give up the other.

There was something cowardly and indecisive in it that I've always blamed myself for. Deep down I was maybe unsure of my feelings, distrusted my ability to take anything seriously enough. Was I looking more for stability than for love?

My husband—I did marry him—loved me, that was enough. I didn't resist. I met him for the first time with my fiancé the law student and I hardly noticed him. He was also a lawyer, with a big corporation, an officer in the reserve. Jeger is my maiden name.

I can't understand anymore why I got married. And that's probably why it failed. Outwardly we had a good life—sailboat, some traveling, backpacking in the mountains in the fall. I had a job at the Industrial Federation, that was before I went over to the Department of the Environment.

My husband's name was Johan, an old-fashioned name in his generation. He was polite and sensible and always right. He ticked along methodically with the same phrases, the same smiles. He was a monument to the indissoluble marriage. To me he was an implacable machine that boxed in and recorded and squeezed dry the all too scanty hours of my life.

It's awful of me to describe him that way. So it was a good thing I eventually managed to break up the tangle. I was a nicer person right away. I must have been defenseless when I met him, afraid of becoming too driving, too cold, promiscuous, career-oriented, things you're not supposed to be.

Because we were very different. He was honest and unimaginative. "Jenny, pardon my saying so, but you haven't straightened out the fringes on the carpet since you vacuumed." He was a better cook than I was. I had the feeling our friends looked up to him and down on me, since I was messy and impulsive. He spoke slowly and never hurried. I'd flame up, get enthusiastic, I could be acid and ironic and tough. When the guests had gone he used to accuse me of letting go too much. He himself didn't have anything to let go of.

"You're so unstable," he'd say. That was an insult. I went to a marriage counselor and found out there was nothing wrong with being a little unstable. You're not supposed to worry about the carpet fringes, or save little bits of soap—that's not bad upbringing but an indication of generosity and big thinking.

Now I have to cry a little. I'm not unhappy, it's just I get angry at myself the way I was then. I was trapped by some idea of togetherness at any price. I gave in to everything so meekly. But there was something that didn't want to give in, so I started being unfair and sarcastic. A lot of awful things came bubbling up, people are full of them.

I'm afraid of the person I was. Even a superficial affection puts your whole personality in motion, charges the atmosphere, makes you active and single-minded. That's why there's nothing more enjoyable than being drawn to another person. But I don't ever want to be a "we" again. I want to be judged for myself and seen for myself.

For Johan, everything was definite. He couldn't look at the world as changeable. You can. Which means we can change our weaknesses into paradoxical strengths, like a couple of clever engineers using buttresses, and exploiting irregularities, and drawing unexpected qualities from a material many people thought had been completely analyzed a long time ago.

I, this person who's now a chief administrator in a government department, who's disciplined herself to overtime and who's come so far that I'm my own boss somewhat and can allow myself so-called creative pauses, which I mostly want to create with you—anyway, this person thought of herself as a despicable artistic personality whom her husband was whipping into shape during life's endless calisthenics.

His parents came to visit. They were Johan squared. They measured everything. The sprig of parsley had to be just so many millimeters from the cheese or the cucumber or the veal roast. I had to go into the other room and clench my teeth, my whole body shook with hatred for them. And I had just let this happen, I, who was so aware of what I wanted—or wasn't I aware of that until afterwards?

He wanted to have children, but we didn't have any. I had myself examined and there was nothing really wrong, but my womb was in a slightly funny position and it was possible the passage to it wasn't quite open. But I let it pass, went home and said there was nothing wrong. Because all of a sudden the thought of children filled me with horror, then I'd be even more helplessly pulled into Johan's family. I'd be caught in the trap and suffocated.

I used to look at him. His face told me nothing, it wasn't mine. I was so much less mature then. I thought if I had a friend or a lover I'd look at Johan with protective tenderness. But feeling duty-bound and loyal against my will that way, he irritated me with his half-presence, his competence. My conventional righteousness made me angry with him. He didn't realize I was sacrificing myself.

I heard him say to friends, "Yes, when Jenny and I get old we'll build on to the summer house. . . ." I went cold inside. I didn't want to get old with him and lie in some family grave.

We lived together for five years. I suffered maybe, but at the same time I must have been standing oddly to one side of what was happening to me, or through me. I must have been living with vague expectations that ran alongside my daily life. That's why I could stay with him such a long time, that's why I could break up with him as quickly as I did.

My feeling of the lack of air grew stronger and breaking up was easy, though I felt awfully sorry for Johan, who hardly understood a thing. I knew it was the last second before I'd be broken by his education program. He realized I was different, but he figured he was doing me a favor by binding me tightly to the kind of life he and his parents and most of our friends found natural.

He got a big job in Brazil. I didn't want to go with him, no more than I wanted to have his child. The company was exploiting the cheap labor in the country, and I was up on the times enough to protest against it. Johan was against it too, but he said if he didn't take the job someone else would, nothing would change anyway, no one was indispensable. It revealed a new difference in temperament and political outlook, but it really only helped me to see how weak my emotional commitment had become.

I used a pang of political conscience to get my freedom. I know perfectly well that if I'd loved him I would have gone along—maybe even if he'd taken a job in South Africa.

The worst feeling of all is when you know something is too late, that you ought to have done it a long time ago. You have to fight that feeling all the time. Why was I so submissive? I thought most people's lives were about the same. There was nothing wrong with me, we had enough money, I was healthy. Why complain when the world's the way it is?

I wasn't thinking in big terms—about living with a person I didn't love and not wanting to change it. In spite of everything maybe one person was better than none. But then it doesn't work any more, you reach a limit you didn't know was there. And it doesn't take another man to get you there.

So now he's with a Swedish company in South America, remarried, with three children. We write once or twice a year. We don't have any reason to accuse each other of anything. I brought about his first depression, but that's over now. He has a better life without me. His wife doesn't work, they have servants. For that matter if your father's out there then he must know him. Swedes in Brazil all know each other. The world is small.

There were a thousand other details, laughter and fun, parties, beautiful lovemaking, security—there's probably a fairer picture, but anyway this was the sum of it.

Jenny's wall

I don't want what you and I have to resemble anything else or be able to be replaced by anything else. But at the same time I don't want to be afraid of everything interchangeable and similar, because it's the earth we're growing in, everything nourishing and recognizable.

People communicate with each other over walls that are really themselves. I move my walls around like dominoes, but they're still there. And since you're a wall you can never get really close to anyone. But without the walls you'd be nothing, no one would recognize you. We talk about defending our integrity and freedom against other people's inroads, but often as not what we're really defending is our lack of freedom and our isolation.

Radio waves go right through us, codes, messages. We don't feel them. They go on through a chimney, a maple leaf, an icebox and a child's head. What I want most of all is continuous contact like radio waves. More than love I want openness— that we're never afraid of each other. That we think it's important to talk to each other. I'd like to work on a clear-sighted tenderness, a feeling for you that had nothing to do with me myself and was therefore constant no matter how stupidly or chaotically you might behave.

Knowing other human beings—that changes a person to some extent. Those dependencies that last your whole life! First you're helplessly bound to your parents, hardly feel a need to get free, the important thing is that they're handy and you're not alone. During puberty you want to be on your own, paddle your own canoe. And then suddenly love and the fact that another, different person can mean so much to you.

When I was a child it amazed me to think that Mama and Papa had once met as total strangers, that they weren't sort of brother and sister, and that therefore, biologically, I was closer to my grandparents than they were.

It's awful to know that maybe other people can't ever change you as much as your own suffering—losing a leg and being confined to a wheel chair, going completely blind.

Jenny then and now

I'm not afraid of you. I don't distrust you. I don't ever want to need your help, but rather take care of myself in the knowledge that you exist. You know so little about me, but I want to be so open to your questions that you hardly need to ask them.

It's never been like this before. No one ever cared about me the way you do, and I never cared about anyone the way we do. I'm starting to use muscles that had atrophied. It feels as if I were carrying something precious, something that wants me to be happy. It ought to make me uneasy, because I've never been through this before. I've come across a room that's always been locked, and now suddenly I can go in there and play.

I'm probably undependable. But I'm trying to prepare you for who I am as well as I can. I don't want to know more about myself than you know. I'd rather be honest than nice. Though I go too far sometimes—I could be more considerate.

I'm willful, destructive maybe, and most of all I have a feeling I'm no one important, no one to waste big words on. It's mainly a need for freedom. The most fun of all—being free with you.

You have to know. That feels more important than anything else. I've never told anyone everything, not even my husband, though there's not really much to tell. My lovers, jobs, deceits, the way I go too far emotionally—I can tell you all of it without fear. And I'm passing a boundary I've never passed before.

I've wanted to be an adventuress with integrity. I sleep with someone but he doesn't know who I am, I have my private world inside me, my solitude. Now I have my own world with you—you know about my one-track imagination, my conscientiously asocial bent, my lack of guilt.

Once in your life everyone ought to be unafraid, take all the risks. By telling everything maybe we'll make it, insured against shock and theft.

Here's a photograph. That's what I looked like. A flimsy dress, folds in the neck, baby teeth in an open mouth. Not much resemblance, though the chin's the same, and the hair. What a turned-up nose! Do you want it? This little girl, passport size, grew and grew until she burst . . . no, till she learned a lot of remarkably pretty and ugly words and collected strange and frightening experiences behind them.

If you look at human beings from the outside you don't make the connections. The ruthless general from World War Two is now in an old people's home, doddering and gentle. The famous prostitute is now half blind, embroidering pillows. But you yourself, seen from the inside, no stage of development seems strange to you. In your own person you combine the meadow full of wild flowers with the battlefield, champagne at the ball with sour milk in a home for the infirm. The terrible part is that you have to live through all of it, relentlessly—I feel an insane defiance against that. I'm not looking for the fountain of youth, but I would like to live undisturbed *between* the strokes of the clock, in real time, and then just chirp-chirp and goodbye.

I'm different with you. I give up gestures I've borrowed someplace, and don't use them any more. All sorts of things in me have only been borrowed, I realize now. The rest is yours. I see your eyes, then I see with them. There's something in me that came into existence for you and was never there before. So it doesn't matter what I did before I met you.

Jenny's stones

I'll tell you about my friend in London some other time. He's still there, I'm going to see him again. But let me tell you about my stones, they're just as important, I've never been separated from them. You can save stones more easily than people.

I've collected them on beaches all over. Flint, shale, quartz . . . I don't know the names of most of them, only where I found them. I've got a big old puzzle box full of them, a regular reliquary. They're shiny, quiet, white or shot with color like birds' eggs, as round as eggs, as soft as skin, bound up in themselves but willing to be warmed by a hand. And every one of them has an inside.

I add new stones from new places. Some have designs all mixed with red and golden brown. They're there. They've been polished by seawater. They're hard. Each is a new way to be happy. You can have them all.

THE THEORY
OF PERSPECTIVE

JAN LEFT THE CAR where the road ended and the neck of land out toward the Water Palace began. It was a fairly uninhabited part of northern Värmdö—fields invaded by young aspen, outlying land that belonged to the farms in the middle of the island. The path ran in stages down a hillside toward a depression that had once been a ford.

Was he afraid to meet Gertrude's eyes? Did he have trouble smiling? Did he feel unnatural? He asked himself the conventional questions. But he experienced nothing without her—she was always built in and taking part, with or against their will. He journeyed with her.

Winding roots broke up the path like a staircase. A bench waited halfway down, from his grandfather's or his father's time, but it was tottering with rot. Jan put his feet down carefully the way he'd done as a child—never step outside the path, balance on a tightrope. If you fell to one side and trampled a flower you lost something; he didn't remember what.

From the sunshine he came into the house. In the initial blindness he thought he saw figures moving among the chairs. But the room was empty. Maybe Gertrude was down by the bay. She knew he was coming, it was Saturday afternoon. He put down the groceries he'd brought from town and opened the refrigerator—mostly buttermilk, butter, and beer. Didn't she eat? He looked at the newspapers. Gertrude's mail from the Academy of Sciences was forwarded out here, his came to Upplandsgatan. He read a picture postcard from Marianne Tidström in Botswana, it had come across the world in five days.

Every time he saw an ad for Nivea or Palmolive—the same woman's face against the sun, the same couple in black tie and décolletage at the dance—he felt the way he did when he came into the Water Palace and the house was quiet and he discovered the knobby alder walking stick and the tennis racket that had dried and split. Europa clung tightly to the bull, together they hid a gilded clock on the mantelpiece, its hands appearing occasionally between the bull's legs.

No time had passed, nothing had happened since the first time he saw all this. And the Jews who'd been murdered, the millions who'd died, the atom bombs, the colonies that had been freed, the refugees, the rootless. . . . For a moment it was as if none of that could have happened, as long as the Palmolive ad and the tennis racket hadn't changed.

Almost everything had been left the way it was. There had once been a zebra skin on the floor in the hall, a diplomatic present to their father, but it had become more and more leprous and was finally carted away by the Värmdö Refuse Company. They had given away a couple of heavy tablecloths with fringes like seaweed beards.

They had inherited the house. It was as if they hadn't dared make it their own. A person is an heir as long as he has ancestors he knows something about. Photographs lay in bundles in the attic—relatives with bulging eyelids, frilled collars. . . . There were also pictures of the Water Palace, atmospheric oleographs on tinted paper. The relatives were his and Gertrude's together.

"I have the feeling we have to change all this," Jan had said, a long time ago. "For your sake."

"No, for your sake," Gertrude said. "We can't both of us decide about surroundings a third person created, a person, what's more, who calls himself our father."

"We could tear out some walls, bring in some modern furniture, Finnish rag rugs, wicker chairs. Make it summery."

Gertrude had looked around and shrugged her shoulders.

"We'll let it stay the way it is. For a while. Then we'll see. But we have to have a washing machine."

Grandfather who'd had it built . . . When he lived in Paris he worked in a laboratory where he took part in the invention of a malt extract that became important in the brewing industry. An incomprehensible diploma bore witness to his success. When the extract was further improved his contribution was forgotten, and the world's beer became neither cheaper nor richer.

Gustaf Backman was by education a chemist but had also picked up some knowledge of mechanics and medicine. Natural scientists weren't terribly specialized, and he remained an amateur in most things. In photographs he looked happy and uncomplicated. He made a good deal of money in a short time on several inventions, invested it skillfully during the European boom of the nineties, moved to Sweden and bought property on Kungsholm.

Right after the turn of the century he acquired a shore lot facing Sandö Bay—a stony realm of bog-myrtle and crowberries and heather climbing on the rocks, but also of meadows that were never mown, full of dropwort and bachelor's buttons and pheasant's eye, and a grass snake who forgot his skin on the path. It was old farmland but seldom cultivated. The coast was windy and the soil thin.

He married late and was over fifty when A. O. Backman was born. He was cremated dust before Gertrude and Jan knew what planet they had come to. Agnes Cecilia Backman, their grandmother, survived him, but she passed away just before Gertrude was born to Adolf's first marriage.

Grandfather, they had been told, lay down to die at regular intervals and issued discouraging bulletins in the hope that some newspaper would publish an obituary and he would finally get to see what he amounted to in the ungrateful eyes of the surrounding world. But no one reacted to the reports from the supposedly dying man, and he eventually lived to be quite old.

He offered the Street Department an easily handled air pump for cleaning sidewalks. That resulted in a dinner with a city commissioner where they drank Punsch and Gustaf Backman described in detail how his invention could be developed for practical application. Afterwards came a regretful letter, and a few years later the inventor thought he recognized his device on the market.

Such discoveries made him paranoid and misanthropic in his old age. The Royal Patent Office became a temple for mankind's most malicious rituals, the abode of jinn, and when he happened to pass the building in a cab he uttered oaths and curses in several languages. So vehemently that on one occasion the driver ordered him to pay and get out, and he found himself standing in the dusk before the closed doors of the Office itself, alone and enraged.

He hit on a preparation that could be used in stuffing animals. What taxidermists thought of it is unknown, but it led him into a new area, zoology. Senile, he went off on an expedition to the Judarn Forest in the belief that he was wandering in Kolmården. His last entry read, "Have finally captured a red mouse." When his death was announced his acquaintances accepted it as one of the old man's customary self-centered reports and discreetly took no notice.

Agnes Cecilia Backman kept a diary in 1904, the first year of the Water Palace. It was in a printed almanac that began with The Royal Family, Postal Information, Swedish Standard Time, and The Positions and Magnitudes of the Major Planets. It lay in the desk drawer in the main room. Jan walked around in the house some sixty years later and looked up corresponding summer days.

"Today we rearranged the rooms. Dinner consisted of bouillon with dumplings, walleyed pike, veal rolls, rhubarb. Miss Lyth sat at table with us. Letter from Betty. Wrote to Jenny in Ramlösa. A little rain. Pastilles 0.50. Nail brush 0.75. Eggs from Höglund's 1.25.

"Magnificent weather. Dinner rose-hip soup, whitefish au gratin, corned brisket of beef, asparagus, marrow pudding. Mrs. Annerstedt, Mrs. Slöörs, and Victorine Ahlberg here. Kerstin altered my black silk skirt. Line a clock cover 2.50. 2 bars of lanolin soap 1 crown. Lisa poorly as usual. Dr. Sjöqvist here. New brown sleeping pills."

For several audibly silent seconds Jan stood and stared straight ahead. Time was everywhere, all around, whirling like the needle of a compass. You made a list of things to do, some of them were attended to years later.

Jan turned over the postcard from Marianne Tidström. Had his grandfather been like Sten? If Gustaf Backman were alive today, would he be out building irrigation canals in Botswana, and experimenting with pressures of six, seven atmospheres in windmills? Why wasn't he there himself, Jan Backman? Why did he fiddle with switches and call out instructions from his tower without ever traveling himself?

He went down to the shore to look for Gertrude. At first he

didn't see her. He looked at the stones. Were these the kind Jenny collected? Shiny, angular, round, chalky, the kind that had clear colors under water and went flat in the air. He thought about the things Jenny had told him—the boys she'd slept with, her marriage. So different compared to him, and still so easy to understand.

"Gertrude!" he called.

And she was right there, resting on her elbows with her hands on her ears, reading, and she hadn't heard him come. She had her bathing suit on, he saw drops of sweat around her waist. He kissed her, feeling cumbersome in his city clothes.

"Have you been having a good time?" he asked.

"Yes. I've been working. I brought down a thermos of coffee and I've been lying here on the rocks reading."

"You've got a tan."

"All over. That was yesterday. Not a cloud in the sky. Do you want to see?"

She pulled her bikini down over her stomach.

"Can't they see you from out in the bay?"

"I lie behind that big rock. It doesn't get in the way—the sun comes from the land side."

He ran his hand over her stomach. He saw the Academy of Sciences stamp in her book, a familiar thing. They knew each other so well, he and Gertrude. No half moments, no half glances.

If everything were the other way around, he thought. If Gertrude were keeping a secret from him. Maybe something he didn't suspect had been going on for a long time. Going on at a distance of light years right before his eyes. Gertrude's project—the one she started talking about that time he forgot his key to the apartment? What if there were a new theory of relativity and his own place in it a flyspeck, a nothing? What would that change?

"I went for a swim this morning," Gertrude said. "The water's still OK. Generally I begin to suspect the worst. The algae . . . ."

It occurred to him that she also read the reports from the Department of the Environment.

"Do you people at the Academy have much to do with the Department of the Environment?" he asked.

"More and more all the time. Have you started getting interested in ecology?"

"It's one of the big political questions," he said.

"Political?" Gertrude said. "It's the biggest question there is. All life depends on how it's solved. Every church in the world ought to get involved—life and death and eternity in one package. It's more important than the existence of God. For that matter, don't you people in Air Traffic come in contact with all this?"

"I think so," Jan said, startled by the sharpness in her tone. "Everyone seems to be working together."

They walked slowly up the hill toward the house. They passed a clump of trees where the ferns were growing high above the lilies of the valley. Soon they would shade everything else, wither, and still be there next year. A cryptogamous forest in miniature, seen through the wrong end of Coal Age binoculars.

"Oh yes," Jan said. "I bought you a book in town. Mostly just for fun. I left it in the hall next to Marianne's postcard."

Gertrude opened it and read, *"Robin Jouet's Travels and Adventures in the Jungles of Guyana and Brazil."*

"I was thinking of Adolf, naturally. And then of your ferns. A popular view of what the world looked like a hundred years ago."

"I don't think you'll ever grow up," she said. "What do I want this for?"

"Look at the list of illustrations," he said eagerly. "The captions for pictures you haven't seen yet. Like a silent movie with nothing but titles."

Jan read them himself, including the numbers.

"1. I sat on deck for hours, dreaming and watching the sea birds in flight.

"2. I was suddenly awakened by a sharp pain near my right eye.

"3. I rowed along the shore looking for suitable place to land.

"4. Each one of them held a piece of their roasted companion in his hand.

"5. I pulled him ashore and refreshed him with a plentiful repast.

"6. Binoculars and surveying instruments went straight to the bottom.

"7. 'Look over there! Your forefathers built that fortress.' "

"I'll think about it," Gertrude comforted him. "Maybe I can use it some way. It depends on your frame of reference."

"Exactly," Jan said. "It's a question of what you let yourself see."

He didn't actually know what it was she was doing. He'd been used to looking at her as his double, his duplicate. Now he realized that other people's lives, even hers, were parallel to his own.

But there was an inescapable lack of privacy between them. They were able to guess so much. What would it be like not to know her? He couldn't say.

With Jenny he could imagine a game—they come toward each other from different directions, having no idea that they are she and he, they catch sight of each other as if for the first time—and then they know.

With Gertrude he couldn't even pretend there was a time before they'd met.

Still both he and the Water Palace had been there before Gertrude. Or did he have no past he didn't share with her, because he and she had arrived in the world at about the same time and from the same source? He saw their common experience out here as children in a strong, feverish light. But for the most part their experience had been individual—stories and unverifiable events.

Gertrude filled the thermos. They sat down on the grass in front of the house and looked out toward the channel, where pleasure boats passed on their way to the outer skerries and left a smell of gasoline in the air, and large ships sailed by with pilot flags flying.

"Take some more coffee," Gertrude said. "And here's some chocolate. We can do anything we want to," she added, as if it were unusual for them to be alone and the fact should be celebrated.

Yes, they were themselves out here. They ruled over a domain. It felt strange, as if it didn't belong to their way of life, to their time at all. They came from their jobs, they got salaries, paid rent and taxes. They were adults but made no more use of the Water Palace than when they were children. They created customs for themselves. Slipperwort and cineraria on the window sill. As if they were imitating the traditional upbringing they in fact had missed, with Mrs. Tapper in the kitchen, their father out of the country, and Gertrude mostly at boardingschool in Switzerland or in Sigtuna.

They were like radio-controlled boats on a pond. An invisible hand held a rod, an antenna. They were forced to navigate accordingly.

FIELD OF VISION

Evening at the Water Palace, the same day.

Gertrude was frying meat in the kitchen, Jan was browning leeks in a pan alongside. Gertrude had put up the thin, white curtains. He brushed his lips against her neck.

He thought he saw something questioning in her eyes, but it quickly disappeared—or else what he saw there was only himself. It occurred to him that he didn't make her life any more exciting than she made it herself. She deserved something better, but she seemed to love him and not to require anything more. And that was, everything considered, a sort of miracle.

The light of the western sun was sharp through the kitchen window, as if it were searching for anything erratic in the expressions on their faces.

He turned on the transistor radio, but Gertrude asked him to turn it off.

"It's hard to concentrate when the radio's on," she said. "There's news every hour. It's as if the same war moved around the world like a swarm of locusts. It's always somewhere. It's been like that for as long as I can remember. Just like there always seem to be crows overhead when I'm sunbathing, I'm never alone. They make a lot of noise and I get sick of them and they don't stop and I leave. But I can't understand them, so I don't really get upset."

"So many things happen to people," Jan said. "When it's important, you're never consulted."

"No," she said.

They drank wine and ate slowly. After sunset the wind came up unexpectedly, trying to force its way through the cracks of the house with a chisel.

"Poor grandfather," Gertrude said all of a sudden. "If he could hear the way we talk, and see us sitting here not doing anything."

"At least we're still here. We haven't sold his house."

"But we're not much of a family."

"The Backmans are on their way out," Jan said. "We've been careful about children."

"There are other people everywhere you turn," Gertrude said.

"You're just like Grandfather. You're working on some mysterious idea."

"Oh, it's nothing," she said, fending him off. "I get that way when I'm waiting for you."

"Waiting for me?"

"No, that was wrong. I'm not waiting for you. You're here after all."

He looked her in the eyes across the supper table and saw himself reflected in her pupils—I'm there in her and here outside her. Was he leaving her in order to follow an unknown scent and be led away by an unfamiliar ecstasy? Was there something horrible in his happiness? She was part of it. It seemed to him his life had begun in her, in someone who was not his mother, and now he moved in an orbit around her.

"Have you been working a lot at night?" she asked.

"A couple of times."

"Don't you have trouble sleeping?"

"I can sleep anytime," he said.

He informed her of the fact as if she hadn't always known his habits. She'd never been out to Arlanda with him. She listened to what he told her, but she seldom called and never came to visit.

"On the other hand, Arlanda never goes to sleep," Jan said after a while. "The rest of us have to sleep and lose out. The world is full of moments, falling dust, a shaft of light. I want to be here every minute."

"You are."

"Not the here that's everywhere."

"You're trapped inside your skin," Gertrude said, as if she were speaking to a child. "It won't do you any good to complain. The world is only a tiny bit bigger than your own body."

"You hear about other people; you don't know them, but they think and feel. And things exist—those piles of barbed wire in a forest, those supplies of bombs and forms and emergency plans. I can't seriously believe it."

Was this part of the significance of their being brother and sister, he wondered—not letting anyone get in close, defending themselves against the temptation of the unfamiliar? Nothing from outside was allowed to threaten their delicate structure.

After supper. Gertrude was going to do some work. Jan poured himself some coffee and set out gin and tonic. It was a warm evening. He picked up a clay apple lying on a shelf under the table in the main room. It had a slot on top, a bank. Gertrude had made it herself, once as a child when he wasn't with her, at her boardingschool in Switzerland, under the direction of Mademoiselle G. . . .

"What *was* her name?"

"Who?"

"Something with 'god.' Your headmistress in Lausanne."

"Gudasnes. And when I say that name I feel like my legs are starting to go to sleep. They remember that short bed. I was taller than the other girls."

"Do you think about that time a lot?"

"Hardly ever. Plaster dust used to fall on my bed in the fall after drying out all summer. We had to go to church. I used to count the thorns on Christ so I wouldn't go to sleep. There was a handsome bus driver we rode into town with. Either you sat up close to him or else someplace you could see his face in the rear-view mirror."

She was his sister then too, though he didn't know he loved her. She was "Gertrude" whom his father used to talk about. Because of the war, several years went by without his seeing her at all.

Had Jenny started collecting stones back then? Did the same yellowish sulphur fumes drift up in the school laboratory in Västerås? Were flushing toilets just as disturbing from one country to another? What did Jenny make in handicrafts?

Gertrude was a maker. He himself imagined that he had inherited some practical qualities from his mother the sculptress—a way with tools, keyboards and simpler machines, an ability to feel with his hands, but hardly the desire to create something out of nothing.

Was there a great deal he'd kept Gertrude from doing? He saw her from in front, and at the same time he caught a glimpse at a distance of the back of her neck in the mirror inset in the tile stove. He had her surrounded.

"What I envy you," Gertrude said, "is your ability to lose yourself in the moment—just the opposite of what you said before. I look at you and I know you're thinking about what's happening before your eyes. I always have a background covered with scribbling. And the minutes ebb away. The day becomes an anticipation that turns into new anticipation."

"But you weren't waiting for anything?"

"Not for you. Not for anything in particular. But I remember the boardingschool—there I really did wait. For the war to end, for boys, for getting away from the other girls."

A bat sailed in, soundless, deaf, and nimble. It obeyed commands beyond their senses. It hesitated and received signals to which they were insensitive. It got ready to land but changed its mind at the moment of touchdown and disappeared, like one of the trainers at Arlanda.

Night. They lay close to each other like spoons in a drawer. He had his knees in the hollows of hers, his stomach against her behind. He didn't touch her breasts, just breathed against the back of her neck. She lay here alone at times. She didn't mind. She coiled up like an armadillo when she fell asleep.

Jan had trouble sleeping. There was so much within his field of vision. He put his leg carefully across her hip, but she didn't wake up. She lived inside something he couldn't guess at, clothed in her own breath.

Because we're brother and sister we don't need to own each other, he thought with tenderness. We're close to each other anyway. Foster siblings. It's important that I like her. For my sake. He didn't know exactly why. She was with him all the time.

He tested various sacrifices in his mind—they were meaningless. For the first time he clearly realized that if he stopped loving Jenny he wouldn't be able to love Gertrude either. It struck him that someone else ought to love Gertrude, not he. He hadn't told her everything. Not sharing his secret conflicted with the family closeness between them. But maybe she understood it anyway.

Then and now and later weren't steps of different heights. They existed all at once and at the same level. The room was all around him even if he looked at one part at a time. Arlanda's flights in his dreams . . . bulbs blinking on the control board . . . Gertrude . . . Jenny. . . .

Done is never really done. He had chased mosquitoes and jumped across her sleeping body . . . a couple of decades ago, in another of the Water Palace's rooms. The mosquitoes still whined. He put a corner of the sheet over her knees, which were sticking out over the edge of the bed.

Nothing ended. Nothing ever became entirely definite. But the things he remembered, the things still there right now—they were not indefinite. They were moments remaining like thumbtacks in wood, long after the poster has been ripped down or dissolved by the rain.

He wanted to take her head between his hands and mumble something into her sleep, so she'd always be secure. But nevertheless she slept, she seemed calm, it was he who looked now at the ceiling and now at her naked shoulders. A thin blue vein ran parallel to her eyebrows. She breathed regularly. She drew nourishment from herself.

SEEDS

JAN BACKMAN GUIDED people out into air channels. He knew approximately where they were going, but could find out little more. He had takeoff bulletins and flight plans from central briefing, he had information on weather conditions, artillery ranges, and other air traffic, but simple facts were no more reliable than the most expansive commentary. Triviality and mystery both increased with the accumulation of detail.

There were thirty air traffic controllers, counting the assistants. Most of them were young, college men with a year or two at Bromma Field and an extra year of on-the-job training. Almost all of them could alternate between control room and tower. Jan was the same age as the oldest among them, and he was their boss, which meant he spent part of his time in an office and had access to the department secretary.

His primary job involved only a few operations, a number of combinations expressed in figures. There were code letters for arrivals and departures. It was all defined and indefinite at the same time. On a foggy morning there are spider webs running every which way across a bush. The same inside the instrument panels. Everything was on its way somewhere and had a function and therefore a pattern.

The policy of the double condom: not pretty but safer. That was what Jansson called the precautions in the tower, with radio checks in every direction and no departures from the established phraseology. And if anything happened, it was all recorded on tape.

The telephone rang at Arlanda. It was Jenny. An electric

arc was thrown between two power sources connected underground. Would she say she couldn't meet him? Half a second's
hesitation, then he could read the tone of her voice. He ran to
the parking lot and drove quickly into Märsta. He had his
checkbook with him, four thousand crowns in the account. He
was short of cash.

At a hardware store he bought a knife with a corkscrew,
paper plates, enamel mugs. He managed to find a bottle of
decent wine at a poorly stocked state liquor store. Then to the
delicatessen section of the supermarket. After that he drove
back to Arlanda, informed the switchboard he was off for the
afternoon, and saw Jenny's car pass the gate and circle the fire
station. She climbed out. They didn't embrace, they pretended
they were only acquaintances.

Jan transferred the groceries and the army topographical
map from his car, got in beside her, she started the engine. He
let one finger brush against her jaw. They drove away from the
airport buildings. The day was shining, unannulled.

"Where are we going?" Jenny asked.

"I'll show you. There's a little lake—doesn't have a name on
the map. I've never been there."

"What's it look like?"

"Sort of a blunt triangle. Open land on one side, trees and
forest on the other two. That's what the map says."

He was wearing a short-sleeved white shirt and thin light-
brown pants. Jenny had on a beige kilt and a white polo shirt.
She was wearing the wide watchband he'd given her.

"There's mud under the gas pedal," she said. She stopped the
car and got out, cleaned off the clutch and the brake as well.
Her shirt slid up around the waist.

"You're tan," he said.

"Sunlamp," she answered. "I haven't had time to get out and
sun myself."

He touched her skin, which had a trace of roughness. She

smiled weakly, resigned. He recognized it—as if she didn't really want what she wanted.

Very close to the lake was an estate called Sigridsholm, but first they came to Lunda church, from the fifteenth century. It was open. There was a medieval baptismal font, and on the wall of the weapon house an almost obliterated wheel of fortune. A demon churning butter could be seen more clearly. They stood in front of the grainy wall. The bell tower was tarred, and the weathervane bore the date 1710. The church had no priest, and the blinds were drawn at the house of the parish clerk. The yellow library was also closed. Sweden was a sparsely populated land.

He held her hand. The thing he found most difficult to comprehend and to believe was that what he felt was mutual.

South of the church there were grave mounds and prehistoric stone monuments. Moss and lichens were growing on the slender granite slabs, birches had shot up around them and roots pressed in under them and set the stones at angles.

She blew on him. Jenny's collected sighs, he thought.

"No one knows we're here," she said.

She kicked at the ground, then leaned against one of the stones, and when he came closer threw her arms around him.

"In graves like these," she said, "they've found seeds that sprouted after hundreds of years. Henbane, red nettles, sage. When the light hits them they start growing."

"Shall we bury some seeds?"

"Weeds are the hardiest. If anyone finds them."

"We'll be parents in another age."

He pulled up her polo shirt from her sunlamp skin and her bra came with it. He took one of her nipples in his mouth and pressed it gently against his palate with the tip of his tongue. She breathed in his hair.

"I saw a seed like that one time," he said a moment later. A cucumber seed. It got caught in the wicker in a basket and one day it started to sprout. It looked like the wicker had started to grow. The basket was muddy—we used to carry plants in it."

"I like to hear stories of nature's toughness," Jenny said, straightening her shirt.

He watched the way she stuffed her breasts into her brassiere, matter-of-factly, as if she were handling ordinary things.

Traces of medieval waterways from Lunda to the sea could still be seen around the church. The cows were grazing on marshy land, mist was rising from a muddy stream.

"One problem for us at the Department," Jenny said, "is that scientific conservation gets pushed aside in favor of social conservation, you know, the outdoor life. But why do you touch me that way? It's as though there were only the thinnest skin between us—a protective membrane against being too happy."

They stopped the car by the lake that wasn't named on the map. Brown spring water lay motionless on bright gravel, and the opposite shore was hidden by reeds. Several pines were drawing nourishment directly from the lake, and between their coarse roots was a shelf of flattened sand.

They lay down side by side. Jenny took off her polo shirt, stretching her arms above her head, and her nipples were drawn to the upper edge of her brassiere. Jan closed his eyes, and inside the lids there was a dance of molecules, bacteria, sperm, and ants—old acquaintances usually viewed through a microscope. When he looked up the clouds had divided, and Jenny sneezed.

As she was sneezing he folded her kilt to one side, pushed both edges of her underpants against one leg and forced his way into her. She drew up her legs so he lay against the backs of her thighs. He kissed her knee, which brushed against his shoulder. She looked at him in surprise and after a few moments he withdrew and ran into the water. She lay where she was, watching him. It was shallow a long way out, he slipped on a stone and fell forward, took a few strokes and was back. She looked at him and laughed.

"Well I see the water has had its effect. So maybe we can eat first?"

It was a lazy summer lake. A little way out, a grebe and a coot were swimming around at an uncertain distance from each other—you might suppose they were a couple, drawn to each other by the solitude. The shadows of the pines were painted on the water in dark green strokes.

"Woodcocks, grouse, brown crakes, horned owls—they've all disappeared I suppose," Jenny said. "We've asked the county for some information on the way the air traffic's affecting the animal life around Arlanda. Have you heard anything?"

Jan knew nothing about it.

"I can bring along some papers on it next time," she said.

She'd brought a tablecloth, knives and forks, glasses. They didn't need the enamel mugs from Märsta. From the market bag he set out whitefish roe, pickles, cured sausage, roast beef, goat cheese wrapped in chestnut leaves, rye cakes, strawberries and cream.

"Sweden has everything," Jenny said contentedly, and started to eat. "It's a good life."

"I probably could have broken into the SAS kitchens and taken some first class dinners," Jan said.

Jenny had a rather short, broad nose and mobile nostrils. With longer hair her whole face would have seemed less wide. He had an impulse to take the measurements of her skull.

"Some things go so fast," he said. "Entering you, for example. Other things take time. Like those seeds. . . . There ought to be a special calendar, one that has nothing to do with days and tiredness and change."

"There is no such thing. No more than a world without horizons. Nothing exists all by itself. Death in itself doesn't exist, death is something that connects, a beginning, like everything else."

"The life after death," he said. "That's the life a person leaves behind him."

Jenny was leaning back with her elbows on a clump of grass. She picked up some gravel.

"Even these are graves," she said. "Slime and moisture and membrane hardened into fossils."

"We're being philosophical," Jan said, and took a drink of wine.

"Scientific," Jenny said. "This is one of my lakes. They think life originated in motionless bodies of water, water where nothing seems to be going on, water beyond the tides. That's where the move toward life begins, toward jellies and slime, the scum that never gets to stiffen into crystals and gravel."

His glass tumbled over in the sand. Crumbs caught in the corners of her mouth. He put his arm around her shoulders and bent her down to the ground, and found his way into her without help. He lay still, fed her some cheese, took a gulp of wine. Between kisses he gave her a strawberry from the paper carton. He was still wet from his swim. She lifted her head and looked at the coot on the water.

When he was with her it was as if he remembered nothing. The hardwoods stood light green against the pines. A dry fir had fallen across the rocks. Here in the woods he felt himself halfway to Bald Mountain, carried off asleep. He looked at the everyday Jenny, at the goose bumps in the hollow of her throat, at the blond hair that didn't really gleam. She wasn't purposely trying to attract him.

And he knew less than ever who he was himself. But between him and everything that moved in the world there was a bond, a blink of recognition, a tenderness for others that was also a kind of indifference for himself. Astonished, he acted as if that were only fair, as if he wanted nothing else.

For the first time, they made love in the clear light of day. Shyness and wonder still. They were uncertain where it led, what the consequences might be. Its beginning had been so full of chance. Jan wasn't used to letting chance control his life. Gertrude was the opposite of chance—his natural sister.

A face could be so neutral, and then suddenly hunger, light, eagerness . . . and from such moments, that couldn't be gauged or gratified, life was stitched together.

He was still frightened and astonished by his feelings. To be the master of the situation—that was called freedom. To get the better of your existence. He felt himself emptied and far from free, but he lived and grew. Better to steal than to have nothing. Better to have nothing than always to possess.

He experienced Jenny with such force that for an instant he wished he had already gone through these stages of feeling, this erratically distributed pleasure and pain, and be left in peace, be done. An inflammation of the lungs, with fever curve, crisis, calmer respiration—and everything would be over, an ordeal, a whim. He tried to imagine it that way; it seemed that was the way it ought to be.

Could a man in the long run live on anything more than diluted feeling? His tenderness for Jenny hurt like a wound being washed with gasoline. An explosion was taking place, with forces trying to fling him away like shrapnel. And yet there were other terms as well. Low voltage can light a lamp as brightly.

Jenny put her palms against his shoulders, lifted him away from her, and stared at him as if to see if he were serious. Then he sank down on her again.

"My darling," he said.

"Let's let everything go slowly," she said. "We've got lots of time."

Fingertips searching, eventlessly, loitering.

And there lay the lake, apparently unpoisoned.

They were starting from scratch. They were satisfied with the fourth part of a kernel. It could easily have been nothing at all.

A breeze heavy with odors came from inside the storehouse of the woods. It was a wind, and it paused in the leaves beside them. When it started to blow again it sounded like two separate voices breathing.

She was his laughter. He saw eyes and smile, wrinkles on her elbow when she held her brown arm straight, lumpy knees, nipples moving slowly under his glance like marine animals. He had sand under his toenails. He held her tightly as though trying to stop the pulse of time.

She drew up her legs a little, and suddenly everything gushed forward through him and he came as she cupped her hand around his balls.

"You've given me a new body," she said, smiling.

Jan reached toward the tablecloth.

"Be a gentleman," she said, "and pour me some more wine."

She ran her fingers quickly and unconsciously through her hair. Her feet grazed his and he held them fast between his own.

Yellow flowering moss carpeted a rock beside them, and dark panes of lichen stood out against the love-in-idleness and wild thyme.

"We couldn't have predicted any of this," Jan said.

"It feels inevitable and easy," Jenny said. "Not a distraction and then 'thanks for everything.' Nor something off in the future."

"I fell into your hands so headlong. You're the most accessible part of me, also the part I most have to hide."

"I'm like other people, and so are you. I don't want to write things into you that aren't there. That would just be playing games with myself."

Jenny sat up and spread out a white bath towel. She picked blades of grass from her vagina.

"I wonder what else got in there."

"I'll wash you," he said. "Sit on the stone here."

"You purse your lips and crook your toes like an ape," she said. "You look so determined when you handle me."

He knew her slender hands by heart, and her body as if he

were the midwife, holding her out in the light for the first time, upside down.

"It's nice we're not seventeen," Jenny said. "We might panic in the face of all this lust."

She kissed his ribs and nipples. She pressed her lips hard against his thigh and let them stay while with one finger she drew circles around his kneecap. His penis was resting against her neck. He looked down at her head and then at the steep pine needle path to the lake. The blueberries were pale rose.

She was tattooing him, invisibly, but it couldn't be washed away. Whatever happened, she could count on some kind of loyalty from him. It seemed to Jan he should suffer more from conflict, and he began to be worried about himself. This is the beginning of a case, he thought.

She had the marks of his buttons between her breasts. At first he'd thrown himself on top of her without taking off his shirt.

"I'm so happy now," she said. "We shouldn't see each other for a week."

They were sitting on a ledge covered with dry reeds. Down by the lake a dog rose had woven itself into the branches of an alder. She moved to the edge, he knelt on a lower shelf and was in her. She lay back so he could come in more deeply.

"Are you cold?" he said. "You're shivering."

"From bravery," she said. "I'm not afraid at all."

"Nothing will happen," he said. "You've taken your pill." But he knew it was something else she meant.

He wondered what was happening—the position of the atoms in their bodies in this microsecond of existence, of cellular activity. Hormones rounded dangerous promontories, the sargasso weed parted beneath him and he felt currents from the deeps. He heard the click of a tape recorder; whatever was taking place was being taken down. But for whose archives?

"It really is spectacular," he said. "I begin to see why people make such a fuss about it. And yet it's mostly pretty simple."

His smile broke down. He flowed into her like a hot drink. "Jan, Jan, Jan," she said.

He could see it in front of him. Words meeting in a crossword, one letter in common. Then for a moment he fell asleep.

He woke up. He'd slipped out of her. The light was different. Alder cones lay by her ear, and she smiled.

"I don't know much about you," he said. "You ought to seem like a stranger."

"I guess the coefficient of misunderstanding is unusually low between you and me," she said prosaically.

A Swissair Caravelle shot past above the spruces. It was used as a trainer for practicing takeoff and landing when regular traffic was low. They got dressed. Jenny picked some midsummer flowers. Jan packed up the remains of the picnic.

"I'm going to a conference with a group of surveyors on the different ways of cataloging lakes," Jenny said.

"This one's been adequately cataloged already," Jan said.

They were ready to drive back to the airport, change cars and go on into Stockholm separately.

"I'll throw out the pickles," Jan said. "Organic waste. Does the Department of the Environment have any objections?"

"No, it won't upset any natural processes."

"Maybe the seeds will grow."

"Things that are pickled tend to keep," she said.

"That sounds unscientific."

"We wouldn't get to see it anyway. Come by here in a week. The grass will be standing again where we were lying. There'll be just as many flowers, in spite of my bouquet. No memorials, no tales. Maybe in a hundred years there'll be a cucumber, or a cucumber leaf. Maybe not even that. The earth isn't a basket you can carry around."

"T# A PROPOSAL

HE MAPS HERE are deceptive. Roads that are being built or only being planned in an office are marked as completed. The cartographer lives in a utopia. He doesn't mark the runnels and ravines that bring the roads to a stop.

"It's no country to take walks in. I walk along the thorn-brake, beside a wall where someone once tried to get grape-vines to take hold and where they are now turning black, down toward the cattle pond in the sink, where there are signs of eland. A dry still coolness in the air and sharp shadows on the ground.

"The light of dawn down here is a thing I can't describe, though it's the Scandinavian hour of the day. Lick the peel of a plum, crumble wormwood in your fingers, look at stones in springwater or at the white-spotted wings of a woodpecker, take a quick taste of a fresh hazelnut. There's a morning experience that compensates for most of it. The horizon is distant but very real—an hour for the future, for the imagination, for planning. The earth demands immediate investment. But maybe only the farsighted can save it."

Jan had emptied his mailbox in the lobby of the Air Traffic Department office building. He had come up to the tower, where Jansson still had the watch. He filled a paper cup with coffee so weak it looked like whisky and read Sten Tidström's new letter to background music that drowned the whisper of the air conditioning.

The letter was addressed to him, The Tower, Arlanda. It must have come on the SAS flight from South Africa he'd guided in on Monday.

Tonota, Northwest Botswana. Make plans for a school along with someone who calls himself a surveyor. Draw up a budget on the basis of what I've read about other school projects in Africa. Know what we can request in subsidies from the government and from FAO. Convince the young people they have to build their own school from scratch to finish while at the same time they start makeshift classes outdoors. The last part is easiest—they want to themselves. And it's because they do that I can work with them.

Nature is hard in Tonota. Dry grass with stalks too stiff to break. Elephant grass, steppe grass. The ground is full of folds and incisions—a record in the process of being deciphered. So much is unworked. The lizards rustle like old newspapers.

Wild geese fly over us on their migration from fall in the south to spring closer to the equator. Great chunks of dried fish have arrived from Iceland—protein for the dry season.

Long-term planning that pays no interest. . . . Concentrate as much as possible on voluntary effort instead of force. But the march of the desert has to be stopped. If the water doesn't start to flow, if forests aren't planted and the soil isn't bound down against the wind, then everything will turn into sand and salt. Even if we get no joy from it, we make repayments on what we've borrowed from the future.

So far, Botswana is a long way from our technological dictatorship. The roar of jet engines, polluted waterways, smog and traffic, DDT and defoliation, two decades of radioactive waste—you get away from all that down here. Soil conservation, nature preservation . . . pretty soon we'll have a Department of the Environment here too, and it'll have to make use of every kind of technology before the country becomes desert forever.

There's a world down here I don't want to see destroyed.

Jan could see Sten Tidström in front of him—long cheekbones like those of an elderly woman intellectual, the corners of his mouth slightly lifted and generally in motion, as if painted on an astonished rocking horse.

He had trouble connecting the letter with the traffic tower where he drank his coffee in the mornings. In Sten's place he would see what Sten saw. They were sufficiently alike for that. It was chance that he sat here looking down on refrigerator trucks outside the SAS kitchen hangar, on woods and farms further away, on the lake where he'd gone swimming with Jenny.

Why not bring Gertrude with you and come? Risks? What do you have to lose? Francistown airport needs help. Even at Serowe the landings are chancy enough. And you've got other things to recommend you.

A person doesn't come here to solve his problems. You can't find any way of measuring. Whether or not I'm saving more people from starvation by doing what I'm doing than by supplying microfilm to Swedish universities —that's hard to tell. Making judgments of that kind is stupid—it's an awkward balance between conceit and a feeling of superiority. It pretends to set up guiding principles for other people.

I'm giving my problems a change of scene and air. They shrink, wither, sprout new roots in some unexpected place inside you and change themselves to new problems and look a little different.

What would he miss in Sweden? Jan asked himself. What was real and held him back? Did he imagine he was firmly rooted here, when in fact he didn't even stand on solid ground? The Air Traffic Department was generous with leaves of absence. He'd known Jenny such a short time.

He sat behind his green window. He documented what took place. Data became information. Information became deposited memory, like Tidström's microfilm. He found himself among tangible things, things that could be put on tape.

But his reality, when he thought about it, was Gertrude and Jenny. The passions were real. That's the way it was right now. Sten had been through that. Later, maybe, came something else.

Reports flowed in according to the daily routine. Jan trusted them. The weather was bad in Rome and Prague. Things like that could be checked. They weren't part of the fabricated news.

This world of corroboration and invention was large enough to hold Jenny too. She lived there independently of his feelings, it meant something to her. That's what was important. It didn't seem to him he needed to be somewhere else. Maybe he ought to want to. But he didn't.

CIRCUMFERENCE

THE DROP OF WATER on the hot plate dances around for a time, enclosed in itself. It gives off steam that settles around it protectively. Inside its own circle of vapor, in immediate contact with the killing heat, the drop of water lives its life until it's blotted out.

There is something helpless in his love for Jenny. Pain, as though from a high-pitched tone that will torment him until he becomes deaf to it.

Strong as a germinating seed. Light as a husk.

The atoms move about in every strand of her hair, like the whirlpools below a waterfall. They move and change. No position stays the same.

Time comes loose like a flake of skin. Eight hours, a working day, has gone. Nothing has been done. The dots on the dice are worn. Soon the six will become a one and everything will start again.

There are no laws of nature, only unprogrammed behavior that can be so described.

There is no love, only something they describe to each other and inscribe in each other. A code they suddenly and simultaneously appropriate.

There are other frames of reference, other methods of perception. With these they would interpret the outer world and each other in a different way.

"I don't want to have a definite idea," says Jenny, "of what is possible and what isn't."

The actions of love are creations, inventions, liberations, difficult to explain in their relation to other actions but carried out without force.

Jan splices himself fast in Jenny. He is so unbound by her that precisely for the sake of his feeling of freedom he attaches himself to her.

From behind his face, he looks out on her. She has a dark transparency. He doesn't want to love her without understanding her.

The course of events in the retina, the stimulation of the eye, the dilation of the pores, the contraction of the nipples, bubbles of carbonation rising up under the skin. . . . To have seen—what does that mean? The first glance is unobservant—he stares straight ahead, reality has no contours, he doesn't evaluate it. It exists, but outside the focused eye.

He sees an optical illusion. He doesn't know it is an optical illusion until the angle changes and he sees something else. Maybe a new optical illusion. Maybe he saw right the first time. Who is she? See her "as she is"? That means see something in her, see her as something. Recognize yourself in her, or find something attractively unfamiliar in her.

She says to him, your eyes give me shape. She is not a given, any more than others with the same bodily functions, hair, and breath. He interprets her, he lives her. What takes place in his retina? What stimuli bring the test picture into focus? He can't fix the border between his reception of her and his reconstruction.

Even she herself knows she now exists in an altered form.

"I want to fold up a huge tablecloth with you," Jenny says, "and come closer to you with each step and each fold. Then our faces and bodies meet and the tablecloth falls to the floor."

They sit opposite each other and enclose each other with their eyes. There is a strange carnality and wonder in this. That tension in the face of the unknown comes back again, the distinct dream landscape beyond all trivia when two people first meet and sense each other's existence, scent each other, in an ambiguous way that includes both worship and distance; both are prepared to flee and give up.

Although they've slept together, there is in them this sexually exciting, enigmatic, unspent distance, as if they have caught sight of a secret precisely halfway between them, and both bend toward it simultaneously.

"I listened to an opera on the Second Program yesterday," Jenny tells him. "All those erotic complications—people behave the same way today. I suddenly felt as old as a Norn. And I thought how you and I are nevertheless adults, we'll cope with our love without thinning it out. And then I was so happy I could hardly sit still. I need you so enormously, though I can get along without you."

To sink down into her, Jan thinks, requires lightness. To be lifted from her requires weight. To reach her, along microscopic paths light years in length, demands a stillness the cat can hardly manage while measuring its prey.

"Maybe I've taken you in," Jenny goes on. "But it must be

your own fault if you're that dumb. You can see who I am after all. I'm nothing more nor less than what you're looking at."

He doesn't know much about himself because he's someone else. But he knows that something in him is a little way ahead, invisible to others. And though he knows it's the same for everyone, it is this movement that prevents his knowing anything definite about Jenny.

What he knows nothing about is how she will move from the point where he sees her now to the point he can't yet see.

"Ten years from now," Jenny says, "I'll be able to tell you how happy I was then, which is now."

THE KEY

THE LOCKSMITH had his shop on Sibylle-gatan. He put a blank in a machine. The whole thing took maybe a minute.

"There, you've got a key to my apartment and a key to the building," Jenny said. "No one else does."

"I won't use them," Jan said. "I only go there when you're home."

"I don't want anything that's mine to be locked to you, even if I'm on the other side of the world."

"I'd rather have part of it locked and have you here."

Six o'clock and the stores were closing. They bought a roast chicken in the subway market at Östermalm Square. He saw her face beyond some shelves, she was coming in his direction from the vegetable counter. He looked at her profile and knew it would be a moment yet before she turned her head and saw him. She existed, they did things, nothing was insignificant—and there was almost nothing they needed to do.

Just for fun, Jan tried his own key from Upplandsgatan in Jenny's door. It turned halfway, only the last half twist wouldn't go—then it went on around without moving the tumblers. It was one of those new police locks. Then he opened the door with the key Jenny'd given him.

"The bathroom is straight ahead," she said. "The hall on the left goes past the kitchen to the dining room. It looks out on the courtyard. And this is the main room, where I work and sleep."

The first thing he saw was the desk, on it a tape recorder, an electric typewriter, and a pile of dictionaries. There were paintings on one wall, several of them, chilly blue and gray—sea and air before the epidemics and the great contagion.

"A friend of mine," Jenny explained. "I bought three of them, he gave me two. They're about climate."

A broad, low bed. An oval pine table. A tall chest of drawers—you could lock them all at once by means of a key in a vertical slat on one side. On one bookshelf there was a blue glass bottle, discarded by some pharmacy, with a Latin abbreviation in gold, flaking off like stars against the blue.

"Here, write your address in my notebook," she said, but stopped herself. "No, on second thought if I crash in the North Sea I don't want anyone to find any definite traces of you."

"In the North Sea?" he said.

"I always imagine I'm going to die there. On my way home to you."

He thought of asking about the man she knew in London. Maybe those papers were messages from him, but all he could see was the official brown envelope of the Department of the

Environment and a pile of photographs of the Vindel River and Sturup Airport. Jenny followed his eyes.

"The threat to the environment and lack of equality, Sweden's two biggest problems," she said matter-of-factly.

Her words went through him like a wind, as if they dealt with a threat to the two of them, four flights up on Nybro Quay, and at the same time with a threat they themselves were creating.

"Did you see this rug?" Jenny said. "A peasant rug from Turkey. So washed out the design is almost invisible. But if you roll it up tight and roll it out again very fast you can get a quick glimpse of a rooster, part of what it used to show."

But they didn't do it. He took the groceries out to the kitchen. In the pantry was a green case full of beer and soda. The refrigerator was new, the stove was electric with coil burners, the sink had been raised. Outside, the courtyard lay in shadow. He looked across it to the building on the corner of Arsenalsgatan—the Fetzo School of the Visual Arts and the Taxpayers' Association. It, too, would be torn down.

He heard Jenny whistling from the main room, as if she were walking along a road by herself or calling a dog from a long way off. She could take care of herself, he thought. Better than he knew.

When he came back she'd changed into a housedress with a big pattern, Finnish, with wide arms. He could see everything. His balls changed their position. He felt it against the inside of his thigh and to his own surprise he told her about it.

"I've never heard that before," she said.

"Like the pans on a scale," he said.

"I'll remember that. Things like that stick in your mind."

"Stupidly enough," he said, "because it's not really all that interesting."

He leaned over and ran his nose along the part in her hair.

"Your hair is like the stuffing in old mattresses," he said jokingly, and her eyes became as clear and trusting as in the childhood photographs she'd shown him at the Hong Kong Restaurant, and he realized how familiar she'd become, like a guest you don't need to meet at the station, a person who's always welcome.

There she was. He could have invented her, but he wasn't so conceited as to imagine that. You don't get used to it, he thought. The unknown spaces of the body. Another climate under my skin.

He noticed she was blowing on his neck. Delight tickled in his armpits.

"I'd like to write to you on my new electric typewriter," Jenny said. "It's calm and cool. The type doesn't tell you how excited someone is. There's a lot more I have to tell you."

A shiver of fear ran through him against his will.

"You're bottomless," he said. "But I'm ready."

"I was sick once for a couple of days in a little town in southwest Ireland. Bronchitis. I rented a room from a family, the man was a metalsmith—window fittings, door handles, jewelry. Every morning either he or his wife came in with a bouquet of flowers from the garden. What I remember best is basil and bougainvillea."

"That makes me feel indecent," Jan said.

"I didn't think that was possible."

"I look at you and I don't feel any desire, but my imagination wants to be full of all the scenes you've been part of before me, everything you've seen, everything you've done with your body. I want your actions and memories to wash over me. And then I forget you as you are now—that's what's indecent."

"You imagine things about me. You have hardly any of my memories yet. We talk a lot. . . ."

"Most people," Jan said, "don't think they have to define what they understand intensively, but they do better if they can. And I've never thought you have to be quiet in order to love."

"It's been quiet around me for a long time. I'm afraid of

disappointing you. I don't want to be an object for love, someone who can be exchanged. Better friendship in that case. An
object is something you want to own, and if you can't then you
get jealous."

"You don't need to say that to me," Jan said. "We happened
to meet. Everything that feels so meaningful was brought about
by meaningless chance."

"I've never loved anyone this much," Jenny said.

"Not right now. But before, and maybe later."

"No. You think I'm lost in this moment. But I can see ahead.
And behind me I can see the faces of the men I said I loved,
and of the men I just went to bed with without loving. I'm
tremendously conscious of time. The things that have happened to me have led me to you."

"And what's happening now can lead you somewhere else,"
Jan said.

"Yes of course. But it'll be hard for the ones who come after
us."

Jan saw her fingertips coming together. Then she ran her
hand along her arm in a long, exploratory movement toward
her elbow. He no longer heard what she was saying. He couldn't
take his eyes off it—her hand and arm, the veins beneath her
skin. He breathed in deeply and gazed at her, puzzled at coming so close to himself. He must have had an expression of
pain. She smiled uneasily, as if from the other side of an
important question.

"What is it we're doing?" Jenny asked.

"Gasping for breath," he answered evenly.

He made use of her without regard to who she was. His
passion wasn't her responsibility. He felt it as a cumbersome
trust.

"Did you hear what I asked?" she said.

"I heard and I'll give you an answer. It's not horniness, not
tenderness. It's a kind of burning heat I've never felt before.
It's the part of me that's never been used, joining forces with

everything else. The muscles contract across my ribs when I talk to you."

"Do you want me to take off my clothes?"

He unbuttoned her housedress, pulled her pants down a little so that he could lick her navel. She laughed because it tickled.

"It's tied there so all the weaving won't come loose," she said, and she looked down at her stomach.

And that made him think of the word "inventorium." He didn't know the dictionary definition. He pictured a room where he could store what he most wanted to hide or save. A room where he could also keep the moments of light, the carefreeness and the speculation, the silence and the desire to say something important, everything indistinct, awkward, timid, ungracious, appealing, stuttering and stumbling that's involved when love seeks a home with lovers.

"I started to wonder what your stomach looks like," he began.

"Wait," she said. "I'll take off everything. I like to be naked with you."

He looked at her standing barefoot on the floor, with her dress unbuttoned and her bra white above a browner stomach, and the triangle of her hair where his penis and his lips were equally at home. A kind of ethics told him he shouldn't feel such cringing joy for a human being but only for a great idea or calling.

She loosened his belt, opened the zipper on his pants, unbuttoned his shirt. It went quickly. Her mouth glided along his thigh.

"Now I'll stand behind you and hold your breasts," he said. "So I'll know what it's like to have breasts myself. We feel our way toward each other."

She laughed.

"We're like fourteen-year-olds who've just discovered sex."

It didn't seem to him he loved her for the sake of anything.

A body told him he existed. But it had to be someone else's body.

The sky over Stockholm deepened toward dusk, violet-gray like a mushroom. He stood naked by the bed, she sat on her knees with her arms around his waist and pressed her breasts against his stomach. He kissed her head.

"My knees are lumpy girl scout knees," she said, displeased.

"When you say that, I remember them better."

She hugged him tightly to her. He saw her pupils narrow quickly as though she wanted to save the light inside, for her eyes remained wide open and undimmed.

The taste on her lips of melted snow, of something that's nothing. His fingers were free to follow the line of her hair at the back of her neck. He sniffed her human scent from head to womb as if he were a giant in search of small creatures to devour.

She lay on her side and he slid down next to her. Then he looked along her thighs, the shallow bowl in the side of her buttocks, the inward curve at her waist, past her ribs up toward the thin hair in her armpits—nothing but curves and hollows to be in.

"You can do what you want with me," she said.

"I don't know what I want," he said from down between her legs. "There's nothing in you I want to change, not even your name."

"Your cock knows more than you do. It's about to creep out of its skin with pleasure."

Her voice was like fingers on his body. In her face there was an abandoned wonder that he loved, a grateful fear that this was possible and never could be taken back. He didn't think he'd ever laughed at anyone so freely. She sat on top of him.

"Sleep," she said. "You don't need to do anything."

He tried not to close his eyes when he came. He saw her screw up her eyes with pleasure. Then he forgot the sudden loneliness and drove away the pictures that usually rained through his head. She fell down on him with her full weight.

In the exhaustion afterwards he felt that nothing more was hidden from them. Life had no more cards to show.

"You have nothing from me," Jenny said, "but I'm filled with you. Not just fluid, but cells, life from you. And we lie here as if nothing has happened."

He sat up and carefully closed the lips of her vagina with two fingers.

"Have you got a bathrobe I can borrow?"

While she was looking in the closet he glanced at the newspaper, lying open on the floor beside the bed, and he read, "Acting as committee secretary is department head Jenny Jeger. . . ."

"That's you," he said. "It's hard to imagine."

"That's silly," she said. "Because it really is me. I exist in different ways, but to me they seem the same. I don't see myself from outside like you."

"It's just that I'm not used to it," Jan said. "Your bathrobe smells of you."

He turned on the radio and pulled her to her feet.

"Come on, let's dance."

The soles of their feet got dirty. It was the first time they'd danced to music. They could feel their muscles, their own and each other's. Eyeless contact was repeated. A city lay outside, but the window mirrored them.

They got out the chicken they'd bought and beer and bread and a white goatcheese from Jämtland that they salted. Jenny boiled a head of iceberg lettuce that they ate with butter; it tasted like asparagus. The table in the dining room was plastic with light metal legs. A brass lamp hung above it.

Jenny had put on blue shorts and a sleeveless white sweater left over from one term of gymnastics arranged by some people at the Department. They sat on a red bench, hips and legs touching. She put one hand on his knee while she ate with the other. He rested his foot on hers.

"You can want to teach someone to love," Jan said, "but it's wasted effort."

"How do you know?"

"It has to be mutual from the beginning. Otherwise there's no point to it. We can teach our values afterwards."

"If I don't live up to your expectations, we've still had a period when it *was* mutual," Jenny said.

He lifted her sweater and rubbed his face against her skin, and her nipple woke up and tried to get into his nostril. He snorted and bit at it in punishment. He wanted to note her down piece by piece, like presenting evidence in court. He wanted to organize and label, justify and preserve, so no change could take place.

"Sometimes the telephone rings and there's no one there," Jenny said. "I pretend it's Miss Weather. She hangs up because all of a sudden she remembers she's absolutely not allowed to make any calls herself. She's not allowed to take the initiative."

"Temperature unchanged, southerly winds. You have to ask her about that, otherwise she doesn't tell."

"You're here," Jenny said. "It used to be I mostly thought of someone's presence as an interval between two absences. Every meeting was a torment, because that first sight of each other contained a farewell. With you I don't think that way."

The street lamps were lit outside. They stood tight around Nybro Square and Berzelii Park—a single huge bulb with threads of tungsten groping toward each other.

"Do you work at home a lot?" he asked.

"Sometimes, to get away from the telephone. But I don't unplug it, least of all these days. I'm working on a proposal for systematizing ecological inventories."

"Inventories of what?"

"Lakes, swamps, glacial moraines. . . . The inventory is the first step. Then you have to plan, evaluate, negotiate, arrange for its protection. How much initiative should we take ourselves? What kind of balance do we want between national planning and local planning?"

He noticed the enthusiasm in her voice. Like him, she had

several footholds. No one's happiness should depend on a single human being, he thought.

"You're a success," he said.

"My mother certainly thinks so. I used to really want to succeed. To show that a girl wasn't just made to have babies and take them to school. So I made myself another kind of happiness. Mama and the rest of the family were just as pleased with it. So I got caught in their toils after all."

"But now you're acknowledged by the world."

"Just as you are. Just as conservation is, at last. And then it depends on what you do with it."

"You get paid more than I do, you'll get promoted," Jan said.

"Does that matter to you? Does it change anything between us?"

"Nothing. I've got no particular ambitions outside myself. I'm quite content."

"Power is fun," Jenny said. "But not fun enough, or I'd be more energetic. The urge to succeed outwardly comes from your upbringing, I guess. But no one talks about the less visible ways. Only the big contests draw the fans."

"I've never thought much about power and success," Jan said. "Sten Tidström—that friend I've told you about—he's always wanted to stir up those impulses in me. I've been happy, but that's something else again."

"I can see which way the wind is blowing easily enough. But my job is too important for tactics."

"The trouble with me, Sten Tidström's told me, is that I don't have anyone standing over me with a whip, neither inside nor outside. I don't even have an inferiority complex about working at Arlanda, or because you and Gertrude are so gifted."

Jenny put her feet up on the bench and rested her head on her knees.

"I can smell your smells," she said. "I love them. Can you hand me my purse over there?"

She opened it a crack and took out some cotton.

"Here's where the bureaucrat has her grown-up toys," she said. "Lipstick, which I hardly use since I met you; my compact, which doesn't have any powder in it but I keep it for the mirror; a collapsible magnifying glass; birth control pills; aspirin; a couple of Tampax; bandages. . . . And then my bankbook, passport, membership cards, money. But no old letters and photographs, if that's what you're thinking. Only one personal thing."

She held up a blue booklet with the SAS symbol. Only the covers were left, the pages had been ripped out. Jenny Jeger: status OK.

"It's my ticket from London to Stockholm that day we met. I like to look at the date and hour. It's funny that chance deals in exact figures."

He followed her out to the kitchen and stood behind her, and while she held the kettle under the faucet he folded aside the leg of her blue gym shorts, removed the cotton ball that was supposed to keep his fluid from running out of her, and forced his way in. She turned off the water and rested lightly back against him.

"It doesn't feel like usual," she said. "You're pointing so far forward."

He held one hand against her breast, the other over her pubic hair.

"Don't come yet," she said. "We'll fall down."

"We've got plenty of time. I'll take a shower first, and then the tea will be ready."

In the bathroom was a wicker basket with a lid. He picked up a handful of her dirty clothes and inhaled their smell. He stood still and loved everything about her and hardly dared move for fear something would change. He didn't think he'd tell her about it.

"We're escalating," he said when they were lying on the bed, on the sheet and foam rubber mattress, the blanket on the floor. "Walls that never existed have disappeared."

"I want to arch against you," she said. "Like sweeping the hair back from my whole body and letting it blow. Come, come in me, don't be cold outside."

"I want you all the time, even when it doesn't show."

Boundless desire all over again, as if they were salt cellars in the hands of some lavish stranger.

He seemed to be trembling under a weight. His breathing was harder. Be with me, his breath was murmuring, and he didn't know to whom.

The movements of love carried him away from himself, away from the void that was plundered from the beginning, toward a world filled with resources, unbounded, without walls.

Afterwards he wet a handkerchief and wiped her body carefully, between her legs, under her arms. He took her hand in his and wiped it too. He hung up the handkerchief and rolled up the rug on the floor.

"What are you doing that for?" Jenny asked.

"Well, you said the pattern comes back when you press the material together. Now the rooster can lie there in the dark and come to life."

Then he lay down next to Jenny and drew the quilt over them.

"Are you a heavy sleeper?" she wondered.

They'd never slept with each other for long.

"Very light," he answered. "Only on the surface, as if I couldn't afford to forget you even for a dream."

It was only half true, and she fell asleep almost as he was saying it.

They'd forgotten to close the door to the hall. The bang of the mailbox woke them at five in the morning. Their thoughts began to grope toward each other like sleepy hands. Then they heard the outer door being opened.

"Hello in there," said a quiet voice.

Jenny jumped out of bed naked and threw on the robe Jan had borrowed.

He heard a man's voice saying, "I could have come right in and picked up any old thing."

"Not any old thing, surely," said the voice he loved. "Anyway, thanks."

To Jan she said, "It was the duplicate key I gave you. You left it in the lock. It's been open all night."

She put the newspaper on the floor next to the bed and stretched out beside him. They didn't go back to sleep. He kissed her throat and ears and felt desire rise in him like mercury. It was the first time they'd slept together from sunset to dawn. They'd seen each other across the midnight line to a new day.

The teapot was on the floor on his side of the bed. There was tea left in her cup, with a dark oily film. He knew how she rested her ear in her left hand. He took the cups to the kitchen and drank the rest of the tea with his lips where hers had been.

He boiled fresh water, rinsed the cups, and put them on a blue tin tray that had once been some other color. He found white bread and a jar of raspberry jam. He put it down on the bed and she was asleep again, with her knees against her stomach and her chin on one shoulder, as if she wanted to make herself inaccessible.

He ate the bread hungrily. Then he licked the small hairs on Jenny's arm.

"It feels like the hair on gooseberries," he said.

A patch of sun drew a yellow ring of light on the wall, which changed its shape as it moved toward them. He looked at the rug over by the desk.

"Now we'll see if it's true what you said about that rooster."

FORAY INTO
THE MIDDLE CLASS

T HE PARTY HAD BEEN going on for several hours.

Gertrude and Jan had planned it carefully. He'd been out at the Water Palace for a couple of days and telephoned a group of friends who also spent their vacations in or around Stockholm. Gertrude had filled vases with cornflowers and daisies, milkwort and babies'-slippers—blue and white, blue and yellow. She'd been going around long-legged in a pair of boots because of the nettles.

When the guests arrived, nearly everything was ready. Jenny was punctual and looked utterly unconstrained. Jan had explained how to get there, and she had clumped her car with the others and tramped down the hill and out onto the point. She was wearing a peacock blue dress, less low-cut than the other women's, and she was paler than those who'd already managed to spend some time at the beach.

Of the fifteen guests, she was the only one Gertrude had never met. Jan had told her he'd been working with Jenny on the matter of measuring noise levels at Arlanda, and that he was in the process of formulating a report on air pollution at public airports which the Air Traffic Department was preparing for the Department of the Environment.

"I asked you the other day if you were working with them," Gertrude said, "but you didn't seem to know so much about it then."

He could see she liked Jenny. She didn't use her reserved hostess smile but said right away, seriously, "There are a lot of things I want to ask you about. I'm tremendously interested in what you're working on."

He left them, at once relieved and worried. He shouldn't have to explain Gertrude to Jenny. He didn't want to point things out to Jenny—in a way, she already knew about everything that was his. But maybe Jenny would want to explain him to Gertrude. He'd never been in this situation before, and he was bad at drawing conclusions.

The food was on the table in the dining room, and the doors were opened toward the bay. The guests could sit at two garden tables on the terrace. Everything was ready in time. Gertrude ran lithely back and forth in a beige dress, low-cut but with a cord at the neck holding together the upper corners.

Jan had mixed a punch of Mosel wine, cucumber, lemon, and sliced strawberries. It was poured out in tureens from the Water Palace's first decade and served with a ladle. Beside the low hedge along the terrace he'd lined up bottles of red wine. The snaps, which he'd obtained from colleagues at Arlanda, bore labels from six European countries. There was also a chilled bitter wormwood that Sten Tidström had given him from his herb garden in Roslagen.

Small, cold Baltic herring lay stacked like logs. There was a green platter covered with smoked Gotland flounder, brown as a mummy's skin. Filets of pickled herring, dark grayish-red like wet outcroppings of feldspar, were spread out on a transparent polar skullcap of ice.

Some Swedish and Hungarian sausages lay on a plank beside a bowl of new potatoes, a salad with shrimp and smoked ham and dill, a basket of slim French bread whose crust had had time to soften. All of it in good supply.

The cheeses arrived on a birch breadboard. One of them rested on straw, others were dusted in white or trimmed with a cloud of the lightest mold. There was a Tilsit with a bitter sawdust dryness you could feel beneath your nails, a Cheddar in a cheesecloth shirt, a Swiss with round holes set in a soft material that was an enticement to murder.

Jan made a little welcoming speech. It was not a success. It bothered him afterwards how unconvincing he had sounded, slightly hostile, in fact. It was as if he had hissed at them: if you really believe that life is bearable, then demonstrate it now with all the wit and balance you can muster.

Nevertheless the meal turned out to be splendid. And a steamer passed by on the channel, loaded with pensioners out on a one-day excursion—they'd had coffee three times and were now singing "Praise to the Earth" from the upper deck. The animated voices from the Water Palace were met out over the water by the hymn. With the help of the bracing punch, the plain and the spiced snaps, the bubbling conversation and the warm summer evening itself, they all soon felt themselves part of a cosmic system in which the advocates of the explosion theory had been temporarily silenced in favor of the spokesmen for a stationary universe.

Between the herring and the salad, Jan took Jenny aside and told her about the other guests.

"Klas Lundin is an advertising man and has a house by the Lidingö bridge. Gertrude and I and Sten and Marianne Tidström took his boat out to a deserted island late last spring. It was a miniature trip to an undeveloped country, Sten's first leap—with the past as a trampoline—and then he surfaced in Botswana."

"Your world, your people," Jenny said. "For the first time. It's fun."

"Should I feel observed and criticized?"

"Then you haven't understood very much," she smiled.

"What other people think about Gertrude," Jan said, "that's a thing I'll never know. Or about me."

"You can know that I like both of you very much," she said.

She emphasized the "both." He looked at her and suddenly couldn't remember her naked. For an instant he regretted having invited her. Did she see him handcuffed to Gertrude? Then he pointed to a bald, suntanned man with very blue eyes.

"He's a meteorologist, used to be at Arlanda, now he's at the weather bureau. He's so shy they haven't let him do the weather on TV yet. They say he knocks before going into his own office. He's already thanked me for our exceptional hospitality and for the pleasure of being among true friends. He's got a year-round cottage with a garage and a hobby room a couple miles from here. There's his wife, in that dress with the big purple and blue checks that makes her look pregnant. She obviously bought it in some shop in the Old City, but he's too shy to ask her about it, or if she's expecting a baby."

"I talked to the girl who works in the Real Estate Bureau," Jenny said. "We know some of the same people. I used to work for the city too."

"She's married to a PR man at SAS," Jan said.

"Now let's mix a little. I'm going to get some salad and cheese, and you've got other people to talk to. You know where you stand with me."

"Do I?" he asked, spoiled but still uneasy.

"If you can't find me, look for Gertrude," said Jenny.

She left him. It seemed to him the party was taking place at a distance. It was always that way when he was host. If he took part as a guest, it was more often the case that the party was wherever he was. Ulla, on the secretarial staff of the county council, had just arrived from Paris.

"The train was packed. I sat on a soldier's knee part of the way, and I pinched him back hard when he pinched me. In Hamburg they were washing the statues with soap. There was lots of room when we got to Sweden, I got a whole row of seats to myself to sleep on. Now I'm a member of the French Freedom Committee."

Jan had wanted to show Jenny the Water Palace, but at the same time it wasn't all his, he didn't want to acknowledge it entirely. He was half a stranger here, and he wanted to share her alien status as well as her curiosity. He no longer wanted to be indifferent and blindly intimate with these surroundings that had been his and Gertrude's since childhood. He pretended Jenny was his secret correspondent, in a world he could imagine leaving. He wasn't sure she experienced it that way. But the Water Palace meant more to him as long as Jenny saw it and Gertrude liked it.

"It may be that most people have no real need for freedom and change," said a doctor and hormone expert Jan had known since his school days.

"What other needs do they have instead?" Jan asked.

"The need for success, the desire to compete and win, the desire to be like other people."

"We're looking for a new human being," Jan said.

"He'll appear the instant capitalism falls," the lawyer said. "He's coming into being in the free time he gets from automation. He's unexploited, spontaneous, uninhibited, and yet still social."

"Do you think you'll manage to be one of them?"

"No, I'm already fixed. That's why it's young people and uncommitted intellectuals who spread the message of liberation. The rest of us have already adapted ourselves to this comfortable, sensible, democratic slavery. We keep calm."

Klas Lundin, whose wife was at a rest home, had his arm around Ulla, who was recently separated and had sent her son to a sailing camp.

"The spirit of enterprise is the important thing," he said. "You have to look at Sweden as a business. Technicians and administrators ought to be making the decisions, not politicians and kids."

"There's a whole generation opposed to that, as maybe you've noticed," said Ulla. "They're absolutists. They claim that we—or you—are intoxicating us with consumer goods."

"Intoxicate?" said Klas Lundin. "I'm alert and sober. I demonstrate with advertising. 'Demonstration' and 'advertising' ought to be neutral words. They can be used for whatever you want—better merchandise, poorer morals, welfare, war, high collars, new unnecessary needs, freedom from stagnation."

"Advertising," said the PR man from SAS, "is the fragmentary folklore of our time, childhood legends about things that are soon replaced by different things. In the days when we drank from Duralex. . . ."

The word made Jan and Jenny look at each other quickly—deeply and happily and guiltlessly.

"Advertising shouldn't be too explicit," Klas Lundin instructed them. "It ought to mystify, leave out the last word in the line. That makes people think."

Did they live only for what was visible? Jan wondered loftily to himself. Did they think everything could be solved with an analysis, a diagnosis, a program, a one- or a five-year plan? They noticed the flaws in an argument and improved the logic. Did they notice other kinds of flaws? Did they notice how the runways at Arlanda rose in the air at the horizon and disappeared? Would it surprise them to know that no coastal survey ship had ever sounded the northeast part of the bay outside the Water Palace—that the unknown was so close at hand?

Was he underestimating both their knowledge and their feelings? Maybe he did so because he himself felt so astonishingly happy, like a child who wakes up one morning and sees blue circus tents being raised on the vacant lot next door.

He'd already had a few drinks, but he hadn't talked to anyone about the odor of honeysuckle whose sweetish astringency increased with dusk, and it seemed to him he was standing on firm ground, one foot in the intangible and the other still among the ordinary things that surrounded him, his temporary present.

A number of people had left the table on the terrace and started to mix. Mårten, the hormone expert, and Sonja, who worked for the city, were discussing the hydrogen bomb and the population explosion and which was worse. Jan went up to them, but Jenny was there before him.

"The hostess has instructed me to tell you not to be so concerned."

"Who are you? Aren't you concerned?" Mårten asked.

"I'm Jenny and concerned."

"OK then. Will you sign an appeal we're sending to the prime minister? We seem to be the most progressive people here. It's about how we've tied ourselves to these magic numbers, five percent rise in the standard of living, one percent in aid. The appeal asks the question, 'Are *we* free so long as *they're* not free?' "

"People play with that word too much," Jenny said. "I'm free as long as I don't give a damn about them."

"It's a question of the terms and the price of freedom," Jan objected.

"But almost nobody cares about the terms," Jenny said. "People care about what they can see, not what they find out about through hearsay. I think that appeal is bad propaganda, and hypocrisy, what's more. Freedom is the fact that I can go home, it's a tacit agreement among us."

"We'll see what the prime minister has to say," said Mårten.

Jan hastily touched Jenny's hand. It was as if she had directed her words to him. Her awareness included what was going on between them. His finger glided across her palm like a secret laugh. The quick movement was an underground contact, while with common sense preserved they led the conversation on to new crests and thoughtful pauses.

"These young people," said a tall middle-aged man, "if only they'd get themselves a little experience. . . ."

"Who's that?" Jenny whispered.

Jan drew her back a step or two.

"A captain with the Coast Guard at Oscar Fredriksborg. He and his wife have a cottage here in the neighborhood. We don't have anything in common with them, but since they're neighbors we always invite them. Listen how firm and modulated his voice becomes as soon as he can talk about the impersonal, about the poor, about our form of civilization and whether it's a yardstick for others and shouldn't we rather hold on to our own values. . . ."

The captain portrayed himself as the Representative for the

people who "can't help it if they live fairly well," for little out-of-the-way Sweden, for us non-Stockholmers, and more. Merely being yourself was not sufficient—he'd learned that much from the very beginning, and the civil service and the regiment that had given him his livelihood had confirmed the security in this form of asceticism. And still he was a tyrant, Jan said. He suspected that his wife and children, more gifted than he, made fun of him or smiled at him behind his back. He therefore required his wife to conduct herself so as to convince him of her respect. In this way he managed to tyrannize her and make a fool of himself at the same time.

"And experience isn't free," the captain emphasized.

"What kind of experience?" said Jenny and moved into the group. "The experience of the old people? The world view that's continually led to war?"

"The end of the world is being prepared all day long every day," said Gertrude severely and without a hostess's tact.

Jan hadn't seen her come. She exchanged a look of such mutual understanding with Jenny that his cheeks went tight.

"Shouldn't we go make some coffee?" he asked Gertrude.

"I'm glad you invited Jenny," she said in the kitchen. "She understands what I say."

"You even talk alike. I noticed it just now."

"You sound worried. We've read the same books, she and I."

"As far as I'm concerned it would be fine if everyone were alike. Exactly like you."

"I miss Sten and Marianne," Gertrude said. "They've always been here before."

Jan suddenly had a hard time picturing the Tidströms in Sweden. It occurred to him that Gertrude missed them more than she would admit. Where would she turn in a serious situa-tion if he wasn't available? He couldn't think of anyone but Sten Tidström. She had no close woman friends. Perhaps from the beginning he and Gertrude had shared an unexpressed need: now at last we can be alone together. No one could intrude on their background and experience. They stood leaning over the same picture, which no one else recognized.

Coffee on the terrace. New conversations, about life's tricks and dodges, about the price of land and overtime compensation, about architecture in the suburbs and how you convert a woodshed into a guest cottage. Jan had most fun at parties during the first half of the evening. Then his ability to socialize decreased.

He wandered around with a coffee thermos and heard someone asking whether the state was the protector of the poor or the cowardly. It was Klas Lundin and the architect.

"The greater the collective security, the greater the number of individuals. The more differentiated society becomes, the more room there is for deviation," Jan remarked ministerially.

But he realized a lot of people didn't want to make room for deviation. Right here in front of you, you have a person who at any moment could get two years in prison, along with the hostess at this charming Swedish summer house, he whispered to himself. There are a lot of dogs buried in the pastures of Our Lord.

"We want to do everything at once in this country," said the architect. "We don't know our limits, because our experience is so limited."

How did they get here? Jan was filled with wonder at these people he regarded as his friends.

Further away the garden darkened and took color from the pansies Gertrude had set out on the tables in glass jars. But light fell across the terrace next to the house as if on a little rectangular stage, and assembled there were the characters Gertrude and he had collected, almost as if they had invented them for their enjoyment. A few with sharper contours than the rest refused to be swallowed by the surrounding blurry night.

While he concentrated on serving the coffee he heard voices but not words, and he felt close to panic at the fact that everything was taking place beyond him, only a few inches outside his sphere of perception, so that he was aware of, and at the same time missed, what he was missing. Let me be an accomplice, he thought. But to what?

Then he caught sight of Gertrude and Jenny talking to each other at a white table. Their voices were low and even, as if they were into a conversation that had started a long time ago. They looked at him simultaneously. It was not his doing they were there. They were not his two women. He was not theirs.

"Sit down," Gertrude said. "You don't have to go around being host any more. They'll take care of themselves."

In the course of a couple of seconds he thought a great deal. They seemed to be as close to each other as he was close to them both. It didn't seem to matter to them whom he was with. They were having a good time, they had other interests, he shouldn't imagine that very much depended on him.

"I was asking Jenny about the Environment Department's research conferences," Gertrude informed him, "but now we're talking about sin."

"Very appropriate," Jan said.

"I was pointing out," said Jenny, looking amused, "that in our times the personal sense of sin has been replaced by an almost impersonal sense of guilt. Our own responsibility has been replaced by collective responsibility. Nothing is our own fault any more—in the old-fashioned sense. The causes always seem to lie outside our immediate control."

He really did love them both when he saw them next to each other. Gertrude was the one anticipated, Jenny the one that couldn't have been foreseen.

They didn't cancel each other out. It didn't seem to him he needed to write into them things they didn't have. But they each had a share in who he was.

"We can always throw the blame on someone else," he said. "Now more than ever. Relentless technology. . . . But even if a person can't always determine the causes of his actions, surely that doesn't mean he's always forced to act as he does or that he acts against his will?"

He sat down between them and tried to brush Jenny's leg with his knee, but she pulled it away without changing expression. He wanted to give both of them a secret signal. He was washed back and forth in a tide he couldn't control.

"So you don't think," Gertrude said, "that it's a mistake based on an illusion to credit human beings with moral responsibility?"

He suddenly felt an unexpected joy. He clenched his fists in readiness. How did this Swedish society they lived in so loyally dare deny their being brother and sister? So they themselves must burst out of all those relationships that were determined from outside and labeled normal and worthwhile.

And this was a beginning—Jenny and Gertrude talking to each other, he between them. Gertrude's and his forbidden life in the shadow of their common fate. Jenny's and his life beyond formal agreements.

There are parallels and antipodes. Insides and outsides.

He was filled with a quiet obstinacy like the time the chain came off his bicycle when he was a child and he held the handlebars and pressed down with all his strength until he discovered a pile of empty paper cartons. There he let himself fall, no one noticed, he realized he'd steered there of his own free will. He lay quietly on his back, beyond time and destruction, wrapped in his stubbornness. That had happened at the Water Palace, a few steps from where he was sitting.

"Sometimes we're the playthings of fate, but not always," was his answer to Gertrude.

His fingers were cramped around the handlebars. The pedals spun around without braking. If he squinted he could see where he was going.

"You can deliberately prepare yourself for the fact that things will happen to you completely beyond your will," Gertrude said. "You make up your mind that this is something I can't do anything about."

"I'd like as little as possible to be decided like that," Jenny said.

"Things happen to you anyway," Jan said. "There's so much that can happen in a moment."

The moment when he hovered between the bicycle saddle and the empty cartons, borne by speed and presumptuous calculation and a fear of breaking his nose.

"By making a choice you know you're not interchangeable," Jenny said. "At first you're attracted by that driving animal freedom, but then suddenly you're forced back to yourself, which you feel you're about to lose. And then you become hysterically clinging. Human beings are judged so deterministically. Someone betrays his closest friend in the face of a weak threat, someone abandons his four children in the middle of the kitchen floor. It happens because of something, and this 'because of' is allowed to excuse everything. By the same reasoning, we're all equally without responsibility for our virtues, effort and success."

Jan listened to her in astonishment. Was she lecturing on ethics with emphases only he would understand? Was she trying to be braver than she was? Did Gertrude have something to do with this?

"I live out here," Gertrude said. "Jan is at Arlanda. He's not taking any summer vacation this year. I'm on a leave of absence to do a thing I want to do. A thing I find it necessary to do. But it's not because Jan's at Arlanda that I'm here. I don't feel like a robot controlled by social and biological factors. After all, there are different ways of behaving in any given situation."

"There are usually alternatives," Jenny said. "That's the freedom you have. It can be overemphasized. But you can also overemphasize the inability to control your feelings, though that's actually another matter."

"There's so much life that's determined in advance," Gertrude said. "You fall into things you hardly have any control over. For the most part you wave your arms around trying to fend things off."

The moon hid behind a corner of the forest, but further out over the water they could see a clothesline of light stretched between two darknesses.

"You don't forget those early disappointments," Gertrude went on, telling Jenny a story Jan had never heard. "They could make you afraid of people. People see you as someone other than the person you think you are. I met a grown-up on a beach one time who told me all about the wonderful travels he'd been on, he'd found a buried treasure, he'd been on a ship where there was a mutiny. I thought it was marvelous that he told me about it. I felt like his secret friend, though I didn't have anything to give in return. Then I happened to overhear him telling another adult that he was amusing himself with a little girl who'd believe anything he told her, how he took stories out of books he'd read and she just stood there with her mouth hanging open like an idiot. So I sneaked away, everything collapsing around me. There was no house to go on living in, no one to depend on. I was forced out into the open air. He had a different picture of me, and he was spreading it around. And for a moment I had thought I was his equal; I thought I had nothing to fear from him."

WITHIN YOU
WITHOUT YOU

WELL YOU'RE hardly weighed down with years. . . ."

Jan caught a disconnected remark as he walked across the

terrace. The trees stood weighed down with leaves. And time stood still as water in a pond, and there sat Gertrude and Jenny discovering each other.

He associated Gertrude with the Water Palace and the Academy of Sciences—an opposite to Arlanda which she had never visited and where he'd met Jenny. But the Department of the Environment and their talk tied them together, to the point he couldn't keep them separate in his mind.

Jealousy of both of them pulsed through him like anxiety. The Water Palace no longer felt like home. It surprised him: jealousy, not guilt. He walked faster. Out of the forest . . . .

The record player was going. Jan asked Ulla to dance—the table had been carried out of the dining room. She rested one hand lightly on his back and held his hand tightly with the other. Bodies function as they will—crooked, laconic thermometers. He was wearing loosely fitting underwear and light summer pants, and to his horror he suddenly felt his penis throbbing, there was nothing to stop it, it would be very obvious. They weren't quite alone. There was nothing he could do but hold her closer. She was silent and didn't seem to notice. She had a narrow, suntanned face, full of summer freckles.

Then, over her shoulder, he caught sight of Jenny standing in the doorway to the terrace laughing, low, mostly with her eyes and the animated corners of her mouth. She was looking at him, not derisively, but as if to say he wasn't the only one such things happened to. The record ended, Ulla held tight to his hand until he'd left her at a table with the doctor.

Then he took Jenny by the elbow and led her into the music.

"I saw the whole thing," she said. "You weren't embarrassed, were you? She's awfully sweet. You could have taken her straight out in the gooseberry bushes and she would have been panting."

"That would have been too mechanical, even if she'd wanted to. It's never that simple."

"It ought to be simple," Jenny said, and it seemed to him she caught her breath. "Why don't you tell Gertrude about us?"

"Because I don't want to make her unhappy for no reason. And because I don't want to like her less, and that's what I'd do if she wanted to keep me from seeing you. I don't want to hurt her."

"Oh, Jan, what does Gertrude stand to gain from all this? I'm much more used to losing than she is."

"Why does someone always have to lose? We could all of us win. . . ."

"Can she win when she doesn't even know?" Jenny said. "I'd like to write a postcard to someone. To some person who is ingenious about solving problems. Dear Euclid, long time since I heard from you. . . . I've gotten into difficulties here, it looks like a parallelogram. . . ."

"I love both of you," Jan said. "It feels so strange to have you here. At the Water Palace."

"Do you understand that I could love Gertrude just so that I could be closer to you? I'd like to caress her whole body just because you've touched her. I can look at the back of her neck exactly the way you do, and my nipples get hard. I have such a desire to experience exactly what you've experienced."

You still don't know she's my sister, he thought. That's the one thing you don't know. And that I love you, that's the one thing Gertrude doesn't know.

Euclid, he wanted to ask, are there destinies parallel to our own that can help us understand all this?

Yes, there always are. Other people's experience isn't ours, and still it helps. This feels so unique it must be told, no, so unusual it must be kept secret, no one else could understand.

"No one's going to know," he whispered in Jenny's ear. "And Euclid will take his time answering. In the meantime, this is happening."

"Let it happen," she said. "Most of all I like to look at you and know you. Next, to look at Gertrude. So actually I'm pretty happy."

"Don't think any more. Listen to the Beatles. That's George Harrison. Can you hear the words?"

We were talking—about the space between us all
And the people—who hide themselves behind a wall
of illusion. . . .
And the time will come when you see
We're all one and life flows on within you and without
you.

They danced. With his little finger he drew a band around her wrist.

"Your hand in the small of my back," Jenny said. "Bodies are so much alike. Just now you were dancing with Ulla the same way. Did that get you more excited?"

"Your voice alone is enough," he said. "A couple of words in a certain tone of voice and my whole body reacts. I can't help it. Don't be unhappy when nothing happens. It's beyond my control."

He wet his lips and kissed her lightly on the jaw. It felt as if he'd known her for a very long time.

"I wonder where Gertrude's disappeared," she said when they stopped dancing. "I don't see her anywhere."

"I'll go look for her."

"You have to find her," Jenny said sharply. "You mustn't let her out of your sight."

Everyone had just seen her. The record player changed records, doors slammed. She wasn't in the kitchen. He pretended he wasn't looking, just talking to people on the way.

"Did you see? Northern Lights in July!" he announced.

He was the only one who'd seen them. Other people jumped up or turned around in their chairs. The people dancing inside didn't hear. There were four streaks crisscrossed like searchlights in wartime, and down by the horizon flames burned as restlessly as sleet, until they were turned down.

He finally saw Gertrude; she was coming through the glass doors from the garden.

"Gertrude!" he burst out, but forgot why he wanted her.

She was pale, and dark beneath the eyes, but she smiled at

him. Had she been in someone's arms? He didn't ask, it sounded too silly.

"You've been gone," he said.

"You can see how well they take care of themselves," she said, and met his questioning look with a smile.

"Have you been doing something fun?"

"Yes."

"What?"

"Do you tell me everything?" she asked. And so he didn't find out what it was. Something mysterious. It didn't have to have anything to do with kisses and contact. It might be something she didn't think he'd understand. Were there many such things? Was there a Gertrude who was different from the one he observed every day?

A moment later he stood alone on the terrace and caught the smell of low tide. In the dining room Gertrude was dancing with Klas Lundin. Maybe they were talking about Sten Tidström. It was midnight at their ancestral Water Palace. Father was far away, mother dead, close relatives they had none. These were their friends. Jan felt warm that they had come at all, and sorry that they didn't mean more. But that was his own fault.

I don't miss the dead, he thought. I miss the living when I can't get them to live for me. I miss those present who refuse to appear.

His father had had parties like this, so had his grandfather. Topics discussed: about the same. Other people's prospects and oblivion. It was criminal of him to stand here by the honeysuckle all alone. He was responsible for his friends, at least as long as his party lasted. Gertrude was dancing. She was always happiest and most herself at the Water Palace.

It's right now we exist, he thought angrily. Don't let your gaze drown in the bay. What kind of a life is it when people die off around us? Suddenly they're gone, though just now they were dancing here in the dining room. They still exist, we say, because we talk about them and think about them. They exist a little bit because we exist. But if we don't talk and think but just stand staring out over the honeysuckle, then we're not even aware that they don't exist.

When he turned around he saw Jenny. She clapped him on the shoulder, a gesture so friendly and forward he felt as if they'd just put their clothes on after making love.

"Jan, you make me feel I'm destructive. I'm harder and less vulnerable than Gertrude."

She isn't clear about Gertrude's role, and she couldn't possibly be, Jan remarked to himself like a narrator.

"I don't often think about what my life is going to amount to," Jenny went on.

"Your life is pretty well arranged," Jan said.

"I mean emotionally. I don't put such a high value on it, I don't expect anything in particular. I care about what's happening now. We have to be careful with Gertrude. I'll always get by."

He looked around, then he took Jenny's face between his hands and kissed her. The tips of their tongues touched, and her breath blew across his throat.

"Within you without you," he sang quietly. "You're so pretty. But maybe you shouldn't have come here."

She shook her head. He didn't know what it meant.

A few of them threw darts in the moonlight. It was one of the Water Palace traditions. The targets were on soft gray cardboard, nailed to a chestnut tree. One of Jan's darts hit the bark above the target, and the point broke off as he was trying to loosen it. He told Jenny about it—it would stay there as their secret sign and no one would ever know. She nodded, but when he brushed against her hand she pulled it carefully away as if she no longer wanted to do anything in secret.

"What's the matter?" he whispered.

"I don't really know. I don't want to have the feeling I'm alien, so that you or parts of you seem alien too."

"Come help me fix the supper," Jan said. "Frozen meatballs, herring and strömming, and beer and wormwood snaps."

"Good," she said. "I'll help you. Though I really think I'm a little drunk. Hold onto me anyway; it's all too much for me. But I have to talk to you seriously. What in heaven's name do you want from me? Are you looking for some kind of assurance that you can attract other women? I don't believe it, but now you have it. Gertrude is prettier than I am, slimmer, lighter. She could have a thousand affairs. Even if she didn't have you I'd be a little jealous of her. She doesn't lack anything you can find in me, even our jobs are sort of related. I don't know much about her social interests. Maybe she's less extroverted than I am, but she likes nature just as much. She's your woman, Jan."

He shuddered. He almost thought he heard "your sister," as if Gertrude had already given that away, to Jenny of all people, and at their first meeting.

"Jenny, I hope you're not making the same mistake Gertrude might make if she knew—I mean that you imagine love depends mostly on sexual attraction, and that a person's opinion of himself stands or falls on how attractive other people find him? It's possible Gertrude has everything you have and then some. I haven't thought about it. I'm not playing the qualities market. You know that. Are you afraid of something?"

"No."

"Are you tired?"

"Not tired, but thoughtful."

At dawn, three thirty, a herring supper for the remaining guests by the bay. That too was a tradition. Strong coffee after the bitter snaps. A slight dizziness in the sunrise, but no deceit. The water floated the smallest pebbles back and forth at the corner of the beach where the wagtails danced. Jenny slipped on a patch of wild chives and her shoes smelled of onion.

One of Jan's colleagues spread out his arms in the air.

"This is one of those relaxed, uncommon mornings when all mankind ought to have something to say to each other."

They swam out from the rock, which was dark with dew. The water rippled against their mouths, and as they looked out over the surface the waves glittered like fish scales, and the islands hung in the air like mirages. They stretched the muscles in their bellies. No doubt everyone took the opportunity to pee. The Department of the Environment directives applied only to collective sewage.

Pleasure returned. Because of his job at Arlanda, Jan was used to the various hours of the day. He put his arm around Gertrude's shoulders, she looked cool and fresh though a little red-eyed. He was struck by a formless admiration for her. She had come so far without tiring—that night, and in life.

He remembered how the trees had been thicker before, as thick as on the tapestry with the lady. Now they thinned out toward the channel. If only everyone could live through this, he thought idly, as the morning breeze reached them and puckered his skin so the water dripped off. But maybe even the most deprived had these brief feelings of abundance, and maybe they'd rather have something quite different.

"There's a message in a bottle, without the bottle," someone yelled, and fished out a floating piece of paper with a boat-hook.

It was a What-To-Do-When-Someone-Is-Drowning of the kind that's usually enclosed with a new lifebuoy. They read the instructions aloud while they stamped themselves dry.

They felt braced and invigorated. When a freighter under the Costa Rican flag slid past, early enough to avoid paying another day's wharfage in Stockholm Harbor, the hormone expert and the architect and the air traffic controller sang, at the tops of their lungs,

> *We are Swedish Boy Scouts we*
> *And our given vows*
> *Sworn on a day both brisk and free*
> *Stand written on our brows.*

There all three of them stopped. After so many years it was no longer clear what those vows had concerned, and it was better not to know.

And so they went to bed. Jenny slept over in the old bathhouse. Jan and Gertrude had long since taken out the rickety hoistable wooden tub with its rusty chains and slippery bottom. They had put in a floor, on which stood oars and boots, a badminton net, a discarded radio. They set up a cot for Jenny, a stool for a night table, mineral water, and a bar of soap. The window looked out north toward the bay.

Jan had a dream that night. He was enormously ugly, both girls despised him, he had big white bubbles on his chest. He lay hidden on a shelf in the pantry behind a row of canned peas and asparagus and mussels. The shelf was gritty with bits of rice and sugar and grated cheese. He was tiny and yet like he always was, as if seen from a distance. If only we can get away without Jan, he heard them saying out in the kitchen in their most everyday laughing voices—they were planning a picnic. He was no invisible bridge between them. They wanted to have everything in common except him. There was a crunching around him like dried insects. But they didn't hear.

He woke up quite late, looked out in the garden and thought he was still dreaming. There were Gertrude and Jenny with their arms around each other, one of them was teaching the other one some kind of folk dance. Jenny made a hop, Gertrude rubbed her temple. They looked fresh, although it was the morning after. Then they compared arms, legs, knees—suntan, length, amount of hair, he didn't know what. He thought of calling, but he didn't. A self-evident physical intimacy seemed to exist between them, as if they'd grown up in the same nightgown.

If she loves me, he thought, maybe she'll notice something in Gertrude . . . something genetic. But that seldom happens.

He dressed and went down to them, stood for a moment smiling on the stairs, the Master of the Water Palace.

"Good morning, ladies. It looks like you were up early."

"I took a bathrobe down to Jenny," Gertrude said. "We went for a swim."

He could picture them swimming naked out into Sandö Bay, which was several miles outside the mercury limit, among the algae and the DDT particles that Jenny knew the figures for.

"I'm afraid the lakes around Arlanda are filling up with mud," he said, in order to offer a secret channel.

"Oh, not all of them certainly?" Jenny said calmly. "I was telling Gertrude about the maritime birch forest zone. Did you know that in the whole world it exists only in the Stockholm and Åland archipelagoes?"

"I'm going to make some tea," Gertrude said, and ran into the house.

"Jenny. . . ."

"I've been rejecting you, haven't I? We're used to nights out in the open after all, and the contrast was too great. I have a lot of thinking to do."

"You don't want to interfere and spoil things."

"Don't think I'm only noble minded. No more than what I think's good for me. But there are all these cogs and gears groping for each other. If it were all superficial and easy, then I could have kissed Gunnar, the one who knows so much about hormones. And you could have gone off with Ulla . . . or with Gertrude, who's after all more attractive than all the others put together."

"But that isn't the way it is," Jan objected.

He was searching for words, weighed down by the serious certainty in Jenny's voice.

"You and Gertrude love each other."

"How do you know?"

"I can tell by looking at you," she decided. "I have a feeling about it."

"It never occurred to me to deny it. I love you. That's also part of it."

"I love you. Like before, or a little more. And that's also part of it."

"It's funny," Jan said. "You've never asked me if I love you. You've never asked for any assurances."

"I've never needed any with you."

"You don't need to worry. My love feels gigantic. A two-man job."

"Yes, we've got possibilities in other directions. Would we dare play this kind of game if we had to depend on each other for life and death? If I was deprived of my love, or yours, we'd manage anyway. Somehow. It's nice to be so adult."

He smelled the honeysuckle. A belt of odors closed around him, sweet and acid and insistently sad.

"Doesn't honeysuckle smell mostly after dark?" he wondered. "I have the feeling I smell it all the time."

"I don't know," Jenny said. "Now I have to get back to town."

"I could lie in the back of your station wagon," he suggested.

But he could see it was a cheap remark.

"I'll stay," he added. "There's a lot of cleaning up to do."

"I could help. I like learning where things go. But I don't have time. Gertrude will be right back. So listen to me. If you decide things are getting too difficult . . . or if I think it's getting too complicated . . . well, why couldn't we pretend I'm your sister?"

A third member of the family, he thought. Had Jenny sought out Gertrude's friendship in order to get her used to this idea?

"Someone who's always there," Jenny went on. "A serving of loyalty you can help yourself to for a long time."

"No, not a sister, thanks," Jan said. "Here comes Gertrude with the tea. Our well water's hard, we let it boil for a long time."

"Don't ever think I'm odd," Jenny said quickly and low. "If I do something I can't figure out, why anyway *you'll* probably understand it."

Gertrude put a tray down on the steps between them. The cups were crackled and brown on the inside.

"I'm going to take a picture of you," she called and ran after the camera.

"Some other time," said Jenny firmly. "I feel too hungover. But I can take one of you."

"No, I'll take a close-up of Jan," Gertrude said. "A meter and a half away. You seldom look yourself in pictures."

MOSS

WHEN JAN CALLED Jenny two days after the party, no one answered. He tried to reach her from Arlanda all through the morning watch. She hadn't left any message with Traffic Control or the switchboard. The Department of the Environment reported that Departmental Director Jeger was on vacation.

It made him restless, but he didn't know what to do. He had a key to her apartment, she'd said he could stay there. Maybe her mother came and cleaned. He went, hesitated a long time before opening the door, but found no particular clues. It seemed more impersonal than before. He looked at the blue apothecary's bottle with its gold writing—it might belong to anyone. The morning paper was on the floor in the front hall, but there wasn't any mail. The traffic went on unaffected down in Nybro Square. She must have gone the day before.

He sat on the edge of the bed and called the local post office. No, they didn't usually give out forwarding addresses. It would be OK just to write to the regular one.

He suspected that Gertrude and the Water Palace had been too much. By disappearing, Jenny would make everything right —that was the simple solution. The self-punishment that satisfies, the passive guilt that turns into active will to self-sacrifice.

He opened her refrigerator. Butter, a piece of salami, beer. It didn't look as though she'd emigrated. But you could transplant most of yourself on pretty short notice these days.

You never own anything, he thought. You exist in others and others exist in you—and cease to exist.

She was an extra in his life. I can take you or leave you, he tried to say to protect himself. She wouldn't leave a visible emptiness. But by thinking away her voice and eyes an emptiness came over him like a cage, and his legs gave a start as if they wanted to run away from him.

He looked at the red bench in the dining room. Objects were made to people's measure and for people's needs, but now they stand there alone, somehow unusable, forgetting all they've been through.

I love you, he said to the nail brush in the silence of the bathroom. For it was worn a little flat by her fingertips, and its bristles had scratched the soap.

It was as if he were in the grip of a forbidden passion—a boy's love for a pretty, full-grown woman, or an older man's attraction to a schoolgirl. His heart was hammering. You're being silly, he said to himself and his heart. Jenny's hands, slender, with coiling veins . . . and higher up . . . he rolls up the arm of her blouse . . . the inside of her arm is pale, the crease where her arm fold ends an inch from her elbow . . . anatomical matters-of-course . . . he sees it, lowers his lips toward it . . . his shoulders draw together as if of their own accord.

Even in her absence he embraced her, persistently. The house doesn't notice the wild vine until it has hooked on tight with its sucking feet and begun to lift the windowsills and force its way into the holes in the plaster and behind the thighs of the caryatids and under the staples of the drain pipes. It finds climbing holds everywhere.

He lifted the spread. The sheets and pillowcases were new, no smells. Pajamas and nightgowns in a drawer smelled only clean. In a winter coat in the closet he found a vague odor in the armpit—a trace of her.

To be beside yourself. He thought about the expression. A kind of obsession, which you could know nothing about unless you'd once been gripped by the desire to surrender, totally, to the unbelievable insight that another human being's existence is for you the only true reality.

He wanted to buy something for Jenny. It was a way of evoking her. He would lure her out of her hiding place. He straightened out the bed and left the apartment, sat down outside the Nybro Pavilion and ordered coffee. A smell of sea and mud from the bay, the same smell you got up at Jenny's when the wind was right.

He went into several jewelry stores along Norrlandsgatan, picked up rings from blue-gray beds of satin, put them back. The clerks were obliging. Was it for a lady, a young lady? He thanked them and disappeared. Jenny owned a smoke topaz, he'd never seen any other jewelry. He went into a shop on Kungsgatan and asked to look at brassieres. A girl waited on him.

"What color?"

"White."

"And the size?"

"Thirty-four B."

There were only women in the store. While waiting, he browsed through some thin negligees. He chose a bra without frills or lace and felt at once fatherly and daring toward the girl who took his money and handed him a sack without a trace of expression. Exhilarated by his knowledge of Jenny's different numbers, he went into a store next door and bought a pair of green slippers, size six and a half. They looked like elf shoes.

Performing these very ordinary actions made him terribly excited. Was this some kind of a double life—or was he living one and the same life divided between two people? Or were Jenny and Gertrude the same person and he the victim of a temporary optical illusion?

He walked faster, swinging his sack. He had a feeling he was the master of his fate, not a marionette in an unknown hand. Still, this wasn't that opera Jenny had been listening to. It wasn't like him to behave this way, and it made him defiantly pleased.

But for the first time he realized it was going to be hard to talk to Gertrude. Not just about this, but in general. Jenny's absence made her slightly unreal. She was sitting out there at the Water Palace. He could call her, but not tell her about his loneliness. He could describe, in general terms, what loss was like, and she would understand—being present in another world than the one around you.

He decided to go have a look at the place where Jenny worked. He got his car and drove out to Solna. The Department of the Environment was in a district where he'd never been. It looked as if they had searched out the one spot in Greater Stockholm where smog, sterility, and an indefinable ugliness had achieved their greatest possible concentration. What he saw was an experiment in environmental destruction, a Hades or at least the domicile of the halfway dead.

Heavy smoke from heating plants and factory chimneys wound around him like a python. He coughed helplessly while his lungs adapted to the altered climate. A couple of trees had been planted on a desolate vacant lot next to the new Department office building. They were the only trees in sight and were obviously growing smaller under the attacks of the filthy air.

It was a frontier region where city and country chewed each

other ragged, the street plan petered out into weeds and wasteland, the neon lights and the imploring ads cried out to no response from the forgotten garden plots and the heaps of demolition debris. In the old days, he thought, people could move to better places where the earth was still fertile. Now the emigrant's day was over. Hello carbon monoxide, welcome sulphur dioxide, he sang softly to himself, in honor of the Department of the Environment.

The ground was eroded, petrified by sun and cold. The water table seemed to have sunk. He caught a glimpse of Bällsta Bay, silted up with decades of industrial waste. Airplanes rose thunderingly from Bromma Field. And somewhere the supersonic transport stood ready to drive mankind insane with its shock waves.

Jan Backman walked in through the main doors of the Department of the Environment. The building also housed the Department of Traffic Safety, a vocational school and a school for kindergarten teachers. He stood in a waiting room and was going to say, which was the truth, that he was from Air Traffic Control and wanted some material on the noise problem. But there was no one to say it to.

He wandered into the longest corridor he'd ever seen. There was light blue linoleum on the floor, and between the doors hung maps marking the locations of the things the Department worked with: crown forests, ecclesiastical properties, crown land reserves, nature reserves, agricultural limits, bird sanctuaries, military preserves, national parks.

A girl in red stockings disappeared through a door marked Coffee Room. Two men pushed past him, one of them saying he had just come back from the Oil Protection Organization in Zürich. The rooms at the end of the corridor were empty, waiting for the occupants of the new posts that air and water pollution would soon supply. They were already furnished like the others—gray striped wallpaper, curtains in white and orange, metal ladder shelves full of green folders.

Several doors were open, men in shirtsleeves worked, looked up, and not recognizing Jan bent down again over their reports on the sewage problems of vacation villages. "Secretary Llife" it said on one door, and encouraged by the name, Jan knocked. He named his errand and was escorted to the library, which was being enlarged.

"You seem to be involved in almost everything," he said.

"There are only about seventy of us out here in Solna, so we can't manage everything. But actually everything in society comes within the scope of the Department of the Environment."

He caught an echo of Jenny.

"Is Director Jeger here today?" he asked.

"No. I just found out she went on vacation yesterday."

"Do you know where?"

"To London probably. That's where she usually goes. It may be she has an assignment from here as well. She handles some of our international contacts, and of course the Council of Europe's Environment Year will be starting soon."

"What about her secretary?" Jan asked.

It was the girl with the red stockings he'd just seen on her way into the coffee room. She was also supposed to be off, she explained. Jenny's mail was coming to the Department. Jenny had a private address in London, as far as the girl knew, but it wasn't certain she was there. She hadn't said anything definite.

"Isn't there some contact address in London?" he insisted. "Doesn't the Department collaborate with some organization that Miss Jeger generally visits?"

"Maybe I can help," he heard a voice behind him say.

A man introduced himself as Dr. something that Jan didn't catch. He kept an eye on Jenny's work while she was gone.

"If it's a departmental matter, you can turn it over to me."

Jan said he was from Air Traffic Control, but that his actual errand was of a somewhat more personal nature at the moment.

"It's possible you can reach her at the Natural Environment

Research Council, Alhambra House, Charing Cross Road," the man said. "Right behind the National Gallery."

It sounded as if he'd just been there himself. Maybe on a business trip with Jenny. Jan knew the official per diem allowance for London had just been raised.

"Have you seen our little exhibit, by the way?" the man asked.

Jan was led to a couple of display cases in the conference room. They contained different kinds of moss that had been exposed for a certain time to the onslaught of the city's fumes.

"We're studying their resistance. And the adaptability that's a part of resistance. I have to go to a meeting, but please stay if you want to."

Jan stayed with the mosses, which were described as frail, hardy, persistent, demanding, or easily asphyxiated. There were common mosses but also some more unusual types: marsh moss, umbrella moss, slender swan's neck moss from lime-rich swamps. Elfin gold that gleams from holes in the rock—strongly arched cells function like lenses, gathering the light. And hygrometer moss, a cosmopolite that follows in the tracks of human beings and twists itself into a moisture-preserving spiral in dry spells.

He understood right away that the thought of this moss was one of the things that could make him happy while Jenny was away.

He left the building with a number of reports on noise, which he meant to return as soon as he could. They know a lot of things here that Jenny knows and I don't know, he thought. He remembered something the Director of the Department had said on a TV program: "There used to be a lot of questions and problems that just whirled around in empty space. Now they've found a receiver that sends out new impulses of its own."

Was Jenny the visible form of his feelings toward the world? A form he had to work within so that everything might take on shape? He could know nothing for sure about who she really was. But he hoped they would make themselves as visible as possible to each other.

He discovered the parking place where Jenny's car must have stood. Someone was changing a tire on a trailer truck. I'm catching your scent, he thought. I can see you sneaking by. Your tracks are everywhere. Other people don't think about it. A strand of hair, a piece of a nail. I sniff my way to your trail. But when I arrive and burrow my nose and mouth in your lap, all I taste is water.

The nauseating smell from a coffee roasting plant drove him into the Smeden Cafeteria. It was a desolate yellow room with tables and curtains in orange. He ate sausage and drank near beer, which was all they had to offer. It was a long time since he'd eaten. He felt a threatening and mysterious atmosphere closing around him. Hydrogen sulphide covered the hollow between Solna and Sundbyberg like a dome. The acidity of the air increased.

A threat to the environment—what Jenny worked with—certainly she didn't see him that way? Was she fleeing him? He made no claims on her. And if she came back, would it be she who came back? If only he had her near—he depended on his hands, on his eyes, she had taught him that.

When he came out it was after four in the afternoon and the area was as deserted as during an air-raid alarm. As empty as the corridors in the Department of the Environment. He'd left his car near the main road to Bromma Field. He stopped outside the Swedish Piano Company, built in dusty brick in the shape of a concert grand. The noise of the traffic was drowned out for a moment by strange bright sounds from inside. Some worker who's gone insane, he thought, and is in there biting the strings.

When he came into town he drove through the gloomy central European neighborhood around Frejgatan, Ynglingagatan and Roslagsgatan. It fit in with his mood. Junk shops full of auction goods from the demolished Klara district had found a temporary refuge here. The Vasa Pawn Shop displayed tools apparently intended for the summer's burglaries, and the secondhand suits retained the forms of bodies that had just made off in their underclothes. Unidentifiable one-crown sandwiches lay behind the misty glass in an automat outside Te-Ge's Cafeteria.

He felt as if he were some stray emotion, an emotion which he failed to recognize because it was pure novelty. It seemed to him his love was sinking down through him and being obliterated, like something losing its contours and its name. He had opened himself for the experience of Jenny. Now she was swallowed and gone and he a different person by reason of that nourishment. He felt empty and impoverished.

Because he had felt love sink and suffer defeat and yet not disappear, it seemed to him he no longer possessed anything except the love he'd lost, no longer had room for anything except the love that, obliterated, filled him to the brim.

Jan took one of the narrow paths up to the Observatory. Around him lay the city and its hills. He had stood here before, wanting finally to make a plan for his life, the way the astronomers in the building beside him circled in the heavens with their compasses.

He looked at Stockholm's geometric pattern. Vasastaden and Östermalm at right angles, Johannes Church on its competing hill, Engelbrekt on another, Marieberg and the newspaper buildings far away, the gas holder in the opposite direction. But if everyone chose the same point from which to view society, then society would be invisible. And if everyone felt what he felt, would this feeling then exist? A new postcard to Euclid. . . .

And then he was forced to think of Jenny in another city— the echo of footsteps on a sidewalk, unexpected silence, the coming attractions on movie theater walls. His feeling of loss frightened him all over again. She could be an opium addict, a doormat, a mole, if only she'd let him know exactly where she was. He decided to buy her something else and leave it in her apartment. Not just a bra and slippers. Perhaps an hibiscus, crooked and angular, and some canned food—tongue and ham, pumpernickel and camembert.

He looked at the blocks nearby, dusty metal balconies like nesting boxes on the outsides of the buildings. Soot and smoke sticking to blind firewalls. The varying fields of plastering, now fallow in a dirty gray, now a blossoming harvest of colors that nibbled at each other. The city was a barrel with space as a lid.

The drainpipes grew up the buildings like wild vines. The displays in Sveavägen's furniture stores looked like living rooms. And the apartments above copied them and were filled with bluish TV light.

Then the buildings darkened and became black dominoes with glowing dots. He saw other buildings further off, irregular, clumped together, like building blocks dumped hastily out of a box.

And he dimly saw the city's smudgy edges, with occasional buildings under construction, and cow barns that had become warehouses and workshops, and hay barns where young people fixed motorcycles and slept with each other, and small factories already driven to their knees by progress, and gravel pits, and compost heaps, and fire-ravaged lots full of wild raspberries and digitalis. And fast on the heels of slum and disorder came the low, pretty schools, the new churches, the youth centers and the educational societies, the row houses, the high-rise, and the covered bus stops for the feeder lines.

It was his city, his world, winking on and off before his eyes like a tremendous instrument panel.

CONTOURS

JAN BACKMAN WAS sitting at home alone. Jenny stood in the door.

"Can I come in and stay tonight?"

They looked at each other, a dizziness on solid ground. He didn't dare close his eyes for fear of losing sight of her. He knew: they would crawl in with each other and no trace of betrayal to anyone or anything would shadow them.

A great silence . . . he himself a liberated musical instrument . . . finally he would sing. When summer comes to the arctic plains, lichens and short grass awaken, rear up for a while, then disappear again but do not die. He felt her breath against his cheek, saw her pupils enlarge in unreserved astonishment.

Such was his dream, sentimental but clear, almost awake.

When he brushed his teeth in the morning he felt this desire for her again, sparked by the thought of her yellow pajamas somewhere far away, in a ship's cabin, in a room where he'd never been. What he wanted was to caress her body through the material, count her birthmarks, kiss her armpit, measure the distance from her navel to her pubic hair with his penis as a ruler. Another thought was equally exciting—to look through a magnifying glass at one square millimeter of skin, between her little finger and the palm of her hand.

He was hounded by pornographic fantasies. Jenny's body bent in a bow against a man he'd never seen. With a superficial, physical lust he couldn't remember ever having felt before, he thought about girls. He guessed it was a need to take revenge, to enjoy them without telling them why. He felt alone. Because Gertrude didn't help. She was the last person he wanted to hurt. He was glad for the unspoken distance she maintained.

He drank coffee and caught sight of a woman in an apartment opposite, one story down. The morning sun was streaming into her kitchen. She was wearing an orange polo shirt, black slacks, moccasin slippers that she suddenly kicked off so she could slide around faster in her stocking feet. She got out the tea and held glasses up to the light to see if they were clean. A little girl was crawling around on the floor. She tied her hair ribbon. She opened a carton of buttermilk, kicked an inflated ball with her daughter, made coffee for herself. She kept pulling her shirt down over her hips as if she thought she were being watched.

He drove out to Arlanda. He'd driven that stretch with Jenny, but in the other direction, and the road looks different then. Everything in him broke loose toward Jenny, like ice floes being carried off by the current. If he forgot her for an hour, his amazement at that fact woke him like a phone ringing.

From his office he checked the SAS passenger lists to London, but Jenny Jeger's name wasn't on them. Then he got in touch with a man he knew at Heathrow's traffic control—he'd been at Arlanda on a study tour. He pretended it was official business, certainly no one would notice the teletype copy. The Englishman reported that a passenger by that name had arrived on a BEA flight on such and such a date. BEA's lists were kept only in London. Jan discovered he'd guided that plane into its flight path during his first watch after the party at the Water Palace. The landing card with Jenny's London address was with the police and couldn't be given out.

On his lunch break, alone at a table at the Gyllene Muttern, he read Updike's *Rabbit, Run*. There was one episode—the young man goes home with an office girl one Saturday night and stays for several days. She's not so young, a bit loose, maybe something of a tart. He asks her to wash off her heavy makeup and to shampoo the chemical smell of dye and spray from her hair. Then he makes love to her, probably more inno-cent and scrubbed than she's been since she was a child. She becomes uglier and more genuine, embarrassed by this new nakedness. When he leaves her to go out and buy food for breakfast she says, tenderly and ironically, "Boy, you want to be a real lover, don't you?"

A fine passage, Jan thought. Her hopeful misgivings, the young man's high demands on himself, which you right away suspect he'll come to abandon. Their mutual desperate invest-ment in something they can only glimpse the contours of, some-thing they've read about, longed for, but can never manage to realize—at least not these two particular people at this partic-ular time.

A pilot came up to Jan's table.

"Can I sit down? I'm just having coffee."

"Well it's been a long time. Where have you been?"

"I've been flying Rio-Santiago. Home for a couple weeks."

"You look tired."

"A lot of parties in Rio the last few days. Now I'll be flying in Africa. Athens-Nairobi, stationed in Athens. I bought a car duty-free in Zürich and I'm going to drive it down through Yugoslavia. Wait, I've got a present for you. From Honduras."

He took out a bronze tapir with two heads.

"Thanks. I'll put it on the windowsill. It suits me perfectly."

He meant it. Two heads, one for Gertrude, one for Jenny. It's insoluble, he tried to persuade himself. He hoped the very statement would feel like a solution. But he wasn't deceived. He loved them both.

When he went back to his office there was a telegram on the desk.

"Old commitments waiting in London. I love you."

No signature or return address.

He ordered a long distance call to the Natural Environment Research Council in London. Yes, Miss Jeger had been there. He left a message that she should contact the Scandinavian operator. Finally she called.

He was so happy his whole body started to tremble. He heard her voice and it didn't matter what she'd been doing. He was webbed between his fingers and toes, nothing was ridiculous any more, everything was possible, and he could find his way. She was his discovery, and he loathed the thought that she might do anything for his sake, be faithful to him, for example.

Specification completed at once. She was there on the map.

"In one way I'm only half of me on a trip like this. But it's a state I'm used to."

"I love you. Your voice . . . I'm full of embarrassed happiness. This isn't like anything else and never has been."

"I came to London to be rid of you, for your sake in other words, and it made me comically happy. Acting against you, after all, meant I was still in your sphere."

Expensive moments of joy through the North Sea cable.

"When did you get my message?" Jan asked.

"Just as I was going to meet John, my friend here. I was swept up in a great cloak of happiness, nothing could happen to you and me, I felt like I could make everyone happy. I was with him and still in your atmosphere and I didn't feel split. That's what's so stupid—I ran away from your message, and still I was as happy as if it were you that sneaked away. I gave John a hug because I felt your presence so clearly."

"Did you?" he said without expression.

"It may be I do things that hurt you, but I won't do anything you don't know about—if you want," she said. "That means I have to come home soon. And that everything that isn't you is a little beside the point."

"So we'll see each other again? When are you coming?"

"I don't know. And it's possible John will come with me."

There the conversation was broken off, and he knew nothing definite, but he'd held her voice like an object in his hand. How important was this man Jenny had grown attached to a long time ago, and who was therefore outside Jan's control?

In reach, out of reach, within you without you. . . .

Now his love was gnawing at its tree like a beaver, and finally two pencil-thin points met each other in a giddy balance while the beaver watched. Then the point breaks and the beaver runs home to the water.

He started to write a letter to Jenny.

"Talked to you. Is it still true that a thousand invisible lamps send signals between us and no one else sees them? I want to be the only one who really knows what your feet look like on the bottom. The rest you can share with other people. So I probably am a leech after all. From writing this, my cock has managed to come to attention under my zipper, it wants to go to you, and the only thing I can offer it is the handle on the drawer. . . ."

He slept over at Arlanda, against the regulations. He took Jansson's watch in return for the time Jenny was there. He sat down at the instrument panel high up in the glass cage.

It seemed to him he had a job where he escaped dead weight. It was unfettered, hardly held him down to earth, to Sweden. A safety net of facts was spread out beneath him in case he was seized by vertigo. There was a continuous documentation of what occurred. Data became information. Information became stored memory. There was a foothold in figures. A security in this limited preserve.

The landscape was in darkness and the stars were bright. The radar revolved.

He imagined he was seeing a billion cells in a glass egg being shaken by a hand, and they rained down like stars and gathered into a person who was loved. And then that combination never came back, even though the glass was still there, even though almost everything seemed, on the surface, to repeat itself.

THE PLATFORM

ANOTHER LETTER CAME from Tidström addressed to Traffic Control, and Jan read it before showing it to Gertrude.

Sten asked again what held him back. Jan could picture him at home on Upplandsgatan in an easy chair where he sank deeper and deeper until his knees began to reach the level of his chin. And he looked at Jan and Gertrude with tired clairvoyance, a look that Jan interpreted as meaning, Yes, I know, you've just been making love, you're still wrapped up in each other.

Sten wrote:

Shall we correspond about life's swarming multiplicity, which threatens all rigid bureaucracy with its rebellion, or about the dead forms that suffocate the living? There's all the difference in the world.

I see you in Stockholm where the streets and squares are dying under the latest traffic reform. I see you in a city where the children have never seen a living horse, but where the equestrian statues still stand, tall and straddle-legged, as if we all would be protected by their chests and testicles. Why did kings always ride stallions?

One shouldn't ask even a close friend about his mission in life. But aren't you in danger of becoming resigned? Call it realism if you want to, but since you're not confronting a larger reality it's really the good old common middle-class onanistic melancholy.

What has meaning? Love? Work? What lasts? What

does a person find most consistently exciting? Or does he have to provide the excitement himself? There's a great drama going on down here in Africa. A tragedy. You have to know that but not look at it, so you remain an observer. You have to work with your little part of it. The perspective of distance falsifies and makes you insensitive—human beings are suffering and dying, everywhere, only in different proportions.

Swaneng Hill is a platform. The universal is a thing you can sense, the particular is a thing you can work with. The face of the universal is hard to recognize, but a man can see faces around him as they build a gymnasium, a new classroom for Standard V, a sink for the kitchen.

The truth in a person's life is outside himself, in actions, in other people. In order to do something with yourself, you have to do something with someone else. In order to talk about yourself, and not about nothing, you have to talk about something else, always about something else.

You know that already, Jan told himself. We're talking about the same things. For him, what Sten was doing was the universal. His love for Gertrude and Jenny was the little platform. But they passed in and out of each other like noncongruent circles.

How could he answer so Sten would understand? Yesterday in Marienbad, today in Stockholm, tomorrow in Vredespoort. Now it was today, and he was here.

"Why do you stay in your tower at Arlanda?" Sten asked in his letter.

"I'm here and still not here," Jan answered him. "I'll tell you about that some other time."

"So what are you really up to? Sensual delights? The adventurous civil servant? I'll stay sarcastic until you tell me more."

"So many people," Jan wrote to Sten, "I among them, think in terms of mechanical opposites, in terms of alternatives that other people force on them. You're forever being asked are you a Christian or a Marxist, do you have a summer house, do you go on charter flights? Have you contributed to the economy? Have you ever been in love?"

He would prefer to stay out of the statistics, but there was a special column even for them.

Tidström wrote:

There's a lot more than I can tell you about. All of this exists all the time, not just in relation to me.

Botswana is a threatened country. South Africans every-where—spies, merchants, farmers. What do they care about political independence? They've got the economic thumbscrews. It's OK with them if the word 'freedom' is on the posters. They don't worry about words. If I have any task here, it's to be a buffer, a presence that keeps the South Africans from pushing too hard. They need to know there's a counterweight.

I live on the surface, which feels so salty it carries me like water and sometimes like thin ice. I sit with a glass of lemon tea, someone comes along and tells me a cock-and-bull story about a group of saboteurs—they've found a model railroad in someone's cellar. Is it a hobby or the Rhodesian Railway?

More than you imagine depends on the setting—the savannah, the office, the living room, the well-drilling camp. They tell you something about yourself. They change the pitch of your voice.

Still I suppose you have to live outward from some kernel, even if it's mostly composed of conventions, acci-dental education, second thoughts. Otherwise you get shrill and peevish and hysterical.

What kind of kernel? Joseph Conrad's Lord Jim was haunted by his treachery all his life, he took the boat and left the passengers. He didn't only betray them, he made himself into another person, and this other person wasn't a person he could live with but a person who tortured him. He constantly had to go back to that moment when he abandoned the most important element in himself.

Every one of us has to figure out where those moments lie.

A child asks for advice, but you don't have time, you hurry away, the child is injured or fails. Someone confides in you, but you gossip and a swindle comes to light or a marriage breaks up. Where's the line between consideration and truth?

How long can a man live with an important lie before he's altered from within?

Jan sat remembering Sten, the way he held his cigarette in both hands like a flute. He was a man who for years had been filling his head with absorbingly worthless knowledge. Now apparently all of it was usable.

Out in the desert near Tonota the other day. We lay down in the open jeep with our clothes on, sprinkled water on our faces and went to sleep. No mosquitoes. The ground strewn with pieces of flint, broken aloe stalks, sepia-colored sun-scorched rock. A hundred and five in the shade during the day. If you've got a cow that's not milking, put your lips to its vagina and blow. One of the things I've learned. We built a fire. Along came a drizzling rain of sand and put it out.

Sweden is giving money for hydrographic studies. A wretched little brook running out of a heap of stones. We're supposed to see what we can do. Dirt-gray huts all around it. Dawn at the edge of the desert was as desolate as at sea. A cattle tender here was famous because he owned a stunted tree. We found some crevices of salty mud. The refraction of the light was curious—we often saw flat ground wake up into mountains. We could hear the tramp of the cattle at a great distance, and clouds of dust swept up and lay like golden braids in the air. Old women were gathering sun-bleached dung for fires. Their eyes were red, almost burnt out.

I don't want to tell about them but rather tell it for them.

Don't let me hear any more about impotence. There's power to be exercised everywhere. A lot of people with a map on the wall act as if they'd been given binoculars.

We can make hydrogen bombs explode two hundred and eighty miles above the surface of the earth and extinguish life in an area the size of Western Europe. Bombs like that can be fired off by mistake. Each new day is given us by chance. And it's only now—when we are maybe the last generation—that a majority of the people on earth begin to open their eyes to what an endurable life could mean.

And in spite of that to act with a feeling of confidence in the future. Not: it could be like this if everything works out. But rather: this is the way it's going to be.

Basically, I believe only in those people and nations who help others in the realization that they cannot otherwise survive themselves.

Sten Tidström still had his old liveliness, his restrained enthusiasm. At the same time he was, in Jan's eyes, a free man, clear-sighted in his passion.

His letter arrived from far away. Jan had finally come to know his antipode.

Jan's Africa was airline routes across the map. Alitalia's new connection to Zambia, Sabena's route from the Congo to the Camerouns, Ghana Airway's old Fokker from Lagos to Dakar, Suid-Afrikaanse Lugdiens that has to go out to sea on its way north from Angola.

Another part of Jan's Africa was Arlanda's reptile house, the pride of the airport, which had burned down. He used to stand

and watch as quietly as the children whose noses snailed across the glass. A mamba shot with emerald green, like wind in the grass in the afternoon sun. He remembered the adders' heraldic pattern in gray and white and beige—a severe Persian carpet. The chameleons—dreamlike, enchanting, their tongues as quick as sharpshooters but life itself in slow motion. They were delicate. After two years in captivity they lost their appetites, and then their desire to live.

Sten held up another picture. Livingstone, Baker, and Speke didn't write guidebooks. These father figures were dangerous. As if other people should follow the same routes and search for notes of guidance in every hollow baobab trunk.

Jan could see Tidström's land—far from Jenny's room on Nybro Quay, far from the signals he directed to Air France Caravelles.

He could also see Jenny Jeger's land—the million-year peace of the morains broken by crushing machines, the air of the city thickening into lead, beaches blackened by oil.

It seemed to him he saw two hemispheres. They were the correlatives of his love.

THE DOOR

THE DETECTIVE creeps along the trail into the past. He sees footprints, all pointing forward, toward him. He walks into the light to the place where the footprints begin, and when he then follows them back to the present he finds the prints of his own shoes, now in their turn facing backwards.

He is forced to interpret the prints in relation to where *he* is coming from, the only point he knows anything about, and not in relation to the point from which the prints themselves originate.

When Jan drove out to the Water Palace he had heard nothing more from Jenny, and no one answered when he called, and for all he knew she was still in England.

He gradually discovered that the rooms were inhabited by something that didn't really touch him, by an odor that was somehow captured by the light, or by a light built into the smell of wicker furniture and wooden floors. He saw that the Water Palace had been built for other people. The grandfather clock, the game table, the reference books they'd left on the shelves— they comprised an atmosphere that Gertrude and he had not created.

It all took place outside him, close by, but not where he was. It existed for someone else. And it didn't matter. It was exhausted for him but maybe existed for others, and that was fine. He stood beside a chasm and felt no dizziness. You never lost your footing out here, you mostly stood still and didn't fall.

Gertrude didn't ask much. She worked and seemed happy. When she needed to think clearly she put her forearm over her eyes as if to shade them from the sun, and he saw the pale hairs against her brown skin. She was hard at work on something he didn't understand much of. Engravings of ferns and other pictures lay stacked up in open cartons, a glass full of pens and the portable typewriter stood ready on the table.

Jan gave her the letter from Sten Tidström, and Gertrude, in return, showed him a letter from their father in Brazil, the first in a long time, outside of Christmas cards. He knew they lived together at the Water Palace in the summers, as was only natural for an unmarried brother and sister with no relatives.

A sudden gust of wind from two continents. But Adolf Oscar Backman didn't write like Tidström. He seemed to live behind wrought-iron gates, guarding an Inca treasure. His company was the only thing he'd ever created with pride and unselfishness. He cared little about his children—they had occurred along the way.

His letter had come by sea. It contained an Indian necklace made of nuts, but it had been chewed up by worms that must have come along in the letter. There was some brown dust at the bottom of the envelope.

Jan remembered his father's hands, thin, hard, sound, though fat altered other parts of his body. Once in a while even now a deep, clear voice made a pronouncement inside his skull, from the days before his father had left the Foreign Ministry and gone into business for himself.

Afterwards they looked at the world map they'd tacked up in the kitchen. The Sandö Light was lit and blinked a streak of light in across the steppes of East Turkestan, on toward the graves of the Scythians and the golden carriages in Altai, and then down toward Botswana and back across Brazil.

"I forgot the wash," she said.

She'd hung clothes on the line outside the kitchen door. They were dancing in the breeze—nightgown, pajamas, pants, bras. As anonymously as on the counter at the department store when they were still unsold. His and hers. The sky was clear, so they let them hang out overnight. They were watched by a flock of crows who'd moved over to the Water Palace, carried by an incomprehensible gust of wind just at sunset when crows always shift their bearings.

He was seized by a tremendous tenderness for Gertrude. Quickly and silently he wrapped his arms around her, and she was more his sister than his love, and for the first time he wanted to sleep with his sister and no one else. Everything had to be possible. But he wasn't able to express it.

Gertrude cleared away the transistor radio and the newspapers and put a thick orange candle on the table. It looked like a tower of juice.

"You're far away," she said. "I hardly dare touch you. I don't exist."

It was true—she was far away because Jenny was far away. He smiled at her without being able to answer the question in her eyes. He looked at her suntanned knuckles. It seemed to him she was at home in the country, in the odor of boxwood and freshly cut grass, among birds as swift as the throw of a stone. She dived off the dock every morning, and white air bubbles rose up as though from a boiling pot. He thought of her skin as being watertight.

Jan ran his fingers along the underside of the table, where he had once drawn some trolls with a fat crayon, one of which represented Auditor Strömberg, his father's confidant. That was a long time ago while he was waiting for Gertrude to come home from Switzerland or Sigtuna. Things like that were still there, like the old books where you could be sure of finding phrases like "I was at that time much too young to understand why my mother turned away and wept," or, "When he entered the room I involuntarily shuddered. I did not yet know he was to play a decisive role in my life."

Gertrude herself was reading one of those old-fashioned novels where the characters seemed to move on orders from a whimsical, playful god. The hero was imposing but doomed by fate, the heroine beautiful but melancholy. There were mysterious sins, an aura of forbidden or perverse sex, a mood of terror, violence, or death, and digressions into the grotesque, capricious, or haphazard. The author joined his characters in a riddle of his own creation. Best to stay on the doubtful side.

Suddenly a fuse blew on the enclosed porch where they were sitting. The bay outside was dark, just visible under the brass crust of the moon, a globe in default. Lights from a few boats, looking fragile. When they opened the fuse box in the kitchen, a dead mouse lay inside. It must have come in through a crack in the outer wall and crept through a conduit until it arrived inside the gray sheet metal of the fuse box, where it was burned dry in one hundredth of a second on encountering three hundred and sixty volts.

Gertrude put the animal on the counter by the sink and shone the flashlight on it. The beam flickered, for an instant the mouse seemed to move as if awakened by the light. Its legs stuck straight out. It was threadbare, used up—a dry muzzle, a skeleton, bluegray fur, eyes covered with a film. It should have been able to turn inside the white plastic conduit. Now it was so shrunken they needed a magnifying glass to make it real.

Jan changed the fuse. His tongue felt as stiff as metal plating. Jenny's Englishman, who'd been there so long, who represented silence. He was incapable of talking about all the sounds that silence made. His voice was indistinct with thirst. The mouse was sucked dry by the heat, its body tight. Best not to dream of expansion. Constriction is a greater test. Small stones escape the crusher more easily.

The next day he painted the balcony railing white. Gertrude stood beside him and watched. She told him about a prehistoric find made recently on Värmdö. Skeletons, weapons, and implements from the Germanic migrations and the Viking times. Epochs before the Water Palace. Things had been happening all that time.

He scraped the old paint from the gray, sun-split wood. When he brushed on fresh, it swelled to bubbles and boils that he stuck holes in with a feeling of doing something forbidden. The smell of paint on sun-warmed wood had been part of his life for as long as he could remember, and now he was back to it as if nothing had changed. He associated the smell with people in white flannel, with summer evening laughter and gramophone music while he peeked through the cracks in the curtains, convinced that every other child in Sweden was still up at this hour.

All at once it was too much for him. While Gertrude was in the house, he ran down to the shore. He jumped into the rowboat but didn't push off, just sat on the front thwart. Through the water he could see the flaking underside of the boat, and deep down in the dim, yellowish light, minnows with eyes bloodshot from constant washing.

Then he saw Jenny, the way they ran toward each other to gain time for a more leisurely pace. He saw her forehead against the car door window, he himself sitting behind the wheel, she standing outside. She was wearing a soft jacket with large knit pockets and a cloth belt around her hips. Behind the eyes, faces, mouths that they could hold so seriously commonplace was hidden the knowledge that they were here, on a sidewalk, in a car, and that this was a thing that could never afterwards be destroyed.

And he felt he was ready to do things for her that he would never do for his own sake. He felt terribly calm and at the same time open to a wind that made him ready for the decisive steps that would deprive him of everything. If Jenny was thinking of leaving him, he would take her by the shoulders, as a friend, with heavy tenderness, and be free himself—because he was constantly forcing himself outside the pattern, beyond what was predictable.

He didn't know where she was—in London, in Stockholm, in her lover's arms. He lived in his emotion, in a state that never abandoned him, and nevertheless he could see it was the result of circumstances, of his having met Jenny and of something having happened that hadn't existed for him earlier. Day after day he tried to formulate this for himself but couldn't quite grasp it.

And what she was doing and how that fit together with his life hardly made any difference. He wanted to tumble into her on time's descent. And then he smiled as if he held a bead of sun in his mouth, looked up from the gunwale, and saw he was alone. He saw a loose door leaning against a tree, a door without a house, so that when it was open it was still shut, and when it was shut it stayed open.

The
Places

THREE

EVENLY MATCHED

THE PEOPLE down below were small. They mirrored their faces in the shop windows, went closer and their faces grew larger. Closer still, and the reflection disappeared. Then they started to nibble on the glass.

There were also a few people playing instruments, and graffiti were being erased and rechalked on the public blackboard, and there was seriousness and music in the air. All over there were people trying to redefine their freedom.

Jan and Jenny had met several stories up in a skyscraper by Sergel Square. They looked at each other and at the city outside. His gaze was unsteady. His picture of her quivered like a shakily held camera. He couldn't get the right distance. Her smells were in reach.

"I dreamed about you," Jenny said. "In my sleep."

"I dream about classmates and clerks," he said. "You're too close. But I've missed you the whole time."

She had finally called, and by then she'd been in Stockholm for several days along with John Bringham, which was the name of her friend, lover, and whatever else he was. Jan himself had probably brought their plane into its landing pattern. Her silence hadn't been a whim. She had installed John at Nybro Quay.

"Why?" he said.

"Don't ask," Jenny said. "I mean, ask what you like, but I'll tell you anyway."

"There's a lot I don't know. I've tried to depend more on what you said than on all the silent days inbetween."

They kissed with their eyes open. They stood on the landing where the fire stairs turned between two floors. The doors out to the office corridors were closed. People rode up and down in elevators with ventilation and alarm buttons.

Pretty soon she would leave him and run down a couple of flights to the architects' office where John Bringham was in a conference. She measured the time for them. Their situation was determined by this borrowed time and by the hunger born of passing seconds and the pulse beneath the skin and by the fever that felt like home.

He held her pressed against him. He was suddenly so happy that he felt not glad but depressed at not being able to use his happiness right now.

Microbe in my hand, bun in the nebulae's pantry. . . . But no symbol made the world larger or smaller. No vague connection between chance and intention could be rummaged forth from the dictionary. Somewhere there was a border between her person and the love he felt for her. Somewhere a pliant barbed wire. What was difficult to capture, what coincided for a part but not all of the way, was her love and his love. How easily she could become someone else. How easily his love could lose its footing.

"You're very close to me right now," Jenny said. "You're locking me up, but I still feel free."

"I don't want to be free any more."

"But I'm destructive and amoral. You haven't had to see so much of that."

"You can do what you want to do. I'll only lean against you as long as you're still here."

"You're much more than only the part that has to do with

me. In London I kept telling myself: somewhere you're walking down a sidewalk, holding Gertrude's hand, you're not alone and that's good, your eyes are curious, taking in the buildings."

"And you've got John. Two stories down. How long have you known him?"

"Six years. He's been to Stockholm a couple of times, briefly. We've been to Paris together. Otherwise we see each other in England."

"Have you been happy with it?"

"With periodic sex, you mean, and nothing in particular in between? It's like being married for a few weeks every year."

"You just left. Without saying anything."

"For the sake of equilibrium. And because I had an assignment for the Department. You had Gertrude. I didn't want to take anything away from anyone. No one should be unhappy. Didn't you say it's a good idea to have several footholds?"

"Oh, what have you been doing the whole time?" Jan burst out.

"Not only what you're thinking. I sat in an armchair at John's and read. All of a sudden I put my hand out in the air and ran my fingers through your hair—you were sitting on the floor and didn't reach any higher. That unpremeditated gesture surprised me and I left the room. Were you just my imagination? Was I losing my mind? Your lips are wet. Everything I remembered of you was in the roots of my nails, they don't get clipped."

"You were far away."

"Don't worry. Presence doesn't have a chance against that kind of absence."

"Does he ask you what you do when you're in Stockholm?"

"No. We've said straight out that when we're together it's for the present. What came before and what comes after don't count. What collisions I've learned to live with! Seriousness and lack of it, foresight and from hand to mouth. And all of it's you. The last time we drove into town—it seems so long ago—in the ordinary daytime traffic, I should have asked you to put your hand on my stomach. Several times I've thought how nice that would have been."

"And still you just disappeared," Jan repeated.

"I was worried about Gertrude and you," Jenny answered. "And John. There are parts of him I've never understood. You and I certainly know each other better than he and I do after all these years. Now for the first time I realize how much in him I've never been able to respond to. I want to but I can't."

"Almost everything depends on how evenly matched people are. And they can't bring that about themselves."

"That's why I think about him. If I don't take other things seriously, I can't take you seriously either."

"Did you make love a lot?" he asked.

"I'll tell you more about that, soon. We've got so little time right now. But another thing I did was sit on a chair in my room and think how it could have held us both. I've held your hands against my breasts and I've kissed your fingers. I've pretended you were deep inside me and I put my arm tight around your back and said everything was the way it ought to be and I'm at home again. Now you know everything I've been doing."

They had so few minutes and he wanted to be in on her tiniest activities. He took her hand and looked at her cuticles and the wrinkles on her knuckles, searching for the impersonal that would contradict his amazement and defy his impression that she was a part of his identity, a thing he hooked onto and touched without owning.

With something like relief he discovered what seemed to be a fault in her appearance—her hair was as straight as an Indian's, her posture a little bent forward as if she were leaning into a wind. She's not terribly pretty, he tried to kid himself, as if he were about to be dragged into some fatal train of events.

But she came close to him on the landing, like a shadow

that unites with another one evening in a park, and the two of them go on to their appointed meeting place without stopping to think that they no longer need to seek it out.

And in her form and most of all in her face and eyes and mouth, its lines trembling between joy and disappointment, he saw a hunger and an eagerness that flowed together into a radiance, and perhaps it was the radiance he loved, because he knew he had the power to wipe it away as if he'd mistaken it for a shadow, and maybe too he could make it last, without her knowing it was the radiance that lasted.

With great caution he put his thumbs against her temples in order to feel her pulse. What he wanted was only the lightest contact—to approach something small and intimate from a great distance but not melt together with it, rather preserve the impression of having approached and finally being close.

He was feather-light elastic, bound to her with skin and thought and with the air deep in his lungs, a newcomer to the world. It didn't matter that it couldn't be described, something glided away and couldn't be grasped and immediately became something other than what had been before. . . .

He remembered her lips against his shoulder, she looked down his body as if it were a mile long. She fell slowly to her knees and butted her head into his stomach. He wanted to understand everything and couldn't understand anything, and she was silent as if she had arranged the world her own way and pressed her head against him so he couldn't see her face.

It was this they were doing—the lightest contact and the heaviest. She swallowed him, she wanted to take her lust into a darkness where she didn't need to see. His skin was tight in her mouth. Feelings stood still like the dragonfly before it lands on a blade of grass.

Just then the world was theirs. Then there was something afterwards, another world, just as there was supposed to be another world when they were dead.

The trembling song of carbon elements inside a bulb. As

inaccessible as a cricket. Don't break the glass, you can't get closer. Her head listened against his stomach. Something throbbed. No closer, then nothing would be heard. Now he hardly breathed, now he no longer tasted even vaguely of salt but of nothing at all.

He gropes across her forehead and eyelids, which are damp with sweat. His face tightens as if everything had long been petrified and motionless. The tall narrow building seems to sway slightly. But the things all around remain where they are. They are calm and dignified, just the opposite of they themselves.

"Your semen is thin gruel," Jenny said. "Without sugar. I'd like to be naked now."

He didn't know what he should say.

"It's funny no one uses the stairs," he mumbled. "Everyone takes the elevator."

He stood absolutely still. Down there far away was the square.

"The gestures are so few, the reasons for making them so many," Jenny said.

Jan wished that nothing else would happen.

"I have to go," she said.

Two stories down John Bringham would come out of his conference room and catch sight of Jenny's face, unmoved, unknown—on loan.

Justice can exist only between the equally matched, Jan thought. At least between themselves they can avoid being cruel and calculating, cautious and helpless.

A few minutes later he stood down on the sidewalk and pretended to look into a shop window. Jenny and John went by, first as a reflection that ended, then he turned around and looked after them.

An invisible protest group was singing nearby, or else it was a record in a record store with the door open. Two girls in jeans sat barefoot on the steps to the rooftop café over the Farmers' Market.

Jan felt light, as if he could at last meet the world without conditions. But it didn't work. Jenny stopped him. She was the condition.

T ON SCHEELEGATAN

HE SUN STOOD eight stories high over Kungsholm.

"We need someplace to meet while John's living with me on Nybro Quay," Jenny said matter-of-factly. "Have you got anything against my mother's place on Scheelegatan? I have a key. I go there anyway to take care of her plants."

Jenny's mother was a retired grammar school teacher from Västerås, now living in Stockholm, and she was spending the late summer at a boardinghouse on a lake in Södermanland.

Straight ahead of them was a bank of clouds like a bumper at the end of the street, but overhead the sky was clear. Jan pointed to the buildings along Kungsholmsgatan, the austere pale buildings from the thirties that had become dark with soot, the lion-yellow and the brick-red buildings with black leaves of sheet metal for balcony railings. Several stone heads with the pupils hollowed out like navels reminded him of the streets around Upplandsgatan.

The breeze was blowing through a room on the ground floor where the windows were open between the street and courtyard, lifting a white curtain and billowing it out like a balloon.

"I can see them falling apart, these houses," Jan said. "Brickwork and mortar, cracks and crumbs—like cells under a microscope. All the tiny electrical jolts, all the invisible bacteria. . . ."

Jenny didn't answer. She had two blue candles tied together by the wick, which they would clip apart and light. He was carrying a sack of food from a supermarket. Jenny was roughly as tall as he, so she seldom wore high heels. She walked almost like a boy, her shoulders moving in time with her hips. It excited him to watch her walk. He imagined there were secret hinges in her body that caused her to open herself to him.

"I guess we're unfaithful, both of us," Jenny said. "In all directions."

"But not in the usual sense of the word," Jan said. "You and Gertrude are my life. I might wish it were larger."

"At least you love two people. I don't. Which makes me more unfaithful—toward you. It seems unnecessary. But maybe it's the word's fault."

"All this talk about love as if it were the possession of one person, instead of both and everyone. What does he do?"

"John? He's an architect. Building consultant to the London City Council."

The interior of Kungsholm was a summer stage set, with bread crumbs left in closed bakeries, and yellowed jasmines, and on the roof of Ulrika Eleonora church, patina bleached by the lack of rain.

"Does he look like me?"

"No. He's smaller than you. A horse face with blue eyes. The corners of his mouth turned down a little. British, once you know that's what he is. His body is more supple, and softer, than you suspect."

On the notice board in the hall there was an incomprehensible map of the escape routes from Stockholm in case of enemy attack.

The apartment was abandoned and cool. The living room looked out on the courthouse and a store that sold burglar-proof locks. The flowered dust covers on the furniture stayed where they were most of the year, Jenny told him, and moving with accustomed steps, she took out teacups from a high glass cupboard. They'd bought some buns across from the Café Marx. She was pretty in her skirt and blouse. He padded around behind her and didn't want to let her out of his sight.

"It's as dark in here as it is in the fall," Jenny said. "Can you light a fire?"

Someone else had the watch at Arlanda this afternoon, and Jenny was high enough in the ranks that she could make up lost time in the evenings.

"Does he sleep in the same room with you?"

"Yes, but not in the same bed. He doesn't like that. Jan, you have to understand a couple of things. I don't love him the way I love you or the way you love Gertrude. But he's an assurance from the past—maybe everything's the way it was before, maybe nothing's happened if you only look at the surface. He's our friend. We share the responsibility for him, the way we do for Gertrude."

Jan got a fire going out of sapless silent logs.

"I want to be in on all of you," he said, "even what can make me unhappy or scared. I even want to be able to confront your desire, maybe, deep down, to overcome what you feel for me."

"Jan," she said, and put her hand on his neck. "You're an experience beyond what I thought I'd be allowed."

"They say, of course, that you only love what you don't own. I don't own you. And you can only be jealous of someone you own. So there's nothing odd about me loving you. When did you sleep with him the first time?"

"The night we met. It happened quite naturally. I don't

think I've ever regretted sleeping with anyone. I regret not doing it a few times."

"And this last time," he said, "didn't you stop to think that he might be crushed by the weight of both of us?"

"I tried to tell myself I was getting free of you through him. I didn't realize that no matter what I do it leads me to you. Since I can change everything into a language that reaches you. But John is still a fever in me, a periodic malaria. We've got a wonderful relationship . . . I mean physically."

Jan turned away, the blood draining from his face. Jenny pulled him to her and put her arms around his head so he could hardly hear what she was saying. The world stopped whirling, he saw her lips moving very rapidly, and a cheekbone with its freckled skin became a mountain that obscured his view. He heard her heart beating under his left ear.

"Among other things, that's why I can't regret it," she added. "Our bodies suit each other, but we don't speak the same language. Are you jealous anyway?"

"It was a sudden close-up," Jan said. "Not the thought of your body with someone else, but the thought that your eyes can look at someone else the same way they look at me. Though I really ought to be happy that you can make someone else equally happy. Damned sexuality—at times we damp it down, reduce it to habit, and at other times the very thought of it raises heaven and hell."

"We want to be claimed, made use of to the limit of our possibilities," Jenny said. "But the ability to love is different."

"People usually deal with jealousy by making demands or withdrawing into indifference. Both those ways are stupid. What I always want to feel is that no matter what you do you're no less close to me, *as long as you feel* you're close to me."

"Jealousy, to me," Jenny said, "is the fact that the big thing in your husband's life isn't you but someone else. But maybe that makes him unhappy too—no longer feeling that you're the big thing in his life. In that way some people have made jealousy a yardstick for love. I don't understand that. By those standards, I'm not in love with you. I don't want us to make great sacrifices for each other or want to do things just to make the other person happy. But it's as if you and I had seen exactly the same thing when we were born. The same picture. We can't help it. Maybe I'm wrong, but anyway I'm being misled by myself, not by you."

"How is it you get to be dependent on a person you didn't really need to be dependent on? Do they fill a space in a puzzle, or do they paste you together, or what is it?"

"You notice it depends on how you put it. Do we like someone because of what they really are? That sounds best anyway. Or for what they can make us feel? That sounds worse, it makes them seem like tools. But it's probably the same thing. Human beings are a kind of wish. I think you're handsome, though I'd never put you in a movie. But when you sit there exploring the edge of that ashtray with your finger, why there's something incredibly sensual in it and I get enormously turned on."

The telephone stood dumb, the grandfather clock had stopped. An upholstered electric cord crept along the molding. There was a soft, gaslike whispering in the bathroom pipes.

"Let's take our clothes off," he said. "We can sunbathe in the firelight."

"Why don't we take a bath?" she said.

They stood in water up to their ankles in her mother's bathtub and moved back and forth. It was their new pantomime— the Marquis de Sade and the housekeeper carousing in the tide.

Then she sat on his feet, they ran more water and she pressed up along his body and down onto his penis.

"As time goes by you get back the childishness you never had," Jenny said contentedly.

They moved into her mother's bedroom. Jan pulled off the heavy spread and opened the window. A ray of sun from between two chimneys reached a withered delphinium forgotten on the dressing table, where Jenny sat down and brushed her hair. He could see she was happy. She made a gesture as if to caress to life the flowers on the wallpaper. She put her hands under her breasts and lifted them slightly. She looked slim and almost boyish.

"I recklessly count on the fact that you understand everything," she said. "There's something about you that will make a lot of people love you. If you let them."

"It seems to me the only way I could really be unfaithful to you would be to keep a part of my experience to myself. For once in my life, no rationalizations, no qualifications. . . ."

Then she told him that after their first night, in the car at Arlanda, she had come back to town and dashed around like a schoolgirl in the morning rush. She'd bought a flower and a pot, ready to burst at being so loved. And filled with generosity —as long as this continued she begrudged him nothing else. But she told him about it only now, on Scheelegatan.

"It was different in London about a week ago," she said. "I was walking along the Thames near Blackfriar's. I'd had dinner with John and he was at a meeting. The air was damp and soft and felt good on my face. There was a light in a surgical instrument store I often pass. Next to it was another store that sells old autographs and manuscripts. When it's dark and you've had a little to drink you can imagine the river is the sea. And then in addition I tried to imagine you didn't exist. Not the way I thought, at least. My senses and my reason could have deceived me, after all. It's happened before. When I was married I used to tell myself: how I need Johan's need for me! But now I don't want such needs. I could see trees in the yards and those tall reflecting studio windows. How easy it would be to end up on the outside of everything, to lose the instinct for self-preservation, to become afraid of people. You're standing outside a door but you don't ring the bell. You go around feeling sorry for yourself and get put down by the people who've organized their lives sensibly."

He didn't answer but kissed both her nipples at once.

"How badly we could have hurt each other," she said, "if this were only a game for one of us. Now it feels as if we were getting light from the same battery."

"I never get used to you," he said into the hollow of her throat. "It feels ancient and new. You're there in everything—as if I were making a film and putting your face on all the characters. I even want to see your sleepy face when you're coming from John."

"We've been given eyes and mouths and sex organs to investigate the world with. After all there's only us, no gods."

She created new erogenous zones on his body, caressed his knees with such concentration that he suddenly had to enter her, and he pressed himself so close to her it didn't matter who was who.

Then they looked at her mother's snapshots of Jenny. He lay naked on his stomach and she sat beside him tailor-fashion. He'd never wanted to have a picture of her, hardly cared what she looked like as a child. Some of them were quite recent—there was the face she had standing by the glass doors at Arlanda. He felt warm and excited by that. She was both a picture and the person sitting beside him on the sheet, his excitement covered them both.

Those first times they met he felt he knew a lot and nothing about her. Later on, she started to tell him about herself, and after a while he knew nothing but what she told. Then he crouched on the starting line—to catch up with what he had known before.

Jenny jumped up and found whisky in a cupboard. They drank out of her grandfather's glasses. Sweden in the nineties —brandy-capacious Masonic gentlemen gone rigid for their photograph beneath the lodge's portrait of the king, already aging in their forties, droopily moustached and to all appearances womanless.

The fire had gone out, but she lit the thin blue candles. Jan stalked around undressed in the apartment and thought about Jenny's mother at a boardinghouse on a lake. There was a pile of green grade books in a cupboard—hundreds of children would never forget her. Jenny looked at the picture of her father.

"Do you know a thing that scares me? The way your feet start slipping, it's all downhill, and you get dumber and sicker and touchier. . . . I think I'm afraid of being reincarnated as a person with a hellish life, a person who's always on the wrong side of the fence and knows it."

"You're class conscious," Jan said. "You'd like to belong to that enormous minority that looks in the weekly magazines to be sure they're sitting in the right kind of clothes in the right kind of home, just in case the Day of Judgment is waiting at the door."

"Almost, but not quite," Jenny said. "That isn't what I meant. No, it's what I was thinking that day along the Thames —can I depend on my senses and my reason? Am I halfway senile already? Is there something I've completely forgotten to take into account? Look at Papa! He was an embezzler. He had his reasons, and I'm sure he never would have done it again, but he couldn't see the consequences. He was thrown out of the bar, out of society, and out of his home. He wasn't prepared, all trace of him was obliterated, and so he killed himself, since he'd sort of disappeared already."

"I feel enormously in possession of my senses," Jan said.

"That's what makes me wonder. When I start to lose my grip, will I notice? And panic? Or will I just gradually land on the outskirts, beyond my field of vision? Embezzlement sets in. Our lives are so damned short and indistinct. I love you, and that's why I'm afraid."

There were stripes of bird droppings on the metal roof across the street. In the apartment were things Jenny remembered from her childhood—the lace tablecloth on a round alder-root table, the upright piano in veined veneer with several oval photographs of women, a bookcase with Strindberg and Bernard Shaw, *Buddenbrooks* and *Les Thibaults*. And in the kitchen, a tub, its bottom warmed by the sun.

"If I could give you life insurance, a bulletproof vest," Jan said. "But I can't. I'd like to discover a new chemical compound. A substance that would correspond to feelings."

He held her close to him. Her nipples tickled his lowest rib. She laughed as if she'd come home free in a game of hide-and-seek.

"The strawberries," she said. "We forgot them. We can crush them with sugar. And you can be a new Scheele. From Scheelegatan. Someone who discovers an element or a new organic compound. What was it he discovered? Something about the composition of light."

Jan was almost hurt by Jenny's sudden frivolity.

"Watch out. What we've already invented may be enough."

"If we knew what it was. . . ."

"The girl in the factory who paints the numbers on watches, she can't feel how deeply the radium has penetrated her marrow. And if it's measured for her, it doesn't tell her anything. And I . . . I don't know myself. . . ."

THE METEOROLOGIST'S DREAM

COFFEE IN THE TOWER at Arlanda. Jan had called down to Eklund, the meteorologist who worked on the floor below traffic control.

"You're an absolutely necessary man," Jan said, "since the

world consists of barely perceptible pressures and complicated light effects and unanalyzed noise."

Eklund poured coffee into the paper cups and pondered the sea-green metal roof.

"If we had a good telescope," he said, "we could see a dim blue point of light near Cygnus."

"Radio star?" Jan asked.

"Forty-five pulsations a minute. The deviation is one ten-millionth of a second a month. A ticking star, a neutron star maybe, no one knows for sure."

"Pretty soon we'll have to get weather reports from space," Jansson said.

"The telescope gathers up the starlight, conveys it to other instruments, writes it into the journal. The stars are in the statistics too—their birthrate and mortality, their ecology, life expectancy, chemical gender. The spectrum dissects their light like a language."

"Have you seen my watch?" Jansson asked.

It was Swiss, smaller faces built into a larger one, and it could show everything from the air pressure over the Azores to the minute and second at whatever meridian he found himself.

"It takes you awhile to see what time it is," Jan said.

"Are these rusks on exhibition?" Eklund asked.

"They're all yours and ought to be dunked," Jansson said. "There's a lot going on over our heads."

"It's easy to imagine little low-browed ape heads on the people getting out of that Caravelle down there," Jan said.

"One of the ramp agents told me he was raised on those old-fashioned pinup magazines where the girls are all hairless," Jansson said, "so the first time he saw his wife naked he thought she was a monster."

"Speaking of surprises," Jan said, "doctors thought the first railroad passengers would go insane from the speed. Who knows what'll happen to us?"

"I had a surprise recently," Jansson went on. "My mother in Ängelholm sent me some stuffed cabbage. She doesn't have any faith in my wife's cooking. I got this notice to pick up a package at the post office, and I knew what it was, so I told her on the phone they were delicious, before I went to get them. Then I forgot all about it. A couple weeks later there's Mother on the phone—she'd got a notice of a package returned, picked it up, and found her stuffed cabbage, rancid of course."

"A catastrophe whose consequences can be appreciated," Eklund commented. "But did you know they've bored through the Antarctic ice sheet? At the bottom, next to the rock, they found water, melted by the pressure of the ice above it. More and more ice and snow produces more and more water."

"My wife's a cartographer," Jansson said. "Now all of a sudden she's going to study architecture. I do all the cooking, she isn't very practical. When I'm on the night shift I leave her dinner in the freezer."

"That explains the stuffed cabbage," said the meteorologist.

"She gives me a lot of surprises. I met her in Rome, on a trip I got from the company. She's Finnish. What does your wife do, Jan? You are married, aren't you?"

It struck Jan that Jansson didn't know anything about his private life, though they'd worked together a couple of years. He didn't wear a ring.

"She gives me a lot of surprises too," he said. "But she does cook. And I didn't meet her on one of your barter trips. She works on reports. She's a scientist. She shakes her head at me. She . . . ."

He suddenly realized he was talking about both Gertrude and Jenny.

"One has to be available in several places at once," Eklund said.

Only the double life. . . . At first he resisted doubleness like one of the body's organs thrusting out a foreign object. Gradually he had encapsulated the double life like a needle in a tapestry.

He looked at the others, his colleagues. What priorities did feeling take? He clenched his hand as if everything that went on between him and Jenny and Gertrude could be compressed to a bright hard stone.

"There's a bat coming toward us," Jansson pointed.

"In the ground wind from the west-southwest. And good visibility," said Eklund, raising himself half out of his rickety folding chair. "You can just see the Märsta water tower four and a half miles away."

"It's the Finnair from Åland," Jan said. "He can handle it by himself. We gave him his pattern right after he took off."

But if something went wrong? In that moment when you no longer figured you were going to make it—did life then expand to a panorama, deepen to a flood? Jan believed it narrowed to something insignificant: the stump of a runway, a little cement, some bits of gravel, dead grass.

"All the worst things we can think of, someone has already gone through," he said. "There are no imagined horrors that haven't already occurred in reality with human beings as the victims."

The meteorologist's eyes sat close together as if they'd really wanted to be a single eye. "I have to tell you a dream I had," he said, "because it took place up here in the tower. I was cleaning that window with a rag. I was looking through it. And then I saw other panes beyond it, dirty or covered with snow. In certain places you could see fine, it would be transparent for a way, but on the whole you couldn't see out. It wasn't like in an elevator with mirrors on both sides where you look out into a narrowing gallery of repetitions. I had a spray bottle too, but it didn't help. And I kept thinking a plane might come, or a whole invasion of them."

"Our windows are always clean," Jansson said. "What you saw was the fog around the Märsta water tower."

"A common sort of dream," Jan said. "The machines, all the computers down in the control room—you forgot about them. You thought it all depended on your eyes, and they didn't work because you couldn't find what they were supposed to see."

"You didn't realize you'd wiped it clean," Jansson said. "It's not the window's fault if it's foggy outside."

"That dream was hard work," the meteorologist said. "I wasn't hired to do your cleaning for you. And then I sit here today with my weather map and I'm supposed to make a summary and inform the prediction room. Lowest QNH 980 MB. That's my world, professionally. Just like you have yours. It has to be laid over other maps like tracing paper in order to be of any use. And those maps in turn are measured against other information, and then we arrive at some sort of knowledge. Meanwhile we have to shovel aside a lot of irrelevant nonsense. Because if we welcomed every different thought, we wouldn't function for long. And then we act according to that knowledge, even if it's incomplete, because we have to act in any case."

"Information is a sign of life," Jan said. "Other people want to get to us and alter our observations. The air around us vibrates. Maybe everything is a consciously directed train of events."

"If so, I suspect Deutscher Wetterdienst in Frankfurt and their main teleprinter, Mufax Recorder," Jansson said. "When its salt precipitates on paper there's no spicier dish in the world."

"The recipe is secret," said the meteorologist resignedly.

His nostrils dilated as if he were on the scent of something rotten.

"That pale moon out there is one and one-third light seconds away," he said. "But the part of the universe we can survey is seventeen thousand million light-years in diameter. We can't reckon on coincidence there. All the breathing space we have is right here on this earth. And it doesn't seem to be enough."

"There's always a chance collision," Jansson burst out. "Just think of the way I met my wife."

"We know," Jan said.

"And how did you meet yours?"

"Not so much by chance. We'd known each other for years."

"As long as we stay on earth," said the meteorologist, "nothing that happens is entirely unbelievable."

Jan suddenly felt Jenny's thighs beneath his hands. He wanted to go to her, all the time. He thought about those Donald Duck films where some character runs out of a house right through the wall, leaving his outline in the bricks.

It was as if he were receiving inaudible orders and obeyed the blinkings of an instrument panel that only he could see.

"I was thinking about those people boarding Lufthansa down there," he said instead. "We show them a part of the way with signals. Then they get off in Düsseldorf or Milan or Beirut, in the middle of the night, a bus takes them to a terminal, a taxi drives them to an unknown hotel. They don't know what the city looks like, they submerge in an organism more complicated than they are, they're swallowed by a giant whale. And in the belly of the whale there's a room, a carafe of water on a dresser, a bed lamp that doesn't work, footsteps in the corridor, emergency fire instructions in five languages, and the night sounds that change every hour. The next day they get a map from the desk and find the main street and so everything becomes recognizable and ties itself together. They forget their lost feeling and don't figure on any further surprises."

Then he remembered how Jenny had come to Arlanda—late one afternoon in the middle of his routine.

"Our experience would be different if we could get more of the brain's ganglion cells to work," the meteorologist said. "Because in part the world looks the way we think it looks, the way we picture it, the way we see the reality we think we've explored. Partly, I say. Because if the world were only a model, then we wouldn't get tripped up."

Eklund built little tents of matchsticks while he talked. On the ramps down on the airfield the gray trucks of the Air Traffic Department mingled with the blue cargo carts from SAS.

"I want to go to Lapland," he went on impatiently. "Pick cloudberries and blueberries, stand in the water up to my ankles and look for salmon, pull up a boat among the birch roots on a rocky point, throw myself down in the heather. The air and the wind get to you without being measured. Make coffee. Take a few pictures. There are only certain things I take—bark and lichens and moss, grass that's moving. A low and all too personal perspective."

The other two had fallen dumb. Eklund stared out through the greenish window.

"Pretty soon it'll be September, at least in the almanac. For that matter, you're more insulated up here than I am."

"And more air-conditioned," Jansson said. "Because of the equipment."

"I mean the jet engines bother me," Eklund said. "My wrist bones are coming loose, my hands are starting to get shaky."

"You're spared the most dangerous sound," Jan consoled him. "There's a siren that sounds the lowest E on the piano. That note could split the tower. There's an infra-tone that gets going in the tower so it vibrates like an organ pipe. It would make our stomachs shake. We'd get nauseous, stop thinking and panic."

"There's something like that going on," said the meteorologist gloomily.

"Why don't we quit?" Jansson asked.

"We haven't taken any monastic vows," Eklund said. "We could make our contributions somewhere else."

"We're in the same position as most other people, neither essential nor free," Jan said.

It seemed to him that a lot of things he used to care about had come loose from their frames, been forced out by the pressure. Only the frame was left, the regulating lights on the instrument panel, vehicle control, the magnetic tapes where he recorded the traffic.

He recognized everything around him, yet not completely—

tall trees were bushes. Jenny existed within him. Without that captivity, his feeling of freedom would vanish faster than a chalk mark from the wall of a building.

"The coffee's gone," said the meteorologist, straightening his tie. "Thanks for the company."

"Don't mention it," Jan said. "See you around."

"No one ever came to see me before I put up that sign, 'Official Business Only.' Now nobody even bothers to knock."

Jan felt in a curious way that he had access to something vital that wasn't his.

Maybe some spray fluid that made the surrounding world more transparent. He didn't know for sure.

He couldn't talk about it. His friends didn't notice anything. What did he know about them? There's never any shortage of secrets.

It's hard to see the hallmark on the inside of a thin ring that's been worn by skin and soap and sweat.

FROG SPIT

JAN BACKMAN WENT into the Nybro Pavilion to see what Stockholm was going to look like in a few years— serpentines of traffic over bumpy plaster. An exercise in Gestalt psychology. The scale was so small that the changes themselves didn't seem great.

He looked up toward Jenny's building, her windows, four stories up. John Bringham lived there. That was part of the exercise.

Then through the glass he caught sight of them coming out the door. They were strolling arm in arm like a married couple, Jenny with her head a little on one side. Instead of jealousy, Jan felt a beautiful distance—let them go, they belong together, he looks nice, there's so much else in life. He noticed with pleasure that he begrudged her nothing. Maybe people were interchangeable pieces in an erector set, instead of in a puzzle.

Jenny and John walked the few steps to the Strand Hotel. And Jan Backman became James Bond, aloof, exploring the possibilities of reaching the focal point in a few simple moves. First, surveillance and information.

Minutes later he called from Jenny's apartment, to which he had the key. He gave the headwaiter a description of a newly arrived couple that hadn't had time to order. Jenny came to the phone out of breath.

"This is Secretary Llife at the Department of the Environment," he announced.

"No, it's you," she cried. "Llife is a woman."

"She's working overtime out in Solna and wants some information."

"But how did she find me?"

"You told her this afternoon that you might be at the Strand."

"OK, then, I did. Actually we hadn't really planned to come here."

"I don't want to make trouble for you," he said. "Or destroy the mood, either."

He asked her if she was unchanged and intact. Had a shadow fallen over them, or was there a singing in her as well?

"I feel like I'm completely yours," she burst out right away. "Are you crying?"

"Only because I'm so happy. John's going to wonder what's happened. Still he makes me happy too. But . . . since Llife doesn't know I'm here, how did you . . . ?"

He told her. In the pavilion with the city of the future we see James Bond on the threshold of a hasty attack, an impulsive plan. . . . The combination being, however, virtually risk-free, unless you count the unpredictable in her reaction. Jenny liked his cunning more than his logic.

"So you're up in my apartment. But what if we'd come back?"

"Now you can stay at the Strand awhile," he said. "Maybe I'll take a shower and go lie down in your bed. I remember how it feels."

He heard her hide-and-seek laugh from Scheelegatan.

"Tell me, can you take me the way I am?" she asked with haste in her voice. "Guilt feelings are so foreign to me. I was thinking about openness today, and about marriage and about how much we think we know about people. You have to have the strength to find out what's happening to the other person and to account for what's happening to you yourself—but that sort of thing can be uncomfortable and dangerous."

"You're using John to build a wall against me, because it gives you better balance. But that's conventional, just as much as . . . ."

He stopped himself. Just as conventional as the fact that he and Gertrude weren't supposed to be able to be in love because they happened to be brother and sister.

"John's no wall," Jenny answered. "I'd like to give you the responsibility for everything I do and don't do. It's true to a great extent, you've made me and the atmosphere I live in now. Actions that look almost schizophrenic from the outside are really happening within your sphere. What does it look like in my room?"

"It's nice and clean. Don't worry, you two haven't left a lot of evidence around."

"Don't be smart. Pull out a hair and leave it on my pillow. Something only I'll notice."

"I can see your sherry glasses. And I thought you preferred whisky. I'll put them out in the kitchen, so only you'll know how they got there. Are you sitting across from each other? Do you know what you're going to have?"

"Yes and no, respectively. My heart's pounding from talking to you. Otherwise I'm quite happy and calm. Here I am—no one's property, lots of nice-looking men. Sort of playing games with freedom—maybe the fault of a strict upbringing."

"We're playing games too, you and I," Jan said. "We're making so little effort it's getting to be serious."

John comes home with me, I've known him a long time, and suddenly we very clearly want each other. That's what I want you to understand. My soul isn't in it, but the physical thing is enough. Tea and intercourse. Our eyes don't meet like yours and mine do, it doesn't have anything to do with you and me. You didn't really exist that evening, you were at the Water Palace, far away, with Gertrude. And that was good. I could be fixed on you in a helpless way. I'm manufacturing balance wheels, not walls. But you're right it seems conventional. Why are you so quiet?"

"I'm lying in your bed listening. It's lucky you have the kind of voice you have."

She said she could explain herself without barricades for the first time in her life. He didn't let any details put him off. He was determined to live up to her expectations.

"We need the other people, Jan," she said. "If we were shut up in a mine shaft, alone, we wouldn't love each other."

"I know that now," he said. "I used to think people fell in love so they wouldn't have to see the others."

Their life together was a giant basket of loose, elastic, willow twigs—other people's light shone through.

"It's not worth talking anymore," he said. "Put on your best conference face now."

"I'll pretend I went to the ladies' room. Run down here as fast as you can!"

He met her on the sidewalk. They embraced each other hard and let go almost in the same instant. She ran her hands across his cheeks and shoulders, borrowing his gesture from the day they met. Then for a second she held out her hands as if she were balancing a globe in each palm.

He breathed the fresh air of deceit from Nybro Bay. At the same time he felt for all of them a tenderness so great he felt he could afford to live without them. He watched Jenny disappear through the lobby door. He heard the restaurant music in the distance. His upper lip was still wet from her tongue. He looked at the city without anxiety, as if it and he had both received a temporary respite from the future.

Along toward three in the morning, Jenny called Upplandsgatan. She knew he was sleeping there alone. She was using the jack in the kitchen. He was familiar with her view—the courtyard in pale gray light, near the water but still hidden in a desert of stone. During the day the shadows of the pupils at the Ballet Academy, at night the silence of the doves.

"What do you have on?" he wondered.

"Striped pajamas, bright yellow and green."

"I saw them under your pillow."

"And your slippers. There, now I've kicked them off."

"To think we're in the same city! I'd really like to come over."

"Don't! You were just here. It'll be morning soon."

"But almost everyone's asleep right now. Except Jansson, who's got the night shift in the tower."

"I'd like to put a glass cover over the city," Jenny whispered. "So everything goes quiet. And in the silence everything could be realized, every wish and desire could be put to use without hurting anyone or anything."

"Did you lock the door?"

"Yes. No one'll come. It's just us. And the yard is empty."

"I know what your stomach looks like," Jan said. "Tan, with a little white place where the skin was shaded around your navel."

"And a big fold, because I'm sitting bunched up on the counter with my forehead on my knees."

"I'm standing here trying to flatten myself down on the edge of a window jamb. I need to. Now I'm lighting a candle. Though it's fairly light, and the ceilings are high. You've never been here. I'm imagining I've got my arm around your waist and my hand inside your pajamas."

"I had a sentimental dream just now," Jenny said. "I was sitting in a train compartment and fell asleep and my head fell down on the shoulder of the man sitting next to me, and he lowered his newspaper so fast it woke me up, and it was you."

Some dried, yellow, long-stemmed asters that Gertrude had put in a pot moved in the breeze from the hill on Upplandsgatan.

"My whole body wants to hug you," Jenny said. "I'm sitting here all hunched up like a turtle from wanting to surround you."

"I'm going to bite your nipples pretty soon. I can feel what it's like to pull your blouse out of your skirt, it's easier with a loose top. I'm holding your right leg just above the knee and lifting it out of your pants. You're the only person I know all that about—in just that way."

"It makes me damp between the legs to hear you say it. I can't understand how I can make *you* happy. Like shining a flashlight on the sun."

"It's your voice that turns me on."

"It seems so exorbitant that we're so hungry," she said. "The sensual pleasure escalates more and more, even though I try to tell myself it ought to be the other way around—a de-escalation to save the openness and the communication and the intimacy."

"Sometimes it seems to me nothing bad can happen to me as long as you exist," Jan said.

"How does your lightness manage to bear my weight? My experience has been more bitter and more brutal, it can't speak with your kind of innocence. I could make you dislike me just in order to protect you."

"Don't say that," he said. "You exist. Every square inch of your body knows my fingers and my mouth and my skin. My lips and your lips and your other lips. One of your breasts is against my cheek, your nipple's in the corner of my eye. Of course I want to use you, as much as I can, till you've run yourself tired and panting in the streets, till you've caught cold in back seats all around Arlanda. . . ."

"It's awful of me to be so realistic," she said. "I'm an unbridled pornographer. I can feel your cock in my ear. The muscles of my cunt are clenching like a fist. I could make love to a doll or a stick of wood. Where are you now?"

"I'm sitting on the edge of the bed. I'm looking down at the old, worn parquet floor I painted gray one time while Gertrude supervised."

"I'm sitting with my back against the cupboard and my feet in the sink," Jenny said. "I feel like a flood."

"Touch yourself a little between your legs. It's my hand."

"Yes, if you'll touch yourself for me."

"I hardly need to."

"It feels like I'm carrying you inside me like security," Jenny said. "So we don't need to live the same life. We look at each other. We know who we are."

"I'm running my lips over your body till I'm down between your legs. I saw some lambs once, licking up water that was trickling out of a wall of rock."

"Sometimes I can hardly tell the difference between the tips of my fingers and the point of your penis. It must feel the same for both of us. Maybe all that about the difference between the sexes is just an invention. Though if we could trade sexes then I could come into you, and that would be fun."

"We're us," he said. "And the other people who know us. . . . A person can be such different things at the same time."

"Maybe there aren't so many other people involved in what we're doing. If we told them, they wouldn't recognize themselves. They might be hurt. That makes me unhappy."

"Maybe it isn't that way at all. We don't know."

"We've gone beyond all the ideas about what people should and shouldn't do. We're damned, we'll have to suffer for this."

"Maybe this kind of weightless happiness can't go unpunished, not even for a moment, because it's a moment we'll want to come back to."

But he wasn't sure he believed what he was saying.

"When I realized I loved you," Jenny said, "I started to like my own body too. Since you wanted me, I looked at myself and was happy. I masturbate now and then, I never used to. That's because my body is more alive now, I can like it the way you do, I want to touch myself."

"That's good," he said. "You're so hypnotically close to me. I can feel exactly how your skin follows your thigh."

"I'll take off the pants," she said. "They're in the way."

"Then I will too."

They said nothing, and the silence felt like an object you could show someone.

"Are you still there?" he whispered.

"Yes. It feels so good. I've never done this before. I've found that soft spot under your balls."

He heard her breathing into the phone.

"I'm eating your breath," he said. "Used air."

"I'd like to watch you come. I've never seen that."

"You can now."

"Wait for me."

"I can see your toes curling down in the sink," he said. "My fingers want to come into you a little way. It feels slightly rough right there. At the same time I'm cupping my whole hand over it like a cap."

"Put your kneecaps against mine, and open your palms. Like that. It's so good you like to come in me."

He felt the tickle in his backbone right before, and for a moment he couldn't keep his eyes open, just for an instant he lost her and landed across a border far away in some indefinable place. But only briefly—he squeezed the receiver, he heard her voice, he was in the pupil of her eye.

"Love, how do you feel? You're not sorry?"

"My body is as wet as yours," he said.

"Go get a towel," she said. "I'll wait."

He did.

"Are you lying in bed now?" she asked when he was back.

"A little frog spit on a sheet. That's all we are."

But his voice didn't sound serious.

"Oh, it seems to me I have all of you in me," she said. "I'm sitting hunched up like a knobby turnip on your knee."

"Was it good for you?"

"I mostly felt how it was for you. I forgot about the orgasm. I only have them once in a while. Do you care very much?"

"No."

"It doesn't matter to me. It feels so awfully good. I've jumped down on the floor now and put on my pajama bottoms. I'm dancing with the phone in my hand. Like a crane, because cranes always dance from joy or excitement or gratitude."

"It's a little lighter now. The street light is stronger on the ceiling over here than in your room, you live higher up. This is the quietest time of the day. I can hear something from down toward Norra Bantorget, or else it's you singing in me like an old worn record."

"Shall we hang up now?"

"Yes. Don't dream anything unpleasant. Sleep tight."

"Go to sleep now, darling. Everything will be fine. We've already managed the hardest part—we've found each other."

THE DEVIL BY NAME

THE HOTEL WAS ON Gamla Brogatan. In the entranceway there was a frieze with a plaster angel. Jan Backman blew in its mouth and powder whirled out between the angel's lips and met his breath. A motherly woman behind a window in a booth on the landing sized up and registered the guest before letting him into the narrow corridors.

Jenny had called Arlanda from the Department of the Environment and asked him to meet her at the hotel. Her mother had come back to Scheelegatan from her boardinghouse in Södermanland. John Bringham was still living at Nybro Quay.

"Room 33," the woman said, looking as if she expected him. "We don't have any hot drinks. Just Pommac and Zingo. We have to vacate the building in a month or so."

Jenny's face was collected and narrow. She was wearing a beige corduroy dress with red buttons down the front. She smiled at him with polite esteem as if he'd been a distant acquaintance. He could see she'd been crying.

"What's happened?"

"I'm going to stay here a couple of nights. John has to calm down. We had a terrible scene all night long. I went to work without having slept a wink. He doesn't know where I am. Sit here next to me against the headboard so we can see out. I want to talk for a long time. How do you like the room? It's thirty crowns a day."

Two beds took up most of it. A worn-out buffalo hide armchair from some bankrupt estate, and a shiny varnished birch chair from one of the installment-plan stores in the Klara district. A clothes hook on the door, another in the process of coming out of the wall. A scorch mark on the panel by the bed lamp. A dark green terrycloth towel by the wash basin, and a white tile stove.

He put his arm around her and rubbed his finger on the faint marks her shoulder strap left on her collarbone. The covers were flowery and old-fashioned, the sheets threadbare. The outside wall followed the angle of the roof. They were in the middle of Stockholm. Its seashell roar could be heard in the distance.

"I've got friends," Jenny said. "I didn't have to come to a hotel. I could have asked Gertrude to let me stay at the Water Palace, couldn't I?"

"Of course. You could sit and chat as if you'd always known each other, and buy ice cream at the store and go swimming. And you could tell her all about John. . . ."

"No. I want to tell you."

They sat leaning against each other, and he now and then caressed her arm or the back of her neck as she talked. The skyscrapers in Hötorget could have been pillars of salt against the sky. A storm was gathering over the city. The sun was shining with a smoky, phosphorous light. He had nothing to say.

John wanted me to go to London with him. Take a couple of months off. His treat. We've done it before. If I hadn't said anything, nothing would have happened. I would have gone to London and thought a part of me is in love with him. But I had to choose. I could have been evasive.

I heard myself saying clearly and distinctly that I'm in love with a married man here in Stockholm. Can you imagine that?

There are choices that deal out death in every direction even as they're being made. They're meaningless and dishonest, because they suffocate something alive inside you.

I don't want to rob anyone of anything. You won't have to choose. There's so much that's indispensable on our separate sides. We can't weed out the one for the sake of the other.

Only we can judge what we do to each other. Measured by other people's standards it might seem evil or good or stupid. What I do has no significance until it bounces off someone else. I realized that something was going to happen when I confessed to John. But I forget to think how much of it is determined by customs and upbringing. I count on people understanding more than they do.

I can't let you meet him. He could hurt Gertrude. We don't know anything about passions. Maybe he's one of those people who don't really fall in love until he finds out I've been unfaithful to him. He might want revenge if he thinks everything is lost. You can hear how conventional and awful it sounds. Lost, revenge, unfaithful. . . . You're not going to lose me like a crystal vase slipping out of your hands. I won't be unfaithful to you no matter how many people I sleep with. We can't cope with indifference, but we ought to be able to flout some of the patterns of behavior.

Oh Jan, you can't imagine how people can change. John's and my frankness fell apart because it consisted of discretion. We've never promised each other anything. But now it's as if we had, by being together for so long. We're close friends. But we've never been as open as you and I were after only a few days.

You can live with someone consciously and evenly matched, the same on both sides. You can live in doubleness, but not in inequality.

John cried and smashed that blue apothecary's flask and stamped on records and ripped up a dress in the closet. He said I'd never spoken an honest word and he could never believe me again. I couldn't see him, he'd become so distant. It was you I heard, whistling in the kitchen. I wanted to go and bite your finger. And watch the corners of your mouth flicker between smiling and seriousness. And still I didn't want to let you take his place, that was too simple, you can't shift around just like that.

There wasn't any logic in his jealousy. Of course jealousy doesn't have anything to do with logic. But I began to suspect there wasn't any love in it either, well, yes, for himself. Where did I come into this drama? His outbursts only made me tired. When a person you like very much is suffering, you get overcome with anxiety because in spite of everything you can't feel his pain the way he does himself. I'm a little bit of a murderer. Suddenly he's intruding on me, wants to be with me everywhere. And I feel loveless and deceitful, a heart of ice. My eyes and ears stop functioning, nothing gets to me. It seems to me I can live without either one of you. All of a sudden investigating natural resources has a lot more to say to me. It is actually more important, gentlemen. Think about that if you sometime. . . . with Gertrude. . . . No, don't ever put her through this!

I understand your love for Gertrude partly thanks to John. It's just that sometimes I don't know what I'm going to do with my understanding. I love you. Therefore I want to identify with you at any price. I've rarely liked anyone as much as Gertrude after so short a time. Not counting you. So if you hurt her I'll have to take care of her.

Love is a desire to understand someone so well that nothing he does can surprise you or scare you.

Jealousy is the opposite of love—a twisted self-love, a stinginess. Just when I'm feeling daring and new, I sink down in a swamp of emotional porridge, I'm full of a sickly desire to possess, and I go off to London and I don't see you wandering around in Sundbyberg but only curling up with Gertrude.

What's the matter with me? First I tell you about John and how wonderful it can be with him. I almost imagine I have John, periodically, the way you have Gertrude constantly. And I love you and don't belong to anyone and the one doesn't exclude the other, you know that yourself. And then I tell John what he suspects—that I'm in love with someone else. And then his blueprints fall apart, he's been following hidden maps, and the Labour party and his new sideburns and the Architectural Design Centre don't help.

I could exercise more self-control. I didn't have to drag you into everything. It's often a bore to find out what people are like and how they see themselves. But there's a lot I don't have the strength to tell you. I've known John for a long time. His violence now may depend on other things too. He's worried about his age. Unnecessarily, I think, but that's probably lack of empathy. My whole existence, my job, make him unsure of himself. I haven't been serious enough. But just the right amount of irresponsibility can be as hard to master as his emancipated theories. Something in me may have made him feel exposed and insecure.

If love is worthless simply because it doesn't last forever, then life must be worthless for the same reason.

My husband and I had a good sex life, but in the end that's all there was. I've liked sleeping with John and talking to him, but only up to a limit. I didn't really know the limit was there until I met you, and you suddenly pulled me across the chalk mark. That's why I'm afraid of hurting you. I used John like a balance wheel against Gertrude, that was wrong. And I can't use you at all.

One morning in London, just recently, I put a greasy kettle on the gas, I remember square milk bottles standing out on the sidewalk and the mail lying there in a bundle. I took everything down to John's kitchen, opened a plastic package of bacon, eggs from Sussex, cream from Devon. That huge city was all around me with similar holy morning rituals.

And I wondered if you were awake, if you were also up making tea, and then it didn't feel as if I'd fled there, there were no problems, only closeness, I was in an unbreakable glass fortress and my happiness sparkled, and my womb was pinched with longing for you to come right into me without caring what I felt.

I thought you were happy and hardly missed me. I walked around London on the verge of a strange untested sensation. I was at an anti-Greek rally in Trafalgar Square. At Speakers Corner there was a fat African dancing like a ball—the Day of

Judgment is upon us, he cried, it's this very day today. Would he be back the next Sunday with the same message? For what purpose had they been invented, all these people and dogs, this grass, this city?

That's how thin the ground is. Suddenly it goes out from under. I never count on that, and yet I've been through it before. The surface you and I are walking on can crack at any moment. It could happen to you and Gertrude, and it would be my fault.

John warned me about guilt and humiliation and pain. He made me see with other people's eyes how you and Gertrude are happily married and I'm the one who's intruding. You can hear what conventional ideas I slip into. And then I get so I don't want to see you any more—mostly for your sake. You don't know what bubbles up from the bottom, the rage and the contempt. A human being becomes tiny and unreal, and yet just now I was holding him in my arms and we were rocked by the same warmth.

A person can be wounded by a passion when he feels it and when he stops feeling it. In war, a whole people becomes alien and so you can do anything to them. When my father killed himself it was because his own feelings humiliated him as badly as his social predicament. And when I think about what I might subject you and Gertrude to. . . .

Oh, Jan, I get bitter when I look back. At first the important thing was love. The important thing was to get a boy. Now it's easier to feel passion for ideas as well, for a great work. But it takes time. It's worse for girls. I tried to have a will of my own. I was an emancipated woman and it didn't work. Beginning with sex is beginning at the wrong end. I needed a father and a best friend and a confidant and a . . . I demanded that every boy I went to bed with give me love. Instead I got a lot of experience, a lot of grief, a lot of good sex, and a lot of expectations. But finally you came along. . . . That's why I told John I loved you. I was about to say your name, as if that would make him understand everything.

I'm unhappy with my job sometimes. So much more has to be done, and I don't know where to begin. But it's better than being unhappy over a person. If I have a job that molds me and makes trouble for me and changes me, that makes it a foothold for me and gives me the strength to care about people without the fear of becoming dependent, without wanting to create a distance so I won't get involved. And when I actually do get involved, then I know that's the way it's supposed to be.

The night after I slept with John for the first time, I stood outside his window in St. John's Wood and cried. I've never told him that. You're the only one I tell everything. I went home and got drunk. The next day I called him and was friendly and well bred.

But I didn't call you after the ride from Arlanda. It was so much more important, though I didn't understand why. I waited. Though if you'd put it off . . . I dreamed you bought me a large ring. I never told you that, it was only a dream. I didn't want to ask you for anything. "Begging Prohibited" it says in the doorway on Nybro Quay.

Some of these secrets maybe hurt you more than they'd hurt all those people who don't care about me. But the last thing for us to lose is our openness. It's a hard thing to say, but that's the only part we can't share with others. Love and laughter and trust are things you can give to a number of people, our houses have many rooms. Jealousy is usually misdirected. That invisible floodgate kept open between us is the only way we truly betray the world around us.

The things you grieve for are the things you don't feel. You grieve that something you once felt strongly now seems unimportant. My fear that you'll leave me or that I'll leave you is nothing compared to my fear of having you with me though you've already gone. That a day will come when we don't automatically think of each other with joy, like breathing.

I'm not particularly nice. I can get to feeling trapped, cornered, crowded. And then I cut my way out. Sometimes I'm overcome with a destructive desire to go outside myself, out into a kind of senselessness and insanity, out into anonymity. You aren't allowed to feel that way—one of us is enough. But the really remarkable thing isn't what we each are independently, but the fact that we are something together.

Everything that exists, exists between us. But it begins just outside us. Beyond us is chaos, inside us is chaos. Only between us is there something we can value.

There's an inaccessible level, that I am who I am. And then the level that's only history and parents and Stockholm and job. You belong to both.

As soon as you're gone I remember you. I see your reflection as if in the back of a spoon. You're the only person who's been able to see all of me. I pretend you've got a particular heredity that makes that possible, otherwise I'd owe you a debt of gratitude.

I ought to be different. I want to lie still and feel your hands. It's as if I were carrying a bowl full of something indescribably precious.

Your hair tastes a little salty. You haven't had a shower since you went swimming at the Water Palace yesterday.

"No," he said. "And there's no bath in the hotel."

The rain had started. The streets rocked in the wind, and the loosely fitting windows gasped for breath. The people down on the sidewalk produced raincoats as if by magic. The hats on the chimneys danced. It sounded as if someone were stamping in the corridor, but it could have been the rain in the courtyard. The sky was a dark rectangle above the buildings, and across the street were only attic offices with skylights in the black sheet-metal roof. No one could see in to them.

"I'm done talking now," Jenny said. "Shall we get something to eat?"

"Yes. Can I stay with you tonight? Or do you want to be alone?"

"I want you to stay. As long as you don't hurt yourself on my unhappiness."

They went out in the drizzling rain. The hotel was surrounded by engraving shops, mattress stores, luggage repairing, surplus stores full of American army jackets, tobacco shops that now sold mostly pornography. The nearest eating place was Katés Bar. The woman who owned it had seen "Kate's Bar" on a sign in some foreign country and mistaken the apostrophe for an accent.

Further down Gamla Brogatan was Clara Groceries, ready-cooked food. In the window there were stainless steel basins of Baltic herring fillets, pork pancakes, raw shrimp, meatballs. You bought lingonberry jam by the spoonful. Some girls on their way home from the post office were standing in line, taking the opportunity to add one more line of melancholy around their eyes.

They bought provisions, and then a bottle opener and knives and forks at a hardware store.

"Maybe the next time we pass this hotel, they'll have the scaffolding up to tear it down," Jenny said. "And it'll be dark in the rooms."

"Then we'll have sackcloth to kiss behind," Jan said, unconcerned.

"Have you ever lost control of yourself?" Jenny asked.

He grimaced thoughtfully.

"I've got no gift for hysteria and tears."

"You've got an advantage over the people who have no control. Over me, for example."

"You say that as if I were missing something essential. It seems to me my life is formless next to yours. I don't take any particular initiative. I lie low. I fall into things, into you. You're more decisive."

"I'm unstable," Jenny said. "I've never attached myself to anyone without thinking almost unconsciously that he'd help me to be different. That's cowardly and unfair."

"You got a divorce, for example. You made a decision."

"If it gets too awful, I take off. I do have the strength to go away."

"Just so long as you say so in advance this time. I want your life to be full of a lot of things. It seems to me mine's fuller because I see for you too. One of those balls that's attached to a long rubber band—I want to throw you out, fastened to my finger, and watch you bounce back."

And he added, "There's a blank spot in me you've filled and colored in. Now it's full of activity all the time, confusion, spring cleaning."

They put the beer in the gutter outside the window. Jenny had a suitcase with extra shoes, skirt and blouse, a toilet case and a nightgown. Her briefcase was packed for the following day. She had a matter-of-factness that surprised him. He wanted to be the one who knew best who she was. She let no one give her orders, and he would make her able to board all the airplanes in the world.

"Did you bring along anything to read?" he asked.

"*The National Surveyor's Journal,* the last issue of *Grottan,* and Ettinger's *Toward a Habitable World.*"

"It feels so commonplace. We're sitting here as if we were at home, only neither of us is."

"There's a building falling apart across the street. And a crowd of young people down below."

"That's one of the activist groups," Jan said. "Alternative Society."

"The plaster is falling apart," she said. "The sulfur dioxide in the air dissolves the mortar, which creates calcium sulfate, and along with the frost, that breaks up the plaster. Darling, I long to go back to my job. It's easier to be a cog in an ideological machine than it is to love. The chanting ought to be antiphonal between the action groups down there and the bureaucracy. We have to create a new kind of caution. And be able to see new categories, the kind we never thought of before. What we do now makes the customs and patterns for the future."

They drank beer out of toothbrush glasses and ate herring and sausage on bread. The food lay on paper napkins along the window sill. She sat on his lap and no one would have guessed he was deep inside her. He took her hand and looked at it while she moved gently over him, and all pleasure was concentrated in a small part of a finger.

Then she stopped moving. They looked at each other. It was as if the tenderness of contact was insufficient, as if they were both overcome by something else.

"The National Museum is open this evening," she said, with a big sudden smile. "Take me quickly and we'll go."

Just her saying it made him stream into her. He pressed his mouth against the inside of her arm.

"You bit me," she said.

"It'll go away."

"I'd rather it didn't. But the body never wants to remember."

They walked to the National Museum and looked at gray and blue still lifes and paintings with water-filled wheel tracks. They were alone in a room of basins and tureens, he loosened her blouse and kissed her waist. Her skin was reflected in the glass, colorlessly, and what happened right then couldn't be called back. He felt an unsolemn responsibility for his existence. There was no way out of death and no escape and freedom was this confinement in life.

They ran back to the hotel, along the back side of Jenny's block and of John's outbursts and of the impossibility of grasping that what was good and necessary for them was malevolent and dangerous for others. They felt they were coming home after a long excursion and Jan was not surprised when she said, "For the first time with anyone I thought—what if we had a child together. . . . There at the museum, among all those things that had been saved so we could see them."

Jan envisioned a pale, lively little girl. Children were a

reminder that freedom doesn't exist. Here I am and I have to be taken care of, an antipode in time, a piece of the past—that's what he had been—and a piece of the future he imagined was his but which was exclusively hers, the girl's.

He was afraid of crippledness, of unfamiliar mechanisms that went out of order. The silent spring, the future's spring, was catching up with man, rolling like a fog across the bent, brown grass. No one was safe, there were only challenges on every side. Take the risk, Jan. Yes, he could take his own risks—since death was a fact and everything else could be changed a bit, displaced, set at new angles—but he was afraid of risking what had neither will nor existence.

He stood before the unaccomplished and the uncreated in himself, that which could come into being, maybe wanted to come into being, maybe wanted to abandon him and leave him empty. But it was his. His seed, on the other hand, was not. It belonged only to others, to those who didn't exist.

He cupped his hand over her eyes and felt he was hidden beneath it. Her face seemed to take form from his exhalation. He kissed her where her skin was thin and drawn—on the knuckles and the collarbone, on the jaw beneath her ear. Bottles rattled in the corridor. His apartment stood empty a little ways away. They were in a strange city.

He lay in her for a long time and she fell asleep, with closed mouth and one knee drawn up toward her breasts. With open eyes he tried to dream for her. The sort of thing she often told him—she invented a bulb that you held against the wall anywhere and it lit up. . . . Then she woke up and wrinkled her brow.

"Did you notice anything?"

"No."

"All of a sudden I couldn't feel you touching me. Maybe I wanted you too much. But something was between us. I was huddled up under you like an animal in hibernation. Have you ever seen a plank being pulled out to sea by an invisible current, even though the waves are driving it toward the beach? You may have thought you were closer to me than you were. I don't want to mislead you."

"There doesn't have to be anything between us," he said. "It's something around us. It's never only us."

"No, but I want us to be able to share an experience down to the last molecule. I would have liked to push myself into you. I could have seen my back. A stranger's view. I can say it was Gertrude's, then maybe you'll understand. It was someone who wanted to understand us but couldn't. That's worse than the other way around."

"Yes, it's worse. Maybe I did notice something. But there are times when you don't want indefinite things to be defined."

"Do you feel how tense we are?"

"It's because we're carrying each other," Jan said.

He heard catastrophe rumbling unexpectedly beneath the surface where he and Gertrude, or he and Jenny, walked. He felt a sudden distance between himself and Gertrude and Jenny—the same feeling he had in the radar cave at Arlanda when he looked at the moving points of light and realized that if a plane caught fire in one engine, he could send signals to various authorities, but that it would be meaningless to get up from his chair and intervene directly. Though the signals collected in him, he was not capable of prescribing the measures that would let every one escape uninjured.

They woke up, one bed unused, to the noise of trucks making deliveries to a department store, and to the sound of blasting somewhere far away.

Jenny called him John once and was very embarrassed, but he wasn't hurt. He stayed in bed and watched her washing herself at the sink, quickly and offhand as if she were alone. She stood naked in front of the mirror and turned toward him.

"I can't understand why you like my body."

"Come here and I'll show you. Come closer than last night."

"Not now," she said. "Your hand's enough. Think how many

other hands it's touched without anything happening. If you change your emotional gears and get tired, tell me. You can live through a lot in one single minute. But if only we call the devil by his name. . . . That's what I did last night."

THE HEIGHT OF VANITY

THE CITY, which Jenny and Jan have never really seen. Now it had to be done. Make a basket of the present and let the unfamiliar seeds take root, before the world grows tired of them.

Jan Backman sat waiting in his car by Sofia Church. The steeple clock was lit. Jenny was at a committee meeting, arranging an exhibition on the destruction of the waterways, and she'd called Arlanda to tell him.

He looked into apartments lit up by TV screens. One on top of the other—a million people. A net of duties and consideration. People exchanging favors, love, and food. The wind that once blew monks and missionaries to Sweden now sweeps in sulfur dioxide from the Ruhr. No one gets to the oil spill on the bottoms of the stones.

Were there lights in the windows on Nybro Quay? What did John think after he broke the apothecary flask and heard Jenny slam the door? Did he hate her, or something in himself? Or did he only feel remorse? And Jenny? Was she ever seized with a wild desire to see everything shatter like the bottle with its gold lettering in Latin? Was there some meaning lost there, or only the label we put on great emotions? Or did she want to be elastic, holding together herself and others?

John had thought himself secure in his freedom. Suddenly he couldn't come up with anything that gave him the strength to accept Jenny's truth. And his behavior thrust away the part of Jenny that wanted to stay with him. The bitter part, Jan thought, was that they were forced to break up for a love that to John must seem romantic and unpractical, maybe destructive.

"Have you been waiting long?" Jenny asked and landed beside him in the front seat.

"There was a police car in front of me—I thought I'd be late."

"The committee works so slowly. The country's surface water is being ruined. Though it's even worse in other places. And if all the surface water in the world . . . ."

"If it's hopeless, there's no point in having an exhibit," Jan said.

"No, what we preach is that industry and ecology have the same interests. Cycle the waste back into production. We can't have all of humanity spitting to windward, we'll get everything back in our faces. Sooner or later we'll suffocate. You laugh? You think I talk too much. Then kiss me."

He ran his hand across her face and her closed eyes seemed to listen to his fingers.

Then he drove toward the candle factory and told her about his day at Arlanda, and how he'd thought about John. They drove under Danvik Bridge and found a parking place and climbed up to Vanity from the East. There was a cottage with a glass verandah, and a pond with slimy, green water, and beds of marigolds steaming after the rain. And there was a funny cage with no door but with wide gaps between the bars, and the pigeons felt safe inside though the wind and they themselves could easily pass in and out.

"I wish you'd come while John and I were fighting," Jenny said. "Leaped in through the window like a trapeze artist. You would have seen something you've never seen before."

The Danvik Bridge lifted for a Spanish tanker, bells ringing like high mass. Cigarette packages and beer cans rustled along the now vertical rails down into the water. The drawbridge to Stockholm, straight up.

"There's a wooden lump in me," Jenny said.

"That's John. I feel the same way."

"And still it's only the thought of your being utterly gone that feels like real catastrophe. But who gave you permission to obscure my view?"

"Only the insensitive can be just," Jan said. "We're forever dancing on someone's body. Injustice isn't thinned by being spread. It may be the best thing we can do is to overstep the bounds we see around us."

"I'm blind and incapable," Jenny said. "I have no trouble believing I can be replaced. That's as dangerous as believing you're irreplaceable. A question of upbringing. If you examined everything around you really closely—like a woman looking at a piece of material, or a carpenter running his finger along the blade of a plane, or like blowing on a spark plug in your car . . . ."

"What then?"

"Well, then you wouldn't want to destroy anything."

Off across the harbor there was a light in the bulb-testing room at the Luma factory. The radio masts in Nacka were exchanging signals with the Kaknäs tower—this loose palisade around the city would tighten with the years.

"It's easier to leave yourself than to tell someone else to leave," Jenny said. "And now I can't go back even out of sympathy, because my words have lost their weight, my actions aren't convincing, I won't be believed. I've glorified my feelings without showing compassion. I've told him I love someone else. That has a different sound than telling him abstractly that he's not unique for me. In that case he always said the same thing back. And I'm not unique for you, and neither is Gertrude. There are other ways in which a person cannot be replaced, but not in relationships *between* people."

"I'm involved," Jan said. "Just the way you have a share in my responsibility for Gertrude. But I don't know what you ought to say to him. Every person has his own sincerity, unlike anyone else's."

They looked down on Stockholm. "Over there beyond Kungsholm there's a plane going in to land," Jenny said. "Now it's on your radar."

"Almost close enough for the tower to take over."

"The same way I've come home from John," Jenny said. "He and I met each other in a different dimension where everything seemed possible, because it was always a foreign country for one of us. The distance was security. With you it's all closer and less certain, there's no comparison. This desire people have to become one. . . . You don't love him, don't delude yourself, I'd think, just as he came into me. And I could already see myself boarding a plane in London."

"You've always been more mobile than I have."

"In the fifties I used to hitchhike around in France and Switzerland. Hitching isn't so common any more. Priests were nice. Sit in back, since you're wearing shorts, they'd say. You got trucks at the top of a hill when they'd shifted down."

"Do you speak French?"

"Badly. I was in science."

He thought of Gertrude in school in Switzerland—she spoke fluent French.

"My English is fine thanks to John. But it probably made it easier for me to stay in disguise. It creates a playful distance, nothing really means as much in a foreign language. Now and then I wanted to make him be quiet. There was something in me he misunderstood from the beginning, a thing you understood that first hour when we talked about cat tracks in clay.

I wanted to preserve our silence, John's and mine. That was often the part I liked most."

Over in the city, the clock on the Great Church gleamed like a cat's eye, and spotlights were playing on St. Gertrude's. The Big Dipper overhead. If the handle fell off, the news might not reach earth until mankind was gone. They were seeing things that were extinct. What seemed to be shining was dead.

"He didn't love me with your seriousness," Jenny said. "Maybe love is a talent and a gift. But it hurt him that I wasn't more affectionate and tender. I could have been more motherly. He'd hid his weaknesses—that was his cowardice. And then when he stood there looking like an injured child, I caressed him in despair at how unjust I'd been. I guess I didn't give him any more than I felt he gave me. In his eyes it was an injustice—in any case it was lacking in love. I know what I've done to him, because I know how I want to be with you, and I know how a word from you can make me cry and how an expression in your face can send me rolling off my hill. I've been cowardly and hard, Jan. I mustn't forget the way I used to be."

"How was that?"

"Never as happy as now. I never dared be satisfied. As if I'd had my fist clenched inside my glove. Now for the first time I'm spreading out my fingers and feeling all the way to the edges. What are we going to do?"

"Nothing. Let fall come, and winter and spring."

"I almost never think ahead except in my job, because after all that's a kind of research into the future—what's happening to the cultural landscape, to the pastureland, to the sparse deciduous forests. The way our whole experience of nature is going to change. . . ."

"You can see how love makes people change," Jan said. "It ought to make us receptive to other changes, in the political reality, for instance. Though nothing we do—our love, our politics, our job—is an excuse. We don't have any alibis."

"In the relationships I've had," Jenny said, "I always found something missing. There was something crippled, astigmatic, a lack or too much of something. It may be there's always a shadow of nonsympathy or coolness that never goes away, that you have to learn to live with in as healthy a way as you can."

"What's happened to us," Jan said, "well, the fairest way is to look at it as undeserved. We're lucky we've imagined the same things about each other."

"Have we? I can think away the men I've liked. You can't think away Gertrude. You've never envisioned a life without her."

He remembered that Jenny didn't know. A wife can be forsaken or forsake. A man can stop seeing his sister, but she's still there.

"Gertrude has what I have after all," Jenny went on. "And a little more. It seems so unnecessary, so turned around."

"I don't confuse the two of you. There's only one Water Palace."

"Isn't she enough for you? You love her out of long experience, and me out of inexperience."

"If not even Gertrude whom I love can get the better of my love for you, then who can?"

"Only me, stupid and spoiled. One day you'll think I've betrayed you for something a lot smaller than you and I."

"We met by chance," Jan said. "Our jobs are less accidental."

"Everything comes in phases. I hope this will be a long one."

"To get to be happy together for a whole day and then get to bed unscathed," Jan said. "That in itself ought to be front-page headlines."

"It's hard to talk about happiness. It arouses envy. It sounds like roasting apples and going on vacation. And that makes you think of accidents."

They sat up on Vanity Hill. Down along the City Quay there was the customs shed and the Frigate Café where Jan had tried to call Jenny two days after the ride from Arlanda. There was blue-white lamplight on abandoned tarpaulins.

"Do you understand?" she said. "If we could give each other life insurance outside our emotions, if only we could feel some newly contrived, impersonal loyalty that would always let us go to each other without fear. I want you to know I'm here, like a part of your breathing, without it having to excite you. I want to feel what I'm living through, not have it make me unconscious, or indifferent either."

He put his arms around her and pulled her to her feet. They were standing on a slope. Three streetlights lit the Vanity café. The chairs were gone. The trees were low and pruned. At the top of the workers' quarters by the candle factory was a little steeple with a light inside—maybe lodgings for the most oppressed.

"I get excited anyway," he said. "And a little sentimental."

"It's nice to hold you when you're wearing all your clothes," Jenny said. "I'm not used to it."

He kissed her ears. He dropped to his knees and kissed her stomach through her skirt. They were alone on an abandoned stage. She watched him pull her top up from her waist and kiss her breasts. She chewed a little on his hair. From inside this sensuality that bore him up and perhaps led him in the right direction, he could, like a blind voyeur, experience the joy she had felt with others and they with her. She had to live the way she wanted to. Nothing bad must happen to her.

Meanwhile . . . Gertrude . . . John . . . Sten Tidström . . . the Water Palace England Africa the world. Someone enjoyed himself while others suffered. Someone ate while others starved. Some people did something about it, others didn't. Many did the wrong thing no matter what they did—you began to see that afterwards. And while some people whiled away their time in innocence, impotence, or corruption, others invented destruction and stored up poisons and bacteria in tubes.

"We stand here and we're not ashamed," Jenny said.

"What's between us is a secret, it envelops us, it's a danger, a comfort and a vanity. It can resemble all sort of things and bring all sorts of things about. And our evasions and stratagems are deceptively as obvious as traffic lights."

"The strange thing is that we know it. And the secret's existence is public."

The hill was undermined with tunnels. A train with old-fashioned brown coaches thundered under the bed of bloomed-out peonies. The rock was shiny smooth and covered with lichens. Different water levels seemed outlined in the stone. Jan felt it with his fingers. His skin sensed fusions for which he knew no chemical terms. He saw other outcroppings in Stockholm . . . islands in the fresh-water belt. And then the Baltic below, the salt and the sweet, the new and polluted, the streams and the rain. Buildings sailed up through the light fog like wrecks from the bottom of the sea.

They drove in to the city, to the hotel room in Klara that was Jenny's retreat for one more night.

PERCEPTIONS

He WAS HAPPY as he drove out to the Water Palace. He missed Gertrude. He felt secure with her. He had been in love with her even as a child. He had wanted to be revenged on time which threatened their love; his salvation was that he grew up quickly. It worked out. He had been the ardent one.

He thought about the small things that meant something to them and didn't seem to exist for other people. In that way they discovered they had a life turned toward themselves. She was complicated. He had a gift for simplifying her. She had taught him a great deal, though he'd begun to cut the classes.

The path out to the Water Palace was all summer paths at once—slippery loam, a high grass rampart in the middle, wild raspberries along the ditch.

There was Gertrude, smiling. He was spoiled. He lived in abundance. Gertrude became more distinct because he loved Jenny. They kissed. Nothing happened at the other one's expense. If he regretted Gertrude he would regret Jenny and finally himself. That was the road to self-destruction.

But how easily he could squander his abundance! Gertrude was at a disadvantage because she didn't know. Being equals is a requirement in the society of the passions too. Live in doubleness—but that mustn't be confused with the old double morality.

How could he make Gertrude see what he saw? If only he could fold up the truth like a napkin and give it to her without a word. Because words never get through before being crushed by pictures. An experience of the same intensity—not necessarily of the same kind—would make her understand.

And still she had said it herself—there were so many ways to live, and it was peculiar that just this combination was theirs —the innermost circle, the shortest distance.

"Some giant company's being calling," she told him. "They want to buy the Water Palace for summer cottages and recreation area. Along with the other land around here. And put up bungalows. First they designate the area and then they want us to talk about it. They didn't name any figures. They've got their nerve."

"They can afford to have," Jan said.

They stood in front of the house. In the lilac hedge that hid the woodshed there were snowball mushrooms growing in relays from August to October. And inside the woodshed there were broken, brown-stained chairs that looked as though they had been gathered from a Sunday school, plus a pile of empty boxes that had once held shotgun shells.

It struck him that he'd lived at the Water Palace much longer than Gertrude. He had without objection accepted a life that others had forced him to live. If they had returned here after being gone for years, they would have noticed what had changed. Instead it all glided together into an extended present, which had always existed around them.

"I feel most real out here," she said. "I need the house. It's probably lack of personality, but I don't suffer enough to have to call for help. I don't even have that nice egoism that satisfies itself by sacrificing for others. When I'm happy or sad I put it away in the house, like into a pantry. It takes care of me just as you do, though in a different way. I thought of asking Viveka out here. I thought she was a grass widow. But she's going to Ireland with her family. I thought of Jenny too. It would be fun to see her again. Then I decided it would be nicest to be alone and work. I'm coming to grips with something important. So I don't care about much of anything else."

This last she said almost apologetically and he felt her head against his shoulder—the light pressure of a human being. He sensed her presence not through his skin, not in direct ways, but beneath his skin, present but hard to search out.

He was mistaken about her frailty. She didn't need as much confirmation as he. She had belonged from the beginning. It was the outer world she couldn't handle. She didn't want to live cut off, she didn't deny that people existed, but how could they behave the way they did? It was only to him she turned with a passion that surprised him, since he suspected other people found her cool. Together, they were back up in the attic, naked in the same darkness with everything else wiped out.

Jenny, he thought, was in society's mainstream. Full of comments and controversy, she entered into what went on around her. He couldn't picture her really abandoned. Did he want to make them into two separate halves that he combined? Did he have to be squeezed between them in order to feel how strongly he existed?

Both had ambitions he lacked. He was not obsessed with planning for the future like Jenny. He allowed his environment to affect him without fighting back. He had no project to hide himself in like Gertrude. He found he rarely drew conclusions from his experience. He was conscious of the determining factors in his life, and of the need to oppose them in work and action. But it stopped with that. The gratuitous element in his existence annoyed him.

It seemed to him he'd had a lot of childhood that led nowhere, and a certain lack of freedom that led to greater freedom that led nowhere. He had an accelerated perception of time combined with a certain lethargy—everything passed by at such speed he hardly had time to acquire memories. He was afraid both of loss of memory and of memories he couldn't handle.

The bay lay motionless, as if covered with an oil spill. Dragonfly larvae crept up the reeds into the air, unfolded themselves, rested on the topmost tufts, and threw reflections back to the water from which they'd come.

"Do you remember I cried several times last spring?" Gertrude asked.

"Yes. I never understood why."

"Maybe because I loved you too much. Maybe for lack of words—like when dolphins jerk out sounds. Now I don't know why. I don't think it'll happen again."

"I can hurt you without wanting to or meaning to."

"Yes, it's not hard. Then it doesn't help that we're brother and sister. Do you think ferns grow in Botswana?"

"Yes."

"They're everywhere, some of them more known than others. But Sten Tidström hasn't seen any."

"You can't write a dissertation with only a minor in botany, can you?"

"It'll have to be in the history of science. The psychology and sociology of perception are things I've worked on before. We've talked about that."

"The way experience is altered by new information? Like using detergent or seeing a lake these days."

"It's the same with us as with my ferns. Nothing has been experienced once and for all. Not even my happiest moments are protected."

She seemed calm. He was the one who wanted to cry. They'd been riding in an old-fashioned elevator and had seen themselves disappearing in its mirrors, Jan and Gertrude, Gertrude and Jan . . . smaller and smaller, until they drowned in each other.

When it was raining or foggy a haze passed through the rooms, or the shadows of large trees. The Water Palace covered itself with spider web. Distances developed between the furniture. The house seemed emptier, its contents harder to localize.

It occurred to Jan that there would soon come a time of overturned taboos, because man had learned to control everything but death. At the moment it was a crime for a mother to make love to her son, while wars were legal as soon as they were declared. But communal heating would become more common than communal death. And what teenagers did out camping in the summers wouldn't worry people as much as the bacteria harvests at the military research institutions all over the world.

He wondered what Jenny was doing. He wasn't uneasy. Nothing she did, he imagined, could reduce the closeness between them by an inch. They were free by means of each other —that was their form of faithfulness. Nothing could take her face away from him. He saw her taut conference expression dissolve into a variety of moods, a complicated code. She was a pestle in him; it crushed and stirred.

"Have you become the person you wanted to be?" Gertrude

asked. "Someone liberated from the things we live through?"

"I don't decide who I am," he said. "Sometimes we're only the surface for someone else's match, don't even feel the spark. And I don't know what liberated means."

"Neither do I. It's conceivable, of course, that my life is mostly what you make it."

She spoke as if she knew and he replied as if he were counting on her knowledge. And in fact she did know more about Jenny than he knew about her book.

Did he love Jenny more easily because no one connected them or formulated their relationship for them? Was their love more real because it was a fantasy they shared, inaccessible for others? Yet his love for Gertrude concealed a corresponding secret, an official illegality.

He was loyal to both of them at the same time. He wanted them to feel secure with him and not to regard themselves as opposites. That had to do with the psychology of perception.

He deceived Gertrude with his silence. He could have deceived her with the truth. But from the beginning she had been effortlessly incorporated in his love. She knew that. That was also a truth.

The remarkable thing was to have a focus, unknown to others, constantly in operation. Jenny was his burning glass. He pointed it at Gertrude and loved her.

"You think you know me all the way through," Gertrude said. "Just because I'm your sister. You're not particularly curious. Maybe I take you for granted, too. But I'm probably readier for surprises than you are."

How should he give Gertrude entry to his experience? It seemed to him he understood her better than ever because he also loved Jenny. It struck him that their jobs, Jenny's and Gertrude's, had begun to resemble each other. He must be the victim of a perceptual delusion, something for Gertrude to take up in her paper.

"Surprises?" he repeated.

"Klas Lundin was here," Gertrude told him. "I must have

told you that on the phone. The same old shaky boat. He had a hard time getting across Kanholmen. His friends had stayed in Sandhamn. We drank beer and ate some cold pork chops he brought with him."

"Did he stay long?"

"All evening. He hadn't seen you for a long time, he said. For a while I thought of riding into town with him. He'd gotten a letter from Botswana. That made me happy. I don't understand why I miss them so much."

"And Klas?" Jan wondered. "Don't you like him?"

"There's something fresh-faced and well-meaning about him. He thinks he knows all the tricks of advertising and the good life. He 'fixes' things, makes a lot of phone calls. He's a nice blockhead, and on the way to finding that out for himself."

"I'm sure he's a little taken with you. Just like Sten. Didn't he show any signs?"

"No. Not this time."

"Some other time?"

"Maybe. We hugged each other and kissed. At our party, out in the garden. That was all."

"But Gertrude, you never told me!"

"There wasn't anything to tell. Would you have bothered to mention it?"

"Have you ever let anyone do that before?"

"Let! I decide for myself for heaven's sake."

Klas Lundin, happy and a little simple in Gertrude's arms— Jan couldn't picture it. At the same time he wished for an instant that Gertrude were doing what he was doing—it would reconfirm their being brother and sister.

"I can long for more passionate caresses than yours," she said. "I know what they ought to be like, but it doesn't help. No body but yours really tempts me. I think women are prettier than men and easier to identify with. No, I didn't kiss anyone else, or wait, I gave Jenny a quick hug."

He looked at her with the curiosity she accused him of lacking. Was there a Gertrude he didn't know, one who let herself be irresponsible? Or was this still the girl from the attic who wanted to try everything, first with him and then—when he wasn't handy—with others?

"We have to do the things we want to do," Jan said in an altogether too generous tone of voice. "Have you been lonely out here?"

"Being alone is easier than being with someone else the right way."

Jan sat thinking that most things could be replaced—one picture or situation with another, a person with an idea. His emotional circumference was accidental—the traffic tower, the Water Palace, Sweden. His range of vision was influenced by his position. He didn't count on the world's answering to his conception of it.

In all of it he saw various missions: his double love, Gertrude's book, Tidström's Africa, Jenny's ecology. These missions all took place on the same earth surface, which was but the thinnest varnish over death, and they all resided in the same cage of gas and steam.

Both Gertrude and Sten saw him only in his role as traffic controller. He had withheld his obsession from them. Maybe Sten, who'd also had his point of view altered, would understand the connection between Jenny and Botswana. Or would he think Jan was loitering in the crowded world of girl hitchhikers and forgotten keys, that he didn't dare leave the shadow of the traffic tower and seriously change his foothold.

At dusk the horizon seemed to draw back to leave more room for the water. The bay with its black pine forest edges widened to a sea. Isolated islands stood roughhewn against the sky. On cold winter mornings, seal could still be seen sometimes, but no one clubbed them any more.

When they went to bed, Gertrude said she was getting a cold. Jan got a copy of Olaus Magnus that he'd borrowed from the Academy of Sciences.

"I can read you whatever you like. What this explorer

thought he saw is wonderful. I can read you about the winter mosquitoes, or the native piety of the stork, or about the semen of the whale, rising to the surface of the water and floating there like glistening oil. You have to gather it quickly, you see, before it dries and gets grainy from the cold, because it's best when it's at body heat and full of fat, then it'll cure your cold and consumption and anemia."

But they fell asleep over the book. Jan was awakened at dawn by a creaking in the house like a door opening on crooked hinges. Still stupefied by dreams, he saw Gertrude's face indistinctly like the face of a clock. He bent over her, carefully folded down her nightgown and let his mouth sink very lightly against one of her pale, unknowing nipples.

It was like the tip of a finger pressed against his lips to make him stop talking. She was still dreaming, off in the land of the ferns. She was his sister. So he could never entirely lose her. In many societies, twins of different sexes were separated. They had lain together so intimately in the womb that their affection for each other might remain. But because they were separated, they might meet again and recognize one another without understanding why.

Gertrude let out a cry and pushed him away. She was back in this world. The sheet felt cool against his elbow. His knee rested against her thigh.

"Nothing's wrong," he said cheerfully. "You dreamed something. I was tasting the day's weather."

"How will it be?"

He reached down to the floor and turned on the transistor radio.

East central Sweden light to moderate northerly winds mostly clear along the coast cloudy with occasional showers or thunder showers during the day inland temperature unchanged.

THE SAVANNAH

IN THE MAIN dining room at Skeppet out by the free port you could take a drink at the bar and study naval paintings, and the customs and harbor men had cognac with their coffee after twelve o'clock when liquor could be served. But Jenny and Jan ate the luncheon special quickly. In a few lunch hours they wanted to get through the greater part of the textbook geography—coast and sea, mountain and forest, plain and savannah. Desert and tundra they could skip.

Jenny had come from the Water Conservation Board in Norsborg. She talked about human institutions—how continuity is established, how instructions and files are passed on more readily than imagination and ideas. And about emergency plans—the way you prepare yourself in advance for the possible threats, and familiarize yourself with conceivable situations you never want to meet, for example, the fluoridation and distribution of drinking water once the enemy has destroyed or poisoned the usual supplies.

The whole idea of preparedness is to make people submit to necessity, not to implement freedoms. Free subways are acceptable in a mobilization plan, not otherwise, and the bays around Stockholm would be cleaned if it were considered essential for dealing with an enemy invasion. But what if the attack was already under way, flying low, beneath the radar?

They went up in the Kaknäs Tower to look at the vulnerable city. A shifting sky, haze, the sun breaking through, Jenny's face reflected in the glass. Views told him little.

"I was out at the Water Palace. Gertrude told me she kissed Klas Lundin at that party when you were there."

"I remember him. And that surprised you? But you didn't say anything yourself."

"The worst of it is I love her. I don't wish her any harm. I don't want her to think I'm a completely different person than I am. A certain compass error is closer to the truth."

Love, politics, work, he thought—in Jenny they're not twisted into layers like English candy, they're kneaded together into a daily bread.

Then they walked through the woods by the tower and followed a path along the shore. They sat down in a little hollow, chased away mosquitoes, saw a dragonfly, kissed each other. Then he kissed her incessantly on a spot near her kneecap, and because he went on doing it for such a long time, all their desire collected there like water in a crevice.

He found matches in the moss. Unknown people had sat here before them. One group relieved another. They hadn't come to the place at the same time. He thought about Stockholm, undermined by pipes in every direction. Precipitation regions marked out on maps you couldn't buy. A net. They swayed in its geography.

"If you were a female," Jenny said, "you could be a kangaroo and take me in your pouch and bound around out there on the savannah. It would all be more practical if you were a girl. I'd like you just as much, but I wouldn't want you so badly. You could hug me a little bit anyway. And I wouldn't get so agitated in the midriff. And you wouldn't have to be so uneasy about Gertrude—oddly enough."

"What happened with John?" he asked her.

"I went back to the apartment, I'd called him from the Department. You were out at the Water Palace. He was leaving. I met a polite, evasive shadow, a polished gentleman, afraid of an emotional outburst in himself. I know how it is, but couldn't bear to see him so distant! There we were, he who was so honest from the beginning and I who'd decided to be honest. And a dam between us. If he'd only understood me I would have thrown myself on his neck."

"Like a child that's forgiven," Jan said.

"No. In order to be friends. Now I don't know how it'll be. I've often broken up, but I've never wanted to say goodbye forever."

"As long as it's on your conditions," Jan said. "Is that right?"

"No, not anymore. I guess I sounded mean. But you've pulled a cotter pin out of me. I confront you and everything else. What I am is what I am toward you."

"Since everyone is mostly faithful to himself, he must figure that sooner or later everyone will let him down," Jan said. "And betrayal and faithfulness are funny words, since everything's only on loan and love and suffering aren't things you can measure."

Jenny looked at him with curiosity so strong it resembled tenderness.

"Don't be sad! I thought I could hear your footsteps next to mine when I was on my way to John. I like the way you walk. I heard you telling me not to be unhappy. And I wasn't unhappy. I loved you. I thought I could see you behind the Nybro Pavilion, on the lookout for me. On the stairs up it seemed to me your love bumped against me like a cat, following me and knocking its head against my legs."

He felt her strength. Everything muddled and turbulent in his body closed around her and wanted something of her.

"Something's happened," she said. "I'm less sure that I have my life in my own hands. You have a priority on everything. You're the point furthest from my egoism and greed and apathetic evil. I look at anyone who looks like you. At John too. The back of a neck, a hairline. I meet someone who doesn't look like you, but there's something about his way of talking. And then I can feel attracted to him, that is, to you. You've shaken me up. I want to use the new part of me. You're a huge sun-heated anthill, you swarm and grow and I haul in blueberries and trash, sticks and pine needles, the fine and the foul indiscriminately, but everything comes home to you."

A long path stretched out diagonally across the field. They sat down in the high grass a little way from it, and the vegetation closed around them. They weren't seen by two older women walking by with bread crumbs for the birds:

"I was lucky, the bus was only half full today."

"I've got such a swelling on my arm, I have to go down to the porter's wife and ask her to help me on with my dress. It's awful to be so helpless. I hate to bother people."

"Being a human being is so funny. You're still the same person, but then everything starts getting heavy, and your coat gets tight on you."

They passed out of hearing. Jan and Jenny saw a straw hat and a shiny patent leather bag. They were quiet. Jan thought: just to be able to deal with the time laid out for you. . . .

"You shrink in toward your skeleton," Jenny said. "Helplessly. In toward your own aches. That thing that squeaks in your joints and keeps you from making coffee and getting fresh air, that's what's left at the end."

"Maybe terribly small things make you happy," Jan said. "Like being able to wiggle your toes. And then you no longer remember that it could be like it is for us now, because after all we didn't know this beforehand either."

"I don't want to try to find time for everything and run a race with my cells that are being replaced and destroyed. Today, on my way here, I took in some laundry, in order to show myself I didn't have to be in such a rush to you. What we're doing ought to be an everyday thing. And then I thought how remarkable it was that I could walk along in the middle of my life like this, alone and in love, with a laundry ticket and your smells that seemed to rise from me."

They lay down in the grass, a tight and soundless forest around them. He folded down the upper edge of her skirt and blew in her navel as though into a shell.

"I've started to bleed," she said.

"I want to come into you anyway. Like nomads mixing blood and milk. No one can see us here."

Stockholm was rural. People were drawn to only a few places. The grass arched in over them. Motors in the distance. Her hands around him like wrapping paper. Fingers against palm, thumb against knuckle—even that was a kind of copulation.

And when they then lay inside each other, he lifted himself up on his arms and laughed. It felt as if his semen had left its storage space and was slowly on its way, it rippled up and down, he held back its progress.

Then the motor noise grew suddenly loud. A yellow tractor went by, its blades shooting far out from the cart and cutting low. A boy sat half asleep in the saddle with one hand on the wheel. They jumped apart and Jenny screamed. Jan noticed he'd cowered into a posture of defense. The machine went on mowing.

"Are you all right?"

"It hit my foot. I was under you, I couldn't move."

It was bleeding. The furthest point of the cutting blade had brushed against it. It was a question of inches. Light and pliant as a feather the scythe had stroked beside them. Jan held up her foot.

"Not deep," he said.

"Will I get blood poisoning?"

"You shouldn't suck your own blood. Let me do it."

He saw the wrinkles on her heel and the fluid from the wound and his fingers searched across her hard sole. His response to this nearness was a mixed feeling of lawlessness and wariness that could not be identified. It gave off sparks. It seemed to him he was seeing her for the first time.

"What's your blood group?" Jenny asked.

"O."

"Like me. Good enough for anyone. I've got antiseptic and bandage in the car. I'll dry it in the sun first."

Then she clenched her fingers around his wrist and started to cry.

"To think he came by right here. He didn't see us and we never knew what was happening. We could have been killed just because we hid so well."

Jan held her tight.

"Can you walk? Come on, we'll find someplace out in the open. We'll be safer there."

He put his arm around her waist. She walked barefoot, holding her shoes in one hand. The grass on the path was the grass of the old drillground, trampled down, yellow-gray like a washed-out military coat.

"You get spared temporarily," Jenny said. "As long as you can blame the bacteria and the poisons in the rivers and other things outside yourself, it sounds plausible. . . . But at night you scream in your dreams. And inside you fall apart and your thoughts get more and more confused and brittle like old glass."

An airplane drew a circle in the sky. A far-off drone, not the mower but the traffic and Stockholm's restless population.

They found a clump of trees. They looked like acacias, flat-topped, and the grass was darker here, there might be springs beneath the sod. He ran his hand across the ground.

"Savannah grass," he said. "Stubby and sharp as barbed wire, but soft in places."

"Here's the skeleton of a locust," Jenny said. "It'll soon be fall."

They sank down beside each other. Dry cherry pits and crushed snail shells gave evidence that people or animals had been there before them. The soles of Jenny's feet were black, and there was dried blood between her toes.

"I'm wearing that bra you bought that day you were so unhappy out in Solna."

"I didn't think you were planning to come back."

"Yes. You were right. Jan, you do understand me? Even what's false and unpredictable?"

He freed her breasts, pressed his cheek against them hard and could feel her ribs. He looked up at her face, her pale throat and her eyes still as water and the hair at her temples pulled back above her ears, while the rest of it fell down straight. Farther away the savannah grass ended and the high plains grass began, mixed with mayweed and chervil. She stroked the back of his neck.

"We're down at the grass-roots level, as we say at work these days," she said. "We're beginning from the beginning."

"Or from the end. After all, we don't know where we are."

He thought about the savannah in Botswana as Sten Tidström had described it—sepia brown, strewn with flint.

"We're surrounded by experiences that have been had. Look at the pits and the trampled yarrow. But we haven't had them yet. I don't want to imitate other people, or invent."

While she talked she opened his pants and ran one finger back and forth across his penis, which was still wet from having been in her. He sat up.

"Do we dare take our clothes off? We can be seen for a long way."

He looked at the skyline of the city—the churches, the military research establishment with its poisons and secrets. A silhouette. Society and the family were built on love, or so they said. And at the same time love was secret and unique, a thing that befell you and dissolved you, something you ran aground on. One of life's exceptions. A strange behavior where you gave without being forced to give. A generosity that might look from the outside like a constraint.

He felt Jenny's hand around his testicles and heard her say they shouldn't take their clothes off, they had to be ready to move. They lay on their sides facing each other, one hip pressed against the soil of the drillground savannah. Her hair fell down toward his jaw when they kissed, and he touched his lips with his finger to feel they were his and not hers. Something was living through them, something could tire of them. They themselves didn't mean so much.

In this large city, he thought, among these innumerable galaxies, two grains of dust run into each other and are aware of it. She and he and this third that's the glue between them. An enforced indistinctness in that. Words encircle but don't capture, leave an undisturbed freedom behind.

Now she was there, her face so close she had a single eye. And the untranslatable in his tenderness and the unattainable in their awareness of each other coincided with their bodies, just as they themselves, pressed against the ground, coincided with their shadows.

Combined—an individual group. Eye to eye. Lies could not be told about this statistically improbable moment when everything grew lighter and rose in the air like a kite.

Her hand closed around him. He felt like a screw twisted into wood and touched by it all over. He held one arm around her like a hoop. He pressed his knuckles into her pubic hair. His semen ran between her fingers and down on the grass. Jenny burst out laughing.

"What is it?"

"I don't know," she said. "It's nice to be able to take these serious things so seriously."

She pressed up against him again. They twisted around each other in a coil. He grasped around her and caught hold of himself. They lay still, as if they were waiting for someone to come.

"I feel like a bowl for you," she said. "And that acacia is one of our milestones."

"The grass is wet from us both."

It seemed to him they bore the city on their backs, like a turtleshell. It closed around them and expanded to their movements.

Waves of shadow followed waves of light across the plain. He had pulled down her skirt a way and there were streaks across her thighs, as pale as the skin of her inner arm against the rest of her body. He wanted to say something about these light stripes but lacked the vocabulary.

"Presence of mind is a good expression," was all he said.

He noticed an unexpected stab of new desire. Like a light that spread diffusely just under his skin. He loosened her hand from his stomach and dried it off on the grass. He bit her gently at the bend of her arm as if making a test. Then she arched up quickly and sank down on him, but he wasn't ready, his stomach was pushed in and she had too many clothes on.

"It came so quickly," she whispered. "Now I don't know what I'm wet from."

She hid her head against his neck and was silent.

"Are you crying?"

"It's just I'm filled with more than I have room for. Don't worry about it."

"Free flow," he said. "A useful bureaucratic notion."

"I didn't know I could be so happy. I've so often thought: 'survive,' not 'live.' Get through the worst of it. I want to die before you. The only sort of immortality I can imagine is one where your eyes see me and your hands touch me."

She looked up at him with a shyness as if she'd said too much. We can look at each other in the midst of our dizziness, he thought. He fingered her smile.

"We must be enormously interested in ourselves," he said.

"Let's say in each other."

"We've got a nice habit of speaking well of present company."

"Quiet! I hear voices."

They jumped up and started to walk. It was the two old ladies, who'd turned back on the diagonal path across the plain. Jenny had her car at the Art School, where the ground was cracked by shiftings of the earth's crust. She drove barefoot, and he washed her wound and put on a bandage when she stopped for red lights.

"It stings a lot," she said. "I notice it now you're not petting me. We pretty near bit the dust."

"Like driving a car," Jan said. "It's all a matter of inches."

"That's a risk we take, of course. But back there in the grass we seemed out of reach and you were hidden deep in me. And then . . . ."

"It's not allowed to hurt," he said, and circled her kneecap with his finger.

"I can still see that kid with no eyes rattling by on his mower. I was so scared. But my stupid insides clamp together with lust at the thought, because you were just about to come right then. And I left my sunglasses under our tree."

"Let me off at the terminal," Jan said. "I'll take the bus to Arlanda. And say hello to the moss and the Secretary, if they're all still there."

POINTS

THEY MET AT Bromma Field. Jan took the transit bus from Arlanda, and Jenny had only a short way to come from the Department. His schedule at the traffic tower had given her a different working rhythm and she now took papers home with her more often in the evenings. He in turn tried to keep a couple of hours free in the middle of the day.

"This could be a business lunch," Jenny said. "There's a roof of poisoned air over Europe all the way up to central Sweden. Crops don't yield as well, and people feel affected without understanding why. So our air section and the Air Traffic Department, which is you, are working together on a plan."

"OK," Jan said. "It'll be a while before Arlanda gets a restaurant as good as this. They do a very good spareribs of alligator."

A Metropolitan came in for landing over the edge of the forest behind the Bromma church. A yellow taxiplane stood waiting to conduct some diplomats on a tour of the Swedish defenses. Jan felt as though he were at work. The faces of the lunch hour customers gleamed like radar screens. He threw a glance at the wind gauge at the end of the runway.

With Jenny these days he walked in a city where he had no past. Everything came by way of her. It was like the Italian monarchy, which didn't exist outside the labels on sardines.

On the steps below the East Asiatic Museum he had followed a butterfly and thought about the fact that if you put it in a vacuum it would go on shining even after death. Airlessness and life could be alike.

They had wandered along the pontoon piers by Kungsholm, where steps led up the hill and the water had shiny streaks as if it were worn by the paths trampled into the winter ice.

And they'd stood beneath St. Erik's Bridge, wrapped in the smells of the chocolate factory, listening to the trains thundering by above them. They were surprised by the things they did, and Jenny said, "We're bumping against the fence of our preserve, that's all. From the outside we probably look like animals of some kind. Equality is the greatest invention because it's a thing that never existed, not in nature and not in the merchants' cities."

"But no one's looking at us from the outside," Jan said.

They'd been to see *The Guests of Night*, Marcel Carné's old film about the two agents of the devil who first intentionally, then unintentionally, break the rules of earthly love. "Can a person belong to another person completely? In that case, love is like death. I'd rather live." Somewhat later, the same woman: "Since we met I have a tremendous desire to live."

And Jan had thought about his present situation—living in

incest, in love with two people and feeling resplendent as an Easter egg in his happiness. He pretended they'd finally invented perpetual motion. Could only the initiated understand? Yet many people love two parents and several children and never question that.

The places where he'd been with Jenny, or where he'd been by himself and thought about Jenny, were points on a halftone screen. In the end they made a picture.

"There are certain places where I've never been," he said. "Obviously."

"I mean on you. I don't think I've ever had my tongue between your little toe and your ring toe."

A man slapped him lightly on the shoulder, asked something about the next issue of the staff newspaper but didn't wait for an answer.

"Recognized," Jenny said.

"He's at SAS domestic. I remember him from the university. There you have my life. The staff paper, foreign visitors, lectures, and trips I've never made. Otherwise I do my job according to the service instructions. That's a difference between us. Because to some extent you can affect the course of change and influence political authority. I can tell myself I work for a collective, for the indefinable best of a great many people, but it's a luxury to believe I'm indispensable. My job could be a little more automated."

"Yes," Jenny admitted, "I can force out information and convey it on, and maybe find some way forward through all the facts. That's fun because it's creative. But I'm on uncertain ground. Who can I count on? Even the experts are subject to other people's formulations and emphases and measurements. They plead premises and rules, directives and limits. It's easy to blame someone else."

"You'd look at society a little differently if you didn't think you were doing something new and important. What kind of a society do you want?"

"One that makes me feel it's exciting to be alive," Jenny said.

"That sounds irresponsible."

"I'm talking about the steps beyond security. It might feel like being in love with you. I want to be a fantasy that meets with yours. You draw out what's hidden in me. Neither John nor anyone else could do that—I mean, I wasn't able to do it when I was with them. I don't want to be blinded by ideas of how one ought to be. I want to get lost with you so we'll find our way after all, since there are two of us, twice as many. This is almost a proposal."

She looked cheerfully matter-of-fact.

It occurred to him they were running the risk of becoming self-sufficient—a community parallel to the existing one and concealed within it. A counterimage that put the rest of society in shadow.

"What do you want yourself?" Jenny asked.

"Any regime can be justified somehow. And if it's necessary, the state is always well enough armed to dispense with justification. I want a society where people can most easily get the society they want."

"Governments and big businesses hardly ever know what they're going to do," Jenny said. "I've had direct experience of that. They have to have suggestions and proposals. There isn't any great conspiracy at work, but there's a void, a dead space. And people can fill it with a desire to live differently. We have to familiarize each other with utopias and ten-year plans, all blending together. The future exists, just like countries we never visit. And the ones who get the ideas are individuals, laboratories, small companies, action groups."

"I find it easy to think of myself as manufactured," Jan said. "Dependent, mechanical. What I want is so little compared with the powers that have me by the scruff of the neck. My duties are determined by the density of the traffic. The larger context is a thing I can't control. Nor do I want to. I don't want to have that kind of power."

"Nor that kind of comprehensive picture," Jenny said.

"That's what Sten Tidström says too. I'm always at the extreme edge of something, at the beginning or at the end. I'm always a middleman, connecting signals, arranging, tying things together. Day after day I make the drive from Stockholm to Arlanda, and I have the feeling I couldn't leave the road."

"Still you know exactly what you're doing. What's more, it's important. Not just to me."

"You don't need to comfort me. I can do my job with blind precision. I know it's a matter of life and death, but that's too much to think about. I knew a traffic controller who killed himself when he saw two planes collide on his radar screen."

He pointed at the plane leaving the terminal for Visby.

"I mostly sit in the control room in front of my radar target, with my buttons and my microphone. The light in there is indirect and dim, I'll show you sometime. I'm alone, writing down figures and code numbers on a form. They're abstractions that shut me off from direct experience. It's not like when I talk to you. And I get so I'd like to leave that hole and declare myself autonomous on the spot. But somewhere in the sky a plane would become equally autonomous for a while, and I'd be turning life and equipment upside down. Anyway, there's no danger, I'm a responsible robot. I can imagine reacting differently, but I guess most of the time I feel uncritically comfortable."

"You can't ever just go away like I did," Jenny said. "You have to give regular notice. Your responsibility is more direct than mine."

"I can see myself from the outside," Jan said, "exactly the way I can see the mentally ill, the people who are anesthetized and satisfied with their routine. Should I change jobs? And what am I best suited for?"

"For making me happy."

"There, you see?" he said. "Successful departmental director comforts housewife with inferiority complex."

"I didn't mean it seriously."

"Me neither."

"You require so much empathy. The bright points on your screen are all human beings."

"You've got exciting projects. Gertrude too, because she's interpreting things that have already been defined, she's filming a vanished milieu with a camera made this year. You're my project, the two of you. I try to find time for us, what they call free time or leisure time."

"So many people are so undeveloped," Jenny burst out. "Think of all those freshly scrubbed vacuum-cleaning kittens of women who go waltzing through the ads. When half the people in the world are a storehouse of talent and there are a million roles and not just this one of sitting with the children at the mouth of the cave and waiting for an exhausted man and being disappointed when he doesn't bring the whole world home with him. What men think of women is less interesting than the fact that girls so often think the same thing. What scares me isn't men's prejudices but women's limited thoughts about themselves, and how ready they are to leave themselves out and become irresponsible."

"At Arlanda we've trained the first woman traffic controller," Jan said. "The world doesn't change by itself. Values play a part in changing it. And knowledge determines action."

"But what kind of knowledge?" Jenny said. "It seemed to me I knew you after an hour. Intuition made me take the risk, just like you."

"Instinct versus the bureaucratic order, that's the conflict of our time. That was in today's paper. But you use both."

"On the very threshold of something new, you discover yourself. At the last minute—or the first. It can be awful."

Jenny stopped abruptly and pointed to a man. His face was boyishly narrow, his hair almost white. He caught sight of them and nodded almost imperceptibly.

"He's an associate professor at the Institute of Technology,"

Jenny said. "I haven't seen him in ten years, except in pictures in the paper. We met at a summer course in Denmark. We swiped a rowboat and rowed out to an island. . . ."

"And?"

"Made love. It was fun. But it was toward the end of the course and then we didn't see each other anymore. I don't know why. I think he was engaged to someone. Now he goes to conferences. He's got a house in Djursholm and a lot of children. Sometimes I can still hear his voice, tremendously friendly, and sometimes I thought I might call him up when I was lonely, just call, we could have lunch, and then I realize all of a sudden that it wouldn't do, not even today, in this country. . . . Or else it would do very well."

"Have you ever called?"

"Once. No one answered. Maybe that was lucky. The telephone fools you. You reach out your hand. You say words to fill up the surprised silence on the other end."

"I've heard his name," Jan said. "Maybe at the Air Department. Sweden is still small. It's funny the way you can still picture them, their faces and bodies. . . ."

"It's not important. Let's get back to you."

Someplace they all exist, he thought. In the city. In a suburb. On their way to a plane. He had known only Gertrude. From the beginning, her and no one else. Brother and sister—society was right, there was between them something so nearly indissoluble that the law must intervene.

A large, freckled hand came down on their blue linen tablecloth and made the beer glasses tremble. It was Klas Lundin.

"I recognize you from the summer's only party at the Water Palace," he said to Jenny. "What are you having? Turbot. And elephant kidney for the gentleman. I've just consumed shrimp and wienerschnitzel and some Norwegian snaps. I came on the plane from Jönköping an hour ago."

"What are you up to?" Jan asked, his tone laboriously casual.

"My advertising agency has to move to 'equivalent quarters,' as they say. The city's tearing down the building. So I was up at the Real Estate Board to talk about it, and I went into that old separator factory next door. Picture it—tarred planks, rusty iron beams. And when my eyes got used to the dark I saw enormous models in plaster and plastic. There was the Stockholm of the future like an accomplished fact. Freeways coiling across unsuspecting islands and forests."

Telling them about it seemed to please him. He sent greeting to Gertrude. With his reddish hair and open laugh he hardly seemed capable of passions any deeper than the smörgåsbord, Jan thought.

"We are not exactly strangers around here. We'd better go," Jenny said. "I'd imagined Bromma like an abandoned steamboat pier."

"Funny we should run into Klas when we were just talking about him," Jan said. "But if the city isn't a meeting place, then it's nothing."

"With nowhere to hide. But cities are getting to be less and less like meeting places. At times they're empty. And it says 'No Stopping' everywhere. Do you want to come to the bank with me?"

Jenny's salary level translated into fifty-five thousand crowns. She put part of it into a long-term savings account. She was thirty-seven years old. She earned considerably more than he.

"You don't think it's odd?" she asked uneasily. "That this is all so everyday, I mean."

"No, you're as tangible as a jar of marmalade. But I get so stirred up from just looking at your hand. What if there was complete censorship. People wouldn't be allowed to tell their secrets. Not even brush against their lover's neck. Your fingertips would burn!"

"Jan," she said mournfully, "if you'd met Gertrude instead of me, the same thing would have happened."

"I don't know. I've never met Gertrude. We've been together from the beginning."

He was afraid he'd said too much, but she didn't ask.

"We mustn't pretend anything about Gertrude," she went on. "She exists. She may be the most like us of all the people we ever meet. If we invent her, we draw a chalk line between ourselves and her. Then we'll feel superior. And then right away we'll draw a line between the two of us.

"Remember one thing," she said as they were leaving the bank. "Your attitude toward Gertrude is part of what I love in you."

"Your saying that makes me feel strong and calm," Jan said.

"It's nice I have some experience," Jenny said. "So I know how it is. You've taught me to distinguish between love and what's really something else—a desire to fasten yourself to someone, to torture yourself. I'm finally free to bind myself as much as I want. You've made me less certain than I was before, and happier. Through you I know there's more in me than I can understand. You've done away with an absence around me, but only now that you exist can I see the contours of that absence clearly."

While he listened to her, Jan watched the students at the Bromma traffic control school walk along the edge of the runway to study the marking lights and the measuring gauges. He caught sight of a round object in the short-cropped grass—a beer can, or an interplanetary guest, recording, with the finest instruments, his impressions of this accidentally encountered world.

"I want to be careful of our love," Jenny went on. "But to hurt myself I can pretend you have other priorities. Then I force you to explain things you're bad at explaining. And then I forget the person you are, though I've known who you were almost from the beginning, ever since the *af Chapman*."

Jan Backman touched her gently. She looked around watchfully so no one unwanted would see.

"The bark is hardening around you," he said. "I'm enclosing you into my tree. You'll have to change your profession to dryad."

S THE PLUNDERERS

SHOUTS FROM THE BAY. In the dark, they could just see two figures out on the water. They seemed to be sitting on an overturned boat. Jan had taken a few days' vacation, and this was his first evening at the Water Palace. Now he and Gertrude ran down toward the shore across the molehills on the meadow. They weren't sure of what they saw. It had grown cooler, the fog was wrapped around the bushes without hiding them, like tissue paper stretched around big presents.

Closer to the shore they were relieved to see the two figures were afloat, not bobbing to the surface for the third time like drowning people. They were drifting past at a pretty good pace, sitting on something that looked like a gymnasium horse. At one end there was a brass propeller, and they were at the bow to balance the weight of the stern.

"It's a little racing boat," Jan said.

The boy and the girl caught sight of them and waved.

"Have you got a boat?" they yelled. "We don't want to leave ours."

"Paddle with your feet!" Jan hollered.

"It doesn't do any good. We tried."

Jan had walked out in the water to his knees and thrown a line, but it didn't reach. Gertrude ran after the rowboat, she moved fast and started to pull it down into the water. Jan put himself at the oars. The gunwales were low and the water splashed in as he rowed. His hands were burning by the time he reached the drifting boat.

Gertrude threw over a line and they tied it around the propeller shaft. Both the boy and the girl slipped into the water before they were pulled aboard. They were younger and smaller than they'd looked from the shore. They dragged the boat up between the rocks, and the children followed them into the house. They took off most of their clothes on the steps. Jan made a fire. Gertrude got out some extra clothes.

The boy said he was twelve, the girl almost fourteen. Their names were Bengt and Monika, they were brother and sister and lived on Vindö in the summers. They were cold and shivering, mostly with repressed fear. They'd been forbidden to go out in the boat, which belonged to their twenty-year-old brother. They'd been drifting for over an hour without reaching land. Bengt had taught himself to operate the motor, he and his sister had been alone, the temptation was too great.

"You'll have to call home," Gertrude said.

"We don't dare. Couldn't you do it?" Monika said.

Gertrude got the number. Jan didn't listen to the conversation. He thought about first aid but all he could think of was putting on water for tea. The girl had on Gertrude's yellow beach robe and she stood shivering with her hands crossed on her breasts. Her brother was naked under Jan's bathrobe. Their jeans and sweaters and Monika's bra lay on the kitchen bench.

Gertrude came back.

"I told your parents you're going to stay here. They sounded relieved, to tell the truth. They'd noticed the boat was gone."

"They think we're a lot of trouble," Bengt said.

He said "we" in an unyielding way, as if everything one of them did echoed in the other.

"Is the boat insured?"

"Don't know. Björn'll probably have to pay. Or Papa."

"Or you two."

"I don't have any money," Monika said. "I'm still in school, just barely. I've only got one year left. I'm not awfully brainy, see. So the rest of them will have to take care of it."

"Do you want your own rooms or just one?" Gertrude asked.

"We'll take one, we're used to that in the summer," Monika said.

Suddenly she started to cry, hard, almost howling. Jan was frightened. Bengt sat deathly still, his shoulders hunched together. It was because they were so scared of their older brother, he said.

"You could have been drowned," Gertrude said. "Did you think of that?"

"We capsized making a hard turn," Bengt said. "I banged my head. All I remember is swimming straight up through yellow water."

"You didn't have any life vests," Jan said.

"We forgot," Monika said. "We decided all of a sudden. It was just going to be a quick run. Then we went out in the bay beyond the Vindö passage. We're good swimmers."

"We didn't want to leave the boat."

"But it got colder and colder," Gertrude said.

"Well it was almost evening, and then it got dark. Then we got scared, it felt like the boat was sinking, we were practically in the water the whole time, every wave washed over us. That's worse than swimming."

"You could have died," Gertrude said.

"I don't ever want to look at water again," Monika said vehemently.

They sat quiet. Bengt took an apple Gertrude offered him and bit into it noisily. It was like packed snow inside. Two drops of blood from his gums showed as he handed it to his sister.

"Couldn't we listen to the radio?" Monika asked.

She seemed unaccustomed to silence. It was a program about millwheels and flysnapper eggs with folk music in the background. Jan served the tea.

"What's this place called?" Bengt asked.

"The Water Palace," said Jan, feeling self-conscious. "And how many of you are there on Vindö?"

"Three plus two," Bengt answered. "And then Grandpa, but he took his sign down a couple months ago."

"What?"

"He died. He's dead. Do you live here all the time?"

"Mostly in the summers."

"You don't have a sailboat! Otherwise we'd have seen you. You have to go pretty close to us through the Vindö passage and we sit on the hill with spyglasses and count and watch what people are doing."

"We know everything," said Monika apologetically. "We've got the Sailing Society's register. We find out everything."

In the next silence she turned up the radio. The volume increased considerably. Bob Dylan's "Like a Rolling Stone."

Gertrude, who was somewhat smaller than Jan, gave them pajamas, but the children were still way too small for them. You could hardly tell which was the boy and which the girl—Bengt's hair was as long as his sister's, they had the same broad front teeth. Jan thought he understood what they were like—they knew a lot the adults didn't know, it was adult knowledge, but of a different kind. They changed their tones of voice as if they were remote-controlled from some hidden instrument panel.

Gertrude pounded warmth into them. She wasn't afraid of touching them. They could have been their own children. Jan looked at their twin-like wrists and was struck by a sensuous desire to touch them, by a need to worm his way into their lives and take part in their growth.

"Do you stick together a lot, I mean, play and think up things?" Jan asked.

"Mostly in the summers," Monika said.

"We put a wasp and a spider in an envelope and sent them to Monika's biology teacher," Bengt said.

"For identification," Monika said.

"Did you get an answer?"

"We generally act anonymously."

"I see. You didn't really mean for your brother to find out about taking the boat."

"Now you'll have to go to bed," Gertrude said.

One room was called the Travellers' Room. Guests could sleep there in emergencies. It was temporary in some inexplicable way. The rug didn't go with the low chest of drawers. And a bouquet of dried flowers failed to give it a stamp of permanence. Every time Jan opened the door he was prepared to find it empty.

Gertrude made up cots and handed out soap and towels. The children watched in silence.

"It's cleared up," Jan said, and threw open the window. "Look at the stars!"

"They ought to have nameplates," Monika said.

"But you can find out everything anyway," Jan said coolly. "You've got those registers."

The girl's fingers drummed on the dresser.

"Have you got bats?"

"Regular bats?" Jan said and looked at Gertrude. Slang changed.

"Did you think I meant ghosts?" said Monika. "Or bats in the belfry?"

Bengt grinned appreciatively.

"Sometimes we have bats," Jan said sharply.

"Have you got a canoe?"

"No."

"Don't you fish?"

"Rarely. We buy fish at the Coop. Sometimes the fish man comes."

"We could fish for you."

"You'll be better off taking it easy."

"We can fix up some stuff for you in the morning," Bengt said.

"I can give you jobs," Gertrude said.

"We have to worry about ourselves first," Monika said.

"And the boat," Jan said. "And your father and mother."

"Have you got any pop?" Bengt asked.

"In the morning," said Gertrude sternly.

In the kitchen Jan smoothed out their wet jeans, worn, almost silver-gray. He looked at the frayed pockets and the heavy double seam down the seat and up to the fly. They had identical pants. He could see their dirty fingers, the girl's thin upper arms and long collarbone.

In the morning it was quiet in the house and the Travellers' Room was empty. Two white enamel mugs stood out in the kitchen, traces of black currant juice on the insides. The sun and the windowpanes made a pattern on the wall.

"Where do you suppose they've gone?"

"Probably down to the bay."

"They can't very well go off in their boat."

Then Bengt appeared, wearing a fencing mask.

"Hi, where did you find that?" Jan said.

"In the attic. Whose is it?"

"My father's," Jan said.

Gertrude was silent, she had almost said the same words.

"Did he get stabbed to death?"

"No, he's in Brazil."

Then Monika came in.

"We found this newspaper in the attic. Look how old it is!"

Jan unfolded it. The first page was covered with news of the atom bombs over Hiroshima and Nagasaki. That was obviously why Mrs. Tapper or maybe Adolf Oscar Backman had tucked it away. They never saved papers themselves.

"Do you know anything about Hiroshima?" Jan asked.

"We saw a movie on TV. And heard about it in school."

"It's not something that's over," he said. "You've got strontium ninety in your bones, both of you. Not even unborn babies are safe. They're affected by this thing we can't stop playing with."

He watched the way Monika pressed her hands against her stomach.

"Are you coming, Monika?" Bengt asked.

"Where?"

"Down to the bay. Are you interested?"

They spoke as if Jan and Gertrude weren't in the room. Gertrude forgot to ask if they wanted breakfast. They'd probably provided for themselves.

"Have you got any ice cream in the freezer?"

"No, we're out."

"Come on, Bengt."

After a while Jan went down to where they were sitting on the rock, knees up under their chins, looking at the water where birds bobbed up and down like floats and an outbound steamer made reflections in its own wake. He brought out some air mattresses.

"I thought you never wanted to look at water again," he teased Monika. "School starts this week. So you'll be going home today and we'll wait and see what's to be done with the boat."

"We don't dare. Can we stay till tomorrow?"

"OK," he said right away. "We won't stop you."

"My tan is starting to peel," Monika said. "Have you got any suntan oil?"

Jan saw in his mind a door loosening from its hinges, and there inside an indistinctly glimmering darkness. He went to find a bottle of oil. Monika gave it to her brother and took off her sweater. She was wearing a bathing suit underneath, and Bengt rubbed her back with long, sure strokes.

"I have to fix myself up a little," she said.

She had a lipstick in her pocket.

"You were certainly up early," Jan said.

"We inspected the house," Bengt said. "In case there was

anything neat we didn't have at home. We started with the attic and then we never got any further."

"Attics are usually best," Monika said. "There's a lot of things people don't dare throw away, because they figure they can use them again for something they don't know what."

Monika handed Bengt her comb. He started combing her hair without a word, tried to make a part but gave up and let it fall the way it wanted. He divided it over her forehead and ran his finger down to the base of her nose playfully, as if it were something they were both used to and liked. Monika tapped on his wrist and got back the comb. She had thin, white blond hair and a straight nose and narrow, pale blue eyes. From behind, they had the same brown, elastic bodies. And their hands were alike. That's the way it was with children.

Boys and girls get along more easily these days, Jan thought. He was surprised and a little excited by their touching each other, code signals on the skin. He couldn't approach them naturally. He began to be very curious about them. If he'd been invisible he would have watched them in their most secret movements. But he didn't know what he wanted. He was gripped by some kind of troubled yearning. They'd moved a little away from him and started whispering.

"What are you talking about?" he asked suddenly.

"We won't tell," said Monika coolly.

He hadn't expected any other answer. He left them and went up to the Water Palace.

"You had lunch with Jenny," Gertrude said. "Out at Bromma. Why didn't you say anything? I'd like to have seen her too."

"It was about air pollution," he said. "That's why we were out at Bromma. What else did Klas have to say?"

"He calls when he hears anything from Sten. Marianne is sick."

"He didn't write us that."

"Sometimes people don't mention serious things to their closest friends. They choose someone a little further away."

"He seldom says anything about Marianne to us," Jan said.

"Maybe that's because he likes you."

"Don't be silly. Marianne is so obvious for him. Botswana is a different story."

"Are they coming home?"

"Klas didn't know."

The false picture, falsehood's own truth, he thought. In his innocence and straightforwardness, Klas Lundin could very well be the one to draw the picture for Gertrude and make it ineradicable.

He went out to see what the children were doing. Gertrude set out buttermilk and sausage. He couldn't find them, so he pushed into the overgrown rhubarb patch to cut some stalks for preserves.

The yard had formerly been cultivated—asparagus and strawberries, beans against the southern wall and cucumbers in frames. They'd let grass and clover grow over everything. The apple trees were mossy and bore spotted fruit. Jan regarded all this with mild alarm. Couldn't he and Gertrude carry on anything, uphold a tradition? Gardening was the impulse that governed other people's lives.

He stood in the rhubarb and saw them. Bengt was flattening out the soil in a flowerbed with a spade. Monika was leaning over him, or over something on the ground. She was definitely holding Bengt's head against her shoulder. Jan was again amazed. Every name for what these children are up to is certainly wrong, he thought. Something eluded him. They had their own lives.

Bengt put down the spade, took Monika's hand, and they curtseyed. He looked at his sister as if proud of having performed something for her. Then they both laughed, to all appearances triumphantly.

The wind ripped up the clouds and the light was strong.

There was something grown-up about their bodies. From behind they looked alike. The tight, gray-white jeans cut in equally below their hams.

He strode up to them. Monika jumped visibly. Bengt braced himself against the spade.

"What are you up to?" he said. "We're about to eat."

"We found a dead rabbit and buried it."

"Dead?"

"Killed by a fox, we think. We buried it here, so there'd be flowers too."

Between art nouveau violet clematis and tall dahlias, the ground was packed and clean. Jan couldn't remember what they might have pulled up, they said themselves that nothing had been growing there. Inside his brain he could see how the flower roots caught a foothold in the rabbit's ears.

"The rabbit was in your yard," Monika said. "We wanted to do you a favor. We can fix the steps down by the dock too."

"No, don't bother. I'll get a carpenter out here."

He suspected they were up to something quite different, for which the steps were a likely pretext.

At lunch, the children were quiet at first, then started a round of precocious, mimicking chatter.

"That sink has seen a lot of winters. . . ."

"Do you never vacation abroad . . . ?"

They were turned toward each other in tasteless understanding. It was as if they owned the Water Palace. Jan wanted to rip down the bridge between them so they'd become more ordinary and helpless.

"Poor rabbit," Monika said. "Worms and loneliness, no food."

"The dead don't care about the view from the cemetery," said Bengt.

Between themselves they carried on a conversation closed to outsiders. Maybe they were nervous after their accident, and from being with strangers. Jan wanted to surprise them with something. All he could think of was mushroom gathering. Gertrude thought it was a good idea. It was like in the old days, except he couldn't remember they'd ever done it before.

It had rained recently, and unravaged fungus beds lay all around the Water Palace. The scaly hedgehog mushrooms were lizards' backs among the moss. The saffron milk caps looked like fallen targets.

"Here's a russula," Bengt said. "Somebody bit it."

"That's impossible," Jan said. "It's still attached to its stem."

He leaned down toward the mushroom. It looked as if some animal had closed its teeth on it and then let go. Did rabbits like mushrooms? He tasted it. It burned like curry against his palate.

"Poison russula, not almond russula," he decided. "Gertrude, this is your field."

There were ants all over, dragging along their trash. Wax agarics shone scarlet in the gray moss.

On a slope by the blackthorn bushes and the alders, meadow mushrooms grew in fairy rings. They were already large when they toiled up out of the earth, carrying wisps of grass and topsoil along on their caps. They spread out in white sheets, were eaten by worms and rot, then sank in brown pancakes onto the grass. Jan picked the fresh ones. They were good, dry and firm.

They walked across the point to the turnaround where the car was parked. So as not to be anticipated, Jan said he was thinking of getting a new one and mentioned different makes. But the children didn't even listen, only Gertrude looked surprised, and he felt outwitted again.

Gertrude showed them a ditch covered with leaves where heavy lilies shot up from invisible water. The lily beetle, like a lacquered nail, had gone over the leaves with its punch.

"The stone altar was around here somewhere," Jan whispered to Gertrude.

"A little further on," she said. "We left our bikes on the path."

Aloud he said to the children, "Do you know what stone raspberries look like? Do you know if they're poisonous?"

"I don't know what they look like," Bengt said.

"I've never seen any," Monika said, "but they're not a bit poisonous."

"That's the first time you've come up with different answers," Jan said.

"What kind of a stone altar?" Monika asked. "We heard."

"Just a sort of hut," said Gertrude. "It's gone."

"What did you do when you were kids?" Monika said.

"We were here," Gertrude answered.

"Both of you?"

"Yes, sometimes."

Jan suddenly expected Gertrude to tell them.

"We knew each other long before you were born," he said, for safety's sake letting them vanish in a prehistoric well.

"When there were still cows here?"

Monika was standing in rhubarb and horseradish in what must once have been a kitchen garden. She was fingering a rotting log, half covered with strawberry runners, where wasps came to get their building materials.

"No," Jan said truthfully. "Not such a long time ago as that. But at the time of Hiroshima."

"Tell something you used to do," Bengt said to Jan.

"When I couldn't afford gum I used to chew pieces of wax and dig for skeletons."

"Did you smoke on the sly?"

"I made my own. I'd roll toilet paper around dead leaves— it wasn't so thin in those days. It was wicked, but it didn't last long."

Jan lost the desire to come up with emergency memories like a little old man. He didn't mention that it was Gertrude who'd offered him his first cigarette. She took it out of their father's desk, and they smoked it up in a tree.

Clouds tumbled over the tops of the pines and dark shadows ran along the ground. A chanterelle turned as brown as a paxil and so it was neither. The usually distant stock doves perched tight in the crowns of the trees.

"Can't we go home?" Monika said. "It's going to be a thunderstorm."

"What are we having for dinner?" Bengt nagged, already.

"Stewed lynx and granite with crow feathers," Jan answered serenely.

He was glad they were staying till the next day. But he didn't want to make an effort for them. He wanted some strange force to hold them at the Water Palace even if they were bored.

Jan cleaned the mushrooms at the kitchen table. He spread out a newspaper, the one the children had found in the attic. Someplace there was his past, which he hadn't wanted to talk about. After the atom bomb on the first page, the ordinary paper continued in its familiar sequence—domestic news, entertainment, home, sports.

He opened to the family page and while he peeled off the slimy cap of a *Boletus luteus* he looked at the engaged girls and the wedding couples leaning toward each other so they'd fit in a single column. All these faces and smiles. How faithfully human beings lived up to their own expectations, how seldom they dropped their masks on life's great occasions, as durable and blinding as the flash of the camera.

Gertrude fried the mushrooms on the stove, boiled some spaghetti and made a meat sauce with bits of ham. Jan ripped off a piece of foil and managed to catch a glimpse of his face in it, distorted and askew.

During dinner the children led the conversation into different ways of killing each other. They took most of it from TV.

"I take a fresh bill and cut his throat and then burn the money," Monika said.

"His?"

"Yes, the victim, whoever it is."

She looked at him calmly. He felt as if he'd been placed on an extermination list.

"I take the victim into the sauna," Bengt said, "and take an icicle and stab him in the heart between the ribs."

"But he was caught," Gertrude objected, "because he took the icicle out of a thermos, and a tea leaf had stuck to it from when the thermos was used before."

"Oh, you know," Bengt said. "Do you remember the woman they locked up in the vault?"

"Yes, she slipped bits of paper out through the ventilator, and to keep herself from going crazy from claustrophobia in the dark, she felt her husband's trophies from various regattas, and she held them in her hands and thought herself out onto the sea one summer in the thirties."

"You know everything."

"How to kill people?" Gertrude said. "That's not hard. Mouth to mouth is harder. Bringing someone to life, I mean."

"In school you learn less about dying than about being born," Jan said. "And what about that rabbit?"

"That was already dead. Do you want us to dig it up?"

The bay outside was wrinkled. The evening sun came in, and the air in the dining room shimmered like green water in a swimming pool.

"What's it like here in the winter?" Monika asked.

"We put papers on the floor by the glass doors," Gertrude said, "but there's such a draught they blow up around the legs of the table. Otherwise we leave everything where it is."

"Doesn't it get scary?"

"Well, yes. Sometimes we don't light the lights. We don't want the night to see us. It presses its huge hands harder and harder on the roof to smother us."

He saw all three of them as if through cloudy celluloid. A tern dived at the water's edge of his consciousness and came up with something glimmering in its bill.

He ought to call Jenny. He wasn't forgetting her, but the

children prevented him. The Water Palace, Gertrude with her project, the boy and the girl who'd come drifting along on the bottom of a boat—they were closed worlds, and he couldn't connect them with Arlanda and the streets in Stockholm.

"Do you think about anything when you're getting undressed?" he heard Bengt whisper to his sister.

She looked at her thin nails.

"I don't know. Sometimes about if somebody should come in real unexpected and put his hands over my eyes."

"But I'd be there for heaven's sake," Bengt said low.

Something stirred in Jan. He wanted to sneak into the Travellers' Room to be surprised himself by what Monika was doing and by her not knowing what it meant.

The children had to be taken for who they thought they were. They used fumbling, grown-up tricks to cover their passion. They imitated and counterfeited with the help of the intelligence that was starting to draw the first adult lines in their faces.

They actually went to bed.

"I thought they'd be going down to the bay or out in the woods," he said to Gertrude.

"They're probably afraid of the dark."

"I'm going to bed too."

"I'm going to work awhile. I've got so much to do. We've gotten to be like a family."

Jan went out in the kitchen, opened the refrigerator, and took out a cup of hardened egg white that fell apart into sharp crystals. He heard them running water in the bathroom, screaming and laughing. He gathered they were brushing each other's teeth with their elbows linked. They snorted and spit. They had ceremonies together. He knew what it was like.

A little later he went out and walked around the house. He noticed swallow nests glued up under the eaves. Otherwise it was starting to get dark with winter seriousness. And today they'd seen fall on its way in from the sea, heather-purple, bog myrtle-brown. The fieldfares sounded as if they were taking up a course in typewriting. But the hazelnuts were still soft.

It was dark in the Travellers' Room. If he called to Monika her brother would wake up, or she might cry out. He stepped in among the poisonous monkshood in the flowerbed under their window, and that was all. An experiment with a mood, with the will to act, with ruthlessness. He thought about gestures that aren't made and words that aren't said, so no single little change will occur in the universe.

He didn't know what he wanted, and Monika wouldn't understand. Did he want to tuck in her blanket? Or hold her shoulders? He was a child again himself, seduced and initiated by Gertrude. He would like to ask Monika—outside the silly roles they'd come to play—whether he should crush impulses, or follow them out to be rid of them.

Because it wasn't her innocence that attracted him, he knew nothing about that. It was her knowledge, which he couldn't reach except maybe through involved and half-unconscious ceremonies like once upon a time with Gertrude. It was the opposite of Jenny's experience, which captivated him equally strongly because it was available beyond all ritual.

He looked carefully in through the window. Bengt had disappeared under the sheet. Monika, as light and quick as a toy only moments before, was sleeping like a woman, with one arm under her head, hunched up on her side, not sprawled like a child.

He went back to Gertrude. She was spreading out photocopies of something in an illegible hand. She had her Project O, as she called it, and he was of much less help to her than Second Lieutenant Gosselman and the volumes of the *American Fern Journal* and what N. J. Andersson had written and sketched during the around-the-world voyage of the frigate *Eugénie* in 1853.

"Haven't you gone to bed? Just think, it was only a hundred

years ago people got the idea that dolls ought to look like children instead of shrunken adults."

"Children sometimes strike me as undiluted adults," Jan said.
"They don't know they've already experienced most things, and
that you are not supposed to talk about the beginning or the
end."

He hugged Gertrude around the shoulders and pulled her
cardigan around her like a quilt. They had protected a secret,
which had thinned out until there was no longer much to reveal. Perhaps it was not the fact of their being brother and
sister but rather their concealment of it that was now the
mystery.

I   LIKE A ROLLING STONE

NSTEAD OF GOING to bed, Jan climbed up to
the attic. He followed in the tracks of the children but found
no newspapers with great events from the past. He looked in
vain for his father's foil. Had Gertrude cleaned up without
telling him?

The dry air under the roofing tiles was the same. His palate
felt dusty with the same unexpected excitement as the time
he'd stood on the crest of his first hill. The girl with the strong
hands and the quick movements had dragged him up there,
and something in him had remained in this attic, where the
height and lack of oxygen made his pulses pound.

She had danced on the unplaned floor. They had squeezed

the loneliness from each other's naked bodies. She had drawn a boundary around him—nothing existed beyond her voice against his skin. If he was her property, then she must be his as well. They had no one else after all. Without her nothing would happen to him, he hardly existed by himself.

But if she lived an unknown life where he wasn't woven in? He wasn't bright enough to comprehend what that would look like, but he had a feeling of how much more her body knew. She was larger than his picture of her, that was the picture's presupposition. His words wanted to capture her in a cupped hand, but they were too few, they were fluttering curtains. Someone in Switzerland or Sigtuna or Stockholm would take her away from him, and then he would land outside the burning instant where he dwelled. The quivering in his arch would disappear.

She was his great discovery. His lesser discoveries were arranged beneath it. When she looked at him with those sparkling eyes in which he had a share, she had a power she would never have again.

Once at a meal he had leaned down under the table and seen her empty shoes and her feet in toe position as if she were about to dance away. Would she live in the eyes of an unknown man as she did in his? Could their love be spread out geographically like some kind of surveying? But he didn't want to be flung out into the world.

At that time he'd had a laugh that was only for her. She knew it, and for just that reason it blew into the corners of her body, the ones she'd shown him without his being able to receive them. He had nothing to express his love with. He fell back into the blindness of his body. The shimmering arrogance in her was a thing he couldn't reach. But she could do whatever she liked so long as she did it with him.

The clothes Gertrude had dressed him up in were gone, the winter apples too. Someone had tidied up. But it seemed to him the entire Water Palace had become a single sound-swept room.

Moths whispered like nerves. He remembered the sandwich and the mouse they'd locked up in a suitcase. The suitcases were still there, it was better not to open them.

Gertrude had given him a desire to leap into the unknown. He gave himself up calmly to her half-maturity and its teachings. A cyclone had swept through him. And it was by common consent he tried to strangle her, so that both of them might experience what was most secret and wild, what in the end would separate them from other living things, or from each other.

He remembered the passion in the despair that followed, the leap that was checked, the action that hardened into ritual, the other people who understood nothing but took them from each other and sank them in indifference. He was no longer permitted to look at her while she slept—those moments of timeless mobility that filled his boy's body with an adult tenderness.

That was his only summer with Gertrude. They lived in a wonderful high pressure. Then others pried them apart and frightened off the echo between them.

In any case, they were brother and sister. In the long run, no one had the right to remove them from each other. Of this he convinced himself in order to protect his love, while Gertrude drew away to new experience that he couldn't share.

Gertrude didn't come home the following summers. The Water Palace was his. He played with other children, but they left a weak imprint.

He didn't go up in the attic until he was fifteen and felt as if Gertrude would never come back. He had no companions there that summer, and didn't miss them. He studied, and his father, expected home, was delayed. Business was more important, and Jan had learned not to wonder why.

Gertrude was lost like a stone in the water. There was a hole in him, with room for many stones. He filled it with a longing that hooked inward and diminished him, and with slime that dried away and movements that remained unseen.

It became a summer of uncontrollable masturbation that afterwards seemed more distant than his childhood. He wasn't prepared for this material that came from his body and smelled of detergent and iodine. He lay doubled up in his bed and splattered his face to see how it tasted. If he wanted to allow himself an extended seance, he would keep his hands under control and let his imagination unload the charge. The bathroom tiles were cold to lean against, he sprayed the mirror and then adjusted his face behind stiffening snail tracks and went out to Mrs. Tapper, whom he called Edith, and who patiently ironed his clothes. His dreams of inaccessible women left no traces in writing, only occasionally on the sheets.

No one had warned him. Sin did not dwell in his world, where an admonishing God was as absent as his parents. Evil had other domains. Mrs. Tapper had on one occasion stated that there was an impurity that had no name. But for this nameless thing, this act that wasn't in the dictionary, he felt not the slightest interest.

Masturbation—the dream of yourself as an isolated destiny. The girls he assaulted in the attic were not boomerangs but remained absorbed in themselves. He didn't demand their attention, only to be allowed to handle them. Gertrude was given no place on this film. But she was allowed to watch, with eyes like mineshafts. In a closet he found a bathing suit that had been hers. Hesitantly, he used it for his purposes, and washed it carefully. Then days went by before he could bring himself to resume his games.

Loneliness was in itself a debauchery. From his confined place in the attic or the bathroom, he glided like a carpenter's plane across the surface of the world. Coiled shavings fell from this plane and nothing hindered his progress. He lacked a counterweight when Gertrude wasn't there.

The wooden steps down from the attic had the same knots, but the soles of his feet had been replaced. When he came into the bedroom, Gertrude had left her kingdom of the ferns and was getting undressed.

"Do you think about anything when you're getting undressed?" he asked her quietly.

"I thought you were asleep," she said, surprised.

"I took a walk."

He didn't say he'd been in the attic, first with her, then alone.

"Did you go far?"

"Into the woods a ways. And back."

On their French tapestry was a lady riding a lion, out of the forest. That was his own route. But it constantly curved in again.

"So you haven't been sitting keeping the children awake," she said, as if it were a question of their own children.

"No, you can rest easy about them. They're asleep."

"Why don't we take out all the rugs?" Gertrude suggested. "The house would be bigger and cleaner."

"And noisier. But that doesn't matter."

In the morning Monika was sitting on the steps making marks on a paper. She didn't see him come.

"What are you doing?"

"Practicing mirror-writing," she said, with a threatening seriousness that made him laugh and shiver both at once.

"I guess you should go home today," he said uncertainly.

"Should we?"

She didn't seem to remember.

"I'm going to talk to your parents."

Then Bengt was standing there.

"In that case, we're going to talk to our parents too. About you."

Jan thought he'd heard wrong.

"About us?"

They both nodded.

"About what you did to us."

Jan couldn't speak for astonishment. The children whispered to each other and looked at him meaningfully.

"Yeah, who knows what we'll think up?" Monika said.

"You're crazy," Jan said. "You're pernicious."

"What's that?"

"You destroy things."

"Have we destroyed anything? You're the one who's crazy."

"I wonder if you didn't turn over that boat on purpose," he said irritably. "As an experiment—for the fun of it? And now your brother has to tow it home."

"There, you see?" Bengt said to his sister.

They seemed calm, as if they had the proof in their hands. What could they say about him and Gertrude? Child molesting? Seduction of minors, aggravated by the use of a disguise and a false address? Or had they seen him with Jenny? Certain children were believed no matter what they said. People were led astray by something collected and sensible in their appearance.

"Your brother isn't the least bit dangerous," Jan declared. "Have you even got a brother? You made him up so you could stay here."

Again the children exchanged a look. Monika made a couple of marks on her paper. She ticked him off on a list.

He told Gertrude about it but she paid no attention. She was working with a concentration he wasn't used to. She fried ham and eggs for all of them, and then he drove the children to a dock on the Vindö passage where they were picked up.

On the way back to the Water Palace it occurred to him that the children were repeating something Gertrude and he had been through. He had behaved himself badly and to no purpose, and now there remained an emptiness and disquiet that the children left behind. He thought he could hear Monika's footsteps on the gravel, he could see her hair straggling with rain. She didn't trust him.

If you just let it all be, he thought, and never touched any-thing, then would all the water be covered with seaweed and algae and all the land with moss and lichens?

He decided to call Jenny. For her, he wanted to be trans-parent. After all, she couldn't know what it was like in the attic. But he let it go.

When he saw Gertrude, his eyes adjusted to a particular distance. She came into focus, other things blurred.

"We ought to go out for a ride on our bikes," he said, "now we're rid of the kids."

"You've got a lot of different ages in you," she answered unexpectedly. "I don't know where to place you. The bicycles are broken. And you know what? I can't find that little cash box. I've looked everywhere. Did you take it?"

"No. But I've got the key."

"It's easy to break open."

The papers had formerly been in a safe deposit box, but that seemed too formal, so they bought a strongbox for their insurance policies, the title to the Water Palace, and some letters from their father.

"Vandals, kleptomaniacs!" he yelled. "It must be the chil-dren."

"Yes, you and I don't have any reason to play tricks on each other."

"We don't know what they did in the mornings. In some way they wanted to surprise us. Or get a hold on us. I told them they were pernicious. I told them what it meant."

"Why should they take it?"

"Because it looked valuable. I'm sure they haven't opened it, but now they can't give it back."

"You'd better call them."

Jan dialed the number.

"Monika? Good you answered. There's a certain thing we're missing, and we wouldn't mention it to you except that we . . . ."

He explained, and noticed that he said "we" just the way she and Bengt did.

"We didn't take anything. We never take things."

"But you find out about things, you said so yourself, so can't you . . . ."

"What do you really want? Or have you gone crazy?"

"I'd better talk to your father again," Jan said.

"Go ahead!" Monika invited him. "If we *did* take something, do you think he knows about it? He knows everything of course."

"Or your older brother," Jan threatened. "He could help us look."

"What was in the box since it's so valuable? Gold?"

"Papers."

"We've got our own papers. I'm talking to *him*," he heard her emphasize to Bengt, who was apparently standing beside her.

"OK," Jan said tiredly. "But in case you happened to take that box along, you might give it back."

"Bengt says if we *did* take it, we could have put it somewhere, like maybe in those mushrooms where you were whispering about your altar."

"I can't get anywhere with them," he said to Gertrude afterwards.

"I thought so. Did you think they were going to confess? But their tone of voice might have given them away."

"They've got a whole repertory. It's for luring intruders up to the barbed wire and then putting them to flight."

"What was in Papa's letter?"

"It's the one where he gives us the Water Palace. It makes it clear that we're his children."

"The surveillance is tightening all around," said Gertrude. "I'd like to go to London and do some research. They've got Carl Christensen's and Johan Smith's fern herbariums from the middle of the nineteenth century."

"London!" Jan burst out.

"I didn't think you were particularly interested in what I was doing."

"Your project? The idea you came home with that time I forgot my key?"

"Yes. I've been thinking about it ever since. All I've wanted to do was sit here and work, with the realization that this exists far beyond the two of us and still depends on how I see it. My field came to life because I finally caught sight of it—like an old deep-frozen giant lizard. Isn't that worth taking a leave of absence for?"

"Sweetheart, I understand that very well," Jan said. "But you haven't been particularly communicative. You've been closed up in your book."

"You too," she said. "I mean, you haven't been saying much either."

The Water Palace now lay inside the Stockholm recreation area, exposed to the enterprise of brokers and agents.

At the same time it was a mirror inscription in his and Gertrude's lives, and a whirlpool whose suction would not let them go. It had been left to them out of nothing. And they themselves had no one who could make legitimate demands upon the house.

"We can't be sure the children have the box," Gertrude said. "I haven't seen it for a couple of weeks."

"They offered to fix things up for us," Jan said. "They said they were looking for stuff they could use for things we never thought of."

"First we saved them. Then they warned us. And finally we were plundered."

"The rabbit!" Jan shouted. "What if that was a lie? They buried the box instead. They wanted to have a buried treasure. No one opens a grave. They always seemed to think everything through very carefully."

"Shall we look?"

"Let it go. Digging up an animal is kind of nasty."

"We can get a copy of the title," Gertrude said. "It confirms the transfer. And the letter doesn't really matter one way or the other. I don't want to have the feeling we really *ought* to be exposed."

The wind blew, as monotonously as in a shell, with an echo of earlier seas. The bubbles in the windowpanes, captive and visible, moved.

A ROPE AROUND
THE MIDDLE OF THE CITY

JAN BACKMAN RANG the bell at Nibro Quay. When Jenny saw him she let out a yell and hugged him hard. She'd been in the bathroom and thrown on a raincoat to come to the door. She was naked under the stiff plastic, he noticed she had just bathed and he fell on his knees and kissed her on the stomach. She closed him in under the coat and from there inside her voice sounded strangely resigned.

"I'm on my way out with someone else."

He saw it in front of him in the darkness against her skin— restaurant, movie, home to the same bed. He stood up. There was nothing alien in her eyes, she looked straight into him.

Self-pity swept through him first, he felt it as a tightening of the shoulders. His hold on vitality slackened, he felt weak.

"Has John come back?"

"No."

He thought he could see in her face that she was more sorry for herself than for him. A sun lit up at the bottom of a well. It didn't matter who it was. It seemed to him he'd grown up, beyond suspicion and evasion. He wanted to take part in Jenny's life without anxiety. And when he thought of Jenny in someone else's arms, he identified with Jenny and not with the other man.

He was filled with a pleasant generosity. They could send each other out to any kind of experience. They had sewn their safety net long before the performance began.

"When is he coming? Have we got time to go out and buy you some red wine?"

Jenny's face between laughter and tears made her look angry.

"He won't be here for a while. I won't let him come in. Don't ask any more now, I'll tell you about it."

She sat down on the edge of the bed and searched with her feet for the green elf slippers.

"I wasn't expecting you. I called Arlanda. You'd be at work tomorrow. I called Gertrude. Yes, we really do have things in common other than you. In the great kingdom of nature. Moraines, for example, which we're buying by the cubic yard. There's a lot of geology at the Academy of Sciences. Don't worry. I felt very sisterly. I play a secret game, and that is that Gertrude would understand me . . . and the whole thing."

"I was on my way here when you called."

"I knew where you were, of course, but you'd been swallowed up by the earth. I called before. No one answered."

"We were out picking mushrooms with two children we saved from drowning."

And he started to tell her about it. But not about climbing up in the attic. That would take too long. Though it didn't seem to him there was any secret to give away. It was true he'd been swallowed up. The children had held up an incomprehensible inscription against a mirror and he'd recognized it. It was very simple.

"I suspected all that," Jenny said calmly. "You didn't call. It was a little thoughtless, or insensitive. You did say I'd hear from you in a couple of days. I was so happy that day. I had a floundering fish in my belly, I only had to look at the oranges in that bowl there and they laughed instead of me. Anticipation happiness. And then you didn't call, and it frightened me that I had to love someone as much as that. You know I don't want to feel defenseless, least of all when I have you. And the fish turned into a heavy, dead cannonball and I threw it up. Then I lay quietly with a blanket over me and was neither heavy nor light, because there was no world around me."

"And so you talked to someone you knew? And you decided on a date?"

"Not out of spite toward you. But to avoid being so dependent on you just when it didn't do any good. And because I was tired after a busy day and tired of waiting for you and tired of myself. I felt deplorably anonymous. I often do. I have no more identity than a vegetable, a carrot."

"And I was far away, getting interested in other things—I wasn't in your waters," he filled in.

"I sort of wanted to show both of us that I *can* have fun without you, because after all that ought to reassure you, or else I'd have to tell you that I can't have fun. I talked to you the whole time, not intentionally, but because I'm made that way."

She was still naked under the raincoat. He pulled her to him, and for a while they lay quietly close to each other on the bedspread. Their bodies waited unexcitedly for signals.

"It's you I tell things to, and everything I do is so you can hear about it. If you didn't let me say all this, then what's between us would be hard to grasp. You're not a father confessor, but you remember what I said about the anthill. You have to confirm the fact that you're with me wherever I am. And I can't know that unless I tell you exactly what I've experienced, even when it's not at all worth telling."

"It's too bad we have so little time," Jan said.

"Wait! I'll call him."

He walked over to the window and looked out at the belt of green to the east—the Nordic Museum loomed up like a huge animal at the edge of a river. Jenny came in from the dining room and threw her arms around him.

"We've got the whole evening! If you want, of course. I begged off. He didn't sound at all hurt, it's a colleague from the Department. Don't think I treat people any old way. I can explain things to him in the morning. There aren't any feelings involved."

"Shall we go out and buy some wine for ourselves instead?"

"I've got some. And we can buy food in the subway if we want to eat at home. But first . . . ."

"Yes, first tell me everything."

Because what Jenny told him seemed more important to him than anything he'd experienced himself.

"I want to make myself as hard to get at as you are, for the sake of balance. But mostly it's some kind of a greed for life, or curiosity. Not a desire to risk anything between us. I've told you that before. I don't know anything that could injure me except the ordinary things—bacteria, an automobile accident. And I so badly want to be yours on our own terms.

"I no longer confuse my little fevers with love. They're not dangerous. I know what you may be thinking: I'd really rather she didn't . . . I guess we're programmed in most things. Violent opposition probably doesn't do any good. You look unhappy. Sweetheart, wait for better reasons!"

"Why did you go to bed with him?"

"Out of desire. Because I want to do things out of desire, not out of need. That's what we said on the *af Chapman* after all— we don't need to compensate ourselves. I spent the night with him. We may never do it again, and if we do it doesn't matter. I hadn't really figured on it. Eat, drink tea, talk, laugh at things—that would have amounted to the same thing. We kissed and petted. If I'd drawn limits, wouldn't it have been a double standard? We were very nice to each other. But it was what I was afraid of—the fun part was you. I knew right away I'd tell you all about it."

"Did you count on my understanding?"

"No. Deep down it seemed the most obvious thing in the world that you'd feel the same as I. But I also felt resigned. I love you, but if you don't understand that I can behave this way in spite of that, well. . . ."

"If I backed off from you, it wouldn't be on any moral grounds but merely out of self-preservation. I don't want to be a barrier between you and something you think is fun. And I don't want to be left in some sort of hazy landscape in between."

"You have me for as long as you want me. I must lack imagination, because I can't imagine your looking at me coldly. I'm the Jenny you know, no one else. You mustn't be unhappy because of anything I do, it's not worth it."

"But you like doing the sort of thing that isn't worth it?"

"Oh, I can get awfully loose. After all, sex is so tremendously much fun. My imagination is too active; I can't put in a lot of time and effort. I like men without gravity and bluster. Quick, light men. You shouldn't be able to see a house and a car in their wake. Those heavy, stiff, successful, plodding men with their fear of emotion . . . their bodies make them fatherly, superior. . . . I've had enough of them."

"Bodies in themselves are nothing special," Jan defended himself.

"I need to learn that a little more directly. You can't possibly teach it to me. It's nice to know an act that's so complex with you can be so simple."

"That's easy to say and hard to understand."

"Sex doesn't have to have anything to do with love. Only with lust, or tenderness, or curiosity."

"You're obstinate," Jan said. "An independence that thrashes out in all directions. You go to bed with other men to convince yourself it doesn't mean anything special, and with me to prove the opposite. But I suppose I might do the same thing. At least for the sake of imitating you."

"I want to do away with false jealousy. For me there's only one kind of betrayal—opening myself completely to someone else and not letting you know. But from time to time I feel an urge for a lesser lust, a commonplace and simple lust that makes no demands."

"Jealousy is mostly plain envy," Jan said. "You begrudge the other person an experience you can't have at the same time. My own jealousy is like this: you can do whatever you like with whomever you like, but don't blur over the remarkable things that have happened to us. We stood up on Vanity Hill and looked at the blue lights from Saltsjöqvarn, and I kissed you on the throat. A thing like that can't ever be remembered completely. But it's there, and moves through me like a heavy swell. And I want that swell to move on through you. It mustn't stop, unless it stops in both of us at once."

"Nothing can take away what's ours," Jenny said. "Nothing. I'm not the least bit uneasy about that. I just don't want to be a hypocrite. I want to be able to tell you I want such and such a person, let me go, it won't hurt us. When I was married I didn't dare say that, and that affected my relationship with my husband. I would like to have had his understanding, that would have been decisive for me.

"You love Gertrude, and when you come here you find me freshly bathed and ready to go out with someone you've never seen. And still I don't doubt for a moment that you love me. Other people probably wouldn't understand that. I myself probably misunderstand other people's motives constantly. No one can understand me if you don't."

"Start with the fact that I can take almost anything," Jan answered. "Once you've been through a closeness like ours you lose your fear. You've made me emotionally free. It's a question of feeling your own freedom so strongly you're not hurt when the person you love feels his."

"I'm faithful on the 'long-term-plan,'" Jenny said. "We can destroy this ourselves, but no one else is strong enough to get the better of us."

"I hope nothing bad ever happens to you through me. If you can't depend on yourself, then you can depend on me. Though it's not so easy to be obliging and passionate at the same time. I'm not the type who's spurred on by your being with other men. I'm the opposite of a duellist, competition isn't my line. I've never liked those stories about suitors and adolescents performing great feats for their beloved. The secret of love, I guess, is that you are recognized even if you're a motionless withered blade of grass."

"If I ever again fall in love with anyone else," Jenny said, "then I'll know it's because of something we're teaching each other now."

It occurred to Jan that he really ought to keep track of what he was going through, because this was the sort of thing people wrote novels about. Those who never went through it wrote about it. The strange part was they sometimes knew anyway.

"Now we're going to have an orgy of food," Jenny said.

She pulled on long pants and a blouse and they half ran to the subway and then back.

And after a lot of activity and slamming of cupboard doors, everything was ready—wine, bread in a wicker basket, a dish of peas. On a shiny granite platter lay a rack of lamb with jagged vertebrae and fat dripping from the abutments of the ribs. Baked potatoes wrapped in silver robes of foil, when unveiled they resembled the embalmed face of a pope at some recent grave opening.

The walls in Jenny's main room were white, the ceilings high. On the floor was a rough gray wall-to-wall carpet. Jan pulled the mattress off her broad bed. It became a raft on the sea. They curled up on its surface and gathered together what they owned, waves raging on every side. The tray of food floated alongside like a dinghy.

Jenny stood long-legged on one corner and changed into a striped cotton nightgown. They danced on the mattress. Jenny reached toward one wall and unplugged the phone. They sank down on their knees, ate peas with their fingers.

He burrowed his face between her legs, separated her pale inner lips with his tongue, her moisture had a reluctant taste, he drank it and she became better able to feel him. He stretched his arms along her body and clenched his fists in her armpits.

He knew what he should say at a moment of such pleasure. But he couldn't say it, for the very reason that he knew. It was too close. And besides, his tongue was occupied in searching out places where she was as sensitive as just inside the corners of her mouth.

Then he kneeled over her and was inside her, and her legs lay straight up alongside his body. He could reach and kiss the soles of her feet; he could finally do what he wanted with her feet, which he loved as much as the palms of her hands. As so often before, he felt they managed to save something worthwhile from remaining undone.

They lay on their mattress raft, a green plaid shawl for a cover. Their bodies were wet. They were breathing hard, but not enough to move a propeller or fill a sail. They weren't carried away.

Some bread crumbs in the bed against his skin and the sensation of a cold spot on the sheet . . . his happiness took up more space than his reason.

"It feels as if you'd been in some deep hiding place," Jenny said. "Some part of me that had never been used before."

You can never be certain, he thought, that your own feelings are echoed in the other person. And yet you feel so certain anyway because they fill you so completely.

In the course of a ninety-minute movie a man can have two

women or a woman three men. In the same length of time a man can manage to shoot ten other men. The extravagance of indifference. . . . When he'd opened the back of Jenny's dress, the zipper had caught halfway down and she had straightened her shoulders until the slightly freckled skin wrinkled along her backbone. She helped her fingers with her body.

To find something longer than time, tougher than habit. . . .

"There ought to be a third sex," he said. "This isn't enough."

Because what he felt was a desire so deep it seemed to represent something else.

"And one conscience," he added. "Not two."

"The food's cold," Jenny said.

They lay at the table. Their mouths became shiny with fat. They rested their elbows against the coarse surface of the sea until their skin burned.

"Shall we go someplace and dance?" Jan wondered. "We've never been out dancing."

"Do you go dancing with Gertrude a lot?"

She rarely drew comparisons between them.

"With friends sometimes. To the radio at home. Gertrude loves to dance. You've danced yourself out at the Water Palace."

They got dressed and went to Domino. The pillars in the dance hall were tall and dark, the loudspeakers black, there were orange lamps on wooden poles, and on the walls flickered color pictures of bodies dissolving in clouds and steam.

"Do you remember on the *af Chapman*?" Jenny said. "We recommended this place to a foreigner."

The musicians and singers wore black trousers and orange shirts to match the decor. There were girls in pink pajamas and transparent dresses dancing on a platform by themselves. Others were sitting on a spiral staircase to the gallery, drinking Florida milkshakes and Iced Coffee Kenny and waiting for something.

Jan and Jenny danced in the dim light a yard or so apart. That was the way it should be—the other's body was a goal and a reflection, and the music alone was the message of the senses. They felt shut up in an underground garage or an atom bomb shelter.

Jan hit on a better idea and they left Domino. At a café in the process of closing for the night they ordered tea in a thermos and left a deposit. Then they went to Riddarholm.

The island monument lay in metaphysical silence. The automobiles had gone. There was a light in the window of a caretaker's family in the Court of Appeals—windows with curtains and cactus instead of white venetian blinds indicated the presence of human life even at night. There was also a light in one of the offices of the Aliens Commission, where some lesser official was writing out deportation orders before dawn arrived with its protests and appeals.

Otherwise there wasn't a soul on the island. The darkness put the gulls to sleep on Riddar Bay. Mälaren's waves were etched in the stones of the quay.

They found a bench at the edge of a bastion. They drank tea, looking out at the arch of lights on Väster Bridge.

"I see this view a different way," Jenny said. "If the green algae are damaged by chemicals, they won't supply the sea and air with oxygen. And then we'll all stop breathing."

"And on the other hand, you can wake up in the morning with a split lip and not think about the seas at all," Jan said. "Or one person touching another person's fingers, the right or the wrong person's—that can seem more important than anything else."

"Yes," Jenny said. "Love in lower middle age. It's strong."

"The earth has its mucous membranes and we have ours, which we have so much fun with."

"I have so much to get to work on. The World Environment Conference in Sweden . . . ."

"Do you mean you get pangs of conscience after our excesses, like a hangover?"

"No. And still I consider myself conscientious. And if we were free to do what we wanted . . . ."

"Then we'd do just what we're doing," Jan interrupted. "Don't you think? Or do you have some other picture of freedom? Some hazy picture of life on the open road?"

"No. I was just thinking that if we lived differently we might not be doing this and wouldn't know about it and wouldn't miss it. It's a dull thought."

Jan poured out the rest of the tea in the water, where interested coots swam over to inspect the leaves. Then they kissed in an entrance arch without either door or house, the beginning of a winding outdoor staircase. They followed it up to a sloping cobblestone square with linden trees between the Revenue Board and the Office of Crown Lands.

At the base of a rock outcropping below one of the old civil service departments they found a cast-iron stove lid. The rock projected from under the building so they could sit down. The lid didn't appear to have been lifted for a hundred years. Perhaps it hid nothing. In which case it was only a sort of street sign or instruction, firmly fixed in the rock.

Without understanding, they read the iron text: Sweden's Standard Elevation.

The Landing

FOUR

OUR LAND

THE METEOROLOGIST produced a photograph of Sweden taken from a weather satellite. Parts of the coast were visible, accumulations of clouds, fog over Gotland.

"This is the way we live," he said. "Occasional cloudiness keeps us from being seen."

"Domestic and International," Jansson said. "At airports, at least, there are limits to stick to."

They don't just go, Jan thought with foolish surprise, a lot of passengers come back too. To what? He was suddenly filled with warmth for this country and for Arlanda, lying so squarely in the mud and yet lifting itself from the ground every few minutes. This miserable makeshift took its illumination from a vision of the future that hadn't yet landed. He liked quite a bit of what he saw, and through it he caught glimpses of the weft in the weave, which it would be unwise immediately to fix in words.

From the tower he had a view of the Arrivals Hall. He had seen Jenny for the first time outside its doors. He noticed he was smiling at nothing in particular. He knew that in the middle of a random daily life, one person could come close to another, a little while, without fear, and then off again. Conversation or coitus, dressed or naked, it didn't matter.

Traffic was light. Jan sat down to read a long letter from Sten Tidström that had been addressed to him at the tower. Sten was his closest friend, and sometimes he didn't understand what it was that separated them.

Jan could more easily imagine changes in himself than in the world around him. He discovered that his small existence, as opposed to Tidström's large one, was in the process of growing happier and more flexible. He saw young people floating idly crosswise through society with no feeling for possessions. He suspected that new experiences were being tested whose results would not affect society for a long time yet. People seemed to touch each other more—they played and tumbled and embraced. The sensuous surfaces had grown.

The two of them weren't so different. They were both very much involved in something. Jan remembered something Sten had said, that Sweden was the condition for his experience of Africa. As long as he was in Africa, he couldn't forget Sweden. And if he'd grown up in Botswana and come to Sweden, it would have been just the same, though the other way around. Both countries were hereditary monarchies. Doubleness. . . .

Jan saw him as the antipode he'd searched for as a child. All the different hours of the day prevail simultaneously some-place on earth.

Jan had written to Sten:

"No one's job or task is indispensable. But no one can be replaced. I and my tower here at Arlanda—that's no symbol of another way of life. Aren't you afraid of making value judgments? You've gone to Botswana in order to alleviate need. Someone else is there to exploit it. You border on each other. Wherever you find the one you also find the other. You're at the same level, like the water in communicating containers."

Sten Tidström answered in his letter:

An airplane flight of a few hours would be enough to change your mind. Remember, I'm not saying there's necessarily anything good about that. Only that a lot of things can change, more easily than you think, if you want them to.

Value judgments? It wasn't until I made a choice that my world became altogether real. I'm in Botswana. I've staked out an area—within it I'll succeed or fail.

The world is something more than the answer to my sensual impressions. At a distance, I register the explosion of an atom bomb as a sunset, but it answers me unexpectedly with dizziness and skin eruptions. My senses recorded falsely. I didn't have enough experience, the wrong metaphors presented themselves, and that can be awfully dangerous.

I admit to what brought me here—not rage alone, but also a desire to let something fill me to the brim. Sometimes I can hardly understand how you can go on living in a country where they advertise food that cannot satisfy your hunger, or how you can sit at Arlanda and guide off planes that won't turn back until they reach Johannesburg.

You talk about "unselfish aggression." The kind that can lead you to hell. Yes, I recognize it in myself—a biological need to attach myself to a group or an idea, to break out of the claustrophobia of my own body and go beyond myself in order to be incorporated with other people. Then it's a question of making a choice.

OK, I wanted a country to love and decided on this one. I go walking on the savannah. Bramble hedges around plowed fields, flashes of heat lightning like in Sweden, the birds look like green insects. Right at the moment we're having a seminar on education in agricultural countries, plus courses in construction, tanning, and developmental studies. I'm teaching design and bookkeeping in the school cooperative. And then we've got a jeep that travels around the villages with an instruction packet.

We're working on the elementary school level. Some

people call it standardization. Others, solidarity. Or community of values. To what end? Human beings are awfully easily influenced. I can put some of them into a position of feeling their dissatisfaction. I can undermine and educate at the same time. Practical knowledge is very nice—it makes you less hesitant about what's right and what isn't. But to keep adaptability from turning into conformity, it's essential that your objectives continue to be ideas.

We know what we want to teach—birth control, proper nutrition, hygiene, better agricultural methods. But we don't know how. Sell half your cattle, I tell them. Grind them down to corned beef and you can get ten thousand in the bank and pay for the children's schools. They don't answer. I watch them scrutinizing not what I say but rather me as a person. Do I have a good character? they ask themselves. Am I honest? Do I have a peaceful disposition?

If I'm to help shatter their traditions in a fruitful way, I also have to shatter mine—but which of them? What's good for them isn't good for me. I don't need land reform, I don't have any sick cows. I amble around the villages for a couple of weeks. There are slaughtered goats hanging by their feet from trees so the blood will run out. The women are mixing potatoes and curry powder. Teacups rattle like in a tremendous parish hall.

And then suddenly I want to go to a museum by myself for a whole day and look at old paintings and furniture. That's a need I can't explain to the people here, not yet. And yet I know they experience the same thing in different terms, because force of habit is no weaker in other people than in me.

When I set out, I didn't know many names. Now I do. I'm here on their terms. Most of the people I work with or teach with have nicknames or pet names—Tsokonombwe, the grasshopper, because he moves like one; Bere, the hyena, because of a story he told; Gonzo, the rat, who was in a movie; Maura, intestines, because of another story; Fullback, because he has such a fat rear end; Dzetze, the frog; Hukurutomba, the lizard; Chigupswana, the cigarette butt; Ndogani, the man who works alone; Ushe, which means "much too new to be given a name."

We've started raising squash. They're swelling. The school farm is pregnant with possibilities. We've squeezed our expenses down to 30 kronor per week per person—food and clothing and shelter. We need money to maintain our three Honda tractors, we've got an old Bedford truck we bought for 1500 kronor to haul fertilizer to the fields and vegetables to market, and then we've got a rusty Opel.

We started the Tonota school at a work camp one weekend. The Serowe Construction Brigade gave up their vacation to put up some classrooms. Seventy Swaneng students and six teachers had a ten-day work camp to go on with building. We've got enough money to take more students than expected—they fix their own food, chop wood, clean, sleep in double bunks for the time being.

Why do we try to cultivate our own garden in a country that's the economic captive of South Africa? I look at it as a defense—we are creating our own currency. Vegetables and literacy—longer lives, a new outlook.

I sometimes fall into a rage over the conditions of life. So then I have to move down to some more basic level so I won't come to a standstill—repair the bus, find pencils somewhere, get people to start eating onions and tomatoes.

The earth belongs to everyone. No one should be allowed to own land anywhere, only have the right to use it. I'm a socialist mostly because I've seen the way ownership creates power. Botswana's banks and corporations and railways are owned for the most part by South African interests. We can never stand completely on our own two feet, all we can do is be free along with other people.

The arms trade and a school of home economics—for a definite cause I'm prepared to work for both. When I see these people and their hunger for so much, then I'm no more interested in the sense of doom in your civilization than I am in a Wagner opera. At such times I see Sweden from a distance—flowers in the window, a few people whose thoughts and gestures I can make sense of.

In Africa are the masses. A throng, a darkness, eyes that never see me. And everything I've worked at and all my plans—no one cares about them. That perspective is dangerous and I close my eyes to it. When it really starts to threaten me, I'll have to come back to Sweden in order to survive.

Maybe Sweden exists to tell us there are individual destinies.

But it may all be an error of vision, false nomenclature. Are we at the tail end of a long evolution, or on the verge of a new epoch? We can't supply any answers without questioning the questions.

Here nothing is certain except sand, drought, and death. My microfilm company in Stockholm is in business to preserve and catalog. Unperforated sixteen-mm. non-inflammable film. The daily papers are saved from pulverization. There at home, everything will remain after us—like the heating pad and the slippers and the box with the cufflinks in the room where someone has died. But here we don't know.

People drag their baggage from place to place as if they were hauling their lives on their backs. They kick at the glittering grains of sand, the ones that sparkle like underground Northern Lights in the hours between day and night. That can mean water. Drill here! And a crowd of people materializes out of nowhere around the hope of water.

What do Swedes know about drought? The sun turns

the surface of the earth to leather. The birds disappear, because the bushes have no leaves to hide them with. A hyena attacks a newborn calf. The vultures look you in the eye. In this country, a long way from the sea, you take care of every green sprout, and you never waste water. The livestock on their grazing migrations turn back to the waterholes and find no water there either, though their mucous membranes tell them the rainy season is beginning. Then, and not before, they stagger and lie down and die, while the vultures gather.

I'm worried about Marianne. She's become terribly low. She thinks everything's going to pieces—not with us, I think, but with the country and the people here. She's become really frightened, and I'm afraid of what's going to happen to her. I notice I have more trouble taking care of my own than of strangers, classes, groups.

I'm terrified by her pessimism and depression. It seems to her the women are slaves. They do the plowing and the men tend the cattle. The women need courses in farming, but only the men come to the classes, that's also part of the tradition. And the boys get preference in school, since there aren't enough places. And then they marry girls who know nothing. They can't be companions, only have children together, and the children are raised by the women, and so it goes. . . .

She sees how the government lacks the money to exploit natural resources and has to borrow in South Africa when no one else offers. And then the country has to promise to stop the guerrillas from the north and the refugees from the south. Why should she teach ceramics and weaving when South Africa is lurking around the corner and the country can be turned into a prison and fall into martial law just like the countries on every side?

Marianne suffers more from what she sees than I. You have to live through everything yourself. Experience is something in the skin. But for her it's like a whipping. And she has a harder time than I do acting out what she feels. She just sits, stunned and subdued, with her head in a cloud of gloom.

I'm forced to leave her alone a lot, with one child of course. The other one lives and eats at the school. I'm on trips out in the country, after all, and often in Tonota.

But then I understood it better from the beginning and have maybe other sources of motivation. But I don't know if that helps. I've seen the white bosses. And for the first time I'm convinced there are thoroughly evil men. They commit no individual murders; they seldom go to prison. But with force, cunning, and extortion, they make their way toward a goal of continued force, cunning, and extortion. It's impossible to talk to them.

All that sort of thing has hit Marianne right in the gut. She hadn't expected it. I couldn't prepare her. She can't experience the kind of emotional liberation I can. She doesn't get mad, only humiliated by the fact that mankind's conditions are what they are. She sits doubled up as if she were slowly being consumed by psychic bilharziasis.

I wish you knew what I should do with her. Shall I talk her into going home? And what if she doesn't want to?

A person's strengths and weaknesses are distributed differently down here. In Sweden we didn't know what might be useful. Sprayed hair never stands on end, but what do Swedes know about the desert winds and the ghosts in Botswana? I've said it before—come down and try!

Jan put the letter in his pocket for Gertrude to read.

THE FERNS

GERTRUDE WAS ON A leave of absence to write her thesis, but she often had errands into the Academy of Sciences. Some of the weekly schedules at Arlanda made it so that Jan hardly saw her. He usually slept at Upplandsgatan.

Jan didn't know much about what she was doing. He opened an essay on circumpolar ferns and didn't understand it. When he saw her periodicals from the Linnaean Society in London, he remembered that she'd wanted to go there and stay in a boardinghouse and spend time at the British Museum. Everyone wants to go to London, he thought. Everyone—that was his vague collective name.

He noticed that he hesitated to read what Gertrude wrote. Nor had she asked him to. Gertrude's book—something to weigh in your hand. A completed thing that was part of the future. She had been occupied with this, while he . . . .

He had never seen her working so intensely and so silently. It was as if she were, maybe without knowing it, packing things for another life.

It was as though she had put up a sign to keep people at a distance: Notice! Creation in Progress! He blamed a part of the distance on her. But it was mutual. Things were happening to them from both directions. How much did she understand?

Jan picked Gertrude up at the Academy. Within this empire of knowledge, whose windows looked out on oaks and freeways, the fugitive might slip a secret message between the pages of Isotope Magazine. Here you could find, in binders full of old letters and letter fragments, directions for measuring the pores of an eggshell. One scholar dozed over his own work on the winter sleep of sea animals. Another resembled more and more the polar hare whose family he'd been studying for years.

Jan felt unsure of himself in Gertrude's professional surroundings. He watched her nod to a stranger and grasp a familiar doorknob. She had a desk in a glass cage, a telephone, her own towel in the lavatory.

He wondered how much she talked to other people, how much about them she wanted to know. He had seen a shyness in her that became open and reckless only for him. But what if he were mistaken? She didn't explain and analyze the way Jenny did. At certain times she was quieter than at others. Processes went on beneath the surface. It had always been that way.

He observed her in the Academy world of other people's calligraphy. Men of action had become stuck like portraits on the walls. There was a lot no one asked for—the catalog's cul-de-sacs.

He tried to understand the way knowledge changed on its way to the recipient and rose like bubbles to the surface of another sea.

The sudden joyous light of moments of genius.

But also the shadow of insane vision, problems that time never brought one step closer to their solutions.

Gertrude saw the ferns change in the research room, while the hygrometer stood at a constant forty per cent.

When Jan picked her up she said, "Sometimes everything seems so monotonous and predictable that I have to hold on to myself to keep from kicking up something we'd regret."

He'd noticed she more often said "I." Maybe she was closer to a life that was only hers, to a face she couldn't call theirs.

"What sort of thing?" he asked, not understanding.

She didn't answer. Had she caught a glimpse of love's destructive side? Invisible birch roots undermining a whole garden? Was she tired of being defined mostly through her relationship to Jan?

"I'm finding something to vent my feelings on," she said. "Something's taking over part of it for me."

"Tell me about your thesis," he said, as they drove out to the Water Palace.

"I'm tabulating the existing plates and descriptions of cryptogams in Swedish botanical and travel literature between 1790 and 1870. The book's to be comparative and interdisciplinary. I'm trying to ascertain how much of that material is taken from foreign works. And how much of it is based on actual observation. I go through the important nineteenth-century European fern scholars—Heinrich Link, Desvaux, Kaulfuss, and especially Adelbert von Chamisso, who went around the world on the *Rurik* collecting ferns for the botanical gardens in Berlin. There were three hundred and ten thousand fern specimens that survived the bombing of Berlin."

"They did better than the people," Jan said.

He thought of the mosses at the Department of the Environment. He'd never been there with Jenny. Gertrude must have been out at the Water Palace, immersed in her studies, that day. His reality took on edges that were vague and frayed, as if he were seeing it through a poorly adjusted telescope.

"I'm writing about perception," Gertrude went on. "How great were their chances of really seeing something new that didn't fit their yardsticks? Individual discoveries, for example in botany—did they see them in isolation, or against the background of a definite world view? For what reasons did they make their observations? They were on the move during the long zealous dawn of natural science. Everything was going to be organized into classes and systems. They thought they were on their way into caverns of secrecy that they would illuminate with reason. In principle, nothing was irrelevant, the meeting of different objects could reveal them or make them mysterious in some new way."

"If you stare at something stubbornly, you can see its negative," Jan said.

"My naval officers discovered giant ferns in the delta of the

Orinoco. Those plants had been in existence since the Coal Age, and they drew sketches of them. They brought home a piece of news. They didn't think it would get out of date. But the ferns they saw were colored in part by their way of seeing, by their technique and their time. As plates, they belong to history. The ferns in Carl Willdenow's herbarium in Berlin are dressed up Prussian Empire style, though maybe it's mostly the violet ink and the straggly handwriting underneath that give you that impression."

Jan pictured the fern forest with its thin, pale trunks. The chill along the ground and the soft moss—if you put your foot in it, it wouldn't recover until the next rain. Blueberries. Mushrooms in crevices. The smell of moose.

And you could see a long way between the trunks—beneath the crowns of the ferns, a world with a high ceiling. A wave of heat passed through him there on the winding Värmdö road. He felt like hugging Gertrude. But he couldn't find the words to tell her. Go your way to the land of the ferns. And then I'll see you approaching me again.

He hadn't said it out loud, not this time either.

Gertrude noticed nothing, she was looking straight ahead.

"They made drawings of the ferns because they wanted to save them," she said. "Maybe those were the only ones in Colombia. If only they were put on paper, the way the dodo was put in a glass case at the museum, then everything would be all right. They didn't care about growth. They didn't understand continuity.

"I've tried putting two fern leaves on top of each other. They don't coincide. The differences exist at an almost invisible level. But they do resemble each other.

"The fern forest consists of separate trees. If you save one, you don't save the others. The people who drew them on plates and fixed them with pins and pressed them on paper didn't know that. They thought they'd captured a type, not an isolated example. But all the others were still there outside, in the open air."

LIKE A FOLDED NAPKIN

ONE DAY Gertrude went in to the Academy and Jan was left alone at the Water Palace. Gertrude's dissertation had been discussed in the doctoral seminar in the History of Learning. She was to enlarge it in the biographical area and then it would be published in *Lychnos*. She was very pleased.

Jan saw poppies bursting once more into bloom, inexhaustible into the fall. He was so used to Gertrude's being there that when he heard a crunching on the gravel walk he thought it was she, not a bird. He was off work in order to put together one of his inauthentic, fact-larded talks on tropical lands.

He walked down to the shore. The bay had lost its color and gone as gray as the skin of a turbot, the waves as stiff as fins. He could see out to bald little islands where they'd gone on picnics with boiled eggs as hard as cannonballs. The white shells would wobble down through the water like bits of porcelain.

At this time of year, when the poplars lined up into a fall avenue, he and Gertrude generally talked about getting a dog, a brown or black animal that would root in decaying leaves and dash around among the alder cones and last year's reeds.

He started skipping stones, flat rocks skimming the still surface. Farther out, a school of stickleback scratched the water from below. He noticed that he'd unconsciously placed himself where he used to throw rocks many years ago, and Mrs. Tapper, or Edith, had been with him and said, "By and by you'll have to start looking after what's going to be yours. Your parents would like that."

She had meant the Water Palace, not Gertrude.

And she added, "You must miss your mother sometimes, Jan."

"I don't know," he'd answered. "I can't remember her."

Afterwards he'd thought out a lot of other answers, equally possible.

But he didn't miss his father. And there was no one else he was expected to miss.

He found a dictionary Gertrude had left out in a pouring rain. He pressed it under a frying pan on the kitchen table. While he ate, he opened one of those novels he found it exciting to think about but dull to read—the author rode his old vehicle like a practiced bus driver, and pulled up dutifully at every chapter stop to let his characters on and off, until it no longer made any difference whether the end of the line was a point where some of them would find or lose each other.

He thought about Gertrude's dissertation. It no more belonged to the two of them together than Jenny did. How had that come about? The book had had about the same amount of time to grow as his love for Jenny. Should he regard it as Gertrude's breach of faith, her way of ridding herself of their sibling dependence? Had the ferns served to sharpen her focus, so that she silently observed things as they were? Was she hiding a dangerous insight from him—like before in the Water Palace attic? Or was that just the wishful thinking of his bad conscience?

When he turned on the radio, it played Maurice Ravel's *Pavane for a Dead Princess*. It made him sentimental. He saw waves rolling in over the beach, and though they were sucked out again, people's footprints were filled with water from beneath. Their love was like that water that stays in the sand when the waves retreat. Theirs? Gertrude's, Jenny's, his own. Other people's too.

Why those calculated, established steps in a pavane? A lot of people were elastic because they were indifferent to each other, others were laced up tight enough to sense the lacing. He wanted them to be open, spacious and able to move in and out of each other because they weren't afraid.

Both of them beat within him—wing and propeller, different kinds of propulsion. He hadn't chosen to love them. But he ought to be able to choose what he wanted to do with his love and with theirs.

He began to recognize what, within him, was himself and what was alien, all kinds of trash and nonsense. A person is constantly being cheated and deceived. What the senses pass on is only a part. The dead princess danced on granite covered with autumn's rust, she had the smell of wet pine bark behind her, and was accompanied by a continuing sound of acorns falling through dry leaves still hanging on the tree.

He thought: you become the person you already are, though you didn't know it or kept it a secret. Like the captions for a film that hasn't yet been filmed. Or the list of illustrations in the front of a book.

He had a certain experience, heavy, but not heavy like a burden, rather like the head of a child resting against the palm of his hand. He had words, light and temporary, scraped together like leaves with a thin rake. And then he heard the sound of raking gravel walks, leaves catching and pulled off by hand; finally you wipe out your own tracks by dragging the rake behind you. . . .

Gertrude called when evening had spread a quiet light across the flat rock outcroppings. There was a smoky streak of mist over the closest island, he'd seen the same above old grave mounds when the moisture left the earth. He described to Gertrude what she'd seen herself many times. That gave it a sort of meaning.

She told him she'd been given a research grant. He felt warm and happy at her success. It had come quickly. Perhaps she'd been carrying that material with her longer than he'd realized. But only this past year had given her the means to produce. She and he had followed the same path. And then a variation on both sides, ordered by the laws or magnetism. The growing distance told them of the altered course.

He walked around in the house and it seemed to him that his eyes fell more readily on what was old and outmoded than on what belonged to the new convenience they would choose if they were forced: the telephone, the record player, the washing machine on wheels, the toaster, electric razor, the paperbacks. He put away the dictionary. Its covers were permanently buckled.

Gertrude drove back to the Water Palace the northern way across Vaxholm. By the ferry from Oscar Fredriksborg, she'd been stopped by some people who'd driven off the road. She'd given them a lift to a rickety house.

"They were American deserters. They're living on military land and expecting their parents to send out a persuading expedition. In the woods on the hill there was a cannon and a cracked gun carriage on wooden wheels. They had a cat on the porch railing, and mattresses on the floors. And a girl sitting gazing out at the fort across the sound. For all I know she belonged to all of them, just like the car in the ditch."

"They don't live so far from us," Jan said.

"I never had any idea they were there. They're living their lives right next door. It looked very makeshift."

Later Gertrude said, "Do you know who I ran into at the Academy of Sciences?"

"No."

"Jenny. 'How's Jan?' I said."

"You did?"

"Yes, just kidding. It just came to me. And then she went all stiff and walked away without a word. Is she mad at me?"

"Jenny and I have gotten to be very close," he said.

He didn't remember if he'd added anything else.

Gertrude looked at him as if he were the alien part of herself, a person she was frightened of but couldn't get away from.

DEVELOPED NEGATIVE

ALL THROUGH the fall they talked.

He tried to look at her afresh, as sister and stranger. The person I love, he told himself, exists for me even when I no longer love her. The certainty of that pleased him. But love was still the only word he could find to describe what he felt for her.

For the first time, it seemed to him his voice had a false tone as he assured her of what was true—that he had never pretended a feeling for her that he didn't actually have. She didn't believe him, a dividing line was drawn between them, a thick filter against sight.

It was his honesty that made the tone of voice between them artificial. Because there exists a kind of honesty that can unintentionally sound triumphant—ask me and I'll tell you something unpleasant. It was hard for him to see that he'd seriously kept anything secret from Gertrude. They grew from the same root after all. Now the truth seemed to limit them, because he had never managed to give it its proper form.

He knew they were capable of so much more. It all seemed enormously unjust.

Is keeping silent the greatest proof of love? he wondered. To want to protect someone like a child? Or had it been a cowardly desire to protect his happiness from inspection? Not until Gertrude looked at him as a stranger could she become strange to him. That's why he had kept silent. The easy naturalness between them was a truer reflection. After all, his love had not diminished by half.

He wanted to make Gertrude understand that he loved both

her and Jenny, and that none of them needed to feel cramped. It was no more unreasonable than the fact that he had spent a large part of his life with his sister. This knowledge was to come to her like the research grant—she could make up her own mind how to use it.

He called Jenny and told her he couldn't see her for a while, that he was having problems. Jenny reacted strongly. She felt alone, and saw him and Gertrude as a twin star, radiating the same light. A magnetic storm passed through the telephone lines. But he didn't go any further into what his problem was.

Gertrude was mending a dress. All at once she took the scissors and cut it to pieces. Then she sat motionless and finally her face crumpled up into tears, like a piece of paper just as the flames catch hold. Jan was in agony—I'm the one who's causing this. And at the same time, an anguish at not being able to make more than a part of her suffering his own.

It's important to guard yourself against becoming invulnerable, he thought.

"Don't you feel well?" he heard himself saying.

"I'm just something that exists," Gertrude said. "Not someone you're moving towards. Like parents. Necessary, but not much fun. You think you love me. I suppose it's true—a stiff, little love that wants to shed its skin. It doesn't have room for me. And I'm in a cage as long as that's true."

How wrong she was! The way she saw herself gliding out of sight! She thought her love fell right through him like a lead sinker. But at times he didn't have the strength to say anything. A dumb emptiness beyond fear and sympathy filled him, it was echoless, a murmur below all words.

"What can happen to us?" he asked without conviction. "We're brother and sister after all."

"What can happen," Gertrude said, "is that it doesn't matter to me anymore. That's the worst of all. I don't care that you're sad or happy. I'm becoming indifferent to what you do and to what I do with you. I feel like I can live without talking to you, without your existing."

"But you're my double. Outside and inside."

"I want to be someone else. I want to be the person you're moving toward, not the person you move within, because I can hardly feel that. Maybe we take for granted that we'll be loved as long as we stay the same person, but you become a different person as soon as you stop loving."

"But nothing's happened between us," he objected.

"We've lost something."

"Or gained."

"Yes, I'm stronger and more prepared. But I'm not sure that's a gain. Once you've been lost then you know how it feels to get home again. Afterwards, you can always say you've become one experience richer."

"I'm not the measure of everything," Jan said.

"No, there really are other scales. That's what I've been studying all this time."

"Maybe we're always happy on false premises, those times we are happy," Jan said.

"Have you ever felt like walking right out of your life?" Gertrude asked. "Down a low esplanade with straight clipped trees. You get smaller and smaller like on those perspective studies you do in school. The sidewalks come together in a point. And the point swallows you up. By that time you're already so small nothing matters."

"It was because I wanted to hold on to you that I didn't say anything."

He caressed her face and head, but she turned almost imperceptibly away. "I realize there was a kind of arrogance in me," she said. "You and I were going to manage what few others have managed. Brother and sister, sex, intimacy, constant companionship. I have the helpless feeling that somewhere along the line I could have molded it right. But your life already looks more different than I'd thought."

"You're Gertrude and I'm Jan, and maybe we're both of us someone neither of us knows."

Still an occasional aftertaste of summer—like the silver-white underside of a raspberry leaf.

And Gertrude said, "It ought to be enough to feel you breathing against my throat when we're going to sleep. There are no running agreements, only isolated situations. The present moments. I didn't need to care about the rest of it."

But the clarity of fall said, it's over now, smell the new smells.

It was as if they'd been using an old box camera to capture situations that were about to dissolve and slip away.

"Jenny?" she said. "No, I don't want to know any more. I'm not curious. Uncertainty is a disease, but I've had enough facts. My reasons are more complicated than you think. Now we have to try to take care of ourselves."

He saw her face smooth out as if it had been plundered.

And then she said, and it moved him and made him warm, "I know. The only way I can really approach you is to see Jenny through your eyes. But I don't have the strength for that right now. We aren't even married after all, in case you thought so. I don't want my life suddenly filled with that part of your life I have nothing to do with. That wouldn't leave me anything of my own."

"I don't want that either," Jan said. "What a waste for you to throw yourself into tortures you invent yourself."

"I could break into two pieces, one of them injured and furious, the other one understanding. But I won't."

"You and I chose each other," he said. "We knew the risks. You can't say it should have been so or so. If we hadn't been in love, there are a lot of things that could have been."

Gertrude answered hesitantly.

"I also love you for that other person you could be and maybe are, the person I don't know. And it seems to me at times that deep down I understand everything. But I'm not sure. I have to get you at a distance. I've never been weaned from you, if you can say that to a man."

Gertrude's calm amazed him. Someplace inside him he believed they were so parallel they couldn't cause each other real pain. The similarities between them almost wiped out the sexual differences which in turn let them feel the similarities more easily. Still he wondered if he were one of the thoroughly evil men Sten Tidström had written about. He wasn't worth her sorrow, and he said it with the same words Jenny had used one time. There was no justice in situations like these, and Gertrude knew that too. But he couldn't manage to regret anything he'd done.

There were three people now, and he belonged with both—whatever they felt for him. It shouldn't be so complicated, he thought, we ought to be able to feel some sort of confidence that everything will work out. No one should be dependent, but a lot depended on each of them, on all three.

"I'm thinking about my work," Gertrude said. "There's a part of me hidden from you that way. But that's how it is for a lot of people; it's a part of their everyday lives. That's the way I try to picture you thinking about another human being—like a difficult and interesting problem you turn over and over in your mind. I've never imagined you thought about me all the time, since I'm with you, after all."

He looked at her with undiminished tenderness. She met him halfway. They overlapped. They had looked at each other for so long.

He sensed how it might be for her—the way it is when a loving husband learns that his wife is expecting a baby but not necessarily his.

She seemed to understand that he carried Jenny within him. And that was a Jan she'd never seen.

"I want to avoid thinking about us within too narrow limits," Gertrude said. "At the Academy I heard about a new microscope. When they tested it on a gray pill bug they discovered a whitish mold on its back. It was the same with all of them. They magnified a thousand times and the mold turned into a kind of white golf balls. No one knows what it is, maybe an infection. But whenever I see a pill bug, all I can think of is that it's actually white."

THE RASPBERRY GIRL

THE WATER PALACE—so much gathered in one place. The air still and insect-free because of the chill. The shiny water waiting for the storms. Later, the wood mice would come out and do their nibbling.

Gertrude was wearing a long necklace of bits of glass and African nuts. Tidström had sent it. Unlike the present their father sent them once, it was not pulverized on arrival. She took it off when Jan got back from Arlanda, it had only been a whim.

He had wondered how he would let Gertrude in on his experience. Now she was there, though she didn't want to know anything concrete. But he was sorry she'd come to the truth by the back door, it would have been easier to explain if he'd done it from the beginning, but he'd thought at the time that it was destructive and rejecting and that it resembled a cliché he wouldn't acknowledge. So it ended with his trying to shield Gertrude *and* the truth, since the meeting of the two would alter both.

"If you do something violent and unexpected, you can become a completely different person," Gertrude said. "You said that yourself once."

"Are you thinking of killing me?"

"You wipe out experiences you've had earlier."

"Maybe."

"I'm thinking of going to Sten Tidström. No, not to him. To Botswana. I'm not going to anyone else. In the end a person has to work out his problems for himself."

Oddly enough, he felt neither fright nor surprise. He wanted to be a safety net beneath her. Nothing in him wanted to leave her. Their experience of life had a wide radius.

"There's so much I could say," Gertrude went on. "There's a lot in me you wouldn't understand, and still you understand even what I don't say. If I hadn't clenched my teeth, I would have had a terrible outburst and thrown things at you. But we don't own each other, we just care about each other very much. And don't tell me you have the imagination to think of a situation you couldn't talk your way out of! A situation where you could be strangled, not me. Then you'd stand there as helpless and defenseless as a stupid saint."

"I don't understand what you've lost," Jan said. "I love you. There's nothing unreasonable about that."

"I've lost my faith in you, or in my picture of you. And then I waver. You believe so much in love—you! But there are other things involved too. Are we equal now that I know?"

"You've written a dissertation. You've discovered something."

"You mean I've placed a book between us, you a human being? The man's love and the woman's work?"

They were talking almost in a normal tone of voice, but persistently and searchingly, as if working their way through a mass of material. But they also talked about everything else that tied the days together.

"It's too easy to love you, too dangerous to be dependent on you," Gertrude said. "A dissertation—what's that? It isn't enough for balance. A person probably has to grapple with something serious, a lifetime plan he's unqualified to see clearly. That's why I'm putting Botswana on the scales too. For our sake, yours and mine. I'm not going with some ulterior motive about how you'll see how much you need me. It's rather a way of not losing you. Or more accurately, of not losing myself in you."

She reminded him that she had once had plans to travel out to their father in South America, but they'd had nothing in common except their kinship and the shell of the Water Palace. She had read Sten Tidström's letters several times, one more had come: in short, Marianne was going home with the youngest child, who probably had bilharzia. The real reason seemed to be Marianne's depression.

"I'm going," Gertrude said, "because I don't want to put barbs on all your actions, so that nothing can be done for its own sake. I don't want to think my way into your secret considerations, in case they exist. I don't want to examine you and label you."

It occurred to him that Gertrude was being uninquisitive and uncurious because she wanted him to remain the person she recognized.

"The surface facts are just simplifications of the truth," he said. "That's not me."

"I want to be happy for waves and sun and for my own good health. I don't want everything to remind me of something quite different. I don't want to hope this day will end, when it's the only damned day I've got. That's being in a cage."

"Do you believe me when I say I don't want you to go?" Jan asked. "I've stifled you."

"You've stifled my love. I don't want to weigh you down with it. I'll pack it away."

Later she asked him, "Do you remember Anna in Antonioni's *L'Avventura*? The mystery isn't why she disappears but where to. I don't have any desire to be mysterious. But neither do I want to sound clearer than I feel. Spraying a foam of common sense over the surface of real life—that's dangerous too. I'm glad it's me who's breaking away, without a fuss."

"I've never wanted you to go away," he said for the third time.

"A person can always go on living. But to keep yourself *alive* is painful. I'd rather it was painful in Botswana than here. If you don't make your own choice, the choice is made for you."

The sound of the sea had reached the inner archipelago—a giant's asthma, choking on stones in his throat, twisting and turning in restless sleep. The waves climbed up on each other's backs, the way they do when you run with a glass of water. There was no doubt that the planet was spinning in space.

"I can do what I want to do, isn't that true?" Gertrude asked. "We don't have any papers between us, no prohibitions. It may seem to you we're inscribed in a magic circle. But I may tell you things it will amaze you to hear. All those things you've never wanted to describe to me. Your presence has often been marked by a considerate silence. I'm going to keep you advised."

Her determination was bitter. But at least he was spared feeling hurt that he couldn't comfort her. He realized he'd known very little about her stamina. He had thought she was more anchored in the Water Palace, less prepared to change her way of life. He was not very much at home in the fern forest.

For the first time, he thought, she was doing something as if he didn't exist. He had brought this about, but she had chosen to go *to* something, not away. The usual associations were replaced by others less obvious. She continued to live, for the time being, by means of new combinations.

And he realized that his love for her would float up to the surface continuously, without respect to any calendar. He couldn't put her behind him. She lay in front of him. When she left he would begin to approach her again.

"We'll stay in touch?" he asked anxiously.

"You're my brother," she said.

Whenever she looked at him for a long time, he pretended he could see in her eyes their common original cell, with its radius of less than two one-thousandths of a millimeter.

"I've got my documents from the Foreign Aid Office," Gertrude said. "I'm going under their auspices, though only formally and temporarily. They're putting me through their channels. My grant is enough for a ticket on a charter flight."

"Do you know how long you'll be gone?"

"No. Let's not talk about time. I haven't decided. I'll write you about it."

"Botswana's prime minister is coming here on a visit," Jan said. "I read it in the newspaper. I can look at him through binoculars from the tower."

"See to it he gets a safe landing," Gertrude said in her most ordinary voice.

There was no mood for farewell between them. Botswana had finally come to seem very close, he expected to see Tidström turn up almost anywhere. It was natural that they had many homes and refuges.

He felt he'd like to show Gertrude his Stockholm, the city of many exits. He would point out colors, buildings, and people, the sort of thing he was more open to these days. What if there were a wall painting he could write to Sten Tidström about, to the expert? A window put on a wall by someone's imagination, out in the open air. But he didn't know of any Sten hadn't taken him to see, and they didn't have time to look.

Gertrude said she wanted to go to the Historical Museum

and see the skeleton of a girl whose favorite food was raspberries. She had eaten herself to death on them one day in Luttra parish, not knowing she belonged to the pit-ceramic race in the Neopaleolithic era.

But nothing came of that either, and he motionlessly witnessed her preparations for the antipodean journey. Had he been afraid she would give him a freedom he couldn't bear unless he took it for himself? Was there a counterpole to what he'd done, from which he'd moved away?

Siblings and children are not allowed to marry. They'd been both at once. They'd been afraid to go beyond skin and origin, but they had also made a gesture of freedom against the rules of their own clan.

"I don't care what I've got in dresser drawers at the Water Palace and Upplandsgatan," Gertrude said. "I'm thinking of taking hardly anything. I can share with others, they can share with me. I've stopped feeling anything is ours or even mine. You don't belong to me. So why should things belong to me? And if we don't like this system anyway, with its marriage, divorce. . . ."

"There are men and women, bread, blankets. . . ." Jan said and was amazed at her. "Put us into a different conceptual framework and we look different."

"Yes," Gertrude said. "That's what I've now learned."

She had come to this point just as he had once been led to her, outside himself and yet bound to him in a dependence that could never be questioned.

One evening they walked down Upplandsgatan toward the Old City, past the tobacconist's where advertisements were still accepted for the daily papers, past Kristian Stoll's Housewares, which announced silver and china for rent. It was raining, and the dampness pressed the exhaust fumes down toward the ground, the air became heavy and sticky like a liqueur extract. They talked as they went, and the pigeons blinked at them as if saying one day we'll start talking just like you.

In a shop on Österlånggatan they saw one of those merry-go-round horses with shiny gold reins painted on brown oilskin. It was no ordinary rocking horse. It almost filled the store. It was still nipping, with its wooden laugh, at the figure in front on the carrousel. It seemed at once newly dead and not yet alive.

"No one has the right to believe he's a world for someone else," Jan Backman said.

"I don't ever want to dictate and predict my feelings," Gertrude said.

They wound up at Zum Fransiskaner on Skeppsbron—fillets of perch sprinkled with dill, a segment of lemon, mealy potatoes, beer. A woman sat motionless behind the gray cash register, the clock ticked, the newspapers hung on their rods.

It was one evening among many in their lives. Something weighed them down and made Jan think of iced-up aircraft that can land but not take off again. Gertrude's departure was not quite imminent, nor did it feel that way.

IN MOTION

WHY DID YOU turn around and run at the Academy?"

"I don't know," Jenny answered. "I lost my head. I'd like to turn around and run now too."

Through several weeks of late fall and early winter, he and

Jenny talked, back and forth. Information was now being given out more densely in all directions, but was misread more often.

He told her about Gertrude. Jenny tried to see him a new way. She wanted to free him, alter their love to a parenthetical happiness. How could she do that? Not by setting him trials like in fairy tales, not by forcing him to choose between them. Those were theatrical methods. But by behaving in such a way that he would quite naturally stop loving her.

"Of course everything is fair in love and war," Jan said bitterly. "Do you remember *The Guests of Night?*"

He couldn't imagine what awful fantasies had infected her. She felt no triumph at being given more of his time. It seemed to her that what she was going through hit her just as hard as it did Gertrude.

He caught sight of her at an intersection in her car, he waved and her face was turned toward him but she didn't stop. Was she really trying to avoid him? Later she said she hadn't seen him.

They were in motion a great deal. The buildings in Stockholm began to be wintry pale and rectilinear.

Jenny asked him to pick her up outside the Department of the Environment.

She knew when he was free. And when he came, she said, "I've got a report on the number of sandpipers observed passing south over Falsterbo, but I've never seen Lövsta dump right nearby."

So they drove there. But first to the slurping drains at Bällsta Bay. It gathered in a pocket of the shore and had long since come to a boil. Remaining was the stiffened froth of something that smelled and looked like urine, a bouillabaisse of decomposed hot dog buns, paper cups, seabird feathers, cigarette packages, and plastic toys.

"Here's my hell," Jan said. "Here's where I looked for you. Funny I didn't see this. But the rest of it was the ugliest and deadest thing I'd ever run across in Stockholm. You weren't there."

"Am I here now?" she asked.

"Now you're here," he said. "All the time."

"You don't want Gertrude to go to Botswana. She's never been out of the country without you. I ought to see to it that she stays."

"Let her be. Maybe it has less to do with you, with us, than we think."

They looked around—the archaeology of the dump. Sewing machines and elevator doors, washboards and stoves, bedsteads and shower nozzles. Wicker chairs. Some of them might have been accommodated at the Water Palace. It seemed to Jan he was seeing this ravine from several directions. In the purifying smoke, he saw how everything there could be used for something, how every form could have its purpose.

Jenny walked very close to the edge. He saw her in silhouette against the incinerator smokestacks by the water. She stood almost leaning over an abyss of rusty plates and twisted iron scraps. She didn't seem to notice him. At any moment she might take a step out into this petrified mess. He approached her from behind and took hold of her arm. Her gaze was preoccupied. In a flash he saw Gertrude's face as he strangled her. Jenny smiled as if at an older relation.

"Now I've seen it," she said tonelessly. "Shall we go?"

On their way into town they stopped in Vällingby. They stood on the square, under a bird-of-passage sky. People came up out of the subway and passed them.

"I was close to kicking the ladder out from under both of us," she said. "There are dogs howling inside me. Self-pity and bad conscience. I don't want to get stuck in love, I don't want to feel helpless and dependent; it makes me nasty."

He didn't know what to say.

"Look at all the people!" he said. "Columns in the phone book. And then you and me in particular."

"And Gertrude," she said sharply. "Among eight million Swedish-speaking people. Figures are meaningless. A little while ago I put John to flight because I didn't love him. Now you're chasing away Gertrude, although you love her. Actually, you'd rather she stayed. It would be better if I left."

"What I'd like is for Gertrude to use her new strength to hold all three of us together. Jenny, do you want to play with catastrophe just so you can feel you're at the controls?"

"No. I want to throw myself on a scrap heap. There's a kind of defiance in me. It's as if you'd become too much for me, or as if I could never get enough of you. I don't want to break any patterns of yours. You have a world where you can feel secure."

"The Water Palace?"

"Yes. Out there you're inaccessible. Your affinity with Gertrude is an invisible Himalaya I can't ever climb. I feel like the shadow of a leaf on your cheek. Gertrude lifts her hand to touch you and then the shadow is on her hand and you look the way you did before, and she recognizes you."

"I thought I'd made the two of you realize you're not interchangeable. But maybe that was arrogant of me. What good does it do for you to sacrifice yourself for Gertrude, you who said that everyone has to live his own life? Would it make my love for her more perfect? If you take off because you're tired of it, that I can understand. But you won't be saving me and Gertrude, that's not your choice."

"I know I'm doing us an injustice," Jenny said, "but I've become a little masochistic, I'm drawn to my own wound. And I didn't have that wound before everything came out in the open. Is it for your sake I like her so much? I ought to see you together a lot, so I could teach myself not to need you. I could stop imagining things and realize that I'm alone and chose to be alone. But I'm also afraid of discovering something in Gertrude that you don't see, something I'd laugh at without her knowing. Because then I'd be laughing at you, and you're the serious part of me."

"Let's not waste time on speculation," Jan said. "I love you in an impractical but very real way."

They stood as if petrified in the moving crowd. Jenny rested heavily against his shoulder.

"Still, believe me, I live inside this miracle. You're here, you breathe, your body moves, I hear your voice. That's all something I set against death, because it feels close today."

"Death is stronger," Jan said. "Why should we help it count the traffic? That's only distracting."

"If a person's expansion is checked he'll explode, or find a leak and lose his pressure with a hiss, like the air in a pressurized cabin."

"Or the other way around," Jan said. "Eklund, the meteorologist, told me that stars contract so they won't lose their heat through expansion. They shrink toward warmth."

They stood silently.

"I'm constantly aware of how happy we make each other," Jenny said. "It comes out of thin air. I don't want to put a price on it. I don't want to say, this doesn't balance out Gertrude's leaving you. Or, for that matter, my own uneasiness."

"How do you measure passion and pain? Through actions? To keep war from looking like a massacre, we give it a meaning. We intoxicate and blind ourselves with motives. I guess we do things with no apparent purpose only when we really want to. You've got a job full of objectives. Can't you and I be purposeless?"

"I wish it were that way," Jenny said.

"And why are we standing here talking in the middle of a square?"

"I was thinking of buying some wool pants," she said.

They went into a large store. He watched her peel off her winter pants in a dressing room. He was strangely excited by the sight of her everyday motions.

"Do you remember the bra I bought when you were in

London?" he asked. "Let's buy another one. All the stupid searching I did that day, the dump just now. A closed circle."

"A bent spiral, not a circle. We'll get one like it."

It was as if nothing serious had passed between them. She tried them on while he watched. There was something in him that responded to her like a blotter. A clerk peered carefully around the fluttering curtain, prepared for anything.

Jenny lay in bed in her apartment. She'd caught cold and was wearing flannel pajamas. Jan had bought some salmon *piroschki* he warmed in the oven. He got undressed, crept in behind her and into her as deeply as he could. He kissed the back of her neck and her hair, thinking he would become infected less quickly that way. She hugged his knees. The tea stood by the bed and, still inside her, he drank and lifted her head on his arm and let her drink.

It seemed to him an anatomical treachery that they should meet at a depth of a few inches when it ought to be at five fathoms and under pressure as in a diving bell. At the same time, he wanted to have her curled up inside his own body.

When she thought he was about to come, she stretched her inner arm back toward his mouth.

They were a pair of scale pans achieving their invisible balance. But she couldn't easily see it that way and turned toward him, red-eyed and runny-nosed.

"You love Gertrude and can still love me. That ought to be a comfort. But sometimes it makes me feel interchangeable, deceived in some indefinable way. I don't want that. And I don't want to turn you into an invention. I've invented enough people."

"You're a slide rule," he said. "If you force me to like you less, you think that frees emotion for Gertrude. On the contrary, it leaves less on both sides."

"My body is less reserved than I am. It goes along with everything you say."

Her voice was cautiously hoarse like the rough tongue of an anteater.

"You have a sun in your belly," he said. "I want to get at it."

He held his hand like a mirror over her body. And she polished a little spot on his thigh with the tips of her fingers and a great deal of pleasure collected there. She huddled up between his legs.

"I'm on a roller coaster," she said. "Impenitence and regret. But when you laugh, I can't hide behind my face. I have to laugh too. I can't hide how much I like to look at you. Why do we have only one word for skin? The skin on the back and the lips and the feet and this soft hollow behind your testicles— they're completely different things. Words are so insensitive!"

One day Jenny suggested they go out someplace for lunch. In the car she pressed his head into her lap.

"You're my hostage. You're not allowed to see where we're going."

All he could see was the sky, the tops of the houses, her chin and hair. From outside it looked as if she were alone in the car. He felt her leg move between the gas and the brake. With one hand she pressed his head closer to her stomach. He fell asleep.

When the car stopped, they were at Drottningholm Inn. It was being remodeled for a new epoch and stood there as lonely and distinct as in a dream. The rooms were empty, no customers, it was the end of November.

"Don't agree with me so much," Jenny said. "Maybe I want you to be right, not me."

"People are right one instant at a time," he said. "Then they're wrong."

"I have a harder time pleasing myself than you. I get a desire to disappear from the world without a trace. What world? Oh yes, I have to remember to give Jan my address."

"Maybe someday I'll manage to forget you," Jan said cheerfully. "But I'll always remember it was you I forgot."

The baroque avenue pointed up toward the castle, asleep beneath the engraver's stylus. But the blue waters were playing summer in the light breeze. A low slanting sun shone into the room. He combed Jenny's hair with a fork. The tile stove was a green servant girl, petrified by a terror-stricken willingness to oblige. She was wearing an apron of polished brass.

"I'll manage no matter what happens," Jenny said.

"For homework I ought to let you brood about whether I'd manage without you. But couldn't you show your breasts the view instead?"

She did as he asked. Her nipples contracted with curiosity like two peering eyes. He put his palm against them for a moment and felt two mute kisses.

Later they walked along empty damp-clean piers, the sun went out in the ponds in the park, and the little grocery store closed. He stuck his finger in a hole in her belt. The wild apples still hung glowing yellow on leafless trees. A spaniel followed them to their car, whining.

"Don't get all excited," Jan said. "You're staying here."

And the dog turned tail and slunk away.

They took turns being the balloon and the person holding the string.

"Sometimes I have no faith," Jenny said. "All I see is the rock, not the shape of the whole mountain. And then sometimes I see every chip in the rock and the whole mountain at the same time. Then I'm happy."

"In optics it's called near point and far point," Jan explained. "A person can be nearsighted in one eye and farsighted in the other. So in certain situations it's a question of knowing which one to look with. So you don't mix things up."

"You have an astoundingly tranquil personality," Jenny said. "I'd like to shake you sometimes. But most of all I want to protect you from danger. How strong is your empathy with other people?"

"I can see you're unhappy, but your face is so pretty it makes me want to run my hands all over you. You excite me in the most unreasonable ways. Love gets in the way of empathy."

"I'm here, I'm me," she said. "Just like Gertrude. But living this way requires a good balance of toughness and seriousness and rashness. Jan, my love is a forest of organ pipes, but it sounds like mosquitoes whining no matter how much I pull at those buttons with the fancy Latin names."

New days kept coming no matter how they behaved. They were held together by a happiness it was hard to wear down. They owned nothing in common except an initial on the wall of a building and a duplicate key. There hadn't been many presents. At Arlanda, he had a bar of soap and a towel she'd given him.

They had a lot to draw on, words and views. They pressed soundless keyboards. He heard the snap as she broke a limb from a linden. She of all people shouldn't have done that, but the tree would be pruned anyway in February. It was late one evening on Kastellholm. He had watched her take part in a panel discussion at the National Museum. Afterwards, some people she knew wanted her to go with them to Cattelin. But she sneaked off with Jan and looked so happy he couldn't manage a bad conscience at taking her from her friends.

And so they'd crossed the bridges just before the watchman closed the gates. Outside the long, low, yellow houses, the wives of noncommissioned officers were taking in wash that had stiffened in the frost. Jenny's earlobe was cold between his lips.

Jenny decided she should make an official inspection of the lakes silted up around Stockholm. They were down by poisoned Brunnsvik Bay and could hear the army engineers blasting in the distance.

Jan noticed how close they were to the Academy of Sciences. The peripheries of circles crossing or gliding together. Professionally, Jenny had more in common with Gertrude than with him.

"Since we're here anyway," he said, "why don't we go in and see Sir Edward Hallström in the Museum of Natural History? For the sake of the contrast."

"Who's he?"

"A Swede who became an Australian nobleman. He sent a tropical landscape from Sydney, with owls and cranes and reed warblers."

It was quiet in the museum, the middle of the day and no schoolchildren. They closed a set of drapes to cut off the daylight. Outside were harbor seals and walrus sleeping in the polar ice. They stood holding each other in the light reflected from illuminated waterfalls and mountain ledges and birds' nests swaying in the most delicate balance. Inside, in Sir Edward's realm, there was no mercury and no sulfur dioxide. No clouds from the Ruhr swept over his province, no chemical waste in his water. Nature there still looked the way it did in color photographs and to the naked eye.

They pushed aside the drapes and were immediately out on the thundering freeway.

"Don't bother about the things I say, but let me say them," Jenny said. "A little skin on the milk at the moment, but everything's still there underneath. Keeping just as well as the accident that made us meet. I'd like to take my air mattress out of the closet and spread it out on the roof. But it may be slippery up there. And cold."

"Let's have a look. The wind won't matter."

They had a look. Chips of the ventilators lay rusting to pieces on the tiles. The old observatory stood on its hill to the northwest, gray against the light. Jan felt no need to go back there.

From a distance, the roofs combined into a landscape without street canyons, a floating model city where chimneys and projections raised patterns in relief and human figures would wander about without seeing the abyss that lay in waiting everywhere.

Jan picked up a rusty key beside the chimney. It came from a padlock.

"Hey, that's mine," Jenny said. "I'd forgotten it. It's an extra, I left it the last time we were here. If we came up again we'd find it, and then we'd have a feeling that it was left long ago and that we'd loved each other all that time."

The sun went into its garage, while the lines of cars grew denser on their way to the southern suburbs. An airplane overhead was a moving star. Jenny followed it with her eyes and staggered.

"We're not as steady as snow-clearers," he said. "Pretty soon we'll fall."

He recognized her dangerous way of leaning forward. He put his arm around her waist and she stepped obediently down through the hatch. Inside the wire netting to the attic storage room he caught sight of a chair and an oil painting he'd carried up when they changed the furniture around. He felt solemnly exhilarated by how strongly they had come to interfere in one another's lives.

THE FOURTH WHEEL

THEY TOOK THE northern route to Stockholm. Gertrude was quiet, but as they drove off the yellow military ferry onto Vaxholm she said she had something to tell him. Just then the car started stuttering mysteriously. Jan got it into the gas station at the ferry berth. There seemed to be something wrong with the fuel pump. A man looked at it with a flashlight and tapped it and nothing helped. They wandered over to the harbor to take the bus, but the *Norrskär* came in just then outside the hotel, and they climbed aboard.

They had a part of the lower afterdeck to themselves.

"What were you going to tell me?"

"Jan, I'm going to have a baby."

He grasped her arm and looked around automatically. The steamer was on course.

"I got word from the laboratory just as we were leaving. I didn't want to say anything until I knew for sure."

"Why? Who? How?" Jan said.

"You remember, I talked about wanting to walk right out of my life like in a perspective study at school. Off toward the point where the sidewalks meet, and where everything gets so small there's no room to think or feel. I went that way, but at the end was Klas Lundin."

"Klas!" Jan burst out. "He's practically a stranger."

"Everyone who isn't you is apparently a stranger," Gertrude said. "I didn't tell him much. He may have figured some of it out, though he's not curious about really complicated things. But he's got wine, and he laughs at a person who cries. I slept with him three nights and didn't have a diaphragm."

The devil by name. The memory of a shudder when Jenny had told him something about John.

"You didn't say anything when you came back."

"You kept quiet about yours. Would you have cared so much?"

"And what about Klas?"

"He won't know. He doesn't want to. It's *you* I'm telling."

The thudding machinery in their ears, the chestnut benches . . . and under the benches, the life belts. There were lots of them at the Water Palace—they'd bought them at an auction of assorted coast guard surplus. They wouldn't keep anyone afloat, but could hover in a limbo between the bottom and the surface.

"When the person you most want to make you happy can't do it, then you have to turn somewhere else," Gertrude said. "I didn't feel I was cheating you of anything. I made myself smaller, I wanted to be someone else."

"You came out of the perspective study and there were two of you," Jan said.

"It wasn't an act of despair. It felt clear and simple. Maybe a kind of countermove . . . an experiment. But the experiment told me it was a question of something else, and of something more than I can manage."

Jan could see Klas's red-freckled hands on the tablecloth in front of him. A big friendly laugh and an advertising man's readiness to be of service in uncomplicated, pleasant things. He thought about the party and about Klas's descent on the Water Palace. The opportunity had been there.

A wave of bitterness washed over him. He braced his feet against it. It seemed to him his hair had gotten wet.

It wasn't enough with the ferns, the book, Botswana, he thought. Only as a child, up in the attic, had he fully appreciated Gertrude's ability to act. He'd never figured on this. Was he her springboard to something else? Or was she on her way in and out through the widely separated bars of their sibling cage?

"I could have turned to Klas to sort of . . . ."

"To kill everything between us?"

"Yes. But it was the other way around. It was in order to give us more room to move around in."

Straight through the Gertrude she now was he saw her a couple of months before, bending down toward the moss, pulling up a white agaric and brushing sticks and straws and an ant from its cap, with him and the children standing around her.

"What would have happened if I'd tried to force you away from Jenny?" Gertrude asked.

He didn't dare answer. If a person is robbed of his love, an empty hole is left, and into the hole seeps hate.

"Come on, let's go out on deck," he said.

Drops of melted snow on the rail. Dried flowers in the dining room, and at every table a varnished button for calling the waiter. Along the shore: buoys not yet hauled up for the winter, slippery with seaweed; lawns with a northern exposure powdered with snow; rocky hillsides where blackberries had grown, coal black and frosty in November, though many had never ripened but fallen to the ground still green.

"You're going to have a baby!" he repeated. "Are you happy?"

"Very happy."

The cat print in the clay. A quick impression in passing. That was the first thing he'd told Jenny in the car from Arlanda. The clay dried, the print remained. The cat didn't know. But Gertrude may have known when she left Klas.

"It's remarkable," he said low.

"What? Getting pregnant the first or third time you sleep with someone, particularly if you know your cycle—I don't think that's as odd as falling in love at first sight," Gertrude said.

Should he be mad, unhappy, generous . . . ? Something was expected of him, he was waiting for a feeling that seemed right. But no one could say what that might be. He was mostly amazed and a little frightened by Gertrude's frankness, and a little moved. And something else—like that morning on Långholm with Gertrude: maybe the pattern in the rock existed more distinctly somewhere else—in the water, the clouds, the moss.

It was as if the roof were lifted off. Emotions came roaring in. One of the ship's fenders was still hanging down at the bow, banging against the prow like a door in an empty house. He was moving between two stages, and he felt the dizziness and intoxication of a whirling turnstile, and the liberality of being able to do two things at once, and the loneliness and the pain of the transition to a new complicity.

At a death or a birth: movement in various directions.

"Can you handle all this?" Gertrude asked.

That came unexpectedly—a moment ago it had been he who was anxious for her. He threw his arms around her with a fierceness that surprised them both. And discovered he was happy on her behalf. Because he had often noticed something in Gertrude that opened up only to figures, the shapes of ferns —as if people were used up.

The sun moved along the horizon until some tall spruce became too much for it and then disappeared. The lights went on in a summer cabin set in a hollow—some people with no apartment trying to survive the winter. A jet fighter drew an enormous zero above the plodding steamer.

They went home to Upplandsgatan. In the bus, among the other people, he looked at her body where the baby was growing. She had done that by herself, as if he didn't exist. He wanted to take care of her. But she didn't seem to need that.

On the floor below the letter slot was a notice that the landlord was looking for new apartments for his tenants.

"Before your baby is born they'll have chased us out of here."

Your . . . we . . . he was suddenly at a loss.

"How's it going to be?" he asked helplessly.

"Our baby, if you're willing," Gertrude said. "We've never been too particular about biology. *Are* you willing?"

He couldn't find anything to say.

"Or all three of ours," Gertrude said. "That would be the best."

"Whose? Klas's?"

"Yours and mine and Jenny's. Because I think about you and Jenny all the time, though I try not to. Like today when I found out, it passed through my mind that maybe I could care about both of you, not just about you. But I don't know yet.

I'm certainly not going to let the baby be used for anything. But since it exists, and the two of you exist. . . ."

"Yes," Jan said. "So you mean . . . ."

"I go to Botswana. Nothing changes. You know how Sten is, he won't notice anything until I'm in my eighth month."

"Are you thinking of having the baby out there?"

Nine months without Gertrude. He felt their painted floor moving like the wooden waves in a stage set.

"The Water Palace doesn't have to be the first place it's carried home to."

This child—an outsider, a part of Gertrude . . . . Should they advise Adolf Oscar Backman or let him die in peace? Did he have anything at all to do with it?

His beloved's child. Niece or nephew. A child whose father was its uncle and still not its father. And who might have two mothers. And no one knew how many fathers—Jan put a lot of faith in Sten Tidström. He burst out laughing.

"What are you laughing at?"

"At the total confusion. At all the mistaken names for human behavior."

"But we put up with most of it. We don't order the trees to be different. But think of the fuss if every single anemone were red this spring."

"A newborn child wouldn't notice," Jan said.

And so they tasted the apprehension of an experience—like the wood mice venturing up to the Water Palace to nibble on the rag rugs long before winter set in.

"I believe you're up to all my honest explanations," Gertrude said. "That's nice to know. But I don't know if it's because you're my brother or because you love me."

They were brother and sister. That gave him a share in her child. His loving her gave him a share in her experience.

He wanted to keep her. After all, she was telling these things to him. He had tried to imagine how Gertrude felt in the face of him and Jenny—like a loving husband when he discovers his wife is going to have a baby, but not necessarily his. Now he drew a breath in order to track down his own jealousy. But it wasn't there, though he knew what it looked like—a lack of perspective, an anxious hoarding inside walls that were closing in.

"Don't bump around in a jeep with Sten Tidström," he said. "We can't afford a miscarriage."

"We"—he dimly imagined four creatures that grew and altered and lived in impermanence.

Things never come apart and set themselves to rights in order to be summarized. No phase of a person's development is any truer than any other. Destinies are not fulfilled. But there is something that spreads and then tightens again, as in a loom.

"I'll keep myself stationary," Gertrude said. "I'm going to build up a library for Swaneng and hopefully one for Tonota. I'm trained for that. But I'm ready to set to work on anything at all. We're all volunteers."

Siblings—the parallel life. But now they'd established oppositions, they could move to meet each other again, or could separate.

Gertrude was going to Botswana for the reason Sten Tidström gave—to see a new distribution of strength and weakness.

Stay here, he whispered to himself. Who? Gertrude. And experience, heavy as a child's head against his hand. And the instant, as alive as an organism, when he saw that all these things belonged together and didn't damage one another.

He had read about blind people who had an operation and could see for the first time. The new sense bothered them. Touch knew best whether things were round or square. They closed their eyes again and felt with their fingers. It took some time for them to learn how eyes were supposed to be used.

He couldn't distinguish clearly what had happened, he wasn't sure what Gertrude really looked like. His love had to travel by roundabout ways. He closed his eyes to understand more quickly.

Before they went to bed, he saw Gertrude naked in the bath-room, on a checkered plastic mat under clothes hung up to dry. He looked at her stomach, smooth and flat, with a curiosity he knew he recognized. And finally he remembered. The first time after puberty that he saw Gertrude, in his rented room, he was seized by the same strange mood—the feeling that they belonged together and still didn't know anything about one another. She had had other men, but nothing had changed, she said. It was their closeness as brother and sister that first shattered all the membranes. In the olden days, Gertrude said, probably everyone had a better idea what they were intended for.

They lay pressed close to each other. Before he fell asleep he thought of something Gertrude had said one day when the Water Palace was being shaken by a fall storm—she intended to keep him informed and maybe tell him things he'd be amazed to hear.

He had listened to the first of those things. It was only natural that others would follow.

BOTKYRKA

JAN BACKMAN MET Jenny the following morning. It was his turn to talk. He already counted Gertrude's baby as his own. He was going to tell Jenny everything, and he expected her to share his feelings.

But he found her gloomy and couldn't bring himself to say anything. He found himself driving south on E4, meeting the early traffic.

Jenny was going to go to London for the planning of the World Environment Conference, and from there to Strasbourg and Geneva. Both she and Gertrude were going away. He asked her when she was coming home, and in a forced tone of voice she answered that she didn't know. But she didn't seem happy about the uncertainty.

They were getting close to Södertälje when Jan said, "Jenny, listen. Gertrude's going to have a baby."

After a while Jenny answered in a tense and artificial voice.

"Good!" she said. "You're building up your water palace again. And you remember what I said—if you hurt Gertrude, I'll have to take care of her. Jan, when the two of you are as close as this, without the slightest chink, then I wish I were your sister."

"I remember you said that once. But I've never wanted that."

The cars they met, mopping up the highway with their headlights, seemed to have no drivers.

"You don't understand," Jan said. "It's not my baby. Not to begin with in any case. It's Klas Lundin's. But you and I caused it."

And he told her how Gertrude felt toward what had happened.

"The time I wanted a child with you," Jenny said, "was that evening we ran from the National Museum to our hotel."

They couldn't tell whether it was starting to snow in the distance or whether it was the first streaks of dawn.

"Jan, sometimes I find my emotions so humiliating," Jenny went on. "I'm several things at once—one part lightheartedness, one part suspicion, one part destructiveness."

"That's your instinct of self-preservation being awkward,"

Jan replied. "I recognize it, though the flaws in mine have a different pattern."

"I don't think Gertrude was trying to understand us better, or to be more like you," Jenny said. "She was acting rather *against* her love for you . . . in order to see where it led. Where it led her . . . and us."

"It depends on our counter-experiment," Jan said.

"Our"—his and Jenny's this time. But what if Jenny didn't want to take part? He was hoping she had the courage to act against her own feelings, at least against her own instinct of self-preservation.

"Can you go on liking Gertrude?" he asked. "And if Gertrude accepts you as her friend, can you feel that Gertrude's child belongs to all of us as long as she wants it to? After all, we haven't cared very much about chronology and rights of precedence."

He saw changes in her face. Like a chemical process—a precipitate occasioned by a new ingredient.

After a while she said, "Most of all I want to be with the person I love. I'm not going to turn around and run away again. We mustn't be afraid."

"Of what?"

"Of taking something completely seriously. I'm going to talk to Gertrude."

Thin frosted wires had been stretched between the buildings in Södertälje to carry sounds more readily. They had driven aimlessly down the highway and were surprised to be there. Jenny wanted to buy some things for her trip. A photocell at a department store opened its glass doors; they walked through a belt of warm air and were inside among goods they hardly saw, surrounded by decisions. As they rode down the escalator, he stood behind her, pressed against her back, and blew on her hair.

"Buy me a bathing cap," she said.

Then he knew she would think about him every day they

were apart. His joy was a vein beneath the grass—you kick at the ground and the mark fills up with water.

"We're still on the same stage," Jenny said, taken aback. "All three of us. And one in the wings."

"Being on my way away from you would feel like the worst kind of bondage."

"I share my job with a lot of people; I share the streets; we don't even get our parents all to ourselves. I share you with Gertrude, and you run the risk of sharing me with someone, though right at the moment I can't imagine doubling my love the way you do."

They drove toward Stockholm. The frozen furrows in the fields showed through the thin snow.

"I'm just getting a lift to town with you," Jenny said. "We'll pretend it's the first time. We don't know anything yet. My luggage is in the back seat. At first we talk about the things around us, about the road, the car, the weather. Then we say something about ourselves, something important but not odd. Then pretty soon we're there."

Then he told her that Gertrude was his half-sister. He had kept the secret because it was Gertrude's too. Jenny had been his secret from Gertrude. Maybe both secrets were unnecessary. Jenny was the first person to know.

"Say something! Do you think it's terribly odd?"

"What a mess! You're not married to Gertrude. She's expecting a baby but not yours. Nothing seems particularly stable. But I'm glad I've got the last piece of the puzzle—if it is the last. In order to be honest, you have to have a mystery. How many secrets are there? Isn't it possible to work out a secret everyone can share?"

"How do you mean?"

"Klas Lundin doesn't know anything. There's always someone on the outside—often because he doesn't want to know. The secret goes on. When will the child be told that its father is its uncle, and that it doesn't matter, that it's just a way of speaking."

"Maybe never. Because that's an unnecessary mystery that covers more important ones. Frankness only on certain points distorts the vision. But it's a long way off."

"I know your secret," Jenny said, "but you still have it anyway. Like a birthmark. For a couple of seconds I felt an unreasonable envy."

"You and I have other symbols. A lot of blue pushpins on a map of Stockholm and environs, including Arlanda and the air channels and the lakes. They're getting to be more and more numerous."

"Do you know something I'd like to do? Go look at Sir Edward's landscape sometime when Gertrude's come home from Botswana."

Jan looked at her surprised.

"At least there nothing will have changed," she said.

"Maybe a piece of the tropical sky will flake loose and land on the head of the reed warbler and turn it into a kingfisher. Or it'll float down to the ground and someone will have to go in and straighten up in all that serenity. What are you going to do before you leave?"

"We've got a report to turn out on the legal right to enter private land. In the long run, we'll have to alter the principles of land ownership. The pressures of exploitation are unequally divided at the moment. Almost every regional plan is out of date before there's time to apply it. We have to have cooperation in the planning in order to avoid battles over jurisdiction. Different kinds of environments ought to be made available to everyone."

"It's fun to hear you talk like that," Jan said. "The brain demands a particular point of view in order to understand foreign languages. It has to be prepared to recognize certain patterns and give them meaning. Otherwise everything is incomprehensible and repellent."

"The things I'm saying are very important," Jenny assured him. "They have to do with us."

The Botkyrka church is close to the highway. It is fortress

gray and seems to stand at an angle to the landscape. The day had grown lighter, and they stopped. The tall purple thistles had acquired seedballs of snow. The stalks wore an armor of frozen drops of rain.

Family graves—an engine driver's, a baron's. Solitary graves. A tremendous load of murmured-out leaves had arranged themselves on the ground. On the stone of one dead man it said that he was only now "in the land of the living."

No one in sight. They went in through the black-pitched armored door. Their eyes followed the sweep of white-plastered arches. In the center aisle was the lid of a sarcophagus, with an iron ring at each corner and a text worn almost smooth.

They carefully turned over the hourglass on the pulpit and listened to the buzz of a winter-awakened fly and the sound of filtering sand.

Jenny turned to him. Her voice was murky.

"Are you sure we aren't documenting something that's disappearing more and more? Something about to be pulled up by the roots?"

The low morning sun was reflected in a painted sun, vertical on a blue door to heaven.

"No," he said. "There's something just starting to grow, though we've tried to describe it so we'd recognize it when it came. Do you remember the seeds from the basket we had at that nameless lake by Arlanda?"

Jenny leaned back against a pillar.

"Come here," she said. "I want to feel your weight."

They had their outdoor clothing on, they couldn't feel the soft and the hard in each other's bodies. Wet rowan leaves were pasted to the outsides of the windows. They stood pressed together as tightly as they could, absolutely still, and looked into each other. He felt utterly accessible, public, without recesses.

Her eyes at an angle under his, clear as sun . . . the worn floor. . . .

So much time passed that a patch of light from a stained-glass window had time to wander across Jenny's forehead like a red planet.

"We're wrapping ourselves in something no one can touch," she said solemnly.

Like climbing up out of a mine—the light closes your eyes but at the same time floods your entire body.

It seemed to him he had reached something untranslatable, a truth that neither replaced nor voided other truths.

"Do you know what we've done?" Jenny said. "We've gotten married. Legalized a child."

"But we don't even have an unwilling, kidnapped priest like in the Westerns. The whole church is empty."

"Otherwise it wouldn't have worked. We wouldn't have been able to look at each other this way. Now we'll have to turn the hourglass again. I can't hear the sand any more."

This, he thought, is our most serious, and my only marriage.

The music on the organ was open to a three-hundred-year-old hymn: What Then Can Satisfy My Soul? He leaned over it.

"What are you doing?" Jenny asked.

"You can hardly notice it. I'm writing our initial, J, very thinly on a staff. The organist will see it as a note, or a rest."

"Can you hit that chord?"

"No. But someone playing the whole piece probably will."

THE AIRWAY

In case he didn't come back out to the Water
Palace for a while, he filled the heating pipes with glycol,
hid the soap and candles from the mice, put out chicken feed
for the rabbits so they wouldn't ravage the plants in the yard,
piled the kitchen drawers on the floor so they wouldn't swell
shut. This was customary procedure decreed by the time of
year, a routine that knew its own prerequisites. Winter dampness, the frozen pipes, and the wild animals were fragments
of something steadfast in the midst of all the interwoven
change.

He stopped by the tapestry in the darkness. What if after all
it were some kind of ferns they were traveling through, the lion
with the lady on his back? Was that why the figures were so
large and the trees only stylized green plants? The sky was
close overhead, but they couldn't see it, it was hidden by the
ribbon of words—soon we'll be out of the forest.

They rode in eternal undergrowth, their vision obscured,
until the fabric itself was worn by their tracks.

He drove into town and helped Gertrude with her final
packing for the trip.

"I'll have a beard when you get back," he said. "It's a way
of becoming three dimensional. Otherwise you're only recognizable by a few stray points, like a blurry picture in the paper.
Women are more distinct."

"So you'll recognize me? And Jenny?"

He noticed she no longer had trouble mentioning Jenny by
name. They had talked to each other. He hadn't heard much
about it. She was leaving anyway.

He went out to Arlanda early. Gertrude and Jenny were leaving on the same day. Gertrude to Copenhagen and then a charter flight to Nairobi and then a local flight to Botswana, Jenny on BEA's regular Trident to London later in the day. None of them wanted to say goodbye on the tarmac or in the transit hall, in front of everyone. But they knew he would be guiding them out of Stockholm.

The wind whistled through the side ventilators as he drove toward the airport. He rubbed the mist from the inside of the window with his elbow. The grass along the edge of the road had been blackened with lye. The stars burned pale green like distant reflectors lining a highway through the wilderness.

Jan glided into the corridor of international advertising that intensified the desolation around Arlanda. The guard saw the permit on the windshield and pressed the gate button. He was there.

The office staff hadn't yet arrived. There were textbooks on the desk in his office—Howsher's *Communication Systems*, J. R. Abraham's *Signal Flow Analysis*. He thought about whether he should continue his education. Gertrude and Jenny were preparing themselves for new work. The amount of knowledge in the world was constantly being doubled. Only he waited for no new assignment. Spreading tourist propaganda for foreign countries out in the provinces no longer attracted him. He ought to do something with his life.

He got out of the elevator at the meteorologist's stage and ran into Eklund.

"How's everything with the quasars today?"

"Toward a new constellation . . . ." Eklund answered darkly, and closed the door to his observation room.

Gertrude had never been out to where he worked. Jenny had driven into the restricted area. Neither of them had been in the tower or radar control.

Planes approaching Arlanda were informed "Rime frost with

good braking. Warning for snowbanks—keep to the center of the runway."

He busied himself with his work. He was in control of signals. Once, without his knowing it, he had brought in Jenny's plane. Everything seemed to occur "for technical reasons."

Nothing unexpected happened.

The instruments recorded the wind speed at fifteen thousand feet. That's where they were found—the low pressure areas, the cold fronts. At a lower level, much further away, were the protracted hurricanes and the sudden typhoons named after ladies in operettas.

He looked at Gertrude's plane through the green, nonreflecting glass. He had no feeling of farewell. It was the same with Jenny and with everything. It seemed to him he'd become a person who could no longer put anything behind him forever.

The ice had melted on the wings, the plane could take off. Nothing held it down. Absence and presence canceled each other out. He hadn't expected to feel such lightness. Like skating across frozen black mirrors of water. Fuel from no one knew where.

Snow crystals moved against the glass, not measurable by weight, but not inaccessible. He followed the course of events. A light blinked on the instrument board. He noted down the radio code. For a while yet Gertrude was still within the circumference of the radar screen.

Jenny took off that afternoon. The snow was heavy with moisture it drew from the air. The clouds revolved like propellers across the sky. It was one degree below freezing.

There are about one hundred international symbols for precipitation.

So far he didn't know when either of them would be back. They were prepared to wear at each other. If they were saving and anxious, nothing would be left. He didn't dare take anything for granted. Maybe nothing would preserve the shape it had.

A huge lock with a lot of numbers—they invented different combinations to see how they worked. They had done that right across Stockholm, out onto the savannah, and up to the baby that resembled a future they had worked out together.

The ground rocked beneath the living, because nothing ever became wholly familiar and they were all unwillingly parts of a treachery so great they couldn't comprehend it, they could only catch glimpses of its boundary lines.

It was like a broad, outspread beginning, which pushed ahead of it an end he couldn't see, or had already experienced.

He guided them out into the ocean of air. But they remained within the same area. You possess no one. Nothing held them captive. How much freedom could the air sustain?

Jan Backman was alone at the instrument panel. The others had taken a break. He went over the light settings, meter readings, control adjustments, and visibility.

The tower vibrated in the wind. Visibility was normal for that time of year—low. He looked down on the mist that covered the runways. It folded and unfolded like the sheet that covers an awakening man.